Large Print Dah
Daheim, Mary.
Silver scream

WITHDRAWN

STACKS

NEWARK PUBLIC LIBRARY
NEWARK, OHIO

Silver Scream

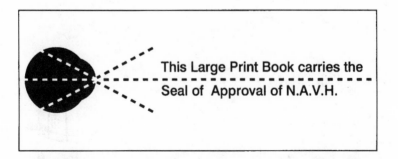

Silver Scream

A Bed-and-Breakfast Mystery

Mary Daheim

Thorndike Press • Waterville, Maine

Published in 2002 by arrangement with William Morrow,
an imprint of HarperCollins Publishers, Inc.

Thorndike Press Large Print Americana Series.

The tree indicium is a trademark of Thorndike Press.

The text of this Large Print edition is unabridged.
Other aspects of the book may vary from the original edition.

Set in 16 pt. Plantin by Christina S. Huff.

Printed in the United States on permanent paper.

Library of Congress Cataloging-in-Publication Data

Daheim, Mary.
    Silver scream : a bed-and-breakfast mystery / Mary Daheim.
      p. cm.
    ISBN 0-7862-4612-X (lg. print : hc : alk. paper)
    1. Flynn, Judith McMonigle (Fictitious character) —
Fiction. 2. Motion picture producers and directors —
Fiction. 3. Bed and breakfast accommodations — Fiction.
4. Northwest, Pacific — Fiction. 5. Businesswomen —
Fiction. 6. Large type books. I. Title.
PS3554.A264 S55 2002b
  813′.54—dc21   2002075920

To Dave —

*As they say in Hollywood,
I couldn't have done this book
without him. Or done much else, either.*

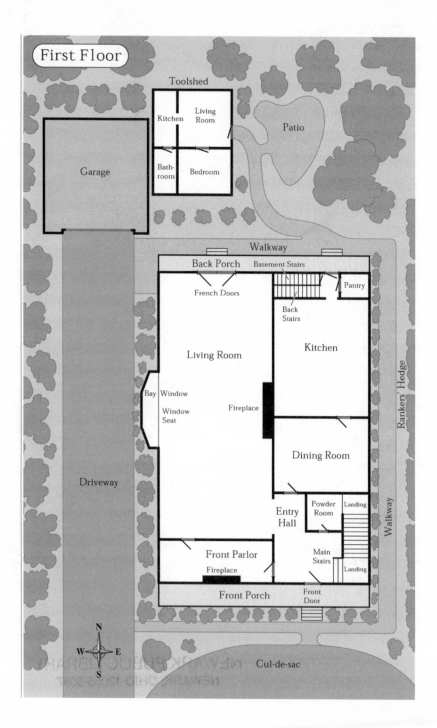

First Floor

Toolshed

Kitchen

Living Room

Patio

Garage

Bathroom

Bedroom

Walkway

Back Porch

Basement Stairs

French Doors

Pantry

Back Stairs

Living Room

Kitchen

Bay Window

Window Seat

Fireplace

Dining Room

Driveway

Rankers' Hedge

Entry Hall

Powder Room

Landing

Walkway

Front Parlor

Fireplace

Main Stairs

Landing

Front Porch

Front Door

N
W E
S

Cul-de-sac

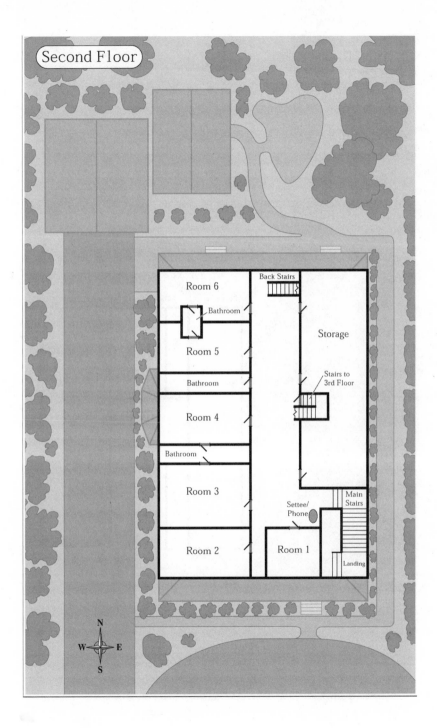

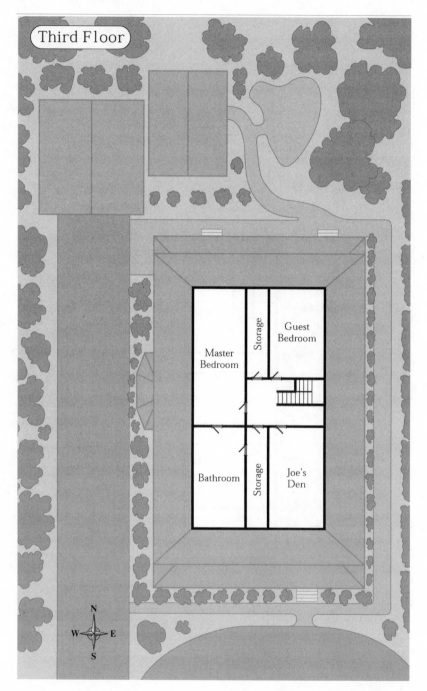

Chapter One

Judith McMonigle Flynn twitched in the kitchen chair, jumped up, paced the floor, and leaned her head against the cupboard by the sink. Desperately, she tried reason, argument, and, finally, bad grammar in an attempt to fend off Ingrid Heffelman from the state bed-and-breakfast association.

"I don't want none of those crazy people at Hillside Manor," she shouted into the phone. "I mean, *any* of them. They're Hollywood types, and they're nuts."

"Just because they make movies doesn't mean they're crazy," Ingrid huffed. "Look, I know this is a big favor. But you had only two other reservations for the last weekend of October besides the producer, Bruno Zepf. I can put those non–movie people up somewhere else to make room for the additions to Mr. Zepf's original guest list."

Since Bruno Zepf had made his reservation two weeks earlier, Judith knew she was on shaky ground. Like many Hollywood big shots, Zepf was as superstitious as he was successful. Ten years earlier, his career as an independent producer had been launched at a film festival in the Midwest. At the time Zepf couldn't afford a hotel; he'd had to stay in a bed-and-breakfast. The movie had won the top prize, launching his Hollywood career. Ever since, he had stayed at B&Bs before premiering a new production. But other members of his company wanted to stay in the same B&B, hoping that Bruno's good luck would rub off on them. Magnanimously — egotistically — the Great Man had allowed at least a half-dozen associates to join him at Hillside Manor.

"Please, Ingrid," Judith pleaded, moving away from the cupboard, "I'm stuck with Mr. Zepf, but I've had my fill of so-called beautiful people, from opera singers to gossip columnists to TV media types. I've had gangsters and psychos and —"

"I know," Ingrid interrupted, her tone suddenly cold. "That's one of the reasons you're going to accept this deal. You've managed to have some very big problems at Hillside Manor, and while they don't seem to have hurt your business, they give the rest of the B&Bs a black eye. Look what happened a year or so ago — your establishment was included in a sightseeing tour of murder sites, and you ended up on TV with a dead body."

"The body wasn't at Hillside Manor," Judith retorted as the cupboard door swung open all by itself. She took her frustration out on the innocent piece of wood, slamming it shut. "And it certainly wasn't my fault. Besides, I got the tour group to take Hillside Manor off the sightseeing itinerary, didn't I?"

"You still looked like an idiot in that television interview about your so-called sleuthing," Ingrid countered. "It was embarrassing for innkeepers all over the state. You owe me — and the rest of the good people who run B&Bs around here."

"That was the editing," Judith protested. "I didn't ask to be on TV. In fact, I begged them not to do the piece. I hardly consider myself a sleuth. I run a B&B, period. I can't help it if all sorts of weird people come here. Look, now you're the one who's setting me up. Who will you blame if something happens while these movie nutcases are staying at Hillside Manor?"

There was no response. The line was dead. Ingrid had hung up on her.

"Damn," Judith breathed. "Ingrid's a mule."

"She always was," Gertrude Grover responded. "Fast, too. She wore her skirts way too short in high school. No wonder she got into trouble."

Judith stared at her mother. "This is a different Ingrid. She runs the state B&B association. She's my age, not yours."

Gertrude's small eyes narrowed. "You just think she is. Ingrid Sack's been dyeing her hair for years. Had a face-lift, too. More than once, I heard."

"Mother," Judith said patiently, "Ingrid Sack — I believe her married name was Grissom — has been dead for ten years."

Now it was Gertrude's turn to stare. "No kidding? I wonder how she looked in her casket. All tarted up, I bet. Funny I didn't hear about it at the time."

There was no point in telling Gertrude that she'd undoubtedly read Ingrid's obituary in the newspaper. Read it with glee, as the old lady always did when she discovered she'd outlived yet another contemporary. Judith was used to her mother's patchy memory.

"I'm stuck," Judith announced, flipping the pages of the American art calendar she'd been given by her cousin Renie. August's

Black Hollyhock, Blue Larkspur by Georgia O'Keeffe was a sumptuous sight compared with the stark, deliberately mundane realism of Louis Charles Moeller's *Sculptor's Studio*, which heralded October. Vibrant natural beauty versus taxing, gritty work. Maybe the painting was an omen. "Come Halloween, we're going to be invaded by Hollywood."

Gertrude pulled a rumpled Kleenex from the pocket of her baggy orange cardigan. "Hollywood?" she echoed before gustily blowing her nose. "You mean like the Gish sisters and Tom Mix and Mary Pickford?"

"Uh . . . like that," Judith agreed, sitting down at the kitchen table across from her mother. "A famous producer is premiering his new movie here in town because it was filmed in the area. He's bringing his entourage — at least some of it — to Hillside Manor."

"Entourage?" Gertrude looked puzzled. "I thought you didn't allow pets."

"I don't," Judith replied. "I meant his associates. Speaking of pets," she said sharply to Sweetums as the cat leaped onto the kitchen table, "beat it. You don't prowl the furniture."

Sweetums was batting at the lid of the sheep-shaped cookie jar. The cat didn't take

13

kindly to Judith's efforts to pick him up and set him down.

"Feisty," Gertrude remarked as Sweetums broke free and ran off in a blur of orange-and-white fur. "You got to admit it, Toots, that cat has spunk."

Judith gave her mother an ironic smile. "So do you. You're kindred spirits."

"He gets around better than I do," Gertrude said, turning stiffly to watch Sweetums disappear with a bang of the screen door. The old lady reached into her pocket again, rummaged around, and scowled. "Where'd my candies go?"

"You probably ate them, Mother," Judith said, getting up from the table. "There are some ginger cookies in the jar. They may be getting a bit stale. It's been too warm to bake the last few days."

The summer had indeed been warm, though not unbearable. As a native Pacific Northwesterner, Judith's tolerance for heat dropped lower every year. Fortunately, there was only a week left of August.

"I should call in person to cancel the displaced guests' reservations," Judith said, scrolling down the screen on her computer monitor. "Let's see — the Kidds from Wisconsin and the Izards from Iowa."

"Those are guests? They sound like innards to me." Gertrude was struggling to get out of her chair. "You got two lonesome old cookies in that jar," she declared. "I suppose that hog of a Serena was here and gobbled them up."

Judith reached out to give her mother a hand. "It wasn't Serena," she said, referring to her cousin who was more familiarly known as Renie. "It was little Mac. Remember, he was here with Mike and Kristin and Baby Joe the day before yesterday."

Gertrude paused in her laborious passage from the kitchen table to the rear hallway. "Baby Joe!" she exclaimed, waving a hand in derision. "Why did Mike and his wife have to name the new kid after Lunkhead?"

"Lunkhead" was what Gertrude called Judith's second husband, Joe Flynn. "Lunkhead" was also what she called her daughter's first husband, Dan McMonigle. Mac was the nickname of the older grandson, whose given name was Dan, after the man who had actually raised Mike. Though Judith had first been engaged to Joe, she had married Dan. It was only in the last year that her son had come to realize that Joe, not Dan, was his biological father. Thus, Mike had honored both men by giving their names to his own sons.

15

"Mike thinks the world of Joe," Judith replied, escorting her mother to the back door. She didn't elaborate. Gertrude had never admitted that her daughter had gotten pregnant out of wedlock. To Judith's mother, sex before marriage was as unthinkable as chocolate without sugar.

They had reached the porch steps when Joe Flynn pulled into the driveway in his cherished antique MG, top down, red paint gleaming in the late afternoon sun.

"Ladies," he called, getting out of the car with his cotton jacket slung over one shoulder. "You're a vision."

"You mean a sight for sore eyes," Gertrude shot back.

"Do I?" Gold flecks danced in Joe's green eyes as he kissed his wife's cheek, then attempted to brush his mother-in-law's forehead with his lips.

Gertrude jerked away, almost throwing Judith off balance. "Baloney!" the old girl cried. "You just want to get my goat. As usual." She plunked her walker on the ground and shook off Judith's hand. "I'm heading for my earthly coffin. Send my supper on time, which is five, not six or six-thirty." Gertrude clumped off toward the converted toolshed, her place of self-imposed exile since she had long ago declared she wouldn't live under the same roof as Joe Flynn.

"Ah," Joe said, a hand under Judith's elbow, "your mother seems in fine spirits today."

"I can't tell the difference," Judith muttered. "She's always mean to you."

"It keeps her going," Joe said, hanging his jacket on a peg in the hall. "Beer would do the same for me. Have we got any of that Harp left or did Mike drink it all?"

"He didn't drink as much as Kristin did," Judith replied, going to the fridge. "But I think there are a couple of bottles left. Kristin, being of Amazonian proportions, has a much greater capacity than other mortals." She glanced up at the old schoolroom clock, which showed ten minutes to five. "You're early. How come?"

"I found Sir Francis Bacon," Joe responded, sitting down in the chair that Gertrude had vacated. "How the hell can you lose an English sheepdog? They're huge."

"Where was he?" Judith asked, handing Joe a bottle of Harp's.

"In their basement," Joe said, after taking a long swallow of beer. "He was trying to keep cool, and in the process, managed to get into the freezer. He found some USDA prime cuts and ate about a half dozen, which gave him a tummy ache. Then he went behind the furnace and passed out. He was there for two days."

"Sir Francis is okay?" Judith inquired, after pouring herself a glass of lemonade.

"He will be," Joe said. "They trotted him off to the vet. I hate these damned lost pet cases, but the family's loaded, it took only a couple of hours to find the dog, and they paid me a grand." He patted the pocket of his cotton shirt. "Nice work, huh?"

"Very nice," Judith said with a big smile. "All your private detective cases should be so easy. And profitable. Maybe we can use some of that money to have Skjoval Tolvang make some more repairs around here."

"How old is that guy anyway?" Joe asked with a bemused expression on his round, florid face.

"Eighties, I'd guess," Judith replied, "but strong as an ox. You know how hearty those Scandinavians are."

"Like our daughter-in-law," Joe acknowledged, opening the evening paper, which Judith had retrieved earlier from the front porch.

"Yes," Judith said in a contemplative voice. Kristin was not only big and beautiful, but so infuriatingly competent that her mother-in-law was occasionally intimidated. "Yes," she repeated. "Formidable, too. What is she not?"

The front doorbell rang, making Judith jump. "The guests! They're part of a tour, here for two nights. I didn't think they'd arrive until five-thirty." She dashed out through the swinging doors between the kitchen and the dining room to greet the newcomers.

The tour group, consisting of a dozen retirees from eastern Canada, were on the last leg of a trip that had started in Toronto. Some of them looked as if they were on their last legs, too. Judith escorted them to their rooms, made sure everything was in order, and informed them that the social hour began at six. To a man — and woman — they begged off, insisting that they simply wanted to rest before going out to dinner. The bus trip from Portland had taken six hours, a result of summer highway construction. They were exhausted. They didn't need to socialize, having been cheek by jowl with each other for the past three weeks. Indeed, judging from some of the glares that were exchanged, they were sick of each other. Could they please be allowed to nap?

Judith assured them they could. Cancellation of the social hour meant that she, too, could take it easy. Following hip replacement surgery in January, Judith still tired easily. But before taking a respite, she had to call the Kidds and the Izards to inform them that their reservations were being changed because of unforeseen circumstances.

Joe had just opened his second Harp when Judith returned to the kitchen. She observed the top of his head behind the sports section and smiled to herself. There was more gray in his red hair, and in truth, there was less of either color. But to Judith, Joe Flynn was still the most attractive man on earth. She had waited a quarter of a century to become his wife, but the years in between seemed to have faded into an Irish mist. On the way to the computer, she paused to kiss the top of his head.

"What's this rash outbreak of affection?" Joe asked without glancing up.

"Just remembering that I love you," Judith said lightly.

"Do you need reminding?"

"No."

She noted the Kidds' number in Appleton, Wisconsin, and dialed. They were repeat customers, having come to Hillside Manor six years earlier. Judith hated to cancel them.

Alice Kidd answered the phone on the

second ring. Judith relayed the doleful news and apologized most humbly. "You'll be put up at a lovely B&B which will be convenient to everything. Ms. Heffelman will contact you in a day or two with the specifics."

"Well, darn it all anyway," Mrs. Kidd said with a Midwestern twang. "We so enjoyed your place. How is your mother? Edgar and I thought she was a real doll."

A voodoo doll perhaps, Judith thought. "Mother's fine," she said aloud. "Of course her memory is sometimes iffy."

"Yes," Mrs. Kidd said in a quiet voice. "Edgar's mother is like that, too. So sad. My own dear mother passed away last winter."

"I'm sorry to hear that," Judith said.

Alice Kidd acknowledged the expression of sympathy, then paused. "You're certain we'll be staying in as nice a B&B as yours?"

"Definitely," Judith declared. Ingrid wouldn't let her down. She'd better not. An inferior establishment wouldn't be a credit to Judith or to the association Ingrid guarded like a military sentry. "Maybe even nicer."

"I doubt that," Mrs. Kidd said as if she meant it.

"You're very kind," Judith responded. "We'll be in touch."

Next she dialed the number of Walt and

21

Meg Izard in Riceville, Iowa. A frazzled-sounding woman answered the phone.

"Mrs. Izard?" Judith inquired.

"Yeah, right. Who is this? We're watching TV."

"I'm sorry," Judith said, then identified herself as the owner of Hillside Manor.

"What's that?" Mrs. Izard snapped. "A rest home? Forget it."

"Wait!" Judith cried, certain that Meg Izard was about to slam down the receiver. "I own the bed-and-breakfast you're staying at in October. The nights of the twenty-ninth, thirtieth, and thirty-first. I'm afraid there's been a change."

"A change?" Meg Izard sounded perplexed. "In what? The dates? We can't change. We're celebrating our twenty-fifth anniversary."

"The change affects your lodgings," Judith explained. "I'm afraid I won't be able to accommodate you that weekend."

"Why not?" Meg's voice had again turned harsh. "You got the Queen of England staying there?"

"Not exactly," Judith replied. "I've had to rearrange my schedule. Unfortunately, there's a movie crew coming for a big premiere."

"Movies!" Meg exclaimed. "Who'd pay

five dollars to see a movie when they can watch it on TV a year later? Who cares? We like our sitcoms better anyway. They make Walt laugh, which isn't easy to do these days."

Riceville, Iowa, must indeed be rural if they only charged five bucks for a first-run film, Judith thought. "It's a big event," she said, with a need to defend herself. "Bruno Zepf is opening his new epic, *The Gasman*, here in town."

There was a long pause at the other end. Finally, Mrs. Izard spoke again: "Never heard of him."

"I don't know much about Mr. Zepf, either," Judith admitted in an effort to appease the disgruntled Mrs. Izard. "You'll be hearing from Ingrid Heffelman soon to make sure you're put up in a very nice inn."

"Hunh." Meg paused. "Okay, we'll stay tuned. But this Heffelbump woman better call soon. October's not that far away."

It was two months away, Judith thought, but didn't argue. She was beginning to feel grateful that the Izards wouldn't be staying at Hillside Manor. Trying to remain gracious, she rang off. The Kidds and the Izards had been disposed of; she needn't worry about Bruno Zepf and his movie people for two months. The waning summer and the early fall should be relatively uneventful.

It was typical of Judith that, as Cousin Renie would say, she would bury her head in the sand. On that warm August evening, she dug deep and tried to blot out some of life's less pleasant incidents.

One of them was Skjoval Tolvang. The tall, sinewy old handyman with his stubborn nature and unshakable convictions had already made some improvements to Hillside Manor. He had repaired the sagging front steps, replaced the ones in back, rebuilt both chimneys, which had been damaged in an earthquake, inspected the electrical wiring, and put in what he called a "super-duper door spring" to keep the kitchen cupboard from swinging open by itself. What was left involved rehanging the door to the first-floor powder room and checking the toolshed's plumbing.

Judith came a cropper with the bathroom repair. On the first day of September, Mr. Tolvang showed up very early. It was not yet six o'clock when he banged on the back door. Joe was in the shower and Judith had just finished getting dressed. The noise was loud enough to be heard in the third-floor family quarters, and thus even louder for the sleeping guests on the second floor.

"Damn!" Judith breathed, hurrying down

24

the first flight of stairs. "Double damn!" she breathed, taking the back stairs to the main floor as fast as she could without risking a fall.

"By early," she said, yanking open the back door, "I thought you meant seven or eight."

"Early is early," the handyman replied. "Isn't this early, pygolly?"

"It's too early for me to have made coffee," Judith asserted. "You'll have to wait a few minutes."

But Skjoval Tolvang reached into his big toolbox and removed a tall blue thermos. "I got my medicine to get me going. I vas up at four."

Coffee fueled the handyman the way gasoline propels cars. He never ate on the job, putting in long, arduous days with only his seemingly bottomless thermos to keep him going.

"I'm a little worried," Judith said, pouring coffee into both the big urn she used for guests and the family coffeemaker. "Having a bathroom just off the entry hall may no longer be up to city code."

"Code!" Skjoval coughed up the word as if he'd swallowed a bug. "To hell vith the city! Vat do they know, that bunch of crackpot desk yockeys? They be lucky to *find* the bathroom, let alone know vhere to put it!"

"It was only a thought," Judith said meekly.

"You vorry too much," Skjoval declared, putting the thermos back into his toolbox. "I don't need no hassles. I quit."

It wasn't the first time, nor would it be the last, that the handyman had quit over some quibble. Skjoval never lacked for work. He was good and he was cheap. But he was also temperamental.

Judith knew the drill, though it wasn't easy to repeat at six-ten in the morning. She pleaded, groveled, cajoled, and used all of her considerable charm to get Skjoval to change his mind. Ultimately, he did, but it took another ten minutes.

Luckily, the rest of the week and the Labor Day weekend went smoothly. It was only the following Friday, when Skjoval was finishing in the toolshed, that another fracas took place.

"That mother of yours," Skjoval complained, wiping sweat from his brow as he stood on the back porch. "She is Lucifer's daughter. I hang the bathroom door yust fine, but vhy vill she not let me fix the toilet?"

"I don't know," Judith replied. Indeed, she had been afraid that Gertrude and Mr. Tolvang would get into it before the job was done. Given their natures, it seemed inevitable. "Did she give you a reason?"

"Hell, no," the handyman shot back, "except that she be sitting on the damned thing."

"Oh." Judith frowned in the direction of the toolshed. "I'll talk to her."

"Don't bother," Skjoval snapped. "I quit."

"Please, Mr. Tolvang," Judith begged, "let me ask —"

But the handyman made a sharp dismissive gesture. "Never you mind. I don't vant to see that old bat no more. She give me a bad time all veek. Let her sit on the damned toilet until her backside falls off." Skjoval yanked the painter's cap from his head and waved it in a threatening manner. "I go now, you call me if she ever acts like a human being and not a vitch." He stomped off down the drive to his pickup truck, which was piled with ladders, scaffolding, and all manner of tools.

Judith gritted her teeth and headed out under the golden September sun. Surely her mother would cooperate. The toilet needed plunging; Gertrude threw all sorts of things into it, including Sweetums. It was either Skjoval Tolvang for the job or a hundred bucks to Roto-Rooter.

Gertrude wasn't on the toilet when Judith reached the toolshed. Instead, she was sitting in her old mohair armchair, playing solitaire on the cluttered card table.

"Hi, Toots," Gertrude said in a cheerful voice. "What's up, besides that old fart's dander?"

"Why wouldn't you let Mr. Tolvang plunge the toilet?" Judith demanded.

"Because I was using it, that's why." Gertrude scooped up the cards and put them in her automatic shuffler. "When's lunch?"

"You ate lunch two hours ago," Judith responded, then had an inspiration. "Why don't you come inside with me? I'm going to make chocolate-chip cookies."

Gertrude brightened. "You are?"

"Yes. Let me give you a hand."

Judith was helping her mother to the door when Skjoval Tolvang burst into the toolshed.

"You got spies," he declared, banging the door behind him. "Building inspectors, ya sure, you betcha."

Judith's dark eyes widened. "Really? Where?"

"In the bushes," Skjoval replied. "Spying."

"Here," Judith said, gesturing at Gertrude, "help my mother into the house. I'll go check on whoever's out there."

But Gertrude balked. "I'm not letting this crazy old coot touch me! He'll shove me facedown into the barbecue and light it off."

"Then stay here," Judith said crossly, and guided her mother back to the armchair.

"Hey!" Gertrude shouted. "What about those cookies?"

But Judith was already out the door. "Where is this inspector or whoever?" she asked of Mr. Tolvang.

"By them bushes," the handyman answered, nodding at the azaleas, rhododendrons, and roses that flanked the west side of the house. "Making trouble, mark my vords."

"I wonder," Judith murmured, heading down the driveway.

There was, however, no one in sight. She moved on to the front of the house. An unfamiliar white car was parked in the cul-de-sac. There were no markings on it. Judith moved on to the other side of the house.

A tall man in a dark suit and hat stood between the house and the hedge that divided Judith and Joe Flynn's property from their neighbors, Carl and Arlene Rankers. The man had his back to Judith and appeared to be looking up under the eaves.

"Sir!" Judith spoke sharply. "May I help you?"

The man whirled around. "What?" He had a beard and wore rimless spectacles. There was such an old-fashioned air about him that Judith was reminded of a character out of a late-nineteenth-century novel.

"Are you looking for someone?" Judith inquired, moving closer to the man.

He hesitated, one hand brushing nervously against his trouser leg. "Well, yes," he finally replied. "I am. A Mr. Terwilliger. I was told he lived in this cul-de-sac."

Judith shook her head. "There's no one by that name around here. Unless," she added, "he intends to stay at my B&B." She made an expansive gesture toward the old three-story Edwardian house. "I run this place. It's called Hillside Manor. There's a sign out front."

The man, who had been slowly but deliberately backpedaling from Judith, ducked his head. "I must have missed it. Sorry." He turned and all but ran around the rear of the house.

Judith's hip replacement didn't permit her to move much faster than a brisk walk. Puzzled, she watched the man disappear, then returned to the front yard. He was coming down the driveway on the other side of the house, still at a gallop. A moment later he got into the car parked at the curb and

30

pulled away with a burst of the engine.

"Local plates," she murmured. But from where Judith stood some ten yards away, she hadn't been able to read the license numbers. With a shrug, she headed back to the toolshed. She'd mention the stranger's appearance to Joe when he got home. If she remembered.

Five hours later, when Joe arrived cursing the dead end he'd come up against in a missing antique clock case, Judith had forgotten all about the man who'd shown up at Hillside Manor.

It would be two months before she'd remember, and by that time it was almost too late.

Chapter Two

Judith recoiled from the obscenity screamed into her ear by Cousin Renie. The four-letter word was rapidly repeated before Renie cried, "You're not 911!" and hung up.

Shaken, Judith stared at her cleaning woman, Phyliss Rackley. "Oh, dear. What now?" she breathed to Phyliss.

"What 'what now'?" Phyliss inquired, scarcely missing a beat as she scoured the kitchen sink.

"My cousin — Serena," Judith said, her high forehead wrinkled in worry. "I think she was trying to call 911. I don't want to call her back in case she's on the line with them. Maybe I should go over to her house to see what's happened."

"You got those Hollywood sinners due in two hours," Phyliss pointed out. "Besides, that cousin of yours is probably in Satan's clutches. I always said she'd end up in the hot spot."

Judith's gaze darted to the old school-house clock. It was two on the dot. Friday, October 29. The day when Bruno Zepf and his Hollywood entourage would arrive for the premiere of *The Gasman* on the following night.

But family came before filmdom. "I've still got some spare time. I'm going to Renie and Bill's. I don't dare call in case she's tied up on the phone with 911."

"Keep away from Lucifer!" Phyliss warned as Judith rushed out the back door. "He'll come after you when you least expect him!"

Judith was used to her cleaning woman's fundamentalism. But like Skjoval Tolvang's obstinacy, Phyliss Rackley's religious mania could be tolerated for the sake of a reliable, thorough work ethic.

Traffic on Heraldsgate Avenue was relatively light for a Friday afternoon. It was just a little over a mile from Hillside Manor to the Joneses' residence on the north side of Heraldsgate Hill. Six minutes after she had left Phyliss in the kitchen, Judith was at the door of her cousin's Dutch Colonial. So far, there were no signs of emergency vehicles outside. Judith didn't know if that was a good or a bad portent.

When Renie and Bill had moved into their home thirty years earlier, the doorbell had been broken. Bill was a psychologist and a retired college professor, a brilliant man in his field, but not adept at household repairs. The bell was still broken. Judith pounded on the solid mahogany door.

No one responded. Anxiety mounting, Judith started to go around to the back but was halted at the corner of the house by a shout from Renie.

"Hey! Come in. I've got this junk all over my hands."

Judith returned to the porch. Renie stood in the doorway, her hands and lower arms spattered with what looked like the insides of a pumpkin. Bill came down the hall from the kitchen. His head was covered with the same orange clumps and he'd left a trail of yellow seeds in his wake.

"What on earth . . . ?" Judith began, her jaw dropping. "I thought you had a catastrophe!"

"We did," Renie replied, moving back to the kitchen, where she ran her hands and arms under the tap. "Bill got a pumpkin stuck on his head."

Judith looked at Bill. Bill shrugged, then took a towel from the kitchen counter and began to wipe himself off. Judith then looked at what was left of the pumpkin. It lay on the floor in several pieces. Only the top with its jaunty green stem remained intact.

Putting a hand to her breast in relief, Judith leaned against the refrigerator. "Good grief. You scared the hell out of me."

"Sorry," Renie said, rinsing her hands. "I hit your number on the speed dial instead of 911."

"Then," Bill put in, his voice muffled by the towel, "she punched the button for her hairdresser. By that time I'd gotten the pumpkin off my head."

"I don't suppose," Judith said slowly, "I ought to ask why you were wearing a pumpkin on your head, Bill?"

Removing the towel, he shrugged again. "It was for your Halloween party tomorrow. I planned to go as Ichabod Crane."

Judith shook her head in wonder, then frowned. "It's not my party, it's Bruno Zepf's. I'm merely catering the damned thing."

"I'm helping," Renie said, looking a trifle hurt. "That's why we're coming, isn't it? We thought it would be more fun if we wore costumes like everybody else."

"What," Judith asked Renie, "were you going as? Ichabod's horse?"

"A tree," Renie said with a lift of her short chin. "You know — the scary kind with a twisted trunk and clawlike branches."

"Don't," Judith advised. "You'll hurt yourself." She glanced at Bill. "One of you already has. I'm going home now. In fact, I might as well stop at Falstaff's Grocery on the way to stock up for the party. Bruno Zepf gave me a list. Some of the items had to come from specialty stores. I hope he can pay all these bills."

"He can," Bill said, his clean-cut Midwestern features finally free of pumpkin debris. "The man's movies make millions. *The Gasman* may hit a billion."

"Good for him," Judith said on a bitter note. "I just wish he wasn't staying at Hillside Manor."

"It's only two nights," Renie soothed. "Look at it as an adventure. A big-time Hollywood producer. Glamorous stars. A famous director. It'll be like having Oscar night in your living room."

"That's what I'm afraid of," Judith said, making her way to the door. "Glad you're not dead. See you tomorrow night."

"I'm coming to help at five," Renie announced. "I'll change into my tree suit later."

"Goody," Judith said in a lifeless voice. "Maybe I'll turn into a pumpkin."

"Hey!" Bill called after her. "*I'm* wearing the pumpkin!"

Judith glanced back at the orange glop that littered the kitchen. "You mean, you were."

An hour later Judith arrived at Hillside Manor with fourteen grocery bags and an entry on the debit side of her checking account for almost four hundred dollars.

"What are you feeding?" Phyliss asked as she put on her shapeless black raincoat. "An army?"

Judith gazed at the paper-in-plastic bags and shook her head. "The problem is, I don't know how many will come here after the premiere and the costume ball at the Cascadia Hotel. Most of the movie people are staying at the hotel. But Mr. Zepf had one of his staff members send me a list of what he'd like served at the midnight supper party. I don't want to run short. He's also been shipping some things that I wouldn't be able to find here in town."

Phyliss gave a toss of her gray sausage curls. "More money than sense," she declared. "What's wrong with meat and potatoes? As for all this shipping, at least two more express trucks showed up today. There may have been another one, but I was upstairs and my lumbago was giving me fits, so I didn't bother myself to come down."

Judith eyed Phyliss. "Are you sure?"

"No, I'm not sure," Phyliss answered crossly. "I've no time for all this fancy-pants stuff. It's gluttony, if you ask me. That's one of the Seven Deadly Sins. I wonder how many of the others they'll commit while they're here."

Judith winced, and based on past history, hoped murder wasn't one of them.

The doorbell rang at precisely five o'clock. By that time Judith had finished organizing and storing the groceries. Feeling nervous, she hurried to greet her first guests.

The middle-aged couple who stood on the front porch didn't look much like Hollywood to Judith. In fact, they seemed more like Grant Wood, or at least his famous painting of *American Gothic*. The thin sour-looking woman with her fair hair pulled back in a bun and the balding gaunt-faced man needed only a pitchfork to complete the image.

"May I help you?" Judith inquired.

"You sure didn't help us before," the woman asserted, "so I don't expect you can help us now."

The voice sounded familiar, but Judith couldn't place it. "I'm sorry, I don't understand. This is a B&B. Have you been a guest here on a previous occasion?"

"Hell, no," the man responded in a deep bass. "We tried, though."

"We need to find the place where they put us instead," the woman said. "Some fool sent the directions to your B&B instead of the one we got changed to."

"Oh!" Judith exclaimed in relief, noticing what appeared to be a rental compact car out in the cul-de-sac. "You must be the Izards. Of course, come in, let me figure out how you can get where you're going."

City maps and guidebooks were kept at the registration desk in the entry hall. Walt Izard showed Judith the address of the substitute inn, which was located about four miles away, near the zoo. She gave him directions while Meg Izard wandered around the big living room.

"I'd like to check out your place," she declared, returning to the entry hall. "I want to make sure we're not getting cheated in case this other B&B isn't up to snuff. We'd stay with my brother, Will, but his place is too small."

"Well . . ." Judith hesitated. "All right, but don't take too long. My guests are due at any moment."

Meg gave a snort. "Movie folks, right?

Think they're big stuff. Bunch of phonies, if you ask me."

Judith hadn't asked, so she didn't comment. "The guest rooms are on the second floor. They're unlocked at present, but please just take a quick look. I have to stay downstairs."

"Will do," Walt replied in the deep voice that seemed too large for his skinny frame.

Judith stayed by the front door, but the phone rang just as the Izards disappeared around the corner of the second landing.

It was Alice Kidd, the wife of the other displaced couple. "We're at Cozy Fan Tutte," she said, "and I wanted to let you know it's not nearly as nice as Hillside Manor."

Judith knew the establishment, which was located north of the university. It was a veritable stately mansion, Georgian in design, and featured amenities not possessed by Hillside Manor, including a sauna and a whirlpool.

"That's very kind of you," Judith said, hearing the Izards' footsteps overhead. "I'd love to have you come to Hillside Manor again. I can't say how sorry I am about the inconvenience."

"I suppose," Alice Kidd said in a slightly wistful voice, "the filmmakers have been given a warm welcome."

"They're not here yet," Judith replied, jumping slightly as the back door banged open. "Excuse me, Mrs. Kidd, but someone has just arrived. Remember us the next time you visit the area, and enjoy your stay."

Clicking off, Judith saw Renie charge out of the dining room. "I'm here. Where's Hollywood?"

"They're late," Judith noted, glancing at her watch, which told her it was almost five-fifteen. "They probably got stuck in Friday rush-hour traffic coming from the airport."

"Probably," Renie remarked, opening the oven. "No appetizers?"

"No guests," Judith said. "I'll wait until they arrive. Hey, what are you doing here? I don't need help until tomorrow night."

"Yes, you do," Renie insisted, pointing a finger at her cousin. "You're already twitching. You're agitated, uneasy, even a little scared. Hollywood descends upon Hillside Manor. You have to be nervous."

"I guess," Judith admitted, "I am."

"So," Renie said, extending her arms in a gesture of goodwill, "I'm at your disposal."

"But what about dinner for Bill and the kids?" Judith inquired.

"Incredibly," Renie said, removing a can of Pepsi from the fridge, "Bill informed me that the kiddies are making dinner tonight. Very brave of them."

"It would be," Judith said dryly, "if they were still kiddies. But since they're all in the thirtysomething range and still living at home . . ."

Renie waved a hand. "Don't remind me. They're merely a bit slow to develop a sense of independence."

"Leeches," Judith said under her breath as footsteps emanated from the front hall.

Renie looked startled. "Who's that? Is Joe home already?"

"No," Judith replied, heading out of the kitchen. "It's my ex-guests, the ones I had to cancel to make room for the movie people. Hang on while I say good-bye."

Renie, however, wandered out behind Judith, but stopped in the archway between the dining room and the entry hall. The Izards were at the door, city map in hand.

"This place isn't too bad," Meg Izard allowed. "Maybe next time we come through here, you'll actually let us stay."

"I hope so," Judith said, not quite truthfully.

Walt Izard opened the door. "Lousy weather, though." He gestured outside. "It's started to rain. Does it really rain here all the time?"

"Often," Judith answered, this time with honesty. "Especially this time of year. Windy, too," she added.

"Halloween weather, all right," Meg said with a grimace. "That's too bad. I hoped we'd have some sun to celebrate our silver anniversary."

"Drive safely," Judith cautioned, moving closer to the Izards in an effort to get them out of the house and into their compact rental. "These streets can be slippery when —"

She stopped, staring into the cul-de-sac as a pair of limos glided to the curb.

"Well, well," Meg Izard muttered, "here come the rich and famous. Let's get out of their way, Walt. We wouldn't want to give them any just-plain-folks germs."

Judith was too flustered to protest. As the limo doors were opened by their drivers, a third car pulled up and stopped in front of the Steins' house at the corner.

"Hey," called one of the other drivers as a diverse group of people began to emerge from the chauffeur-driven cars, "will somebody move this crate?" The young man gestured at what Judith assumed was the Izards' rental.

Both Meg and Walt froze momentarily on the threshold. "Big-shot bastards," Walt muttered. "To hell with 'em."

But Meg had already started for the car. With an annoyed shrug, Walt followed his wife. The couple drove away as Arlene Rankers appeared from the other side of the hedge and the first of the celebrities made their way toward Hillside Manor.

Although at least a half-dozen people were approaching the front porch in styles ranging from a brisk trot to a languid lope, Judith's gaze was fixated on just one man, who held a cell phone to his ear: He was almost bald, with a short grizzled beard and a fireplug build. What little hair he had left had grown out and was tied with a black ribbon into a thin, foot-long ponytail. His cheeks were pitted with old acne scars, and while his movements were controlled, energy exuded from him like sparks from a faulty toaster. Judith realized that she recognized him from casually glimpsed photographs. He was Bruno Zepf, megaproducer and Hollywood legend-in-the-making.

"Mr. Zepf," Judith said, putting out her hand.

"Mr. Zepf," echoed Renie and Arlene, who had joined Judith on the porch. Renie looked as if she were trying very hard not to be impressed; Arlene appeared close to bursting with unbridled gush.

Zepf clicked off the cell phone and zeroed

in on Judith, his shrewd blue eyes narrowing a bit. "You're Mrs. . . .Flynn?"

"I am." To her horror, Judith dropped a slight curtsy.

"Welcome to Hillside Manor," Arlene burbled, grabbing the hand that Judith had just released. "This is a wonderful B&B. This is a wonderful neighborhood. This is a wonderful city." She lowered her voice only a jot. "That's why we're thinking of moving."

Judith and Renie were used to Arlene's contradictions. Judith flinched, but Bruno apparently hadn't heard Arlene. He had already moved on to shake Renie's hand without ever looking right at her, and was now in the entry hall, surveying his new surroundings. Such was his air of possession that Judith felt as if she'd not only rented Bruno a room but sold him the entire house.

Judith had to force herself to take her eyes off the great man and greet the other guests. She immediately recognized Dirk Farrar and Angela La Belle, whose famous faces had appeared in a series of hit movies. Judith had actually seen two of their films, on video. Just as the pair reached the porch, Judith noticed that Naomi Stein had come out of her house on the corner and Ted Ericson was pulling into his driveway across the street.

As Ted got out of his car, Dirk Farrar also saw the newcomers. "Beat it, scumbags!" he yelled. "No paparazzi!" Pushing past Angela La Belle and the three-woman welcoming team, he disappeared into the living room.

With a faint sneer on her face, Angela La Belle ignored the gawking neighbors along with her fellow actor and proceeded up the front steps.

"Ms. La Belle," Judith said, gathering her aplomb, "I so enjoyed your performance in" — her mind went blank — "your last movie."

Angela's face, which seemed so angelic on the screen, wore a chilly smile. "Thanks. Where's the john?"

"Straight ahead," Renie said, pointing to the new door that Skjoval Tolvang had recently installed.

Judith was left to confront a somewhat less familiar face. She racked her brain to recall who else was on Bruno's guest list.

"Hi, Mr. Carmody," Renie said, coming to the rescue. "My husband and I were sorry you didn't win Best Supporting Actor this year. You were a really great villain in *To Die in Davenport*."

"Thanks," Ben Carmody replied with what appeared to be a genuine smile. "Face it, I was up against some pretty tough competition."

Judith was startled by Carmody's benign appearance. She was so used to seeing him as the embodiment of evil that she scarcely recognized him. He was tall and lean, much better looking in person than on the screen. Judith shook Ben Carmody's hand and also received a warm smile.

Like Dirk Farrar, the next arrival ignored Judith and the others. Unlike Dirk, the pencil-thin black woman in the gray Armani suit glided over the threshold as if she had wheels on her Manolo Blahnik pumps. Once inside, she joined Bruno Zepf, who had migrated into the front parlor. The woman closed the parlor door behind her, leaving the cousins and Arlene staring at each other.

Last but not least was a small, exotic creature who apparently was communing with the squirrels in the maple tree near the front of the house.

"Who is that?" Arlene inquired, her pretty face perplexed. "She reminds me of someone."

"Ellie Linn-MacDermott," Renie said. "Except I think she's dropped the Mac-Dermott."

"Y-e-s," Arlene said slowly, "that's who she reminds me of. Ellie Linn-MacDermott. I've seen Ellie in two or three movies. Funny, this girl's a dead ringer for her."

"She *is* Ellie Linn," Renie responded, making way for the chauffeurs, who were carrying in the luggage. "She has a role in *The Gasman*."

"Oh!" Arlene's hand flew to her mouth and her blue eyes widened in surprise. "Of course! The actress! Or is it hot dogs?"

"Both," said Renie, then jumped out of the way as the wheels of a large suitcase almost ran over her foot. "Her father, Heathcliffe MacDermott, is the Wienie Wizard of the Western World."

Arlene again looked puzzled. "But this girl . . ." She waved an arm toward the young woman who was trying to coax one of the squirrels down from the maple tree. "She looks Chinese."

"Her mother's from Hong Kong," Renie said. "Or Shanghai. Or someplace like that."

Judith excused herself to show the drivers where to stow the luggage upstairs. When she started down again, Angela La Belle met her on the second landing.

"Where's my room?" she asked, blinking big brown eyes that were offset by long lashes that might or might not have been her own. The lashes, like the eyes, were dark, and made a striking contrast with the actress's waist-length blond hair.

"Um . . ." Judith hesitated. "Let me get

48

the room chart. I'll be right back. There's a settee in the hallway and a phone, if you need it."

Without any response, Angela passed on to the second floor. Judith hurried to fetch the room chart, which she'd left on the entry-hall table. The only thing she remembered was that Bruno Zepf had the largest room, Number Three, to himself, though he shared the bathroom with Room Four. Judith couldn't believe that she was so rattled by a bunch of Hollywood hotshots. After ten years in the hostelry business, she thought she'd met just about every type of person from every level of society. Maybe she was more impressionable than she realized.

Swiftly, Judith tabulated the guests who had arrived so far. Unless she was mistaken, at least one of the members of Bruno's party hadn't shown up yet.

"Psst!" Renie hissed from the hallway. "We're on the job."

Judith turned sharply. "You are? Doing what?"

"Plying your guests with adult beverages," Renie replied. "Or, in some cases, the freshest of springwaters and a vegetable drink that looks like a science experiment."

"Thanks, coz," Judith said with a grateful

smile. "Thank Arlene for me, too. I'll be right with you."

Checking the chart, Judith noted that Winifred Best, Bruno's special assistant, was slotted for Room One. Since there were only three women in the party and Judith had recognized the two actresses, Winifred must be the Armani-clad black woman who had sailed into the house and closeted herself with Bruno.

Dirk Farrar and Ben Carmody were sharing Room Four. Judith wondered how — and why — they'd put up with such an arrangement. The same could be said for Angela La Belle and Ellie Linn, who would be staying in Room Six. Of course it was only for two nights. Perhaps the proximity to Bruno was worth the sacrifice. Still, Judith wasn't accustomed to such self-effacement among the Well-Heeled.

Room Five had been assigned to *The Gasman*'s director, Chips Madigan; the film's screenwriter, Dade Costello, was set for Room Two, the smallest of the lodgings. Chart in hand, Judith went back upstairs to find Angela La Belle.

"Room Six," Judith said with a cheerful smile.

Angela was sprawled on the settee in the hallway, leafing through one of the magazines Judith kept handy for guests. "Okay." The actress didn't look up.

"Your key," Judith said, reaching into the pocket of her best black flannel slacks. "I'll give the other one to Ms. Linn."

"Fine." Angela still didn't look up.

"Your baggage is right there," Judith said, pointing to the piled-up suitcases and fold-overs the drivers had placed in front of Grandma and Grandpa Grover's old oak book shelving. "Only Mr. Zepf's has been put away because I wasn't exactly sure who was staying where. Some of his belongings arrived earlier today via UPS."

Angela yawned. "Right."

Judith gave up and headed past Rooms Four, Five, and Six to the back stairs. She wanted to pop the appetizers into the oven before she joined her other guests. Halfway down, she realized she hadn't given Angela the front door key along with the one to her room. Though her hips were growing weary, Judith hurried back to the second floor.

The settee was empty, the magazine that Angela had been perusing lay on the floor. Judith frowned. Could Angela have already collected her luggage and gone into Room Six so quickly?

The stacks of baggage sat untouched. But

the door to Room Three, Bruno's room, was ajar.

"Hunh," Judith said to herself. When she picked up the copy of *In the Mode* magazine, she noticed that it was open to a spread on a recent Hollywood gala. The large color photo on the left-hand page showed Dirk Farrar and Angela La Belle with their arms around each other. The caption read, *Super Hunk and the Ultimate Babe get cozy at the annual Stars for Scoliosis Ball. Are Dirk and Angela hearing La Wedding Belles?*

Judith wondered if Angela and Dirk had no intention of staying in different rooms.

Chapter Three

Renie and Arlene seemed to have everything under control. Arlene already claimed to have formed a fast friendship with Ellie Linn, and insisted that Ben Carmody would be the perfect husband for her unmarried daughter, Cathy.

"They're not snooty," Arlene declared, putting another batch of puff pastries into the oven. "You just have to go about it the right way when it comes to asking questions. For example, when I spoke to Dirk Farrar about the paternity suit that was in the news a year ago, I mentioned how wonderful it was to be a parent. Then I asked how he liked being called Daddy. So simple."

"What did he say?" Judith inquired.

"Oh, it was very cute," Arlene replied breezily. "He sort of hung his head and mumbled something about 'mother' and

'Tucker.' I think he said 'Tucker.' That must be the little fellow's name."

The cousins exchanged bemused glances before Judith carried a tray of French pâté and English crackers into the living room. Dirk Farrar, with a cell phone affixed to his ear, lazed on one of the matching sofas by the fireplace while Ellie Linn and Winifred Best sat opposite him. Winifred was also using a cell phone. Ben Carmody was examining the built-in bookcases next to the bay window. A big shambling man in khaki cargo pants, plaid shirt, and suede vest had his back turned and was staring out through the French doors. There was no sign of Bruno Zepf.

Judith cleared her throat. "I'll be serving the hors d'oeuvres in just a few minutes," she announced.

Only Ben Carmody looked at her. "Sounds good. I'm kind of hungry."

Winifred Best's head twisted around. "You should have eaten more of Bruno's buffet on the plane. You know he always serves excellent food."

With an off-center grin, Ben shrugged. "I wasn't hungry then."

Renie, who had been out in the kitchen with Arlene, joined Judith. "Hey, coz," she said brightly, "have you met Dade Costello, the screenwriter for *The Gasman*? He's been telling me all about the script."

Judith nodded toward the big man by the French doors. Renie's nod confirmed his identity.

"I'll introduce myself," Judith murmured. Passing through the living room, she caught a few cutting remarks:

". . . worse than that no-star hotel in Oman . . ."

". . . If I'd wanted to stay in a phone booth, I'd prefer it was in Paris. . . ."

". . . bath towels like sandpaper. Whatever happened to plush nubbiness? Atlanta was nubby, but Miami was the nubbiest . . ."

Wincing, Judith arrived at Dade Costello's elbow before he turned around. "I'm Judith Flynn," she said, putting out a hand. "Your innkeeper."

"That right?" Dade shook Judith's hand without enthusiasm. Or maybe because he was so big, he'd learned to be gentle with somewhat smaller creatures.

"Yes." Judith's smile felt false. "I'm interested in the story behind *The Gasman*. Your story, that is."

Dade's ordinary features looked pained. He had bushy dark hair dusted with gray, and overly long sideburns. "It's not my story," he said, with a trace of the Old South in his voice.

"Oh." Judith's phony expression turned to genuine confusion. "I thought you wrote the script."

"I did." Dade stuck his hands in his pockets. "But the story isn't the script."

Judith waited for an explanation, but none was forthcoming. "You mean . . . you adapted the story?"

Dade nodded. "My script was based on a novel."

"I see." Judith understood that this was often the case. "Did the book have the same title?"

Again, Dade nodded, but offered no details. For a man of words, Dade Costello didn't seem to have many at his command in a social situation. Maybe, Judith thought, that was why writers wrote instead of talked.

"I never heard of the book," she admitted. "Was it published recently?"

This time, Dade shook his head. "No. It's been around awhile."

"Oh." Now Judith seemed at a loss to make conversation. She was about to excuse herself when Dade rapped softly on one of the panes in the French doors.

"There's a head in your backyard," he said.

Judith gave a start. "What?"

Dade's thumb gestured out past the porch

56

that flanked the rear of the house. "A head. It's been sitting there for at least five minutes."

Judith tried not to shriek. "Where?"

"There." Dade pointed to a spot almost out of their line of vision. "See it? On top of those bushes."

Judith stared. "Oh!" she exclaimed in relief. "That's not a head, it's my mother. I mean . . ." With a rattle of the handle, she opened the French doors. "Excuse me, I'd better see what she's doing out there."

Despite the rain, Gertrude wore neither coat nor head covering. She stood next to the lily-of-the-valley bush, leaning on her walker and panting. At the foot of the porch steps, Bruno Zepf hovered in the shelter of the eaves with his head cocked to one side.

"So," Bruno was saying to Gertrude, "you actually survived the *Titanic*'s sinking?"

"You bet," Gertrude replied, catching her breath. "It's a good thing I could swim."

"Mother!" Judith spoke sharply as she moved to take Gertrude's arm. "It's raining. What are you doing out here?" She darted a glance at Bruno. "Excuse me, Mr. Zepf, but my mother shouldn't be outdoors without a coat or a rain hat. I'll take her back inside."

But Gertrude batted Judith's hand away.

"Stop that! I'm not finished yet with this fine young Hollywood fella."

Bruno, however, held up a hand. "That's all right, Mrs. . . . ?"

"Grover," Gertrude put in and shook a crooked finger. "You remember that when you make the movie about me."

Bruno forced a chuckle as Judith tried to move her mother along the walk toward the toolshed. "The problem is," Bruno called after them, "someone else already made a movie about the *Titanic* not very long ago."

Gertrude refused to move another inch. "What?"

"Yes," Bruno responded, backing up the porch steps. "It was a big success, an Oscar winner."

"I'll be," Gertrude muttered, allowing Judith to make some progress past the small patio. Then the old lady suddenly balked and turned around to look at Bruno Zepf. "Hey! Did I tell you about being on the *Hindenburg*?"

"Keep moving," Judith muttered. "We're both getting wet."

"You always were all wet," Gertrude grumbled, but shuffled along the walk under her daughter's guiding hand. "Who was that guy? Cecil B. DeMille?"

"No, Mother," Judith replied as an ago-nized scream erupted from behind her. She turned to see Bruno Zepf clutching at the screen door and writhing like a madman.

"I can't get in! I can't get in!" he howled.

Abandoning Gertrude, Judith rushed to the back porch. "What's wrong? What is it?"

Bruno swung his head to one side. "There! By your foot! It's a spider! Help!"

Judith peered down at the tiny arachnid that was scooting toward the edge of the porch. A moment later the spider disappeared into the garden.

"It's gone," Judith said, over Bruno's wails. "That is, the very small spider has left the building."

Bruno's head jerked up. "It has? Are you sure?"

Judith was about to reassure Bruno when Winifred, with Dirk Farrar right behind her, opened the back door. Bruno all but collapsed into Winifred's arms.

"What's going on?" she demanded.

Judith grimaced. "Mr. Zepf saw a spider on the porch."

"Oh, no!" Winifred looked aghast. Dirk snickered.

"Does Mr. Zepf have arachnophobia?" Judith asked as Bruno's shudders subsided.

"Not exactly," Winifred replied, patting Bruno on the back as if he were a frightened child. "They're bad luck." She managed to disentangle herself and took Bruno's hand. "Come inside, it's quite safe."

Dirk lingered at the door. "Twerp," he muttered. "Chickenhearted twerp."

"Why are spiders bad luck?" Judith asked.

Dirk shrugged his broad shoulders. "Something to do with a spider during the shooting of Bruno's first picture. Somehow, one got on the camera lens and ruined a perfect take. The crazy bastard's never been the same since." He stopped and turned quickly to look over his shoulder. No one was there. "Crazy like a fox, maybe I should say." With another shrug, Dirk Farrar moved down the hallway.

Judith went back to the toolshed, where her mother was still standing in the doorway.

"What caused that commotion?" Gertrude asked in her raspy voice.

"The guest you were talking to doesn't like spiders," Judith explained, steering her mother inside. "He's okay now. Say, what were you doing out in the rain? Were you trying to come into the house?"

"Of course not," Gertrude huffed. "Why would I do that?"

Judith eased the old lady into the overstuffed chair behind the card table. "You do sometimes."

"When Lunkhead's not there, maybe," Gertrude allowed, then gave Judith a sly look. "I don't see his car. Maybe I wanted to meet those movie stars, like Francis X. Bushman and Clara Bow."

Judith didn't feel up to adding her mother to the already motley mix. "How about seeing them tomorrow when they're all dressed up and ready to leave for the premiere?"

Gertrude flopped into the chair. "Tomorrow? I could be dead by tomorrow."

"You won't be," Judith assured her mother. "Besides, not all of them have arrived yet."

Judging from the pinched expression on Gertrude's face, the effort to reach the house had tired her. "Well — okay. Who's still coming? Theda Bara?"

Judith gave her mother's shoulder a gentle squeeze. "Someone more recent. I'll be back with your supper in just a bit."

The truth was, Judith hadn't even begun to prepare the family meal. Gertrude didn't mind a TV dinner, but Joe was another matter. As soon as the hors d'oeuvres were served, she would start the evening meal.

Arlene, however, had already brought the appetizers out to the guests: crab cakes, mushrooms stuffed with shrimp, teriyaki beef on skewers, tea sandwiches with smoked salmon, and — courtesy of Bruno — an exotic caviar from a shop and a city Judith had never heard of.

"Thanks, Arlene," Judith said when the two women were back in the kitchen. "You saved my life. Now I can get dinner."

"No need," Arlene said, opening the oven. "I made a chicken casserole this afternoon. It's heating right now. I put the green salad in the fridge. The homemade rolls can be heated up in five minutes."

Judith beamed at her friend and neighbor. "Arlene, I could kiss you. In fact, I will." She leaned forward and gave Arlene a big smack on the cheek.

"It's nothing," Arlene said, her expression suddenly gone sour as it always went when she was complimented for her charity. "I knew you'd have other things on your mind. By the way, the last guest just arrived. Serena took him upstairs to his room."

"The director, Chips Madigan," Judith murmured. "I'd better say hello."

But Renie and Chips were already coming back down the stairs when Judith reached the entry hall.

"Hey, coz," Renie called from over the balustrade, "meet the Boy Wonder of the movies."

Startled by Renie's familiarity with the famous director, Judith was even more startled to see the Boy Wonder. With his red hair, freckles, and gawky manner, Chips Madigan looked like a college freshman. Half stumbling down the stairs, he grinned at his hostess, put out a hand, and almost knocked over a vase of flowers with his elbow. He wore a viewfinder around his neck, which he put to his eyes as soon as he reached the landing.

"Wow!" Chips cried in excitement. "A great tracking shot into the living room. Bookcases, silver tea service, lace curtains — this angle reeks of atmosphere." He let the viewfinder dangle from his neck and loped over to Judith.

"Hi," he said with a big smile. "You're Mrs. Flynn, right? This is one swell place you've got here." Chips got down on his haunches, the viewfinder again at his eyes. "Great elephant's-foot umbrella stand. It doesn't have a bad angle."

Recalling the critical comments she'd overheard from some of the other guests, Judith grinned back. "Thank you, Mr. Madigan. I appreciate that."

"Hey," Chips responded, "my mom runs a bed-and-breakfast in Nebraska, right on the Missouri River. It's an old farmhouse. I'll bet the two of you would get along real well."

"I'll bet we would," Judith agreed. Up close, she could see that Chips wasn't as young as he looked. The red hair was thinning and there were fine lines around his eyes and mouth. Maybe behind the camera he coaxed rather than commanded his actors. Certainly he emanated no aura of Hollywood's legendary directors. Judith found Chips Madigan's friendly, boyish demeanor refreshing. Even endearing, she thought as he turned toward the living room, tripped on the Persian area rug, and sent his long, lanky frame sprawling across the floor.

"Whoa!" Chips cried. "You'd never know I got my start directing musicals!"

Though both Judith and Renie offered to help, he politely brushed off their outstretched hands and scrambled to an upright position on his own.

Judith noticed that none of the guests made the slightest move to aid their fallen comrade. Indeed, Chips Madigan's unorthodox arrival was virtually ignored. Perhaps that was because Bruno Zepf was standing in front of the fireplace, obviously over his fright and looking like Napoleon about to rally his generals.

Chips, however, seemed undaunted. With a cocky air, he strolled into the living room and plopped down on the window seat next to Angela La Belle, who had also joined the company. At least three cell phones were swiftly turned off. Judith was beginning to wonder if the devices were permanently attached to their owners.

The director's arrival was apparently a signal for Bruno to shift gears. He took a cigar out of the pocket of his denim shirt, rolled it around in his pudgy fingers, and stuck it in his mouth, unlit.

"We're assembled here on an historic occasion in the annals of the motion-picture business." The producer paused to gaze around the long living room, from the plate rails to the wainscoting. Several of his listeners' expressions of distaste indicated that Hillside Manor wasn't worthy of so momentous a pronouncement.

"As you all know," he continued after a sip of the thirty-year-old Scotch he'd brought with him, "when I first conceived *The Gasman*, most people in the business told me it would be an impossible film to make. The scope was too big, the concept too ambitious, the goal too lofty, and the movie itself far too expensive given the audience we're aiming for." He paused again, this time gazing at the cousins, who were standing under the archway between the entry hall and the living room. "Excuse me, ladies.

65

This is a private meeting. Do you mind?"

"Not very well," Renie shot back before Judith could interfere.

"I'm sorry," Judith broke in, yanking on her cousin's arm. "We were just checking to make sure you had everything you needed for the social hour."

Winifred Best glanced at Judith in amusement. "The social hour. How quaint."

Bruno made a little bow to Judith and Renie. "We have everything for now. You may go."

Judith shoved Renie back into the entry hall. Renie dug in with her heels and came to a dead stop at the head of the dining-room table.

"That egotistical dork is treating us like slaves!" she railed. "Who the hell does he think he is? I've faced off with bigger fish before he came along!"

Judith knew that her cousin could back up her bluster. In Renie's graphic design business, she had gone up against everybody from Microsweet to the mayor. She didn't always win, but even if she lost, she still managed to save face. Renie's small, middle-aged matron's appearance was deceptive. It concealed an abrasive manner that, upon occasion, could get physical. Which was all the more reason why Judith had to keep her cousin out of Bruno's sight.

"Don't even think about it," Judith said under her breath. She loomed over her cousin by a good five inches, outweighed her by some forty pounds, yet Judith knew she was outmatched. Renie had had shoulder surgery on the same day that Judith had undergone her hip replacement. If nothing else, Renie could still run.

"Hey!" Joe Flynn's voice cut through the kitchen and into the dining room. "What's going on? Still fighting over who has the best Sparkle Plenty doll?"

Judith backed away from her cousin. Renie's ire evaporated, as it often did after the initial outburst.

"Not exactly," Judith said, meeting her husband at the swinging doors and giving him a big kiss on the lips. "Boy, am I glad to see you. I'm not sure I'm ready for the movies."

"What's wrong?" Joe inquired. "Aren't your guests behaving themselves?"

"It's attitude," Renie said, joining Joe and Judith just inside the kitchen. "These creeps are loaded with attitude, and some of it's bad."

"Relax," Joe urged. "Years ago, I made big bucks working security for location companies shooting around town. I could keep the rabid fans and the celebrity seekers and the nutcases away, but I couldn't offer the kind of security they really needed. The problem with these movie types is that they're basically insecure."

"That's true," Renie agreed. "Bill says that because of the capricious nature of the business and the personalities involved in moviemaking, they're constantly seeking reassurance that they're loved and wanted. Bill sometimes uses feature films to study the behavior of —"

Renie's latest parroting of her husband's expertise was mercifully interrupted by Arlene, who poked her head in the back door. "I took your mother's supper out to her. I've got to go home now and feed my darling, patient Carl. To the dogs," she added with a sinister expression.

"Thanks again, Arlene, I really appreciate . . ." But Arlene was gone before Judith could finish the sentence.

"Have a drink on me, ladies," Joe offered, taking down a bottle of Scotch and a bottle of Canadian whiskey from the cupboard. "What are the guests up to?"

Judith slumped into one of the kitchen chairs. "Listening to how wonderful Bruno is, from Bruno's own lips."

"And," Renie put in, opening the cupboard door by the sink to get three glasses, "listening to Bruno tell them how marvelous *The Gasman* is, which I assume they already know, having been involved in the making of it." Handing the glasses to Joe, she closed the cupboard door behind her. Or tried to. "Damn! What's with this thing? It won't stay shut."

Judith heaved a sigh. "Mr. Tolvang supposedly fixed it when he was here, but the door still swings open on its own." She gave Joe a plaintive look from under her dark lashes. "I don't mean to nag, but I have mentioned that you might look at it. I hate to ask Mr. Tolvang. He's so stubborn, he'd probably tell me I was imagining the problem."

"I'll give it a go," Joe answered airily, handing Judith her Scotch. "I've been kind of busy lately."

Judith didn't respond. While Joe was slightly more adept at household repairs than Bill, the Flynn to-do list was never a priority.

"So what's this movie about anyway?" Joe asked. "A public utility?"

"Not exactly," Renie replied. "Dade Costello — the screenwriter — explained the basic plot to me."

"That's more than he did for me," Judith remarked.

"Maybe you used the wrong approach," Renie said. "He's kind of touchy. Sullen, too. Of course I'm used to moody writers. Freelancers are the worst. They can't bear to have their precious copy rearranged so it will fit the graphics. Anyway, the bare bones Dade sketched out for me involve the entire history of the world as seen through the eyes of a simple gasman. That is, an employee who works for a gas company somewhere in the Midwest." Renie paused for effect. "Get it? Everyman in the middle of the country, the center of the universe."

"I got it," Joe murmured into his Scotch.

"Anyway," Renie continued, sitting on the counter with her glass of Canadian whiskey cradled in her lap, "Bruno shows the viewer how certain periods of history contributed to our evolution as a civilization. He puts a positive spin on it, concentrating on early forms of writing, the invention of paper, the printing press, and so forth. Thus, he jumps from ancient Egypt and China all the way up to the present. The only problem that I can see is that it takes him four hours to do it."

"Wow," said Judith. "I knew it was a long movie, but isn't that *too* long?"

"There's an intermission," Renie responded. "I gather Bruno wanted to do a real epic, sort of the upside of D. W. Griffith's *Intolerance*."

"I'll wait for the video," Joe said. "I prefer scheduling my own snack and bathroom breaks."

"I don't blame you," Renie said, "except that you'll miss the spectacle unless you see it on a big screen."

Joe shrugged. "I'll use my imagination. Besides, how spectacular can it be watching Gutenberg set type in his basement?"

The question went unanswered as Winifred Best entered the kitchen. "Where are the truffles?" she demanded. "Bruno must have his truffles. Served raw, of course, with rosy salt. I assume you know how to prepare rosy salt?"

Joe's expression was benign. "Three parts salt, two parts paprika, one part cayenne pepper."

Judith was always amazed by her husband's knowledge of fine cuisine. But she looked blankly at Winifred. "I don't recall seeing any truffles. Were they shipped with the caviar and the other delicacies?"

Winifred's thin face was shocked. "No! They were shipped separately. Périgord truffles, from France. They should have arrived this afternoon."

Judith thought back to Phyliss's comment

about the delivery truck that may or may not have stopped at Hillside Manor. "I'll check," she said.

"You certainly will," Winifred snapped. "And you'll do it now. Do you have any idea how rare, how delicate, and how expensive those truffles are?"

Judith didn't, but refused to admit it. She immediately dialed the number of FedEx's tracking service. They had made all the previous deliveries, so she assumed they had — or hadn't — shipped the truffles.

"Yes," the woman at the other end of the line said, "that parcel arrived at your house and was signed for by a Mrs. Gertrude Grover."

Judith sucked in her breath, barely managing to gasp out a thank-you. "Could you wait here?" she asked Winifred. "I think I know where the truffles are."

Winifred was aghast. "You *think?*"

Judith didn't pause for further criticism. She rushed out to the toolshed, where Gertrude was watching TV and finishing supper. The volume was so loud that Judith cringed upon entering the tiny living room.

"You'll never guess what I saw on one of those talk shows," Gertrude said. "Men who love men who love monkeys. What next?"

The query was ignored. Judith picked up

the remote and hit the mute button. "Mother, did you sign for a package this afternoon?"

"A package?" Gertrude looked blank, then scowled at her daughter. "Hey, turn that thing back on. I can't hear the news. There's a bear loose in a used-car lot on the Eastside."

Judith put the remote behind her back. "Did someone deliver a package to the toolshed this afternoon?"

"Oh." Looking distressed, Gertrude tried to sit up a little straighter. "Yes, they did, and I've never seen anything so disgusting in my entire life. Who'd play such an awful joke on an old lady? If you can call it a joke," she added in a dark voice.

Judith realized that her mother was serious. "The package — where is it?"

Gertrude's expression was highly indignant. "Where it ought to be — down the toilet. At least it didn't stink. Much."

"Oh, no!" Judith gasped. "That was . . . that wasn't . . . what did it look like?"

"I told you," Gertrude said. "Like . . . you know what. It was dark brown and all bumpy. It was just . . . horrible. Now who would play such a filthy trick?"

Judith recalled seeing truffles in Falstaff's delicacy section. They had been grayish white and came from Italy. Maybe French truffles were different. If their appearance was as loathsome as Gertrude had described, she couldn't blame her mother for flushing them down the toilet.

"It wasn't a joke," Judith said, patting Gertrude's shoulder and handing over the remote. "It was a box of truffles — sort of like mushrooms — and it was intended for the Hollywood guests. I've never eaten them, but I guess they're extremely delicious."

Gertrude gave Judith an elbow. "Go on with you! Nobody, not even those movie people, would eat anything that looked so foul."

"I'm afraid they would — and do," Judith replied. At least they would if the truffles weren't floating somewhere in the city's sewer system. "Don't worry about it, Mother. It's not your fault."

"Of course it isn't," Gertrude huffed. "What are they having for supper? Bacteria?"

Judith couldn't discuss the matter further. She headed back into the house, trying to come up with one of her well-intentioned fibs to stave off the wrath of Winifred and the rest of Bruno's party.

As Judith entered the kitchen, Joe was answering the phone. She gave him a questioning look, but he shook his head. "It's Bill," he said, handing the receiver to Renie.

Winifred was waiting under the archway between the entry hall and the living room. "Well?" she demanded, tapping a toe on the bare oak floor.

"The truffles were stolen," Judith said. "A bushy-haired stranger burst into my mother's apartment and grabbed them off the table. He fled through the hedge on foot."

"What?"

Judith nodded several times. "I'll notify the police at once."

Winifred looked homicidal. She also seemed incredulous. And, in fact, she was speechless.

Ben Carmody came to her side. "The truffles were stolen?" he inquired in a mild voice. "That's too bad. But then I don't like them." As soon as the words were out of his mouth, he shot a furtive glance at Bruno, who was still standing by the fireplace. "I mean," Ben explained, "they're not my favorite."

Bruno eyed Judith, Ben, and Winifred with curiosity. "Did someone mention the police?"

Winifred pointed a long, thin finger at Judith. "She claims the Périgord truffles were stolen."

Bruno frowned. "Really?" He hesitated. "Calling the police is a bad idea, even for a thousand dollars' worth of truffles. We don't need that kind of publicity."

Chips Madigan jumped up from the window seat. "How about a private detective?"

Bruno looked dubious, but before he could speak, Judith broke in: "That's a good idea. I know just the man." She paused and gulped. "I mean, my husband is a private detective. I'm sure he can clear this up."

Bruno shrugged. "Then let him do it."

Winifred gave Bruno an inquiring look. "Are you certain you want to do that? What do we know about Mrs. What's-her-name's husband?"

All eyes were on Bruno. He scratched his bearded chin before responding. "Why not? Maybe losing the truffles isn't our biggest problem."

Nobody spoke, but there was much shifting of stances and staring at the floor.

Finally, Winifred turned to Judith. "Very well. Let's have a word with your private detective husband."

Judith tried not to grimace. Joe would not take well to supporting his wife in one of her bold-faced lies. "I'll get him," she said in a weak voice.

She went back through the dining room and into the kitchen. As she opened her mouth to explain the situation to Joe, Renie dropped the phone, let out a high-pitched shriek, crawled under the kitchen sink, and slammed the cupboard door behind her.

Chapter Four

"Renie!" Judith cried, pulling on the handle of the door beneath the sink. "Come out right now!"

"What the hell is she doing?" Joe demanded.

"She's in shock," Judith replied as the door — or Renie — resisted her tugs. "I've seen her do this before. Once, when she found out she was pregnant the third time, and again when she got the kids' orthodontist bill."

Joe bent down to pick up the receiver, but heard only the dial tone. "So what is it?" he asked with a worried expression. "Has something happened to Bill?"

Placing the receiver on the counter, he nudged Judith aside and gave the cupboard door a mighty yank. Renie was folded up inside, pale of face, with her chestnut curls in disarray, her mouth agape, and her eyes almost crossed.

"Coz!" Judith urged, hampered by the hip replacement in her effort to kneel down. "What's wrong? Is it Bill?" Maybe he had another pumpkin stuck on his head, Judith thought wildly. Maybe he was suffocating. Maybe he *had* suffocated. Maybe Bill was dead.

But Renie shook her head. "No," she finally croaked, struggling to crawl out of the small, cramped space. "Where's my drink?"

"You dropped it in the sink," Joe replied, giving Renie a hand. "The glass isn't broken. I'll make you another."

"Make it strong," Renie said, then got to her feet and half fell into one of the kitchen chairs. "After all these years . . ." Her voice trailed off.

Judith sat down next to Renie. "Coz, if you don't tell us what's happening, I'm going to have to shake you."

"I'm already shaken," Renie replied. "Down to my toes."

Joe gave Renie her drink, then reverted to his role as detective. "Bill told you something. Therefore, he must be alive and telephoning. Bill doesn't like talking on the phone. Thus, he must've had urgent news. Come on, what was it? Something about your mother?"

Judith's aunt Deb was the same age as Gertrude. She, too, was in frail health and had been virtually confined to a wheelchair for many years. Judith knew that it wouldn't be surprising if Renie's mother had . . .

But Renie was shaking her head. "No," she said after taking a deep swallow from her glass. "It's our kids. It's why they made dinner. They thought I'd be there, along with Bill."

Joe frowned. "Your kids? All three of them?"

"All three of them," Renie replied after another quick quaff. "Tom, Anne, and Tony."

"What about them?" Judith asked, beginning to calm down. If the Jones offspring could make dinner, they must be in one piece.

Renie set the glass down and wrung her hands. "They're getting married. All three. I think I'll faint." She put her face down on the table.

"They're getting *married?*" Judith cried. "Are you serious?"

"Of course I am." Renie's voice was muffled.

"Why, that's wonderful!" Judith beamed at Joe. "It's what you hoped for, dreamed of, wanted to . . ."

Renie's head jerked up. "But it's such a

shock. I don't know any of these people they're marrying. Our kids have had romances that went on and on and on, then they all broke up at one time or another. But these . . . future in-laws . . . are strangers. What if they're crazy or wanted by the police or . . . *poor?*" Renie wrapped her hands around her neck and made a strangling gesture.

"Oh, good heavens!" Judith exclaimed. "Don't be such a snob! Why, when Mike and Kristin got engaged I never cared for one minute if she or her family had a dime."

"Mike had a job," Renie pointed out. "This is different. This is . . ." She swigged down the rest of her drink and stood up. "I have to go home. Poor Bill. Poor me. Goodbye." Grabbing her jacket on the way out, Renie dashed off into the rainy night.

"I hope she's okay to drive," Judith said with a worried expression.

"She only had one serious drink," Joe responded. "She'll be fine." He patted Judith's shoulder. "Hey, can I do anything to help with dinner?"

"Oh!" Judith jumped up. "Arlene did everything for us. I just need to heat the rolls."

"Sounds good," Joe said. "I'll wander out to peek in on the guests."

Judith clapped a hand to her head. In all the excitement over Renie, she had forgotten about the proposal to hire Joe as a private detective.

"Joe," she said with her back to the oven, "wait. Bruno Zepf wants to hire you."

Joe's round face was puzzled. "Me? Why? Didn't they bring their own security?"

"If they did, they're at the Cascadia," Judith replied. "I mean, they'd want their own people for the premiere and the costume ball, right?"

Joe gave a nod. "So they want me to watch out for them while they're here?"

"Sort of," Judith hedged. "They also want you to find out what happened to their thousand-dollar truffles."

"Good God!" Joe paused, taking notice of Judith's jittery movements with the oven door. "What *did* happen to the truffles?"

The answer came not from Judith but from Winifred Best, who had reentered the kitchen. "They were stolen by a bushy-haired stranger."

Judith froze with her hand on the oven door. "I think I'll let Ms. Best explain it." Putting the rolls on to heat, she scooted out of the kitchen and into the pantry, where Sweetums was sitting by the shelf that contained his cans of food.

But try as she might, Judith couldn't hear the conversation between her husband and Winifred Best. Winifred had lowered her usually sharp voice a notch or two; Joe always spoke softly when he was in his professional mode.

Instead, Judith heard other voices, loud and angry, coming from the backyard. The pantry had no windows, so she tiptoed into the hall to look out through the door. Sweetums followed, meowing pitifully.

The wind, which was coming from the north, splattered rain against the glass and blurred Judith's vision. Ignoring Sweetums's claws, which were affixed to her slacks, she carefully opened the back door.

In the darkness, she could make out two male figures near the driveway. They were arguing loudly, and it looked as if they were about to come to blows.

The wind caught just a few words, sending them in Judith's direction: ". . . trashed what was a solid piece of . . ."

". . . bitching when you got paid as if you'd come up with the whole . . ."

". . . Why not? I had to virtually rework the damned thing . . ."

The door blew shut, clipping Judith on the arm. Sweetums continued to claw her slacks. With an air of resignation, she opened a can of Seafarers' Delight and spooned it into the cat's dish.

"Enjoy it," she muttered. "It looks better than the way Mother described those blasted truffles."

There was a sudden silence in the kitchen. Winifred must have returned to the living room. Judith took a deep breath before rejoining Joe.

"Why?" The single word was plaintive.

Judith flinched. "I had to tell them something."

Joe took a long sip of Scotch. "What really happened?"

Judith explained about the disgusting appearance of the truffles and how Gertrude had — not without reason — flushed them down the toilet.

"Great." Joe leaned against the counter. "How about telling the truth for once?"

Judith sighed. "I know," she said, taking the green salad out of the refrigerator. "Maybe I should have. But I didn't want to be liable for the loss of the truffles and I didn't want to get Mother in trouble."

"You could have explained that your mother is gaga," Joe said. "That would have been the truth."

"Well . . ." Judith swallowed hard. "It's hard for me to admit that sometimes she *is* gaga. And in this case, what she did made sense." Taking silverware out of the drawer, she gave Joe a bleak look. "What did you tell Winifred?"

"That I'd check around," Joe replied. "Without charge. Tomorrow, I'll them what really happened."

"Oh." Judith arranged the place settings, then started out of the kitchen. "I want to check on something, too."

Peeking around the corner of the archway into the living room, she counted noses. Everyone was there.

But Chips Madigan and Dade Costello looked as if their clothes were half soaked by rain.

Judith kept out of the visitors' way as they lingered over the social hour. Hillside Manor's rule, though never hard-and-fast, was that the hour was just that — from six to seven. Most guests were anxious to leave by then for dinner reservations or the theater or whatever other activity they planned to enjoy during their stay.

The visitors from Hollywood were different. Apparently they dined later. Or maybe they never dined at all. Perhaps they really were lotus-eaters, as depicted by the scribes.

But they did leave eventually. Sometime between eight-thirty and nine, the company trooped out to their limos and disappeared into the October night. Joe helped Judith tidy up the living room, which looked not very much worse than it usually did after a more conventional gathering of guests.

There was something different about the downstairs bathroom, however. It wasn't obvious at first. Judith, who had started sneezing after dinner and fervently hoped she wasn't catching cold, sneezed again as she rearranged the toiletry articles by the sink. A bit of white powder floated up into the air and made her sneeze again.

Judith looked at herself in the mirror. Ellie Linn had almond-colored skin. Winifred Best's complexion was the color of milk chocolate. Angela La Belle was fair, but not that fair. None of them would have worn such a pale shade of face powder.

"Joe," she called from the entry hall, "come here. I want you to see something."

Joe, who'd just dumped what he estimated to be about three hundred dollars' worth of uneaten hors d'oeuvres into the garbage, came in from the kitchen.

"What is it?" he asked.

"You used to work vice years ago," Judith said, pointing to a small film of white powder at the edge of the sink. "Is that what I think it is?"

Joe ran his finger in the dusty residue, then tasted it. "Yes," he said. "It's what you think it is. Cocaine."

"Damn!" Judith swore. "I suppose it's to be expected."

Joe nodded. "I'm afraid so. Too many Hollywood types get mixed up with this stuff."

She sighed. "Well, it's only for one more night."

He chucked his wife under the chin. "That's right. Face it, they're probably not the first guests you've hosted who've had a habit."

"That's true." Judith gave Joe a weary smile. "I'll just be glad when they're gone. I prefer normal people."

Joe lifted an eyebrow. "Like the gangsters and superstar tenors and gossip columnists you've had in the past?"

Since all of the guests that he mentioned had been murdered or involved in murder, Judith shuddered. "No, not like that. I was thinking of the Kidds and even the Izards. They're the ones who should be here this weekend, not this crew from L.A."

Joe shrugged. "As you said, it's only for one more night. What could possibly happen?"

Around two A.M., Judith was awakened by muffled noises from somewhere in the house. The guests, she thought hazily, returning from their revels. When the Flynns had gone to bed around eleven, the Hollywood crew had not yet come back. But, as with all Hillside Manor guests, they had keys to the front door. Judith rolled over and drifted off again.

But moments later louder noises made her sit straight up in bed. She glanced at Joe, who was snoring softly. He'd put in a long day; there was no need to rouse him. Judith donned her robe and slippers, then headed down to the second floor.

The lights were on in the hall. Bruno, clad only in underwear decorated with Porky and Petunia Pig figures, was collapsed on the settee. Winifred and Chips Madigan stood over him while Dirk Farrar peered out from behind the door of Room Four. Angela, Ellie, Ben, and Dade were nowhere to be seen.

"What's going on?" Judith asked, noting that Bruno was shuddering and writhing just as he had done on the back porch.

Dirk opened the door a few more inches. "Another damned spider. Big as a house. Or so he says." He smothered a smile.

"No!" Judith couldn't believe it. In late summer, harmless, if imposing, wood spiders sometimes crawled into the basement, but it was too late in the year for them to show up. She marched to Bruno's room, where the door was ajar.

Ben Carmody was standing by Bruno's bed, laughing so hard that his sides shook. "Look," he finally managed to say. "It's a spider, all right, but . . ."

Judith charged over to the bed, then gave a start. "Ohmigod!"

A black, long-legged creature with a furry body lay on the bottom sheet just below the pillows. Judith stood frozen in place until Ben picked the thing up by one leg and bounced it off the floor.

"It's fake," he said, still chuckling. "It's one of those rubber spiders kids have for Halloween. Where's your garbage? I'll take it outside and dump the thing in there."

"Oh!" Judith put a hand over her wildly beating heart, then reached out to Ben. "I'll get rid of it. You tell Mr. Zepf that the spider wasn't real."

Ben had grown serious. "Some prank. It could have given old Bruno a heart attack."

Judith stuffed the rubber spider in the pocket of her bathrobe and went back into the hall. No one except Dirk seemed to notice her passage as she headed for the back stairs. Five minutes later she returned to the second floor, where Ben and Chips were helping a rubber-legged Bruno back into his room. Winifred had already disappeared and Dirk had closed his door. Judith continued up to the family quarters. She didn't get back to sleep for almost an hour.

Meanwhile, Joe continued to snore softly.

As usual, Judith had breakfast ready to go by eight o'clock. Since it was a Saturday, and Joe had the day off, he didn't come downstairs until eight-fifteen.

"No-shows, huh?" he inquired, pouring himself a cup of coffee.

"So far," Judith replied. "I think they were out very late." She then recounted the incidents with both the real and the fake spiders. "Bruno certainly is superstitious."

"Typical," Joe remarked. "Bill once said that Hollywood types were like gamblers. It makes sense. People who make movies are gamblers."

An hour passed before Judith heard anyone stirring upstairs. Finally, Winifred Best appeared, her thin face drawn.

"Very black coffee, please. With heated rusk."

Judith didn't recall that rusk had been on

the list of required grocery items. Still, Winifred wasn't the first guest to ask for rusk instead of toast. With considerable effort, she got down on her knees and foraged in the cupboard next to the sink.

"Ah!" she exclaimed. "Here it is." She got up slowly, which was fortunate because the temperamental cupboard door had swung out on its own. Judith hit her head, but not very hard. Muffling a curse, she looked around for Joe, then remembered that he'd gone to the garage to tinker with his beloved MG.

"This coffee isn't strong enough," Winifred announced from the dining-room table. "Please make another pot, and double the amount."

Winifred Best wasn't the first demanding guest that Hillside Manor had ever hosted, so Judith calmly put a percolator on the stove. She kept reminding herself that the current visitors were no worse than many she'd had stay at the B&B. It just seemed that this bunch was a wide-screen version in Dolby sound.

Moments later the rusk had been warmed in the oven. Judith brought it out to the dining-room table.

"Has Mr. Zepf recovered from his latest fright?" she inquired.

"Yes," Winifred responded, giving the rusk a suspicious look, "though the rubber spider was a bit much."

"Do you know who put it in Mr. Zepf's bed?"

Winifred shot Judith a withering glance. "I do not. Was it you?"

Judith recoiled. "Of course not! Why would I do such a thing?"

"Because," Winifred said with ice in her voice, "no one else would dare."

"Well, I certainly didn't do it," Judith huffed. "Nor would anyone else around here. In fact, my husband and I are the only residents in the house."

"As you say." Winifred took a small bite of rusk.

"The coffee will be ready shortly," Judith said in stilted tones.

"I should hope so," Winifred said. "Rusk is hard to wash down with weak coffee. By the way," she added as Judith started back to the kitchen, "we'll bring the costumes down later so that you can press them."

Judith turned on her heel. "I don't do ironing. I have a cleaning woman who takes care of the laundry."

"Where is she?" Winifred asked with a lift of her sharp chin.

"She doesn't work weekends," Judith replied, fighting down her annoyance. "If you want something pressed, you'll have to take it up to the cleaners at the top of the hill."

Winifred's dark eyes snapped. "We're not running errands. Since you don't have a laundry service today and it seems you're the innkeeper and concierge, taking care of the costumes falls on you. The costumes must be back by four. Don't worry, you can send the bill to Bruno."

For a long moment Judith stared at Winifred, who was again attired in Armani. Her only accessory was a slim gold bracelet on her left wrist. If she wore makeup, it was too discreet to be noticeable. Late thirties or maybe forty, Judith guessed, and a life that may have been difficult. The Hollywood part, anyway. Judith wondered what it was like for a woman — a black woman especially — to wield such power as assistant to the biggest producer in filmdom.

Nor were Winifred's demands entirely outrageous. If it hadn't been for Bruno's superstition about staying in a B&B before a premiere, Winifred and the others would be ensconced in luxury at the Cascadia Hotel with every convenience at their fingertips.

"Okay," Judith said. "I'll take the stuff up to Arlecchino's. It's a costume shop, so they'll know exactly how to handle the garments and whatever other items need to be fluffed up."

The faintest look of relief passed over Winifred's face. "Thank you," she said.

Judith thought the woman sounded almost sincere, though that was a word she knew she probably shouldn't apply to anyone from Hollywood. The coffee, which looked strong enough to melt tires, was ready just as Chips Madigan loped into the dining room.

"Hey, Win, hey, Mrs. Flynn," he said with a cheerful expression. "Hey — that rhymes! I should have been a writer, not a director." Abruptly, the grin he'd been wearing turned down. "I guess," he muttered, pulling out one of the chairs from Grandpa and Grandma Grover's oak set, "I shouldn't say stuff like that."

"No, you shouldn't," Winifred said with a warning glance.

The guests trickled down for the next hour and a half, creating a frustrating breakfast service for Judith. Normally, she prepared three basic items and offered appropriate side dishes. But the menu requirements for the Hollywood people were vast and varied. Angela La Belle desired coconut milk, kiwi fruit, and yogurt. Dirk Farrar requested a sirloin steak, very rare, with raw eggplant and tomato slices. Ellie Linn ordered kippers on toast and Crenshaw melon. Ben Carmody preferred an omelette with red, green, and yellow peppers topped with Muenster cheese. An apparently restored Bruno Zepf downed a great many pills, which may or may not have been vitamins, shared the strong coffee with Winifred, and ate half a grapefruit and a slice of dry whole-wheat toast. Chips Madigan asked for cornflakes.

Dade Costello never showed. The moody screenwriter had gone for a walk, said Ellie Linn. He wasn't hungry. Nobody seemed curious about his defection.

The omnipresent cell phones were in use again, especially by Bruno, Winifred, and Ben. Somehow they all seemed capable of talking to whoever was on the other end of the line and to members of the party at the table. Between rustling up the various breakfast items and making what seemed like a hundred trips in and out of the dining room, Judith caught snatches of conversation. Most of it dealt with the logistics of the premiere and how to deal with the media. It struck Judith that the only topic of conversation the group shared was the movie business. Maybe it was the only thing that really mattered to them. She tuned her guests out and got on with the task of running Hillside Manor.

As soon as she finished clearing up the kitchen, Judith called Renie. "Give me the details," she requested. "Who's marrying whom?"

An elaborate sigh went out over the phone line. "I'm not sure I've got all this straight myself. Tom's fiancée is the daughter of a local Native American tribal chief. Her name's Heather Twobucks, which is symbolic, since that's about all the money Tom has managed to save over the years. But at least she's got a job — she's the attorney for the tribe."

"That sounds very good," Judith put in.

"She's also one of seven kids and does most of her work pro bono," Renie said. "As for Anne, the man of her dreams is in medical school. You know what that means. Anne will have to get a real job instead of making jewelry out of volcanic lava and selling it at street fairs."

"Mmm — yes, she probably will," Judith agreed. "What's the future doctor's name?"

"Odo Mann," Renie replied. "She'll become Anne Mann. Personally, I wouldn't like that."

"Mmm," Judith repeated. "And Tony?"

Renie let out another big sigh. "Tony's beloved just returned from Tangiers, where she was Doing Good. She works for a Catholic charity and makes just about enough to pay Tony's monthly milk bill. She — her name is Cathleen Forte — wants Tony to join her in the leper colony over there."

"Oh, dear."

"That's what I said," Renie responded. "Except not quite those words and much louder. Bill's in a daze."

"Yes, I can see that he might be," Judith allowed. "Have any of them set the date?"

"Not yet," Renie said, "though Anne and Odo are talking about next spring."

"That gives you some time," Judith remarked.

"Time for what?" Renie demanded. "Time to kidnap our own children and seal them in the basement?"

"I mean," Judith said, "to . . . um . . . get used to the idea."

"You're no help," Renie snapped. "I'm hanging up now. Then maybe I'll hang myself." The phone went dead in Judith's ear.

It was noon before Winifred began bringing the costumes downstairs. Judith was astonished by the detail. They had come, Winifred informed her, from one of the big L.A. rental warehouses that stocked thousands of garments, many of them worn in movies from fifty and sixty years ago and lovingly restored.

"Bruno and I considered using the costumes from *The Gasman*," she explained, "but only Angela, Ben, Dirk, and Ellie appear in the film. We could have drawn from Wardrobe's collection for bit players and extras, but we decided it would make a statement if we used older costumes. More in keeping with the picture's theme, you see."

Judith thought she recognized Ellie's outfit. It looked very much like one of Elizabeth Taylor's gorgeous gowns in *Cleopatra*. Angela's was familiar, too, though seen only briefly on the screen — Scarlett O'Hara's honeymoon ensemble from *Gone With the Wind*.

Pointing to the flowing robes and burnoose for Bruno, Judith made a guess: "*Lawrence of Arabia*?"

"*Khartoum*," Winifred replied.

"Is this yours?" Judith gestured at a nun's white habit.

"Yes." Winifred's expression was rueful. "It's a generic nun's costume, depicting the growth of the monastic movement. We're representing the eras the movie focuses on. I preferred wearing something closer to my own heritage, maybe Muslim dress, from the period of Muhammad. But Bruno insisted that *he* be Muhammad." She waved a slim hand at the *Khartoum* robes. "So I end up being a nun, and I'm not even Catholic."

"I am," Judith said, "and I think it's a lovely habit. Very graceful. You'll look terrific."

Winifred gave an indifferent shrug. "Whatever. Dirk Farrar symbolizes the early Renaissance while showing off his manly physique in that silver-and-gold-slashed doublet and tights. Tyrone Power wore it, I think. The less lavish doublet and the fur-trimmed surcoat came from an MGM historical epic. Or maybe it was Fox. Dade Costello's wearing that for the era of the printing press. The nineteenth-century frock coat and top hat belong to Ben Carmody. The industrial revolution, of course. And Chips Madigan gets to dress as the computer whiz kid."

Judith smiled at the suntan pants, the flannel shirt, the horn-rimmed spectacles, and the box of Twinkies. Living in the land of Microsweet, she was familiar with the outfit.

"What about the rest of the movie company? What will they wear?" she asked.

"Whatever suits *The Gasman*," Winifred replied. "We left everybody else pretty much on their own. They'll conform, of course."

The statement seemed to reflect the general attitude of Bruno Zepf's circle. Winifred had no need to add, "Or else."

Pointing at a stack of garment bags that lay on the living-room floor, Winifred commented, "We'll put them in those. Remember, they have to be back by four o'clock. The premiere is at six."

Carefully, Judith picked up the Scarlett O'Hara costume. "I understand that the ball is at ten. What time do you think you'll be back here for the midnight supper?" She dreaded the idea of putting on such a late event, but Bruno had consented to pay an extra two grand, and Judith couldn't refuse the money.

"A midnight supper is just that," Winifred replied, tucking her nun's habit into one of the garment bags. "We should return shortly before twelve."

Judith gave an absent nod as she fumbled with the silks and taffeta that made up Angela's post–Civil War era gown.

"Careful!" Winifred cried. "Watch out for the decorative trim!"

"Right, okay," Judith agreed. "Maybe I should turn it over to protect the front of the outfit."

Since Winifred didn't argue, Judith did just that. And stared.

The long black-and-white silk skirt and

taffeta petticoat had been slashed in a half-dozen places from the waist to the hem.

Winifred screamed.

Judith couldn't stop staring, but a cold shiver crawling up her spine set off a familiar, terrifying alarm.

Chapter Five

"Win?"

Ellie Linn was standing at the bottom of the stairs, gazing into the living room. She saw Judith and Winifred's horror-stricken faces, and moved quickly, if softly, to join them.

"What's wrong?" Ellie glanced down at the torn costume. "Oh, wow, that looks bad! What happened?"

Winifred was kneeling on the floor, pounding her fists on the carpet. "Sabotage, that's what happened! Angela's gown is ruined! Who would do such a thing?"

Ellie rocked back and forth in her expensive cross-trainers. She was wearing jeans and a long-sleeved tee that didn't quite cover her midriff. Judith figured her for a size three at most.

"Golly, I don't know," Ellie said, gazing at

the ceiling. "Couldn't Angela wear a bedsheet, cut two eye holes in it, and go as a ghost?"

"Ellie!" Winifred's voice was sharp, then she turned to Judith. "Do you think your local costume shop could fix this?"

Judith studied the garment. "They'd have to replace the overskirt. I'll ask them."

"The skirt — or what's left of it — will have to be saved," Winifred declared, finally regaining control of her emotions. "It's the original." She paused, tapping a finger against her smooth cheek. "Yes, maybe an overskirt will do. But make sure it matches."

Judith promised that she would. "By the way," she asked, "were these costumes still in Bruno's room where I had the UPS man deliver them?"

"Yes," Winifred replied. "He was the only one who had enough space."

Ellie was kneeling down to study her *Cleopatra* outfit. "You know, this really looks okay," she observed. "Don't you love the gilded headdress? It'll look way cool with my long black hair." For emphasis, she ran a hand through her raven tresses. "Hey, Win, where are the masks?"

"They're still in Bruno's room," Winifred said, exhibiting the delicacy of a neurosurgeon in placing the damaged Scarlett

O'Hara costume into a garment bag. "The masks are ready. Yours is marked with your name on the inside."

"Great." Ellie stood up. "Wow" — she giggled — "Angela's going to be wild! I'll tell her what happened to her costume. You know — it'll save you the trouble, Win." This time, her giggle sounded slightly sinister as she headed for the entry hall.

"Ellie," Winifred called after her, "don't be mean! Angela has enough problems as it is."

Halfway up the stairs, Ellie leaned over the banister. "Hey, Win, that's not entirely my fault, is it?" The young actress skipped up the steps, long hair swinging behind her.

"I suppose," Judith said in a musing tone as she put Dirk Farrar's doublet and hose into another garment bag, "there's bound to be jealousy between actresses like Ellie and Angela."

Winifred shot Judith a sidelong look. "Oh, yes. You've no idea."

Judith dared to risk a thorny question: "Enough that Ellie would slash Angela's gown?"

"No," Winifred said flatly. "Ellie Linn doesn't have to resort to cheap stunts like that."

Emboldened, Judith was about to ask why

not when Renie gave a shout from the kitchen.

"I'm here. I'm early. I'm out of my mind."

Judith looked at her cousin, who had come into the hallway and definitely appeared a little deranged. Her hair, which was rarely combed unless she was attending a business meeting or a social event, was going off in every direction of the compass. A smudge of dirt stood out on one cheek and a pair of red socks peeked through the holes in her shoes. Even the ratty-sweatshirt-and-baggy-pants combination that made up Renie's working ensemble was more disreputable than usual. And old. The sweatshirt featured the Minnesota Twins World Series victory in 1991.

"Good grief," Judith breathed, "you do look sort of awful."

"I know." Renie, who was carrying a large suitcase, offered Winifred a desultory wave. "I had to get out of the house. The children are arguing about who should get married first. Bill left early for a very long walk, maybe all the way to Wisconsin."

Judith pointed to the suitcase. "Is that your costume?"

"Mine and Bill's," Renie replied. "We dumped the pumpkin idea. Bill's glasses kept getting steamed up. Oh!" she exclaimed, showing a spark of animation. "Look at those costumes. They're beautiful, and they look familiar."

Judith and Winifred explained how and why the costumes had been chosen, then told Renie about the damage that had been done to Angela's.

Renie was genuinely upset. "That's horrible. Bill and I watched a special on TV a while ago about movie costume restoration. It was criminal the way so many of those gorgeous outfits had been left to deteriorate and rot. If I hadn't become a graphic artist, I might have been a costume or a dress designer."

"Then maybe you can help your sister here with getting these costumes to wherever she's taking them," Winifred said briskly. "It's almost twelve-thirty. We don't have much time, especially if Angela's is to be ready."

Renie had bristled over the commanding tone in Winifred's voice, but Judith intervened, putting a hand on her cousin's arm.

"We're not sisters," she explained with a smile. "We're cousins. But we've always been as close as sisters. Closer, perhaps, without the sibling rivalry."

"Lovely," Winifred remarked, putting the last costume into a bag. "I'll see you later."

She marched toward the stairs and out of sight.

Driving to the top of Heraldsgate Hill, Judith allowed Renie two minutes to vent her ire about Winifred's high-handed manner. As they unloaded the car in Arlecchino's small parking lot, Judith gave her cousin another three minutes to complain about the Jones children. Then Judith insisted that Renie stay in the car while she dealt with the costume store's owner. The cautions about the valuable ensembles and the discussion of how to repair Angela's Scarlett O'Hara gown took a full ten minutes. By the time she got back to her Subaru, Renie was fuming again.

"You should have let me help you in there," Renie declared. "I'm not exactly a dunce when it comes to color and fabric."

"No, you're not," Judith acknowledged, "but it would have taken twice as long with two of us. Time is of the essence. Besides, I want to tell you about some weird things that have been happening. Let's drive to Moonbeam's, where we won't be overheard by my very peculiar guests."

Moonbeam's, however, was jammed and there were no empty parking spots. On the Saturday before Halloween, the Heraldsgate Hill merchants had opened their doors to all the trick-or-treaters in the area.

"I could have told you that," Renie grumbled. "While I was wasting away in the car, I counted eight Harry Potters, four bunny rabbits, six fairy princesses, three crocodiles, and two skunks. Not to mention assorted ghosts, witches, and skeletons. This part of the avenue is a zoo — almost literally."

Judith, who was stalled at the four-way stop between Moonbeam's and Holliday's Pharmacy, watched the passing parade in awe. Not only were the children — from infants to teenagers — in costume, but so were many of the parents. Adults dressed as prima ballerinas, football players, sheikhs, African warriors, Argentine gauchos, and a very realistic-looking gorilla were strolling the sidewalks and filling the crosswalks along with their offspring.

"I forgot about all this," Judith said. "They only started doing it a couple of years ago. I guess I've been too caught up with my guests to think much about Halloween."

"You'd better have treats in store for tonight," Renie said. "I understand some of the kids will be going out a day early because Sunday is a school night."

"I bought all my candy a week or so ago," Judith replied. "Hey, where are we headed?"

"Let's go down to the bottom of the hill,"

Renie suggested. "I haven't had lunch. How about you?"

"I forgot about lunch," Judith admitted. "Okay, I'll turn off by M&M Meats and we'll take the back way out of here."

Ten minutes later, the cousins were sitting in a wooden booth at T. S. McSnort's. Even there a handful of customers were dressed for the holiday.

"Would it be terrible to have a drink?" Judith asked. "I could use one."

"So could I," Renie responded. "It's been a rough outing at our house the past few hours."

The cousins ordered screwdrivers, telling themselves that the orange juice would provide them with a healthy dose of vitamin C. To Judith's surprise, Renie didn't even bother to study the menu.

"Aren't you hungry?" Judith asked. Renie was always hungry. Her metabolism could have permitted her to gobble up at least two aisles of Falstaff's Grocery in a single day.

Renie shook her head. "I've lost my appetite. Besides, Bill and I can't afford food anymore. We have to pay for all of Anne's wedding and pony up for our share of Tom and Tony's. Are you forgetting how Kristin's parents tried to fleece you and Joe when Mike got married?"

Judith hadn't forgotten, but as usual, she tried to be charitable. "I think it was mostly a misunderstanding."

"Ha." Renie looked up as their waitress brought the drinks and asked if they wished to order their meal. "I'm having just a cup of clam chowder," Renie said.

Judith quickly perused the menu. "That sounds good. Your chowder is so delicious. I'll have the small Caesar with it."

Renie looked at the waitress again. "Yes, I should eat some greens. I'll have the Caesar, too. You can put smoked prawns on it along with the anchovies. Oh, and maybe I'll make that a *bowl* of chowder."

The curly-haired waitress smiled. "Got it. Anything else?"

Judith shook her head, but Renie held up a hand. "How about the lox platter with the thin slices of rye and onion and cream cheese and capers? That should give me some strength."

"Gee," Judith said as the waitress trotted off, "I'm glad you're not hungry."

"I'm not." Renie sighed. "But I can't allow myself to become frail. Now tell me what's going on at the B&B."

Judith complied, relating the rubber-spider incident as well as the quarrel between Dade Costello and Chips Madigan.

"Chips?" Renie said. "He doesn't seem like a fighter."

"He's tougher than he looks," Judith said. "He has to be, to deal with all those inflated egos when he's directing a movie."

Renie tipped her head to one side in a gesture of assent. "Could you catch any of the exchange between Chips and Dade?"

"Not much," Judith admitted. "It sounded as if they might be arguing about the script. They disagreed about something or other. Maybe interpretation? Would that make sense?"

"Yes," Renie said slowly, "it could. Dade told me *The Gasman* is based on a novel."

"He told me the same thing." Judith paused as the salads arrived and the waitress sprinkled black pepper over them. "Have you ever heard of it?"

"No," Renie replied, attacking a plump pink prawn. "I got the impression it was published years ago."

"The concept for the movie sounds kind of weird," Judith said, "though I'm no film expert."

Renie nodded. "I thought so, too. But I guess we'd have to see it first. Bruno Zepf is a remarkable filmmaker. Remember his last movie, *They All Had Influenza*?"

"I remember when it came out," Judith

said, savoring the tangy dressing on her salad. "But I didn't see it."

"Neither did I," Renie responded, buttering a slice of Irish soda bread. "I heard it was a big hit, though, and I think the critics liked it. It was about the terrible flu epidemic of 1918, with imagery of the Black Death. Or so Bill told me. He watched it on video one night while I was at a baby shower for one of Anne's girlfriends." Renie's face fell. "Oh, gosh — do you suppose I'll end up being a grandmother after all?"

"Why so glum?" Judith queried as the rest of their order arrived. "I thought you envied my status."

"I did. I do." Renie sprinkled salt and pepper on her bowl of chowder, then broke up a handful of water crackers. "It's just that . . . it's kind of a shock somehow. All of this is a shock," she said, dumping the crackers into the chowder. "What if our kids all get married at once?"

"That would save money," Judith said dryly.

Renie brightened. "That's a great idea. It would cut down on arrangements, too. Anne's already talking about where she wants to have the reception."

"Are you going to suggest a triple wedding?" Judith asked.

Renie grimaced. "It sounds a little like the Reverend Moon extravaganzas. I don't know that the kids would go for it."

"It's an idea," Judith said as a familiar figure at the bar caught her eye. "Hey — coz," she said in a whisper, "turn around as discreetly as you can to see who just showed up for a drink."

"Let's try this," Renie said, dumping her knife on the floor. "I prefer using my hands when I eat anyway." She bent down to pick up the knife, then glanced up to see Ben Carmody a mere ten feet away.

"Why isn't he swilling down Bruno's expensive stash of alcohol at the B&B?" Judith murmured, noticing that some of the other customers were trying not to stare at Ben. "Why is he here, alone?"

"Because," Renie replied, loading a slice of rye with lox, "he wants to be just that — alone. You know, like Garbo."

"I suppose." Judith kept her eye on the actor. "He's ordering what looks like straight vodka. Two, in fact. Uh-oh. Here comes Ellie Linn. Now what?"

"Maybe the second vodka is for her," Renie suggested.

Between bites of salad and spoonfuls of chowder, Judith watched the couple at the bar, who were now being eyeballed by at least a dozen other customers. Typical of a city known for its good manners, none of the oglers approached the famous pair.

A glass of white wine was placed before Ellie; Ben downed both shots of vodka.

"They're having a very serious conversation," Judith said. "I'm trying to read their body language. Oddly enough, Ellie seems to be in control. She's all business. That strikes me as peculiar. I figure her for no more than twenty or twenty-two at most."

Renie had lapped up her chowder and almost finished the lox plate. "The control factor is money," she said. "Her dad, Heathcliffe MacDermott, is the hot-dog king, remember? I heard he put money into *The Gasman*."

"Why? To ensure that Ellie got a good part?"

"I suppose," Renie replied, breaking up more crackers. "I don't think she's made more than two or three movies before this."

When the cousins had finished their meal and paid the bill, Ben and Ellie were still head-to-head. Ben was on his third vodka, though Ellie had barely touched her wine. Unnoticed, Judith and Renie left T.S. McSnort's and headed back to Hillside Manor.

Joe met them in the driveway. "Nobody's

home except that writer, Costello. I tried to tell him about your mother's mistake, but he blew me off. I still think that it serves them right. A grand for a bunch of mushrooms. Sheesh."

"I know." Judith started for the back door with Renie behind her.

"Do you need some help?" Joe called after them.

"Not yet," Judith replied. "You and Bill and Carl Rankers will be waiters at the midnight supper, remember?"

Joe looked amused. "I remember. I'm dressing as a choirboy."

"So you are." Judith sighed. "I'm dressing as a Roman slave. It fits my role to a *T*. Oh," she added as an afterthought, "you'll have to pick up the costumes from Arlecchino's before four." Keeping it brief, she explained the damage that had been done to Angela's Scarlett O'Hara outfit.

"Sabotage?" Joe said. "What's with this bunch?"

"Jealousy, hatred, malice, hostility," Renie put in. "All the usual Hollywood emotions."

Joe shrugged. "I'm glad I never wanted to be a movie star. Being a cop seems like a breeze by comparison. Perps aren't nearly as vicious as people in the movie business. Though," he continued in a musing tone, "I

115

suppose a cop's life is always interesting to filmmakers."

Judith scowled at Joe. "What are you thinking of?"

Joe gave Judith an innocent look. "Nothing. Not really."

"Good," said Judith, and went into the house.

For the next hour the cousins worked in the kitchen, preparing the supper dishes that could be made ahead. Joe finally came in from the garage around three. He was carrying a battered FedEx package.

"The deliveryman just brought this," he said. "Shall I?"

"Go ahead, open it," Judith replied, wiping her hands off on a towel. "It must be more exotic items for tonight, though I thought we already had everything on hand."

"Whatever it is, it's marked *perishable*," Joe said, using scissors to cut the strong paper wrapping. "In fact, I guess this was supposed to arrive yesterday. The driver apologized, but explained that because it came from overseas —" He stopped cold as he saw the box. "It's French truffles."

Judith stared at the embossed gold lettering. "Périgord truffles. Dare we?" She cut away the tape that sealed the box and lifted the lid. "Yuk! No wonder Mother threw the other box out!"

Renie peered around Judith's arm. "Oh, for heaven's sake, it's just a bunch of brown truffles! I wouldn't mind tasting one."

"Bleah!" Judith stuck out her tongue. "Go right ahead. I wouldn't touch those things with a ten-foot pole." But even as Renie picked up a paring knife, Judith smacked her hand. "No, you don't! These are for the guests, and now that they got here, Joe can pretend he found them."

"Hey," Joe cried, "that would be a lie! I'm not accepting a fee on false pretenses."

"Ooh . . ." Judith ran an agitated hand through her salt-and-pepper hair. "It just seems to me that after all the —" She stopped and sighed. "You're right, we'll tell them the truth. The truffles got held up because they came from" — she looked at the mailing label on the wrapper — "Bordeaux."

"Makes sense," Renie remarked.

Judith turned to her cousin. "What does?"

Renie held out her hands. "That it would take longer than if they came from Butte, Montana."

Judith blinked at her cousin, then looked at Joe. "True," she said in a distracted voice. "But would they send two boxes? I wonder

117

what was in the package that Mother flushed down the toilet?"

Judith offered up a prayer of thanksgiving when Joe brought the costumes back from Arlecchino's at three-fifty. The Scarlett O'Hara costume had been mended, if not restored. While Judith and Renie were examining it, Angela La Belle wandered into the living room.

"Oh," she said in a disinterested voice, "that's mine, isn't it?"

"Yes," Judith replied. "I had the costume shop put on a different skirt. It looks rather nice, doesn't it?"

Angela barely glanced at the costume. "I guess. Where's Dade? Bruno's looking for him."

Judith said she hadn't seen him, but understood that he was the only member of the Zepf party who hadn't gone out that afternoon.

"Well, he's not down here, and he's not in his room," Angela declared. "Maybe he flew back to Malibu." With a languid toss of her long blond hair, the actress wandered out to the front porch.

Renie gave Judith an inquiring look. "She doesn't seem very upset about her costume, does she?"

"No," Judith said. "I thought she'd pitch a fit."

Renie got up from her kneeling position. "What time do they leave for the premiere?"

"Five," Judith replied, heading for the kitchen.

"That doesn't give them much time to dress," Renie pointed out.

"They're dressing at the hotel with the others," Judith said, putting a mixture of salmon pâté into the food processor. "The movie theater is just a minute's walk from the Cascadia, but they'll still show up in limos, so I suppose they'll drive around the block a couple of times first."

"It'll be a mob scene," Renie remarked, cutting up scallions. Her gaze traveled to the American artists' calendar she'd given Judith for Christmas. "Say, how much have you learned about twentieth-century painters from that? I hoped it would be a teaching tool."

"I've learned there are a lot of them I don't like," Judith replied. "I must admit, though, September taught me something. I didn't realize that John Singer Sargent painted anything but portraits."

Renie went over to the wall and flipped back a page. "Ah — *Spain*. Sunlight and tiled roofs and fat green plants in terra-cotta pots. Done with daubs and blobs. Very different from *Madame X.*" She returned to dicing vegetables. "How many are coming for the midnight supper?"

"The current guest list," Judith said, "plus a few others connected with the film."

"Not the entire Hollywood crew?"

Judith shook her head as she went to the pantry to get a jar of mayonnaise. "This bunch will mingle with the others at the costume ball in the hotel."

"I hope they don't stay late," Renie called after her cousin. "You know how Bill likes to make an early evening of it."

"He'll have to tough it out tonight," Judith said, holding the jar of mayo and glancing out the back-door window. "I really appreciate —" She stopped. "There's Dade Costello. He just came out of the toolshed."

The screenwriter shambled along the walk, indifferent to the rain that had begun to fall again. Judith opened the door for him.

"Hi," she said. "Were you visiting my mother?"

"Mrs. Grover?" Dade nodded. "Interesting woman."

"She is?" Judith bit her tongue. "I mean, you found her interesting."

"Yes." Dade proceeded down the hall,

through the kitchen, the dining room, and disappeared.

"Good grief," Judith muttered. "I hope Mother wasn't telling Dade a bunch of tales like she did with Bruno."

"I wouldn't put it past her," Renie said.

Half an hour later the limo drivers arrived, along with a small van in which the other costumes were loaded. The guests straggled downstairs, Bruno and Winifred first, then Dirk Farrar, Chips Madigan, and Angela La Belle. Ben Carmody came next, apparently none the worse for his three shots of vodka. Ellie Linn descended the stairs backward, humming to herself. Finally, Dade Costello appeared. As usual, he seemed to detach himself from the others as the limos filled up.

Judith and Renie watched from the entry hall. At precisely five o'clock, the trio of sleek white cars pulled out of the cul-de-sac like so many ghosts floating just above the ground. Blurred by the rain, even the headlights seemed ethereal in the gathering darkness.

"To work!" Renie exclaimed, holding up a finger and marching into the kitchen.

But Judith paused at the foot of the stairs. "Now that they're gone, I'll straighten their rooms. Arlene should be here to help in about twenty minutes."

The state of the guest rooms was no better and no worse than when they were used by more ordinary mortals. Indeed, Dade Costello's small quarters looked as if it had never been occupied. The bed was made, the bureau was bare, and no clothes had been hung in the closet. Everything that Dade had brought with him appeared to be contained in a suitcase and a briefcase. Both were locked.

Though it showed signs of human habitation, Winifred's room was also orderly; so was that of Chips Madigan. The bathroom that Chips shared with Ellie and Angela was another matter. Hairdryers, curling irons, magnifying mirrors, and at least two dozen beauty products were strewn everywhere. Judith looked around the sink for any signs of what Joe had deemed to be cocaine. There were none.

Room Six, where the two actresses were bunking together, was as untidy as the bathroom. Clothes were everywhere, all casual, all bearing designer labels. At least ten pairs of shoes littered the floor. Upon closer scrutiny, Judith saw that except for some size-four cross-trainers and strappy sandals, the rest belonged to Angela's size-seven feet.

In Room Four, Dirk and Ben's movie stardom was made known by a pile of scripts and a file folder marked *projects*. Judith glanced at the script on top of the stack. *All the Way to Utah*, by Amy Lee Wong. Flipping through the script, she saw severe editing marks on almost every page as well as derogatory comments, some of them obscene. She replaced the script, then dared to look inside the project file, which contained loose newspaper and magazine clippings.

Judith extracted one of the clippings, which was printed on slick paper. The headline read, MUCHO MACHO COSTS FARRAR A GAUCHO.

Hunkster Dirk Farrar's two-fisted attack on Mighty Mogul Bruno Zepf has cost the actor the lead role in Zepf's Argentine epic, *El Gaucho Loco O No*. The brouhaha occurred outside a restaurant last week in Marina Del Rey when producer and actor got into an argument over who would star in *All the Way to Utah*, a project Zepf has temporarily put on the back burner.

Judith slipped the clipping back into the file. She shouldn't be wasting her time snooping. There was work to be done. Briskly, she went into Bruno Zepf's room. On the nightstand were at least ten pill bottles along with a couple of tubes of ointment, an inhaler, and two small brownpaper packets that felt as if they held some kind of tablets. A tiny scrap of paper that looked like part of a prescription lay on the floor. Judith picked it up, but could only make out the words *pharmacy* and *thalidomide*. She looked at the medications on the nightstand, but their labels were intact. With a shrug, she put the little scrap in the wastebasket, then returned to her tasks.

Straightening the bed, Judith noticed a thick book with a tattered cover and frayed pages slipped under one of the shammed pillows. She picked it up, barely making out the sunken lettering on the cover.

The Gasman.

Opening the book, she noted the author's name — C. Douglas Carp. The copyright was 1929. The publisher, Conkling & Stern of St. Louis, was unfamiliar to her. What struck Judith was not the density of the prose but the well-fingered pages. It reminded her of an aged, much-loved, wellthumbed family Bible. Fragile pieces of leaves and flowers, brittle with age, had been placed between some of the pages. There was a small lock of hair so fine it could have belonged to a baby.

Then, as she riffled through the last chapters of the nine-hundred-page novel, a photograph fell out onto the bedspread. It was a wallet-size picture of a young woman, perhaps still in her teens. Like the book, the photo was well-worn, but the girl's face was fresh, innocent, pretty. Judith thought it might be a high-school yearbook picture. She flipped it over, but nothing was written on the back. The blond bouffant hairstyle indicated the sixties. Judith stared at the photo in fascination. She'd seen that face somewhere else, not so young and definitely not so innocent.

But she couldn't remember where. Or who.

Chapter Six

When Judith got back downstairs, five early young trick-or-treaters came to the front door. While Renie doled out candy to the zebra, the gorilla, the fairy princess, and two wizards, Judith welcomed Arlene, who had just reported for duty.

"I watched everyone leave for the premiere," Arlene said, rolling up her sleeves to pitch in with the cooking. "I hope Ben Carmody will like Cathy. I've asked her to stop by for the midnight supper."

Judith's mouth fell open. "You have? But it's supposed to be strictly for the movie people."

"That's all right," Arlene replied. "Cathy's going to tend bar. She's dressing as a panda."

"Surely," Renie remarked, "that costume will conceal her charms."

"And hide her flaws," Arlene replied. "Mystery, that's what intrigues men. Ben will be able to see her very attractive hands. She can't wear paws if she's going to mix drinks."

Judith didn't contest Arlene's decision. If Cathy Rankers played bartender, Judith and Joe would not have to share her duties. For the next few hours the women worked side by side until eleven o'clock when all was in virtual readiness.

"I'm already exhausted," Renie announced, leaning against the sink. "Is Bill still napping on the sofa?"

"Yes," Judith replied. "So's Carl. On the other sofa. Joe's watching TV upstairs. He should be down in a few minutes. Unless he's napping, too."

"Hey," Renie said, suddenly rejuvenated and jumping away from the sink. "Let's turn the TV on to see —"

The cupboard door behind her sprang open, narrowly missing her head.

"Oops!" Renie exclaimed, then firmly closed the door. "I wish you'd fix that thing."

"Me too," Judith agreed. "If Joe doesn't give it a go, I'll have to call Mr. Tolvang next week. Say, do you think the premiere is on the news?"

"Probably," Renie replied, testing the cupboard door to make sure it was shut.

Judith clicked on the small color set she kept on the counter near her computer. Mavis Lean-Brodie, a familiar face from murders past, was making dire predictions about a storm blowing down from the north.

". . . with winds gusting up to forty-five miles an hour and heavy rains. Small-craft warnings are out on the . . ."

"She changed her hair again," Renie remarked. "Now it's pink."

"I hope the rain lets up," Arlene said in a doleful voice. "It always seems to be nasty when the trick-or-treaters are making their rounds."

"That's because it's late October," Renie replied. "We get some of our worst wind storms about now."

". . . For more on the weather," Mavis was saying, "our own Duff Stevens will be along later in the broadcast. But," she added, now all smiles, "despite the rain, the stars were out tonight downtown. Here's KINE-TV's entertainment editor, Byron Myron, with more on that big event."

Byron Myron was a jolly-looking black man whose appearance belied a rapierlike tongue. He was shown outside the movie theater holding an umbrella.

"*The Gasman* arrived here this evening," Byron said, "and blew out the main line." The camera traveled to the glittering marquee, followed by clips of the celebrity arrivals. "Bruno Zepf's four-hour, hundred-million-dollar extravaganza proved that money can't buy you love — or a good movie."

"There's Angela in her *Gone With the Wind* costume," Renie whispered as the female lead was shown entering the theater.

"How can you tell?" Arlene whispered back. "She's wearing a mask."

"I saw the costume here," Renie said. "In fact, somebody ripped —"

Judith waved a hand to shush the other women.

". . . story which was based on an obscure novel of the same name," Byron Myron was saying, "doesn't merit four minutes, let alone four hours. As for the acting, the performers are in the unenviable position of creating several different characters during the various historical periods Zepf has chosen to make his statement about humanity's progress over four millennia. Or was it five? I'm not sure. The movie seemed to take almost that long. This is Byron Myron, reporting from —"

Judith switched off the set. "Goodness.

That doesn't sound so good for Bruno."

"Maybe," Renie suggested, "Byron Myron feels he ought to trash the movie because it was filmed on location around here and the city hosted the premiere. He may feel that if he praised it, he'd sound like a homer."

"Maybe," Judith allowed, then started turning on ovens and putting dishes on to heat. "The Zepf gang will be back here in a little over half an hour. We should get into our costumes. So should the husbands."

As the three women changed in the third-floor bedroom, they could hear the wind begin to pick up in the trees outside. The rain was coming down harder, too, spattering the windows and running out of the downspouts.

Judith stared at herself in the mirror. She looked more like a noble Roman lady than a humble slave. The off-white gown was held on one shoulder by a brooch that had belonged to Grandma Grover. An old drapery cord served for the belt, and the scarf that hung from her head was anchored by an ivory comb that was a castoff from Auntie Vance.

"Gee, coz," Renie said, "you look pretty hot."

Judith had to admit that the long, graceful gown suited her statuesque figure. "Thanks," she said. "I wish I could say the same for you."

Renie tucked the head of her Daisy Duck costume under her arm. "I thought my tail feathers were kind of sexy."

"Not as sexy as your big webbed feet," Judith said, then turned to Arlene, who looked somewhat more enchanting as Gretel, complete with long golden braids and a gingerbread cookie embroidered on her apron. "How does Carl feel about wearing Hansel's lederhosen?"

"He loves it," Arlene declared as a knock could be heard on the door.

"We're decent," Judith called out.

Carl stuck his head in. "I hate lederhosen. Why couldn't I wear pants?"

"There's nothing wrong with your legs, Carl," Arlene retorted. "Just don't walk like you're knock-kneed. And don't forget your hat with the feather."

The women joined the men, who had been changing in Joe's den. Judith thought Carl looked cute in his Hansel outfit. With his round face and ruddy cheeks, Joe made a presentable, if aging, choirboy. And Bill certainly looked like Donald Duck. He couldn't appear otherwise, since he had his head in place along with the rest of his costume.

"Quack, quack," said Bill.

"Yes, you look terrific," Renie replied, giving Bill's bill a tweak.

"You understood that?" Judith asked in surprise.

"Of course," Renie answered. "Bill and I have been married so long we can communicate in any language."

Downstairs, Cathy was pounding at the back door. Arlene let her daughter in. It was a tight squeeze, the panda suit being very round and very wide.

"The head ruined my hair," Cathy complained, batting at her blond locks with the hand that didn't hold the head itself. "This thing is hot. And now it's wet from the rain. I smell like a sheep, not a panda."

"What does a panda smell like?" Renie inquired in a musing tone.

"Not as bad as I do," Cathy complained.

"Now, dear," Arlene soothed, "we all have to suffer for love." She gave Carl a sharp glance. "Think of what I've had to put up with over the years."

"Stick it in the oven, Gretel," Carl shot back.

Bill waddled over to the cupboards by the work area. "Quack, quacky, quack?" He addressed Renie.

"In here," Renie replied, opening a cupboard underneath the counter. "Judith has four kinds of cocoa. You choose."

"Quack," Bill said, pointing to the German chocolate brand, then to a row of cereal boxes on the bottom shelf. "Quack," he said, indicating the Cheerios. "Quack," he continued, tapping the Grape-Nuts. "Quack," he concluded, nudging a box of bran.

Renie placed her Daisy Duck head on the counter. "You should have had your evening snack at home," she said in mild reproach. "I'll have to heat the cocoa in the microwave. All the burners are in use."

"Quack," said Bill.

Judith shook her head. She'd never understood how her cousin, who was usually so fractious, could wait on Bill hand and foot. At least some of the time. But Renie was equally willing to spoil their children. It seemed out of character, and therefore illogical. And logic was the cornerstone of Judith's thought processes.

Bill had finished his snack and the final preparations were being made when the first of the limos arrived back at Hillside Manor. Judith went to the door.

The wind and rain seemed to blow the trio inside. As Cleopatra, Ellie Linn was shivering with the cold, despite the black cloak that hung from her shoulders.

"T-t-this awful weather!" she cried. "I'm

g-g-going t-t-to catch pneumonia!" She burst into hysterical laughter and fled into the downstairs bathroom.

"That's how she handles adversity." Winifred sneered. "The silly twit." In her nun's habit, Winifred moved closer to Bruno. She seemed to be holding him up as he stumbled through the entry hall. "Scotch, quickly!" she cried. "Mr. Zepf isn't feeling well."

The liquor bottles that the guests had brought with them were on the makeshift bar in the front parlor, but Bruno's favorite Scotch remained on the old-fashioned washstand that served as a smaller bar in the dining room. Judith grabbed the bottle and a glass, rushed to the kitchen to get ice, and hurried back to the living room, where Bruno was now slumped on one of the sofas. His flowing robes and burnoose from *Khartoum* sagged along with the rest of him.

"My God," he whispered as Winifred took the drink from Judith and raised it to his lips. "I'm ruined." He took a deep sip from the proffered glass, then raised his white-robed arms as if invoking the gods of filmdom. "*The Gasman* had everything to please audiences — sex, violence, art — even a small cuddly dog."

Chips Madigan paused in his path across the room. "I told you to leave the chimpanzee in. Chimps are always good."

"Chimps are a desperation measure," Bruno muttered as Chips moved on. "He's a director, he knows that. My God, think of the money we wasted on the TV advertising budget alone!"

The cell phone in Winifred's lap rang. She picked it up, but had difficulty getting the earpiece under her wimple. "Best here," she finally said. Then she lowered her eyes and her voice. "Yes . . . yes . . . we know . . . morons . . . imbeciles . . . philistines . . . yes . . . I'll contact them first thing tomorrow, before we leave for the airport . . . yes, have an ambulance waiting . . . good." She clicked off and suddenly looked up at Judith. "What are you waiting for? Mr. Zepf has his drink."

"I wondered if there was anything else I could get for him," Judith said as a small man in a matador's suit of lights and a large woman dressed like Carmen in Act IV of the opera entered the living room. "Is he ill?"

"Yes," Winifred replied tersely, then caught sight of the new arrivals. "Oh, damn! I must speak to Morris and Eugenia." Her gaze softened. "Mrs. Flynn, would you sit with Mr. Zepf for just a moment?"

"Of course," Judith replied, and perched on the edge of the sofa.

A deep groan was coming from somewhere in the folds of the burnoose. "It's plague! It's devastation! It's . . . the end."

"Goodness," Judith said. "Do you need a doctor?"

Bruno pushed the folds of his robes aside and looked at Judith with bleary eyes. "It's the critics. We flew them in from all over the world. Those damnable thickheaded critics. They hate *The Gasman*. Every one of them so far has trashed the picture. And how they ate at the masked ball! They savage me, then they gobble up everything but the silverware!"

Judith tried to think of something positive to say. "What about the audience? Sometimes, I've heard, critics may hate a movie, but audiences adore it."

Bruno's head fell back against the sofa. "They walked out. The theater was less than half full after the intermission. We should have barred the doors. Oh, my God, what's to become of me?"

Ellie entered the living room with great caution, as if she expected someone to hand her a poisonous asp. She was still shivering inside the heavy black cloak as she sidled up to Bruno and leaned down. "Hey, maybe it's not so bad. You know — every great producer has a flop sometimes. Look at all the successes you've had."

"That was then," Bruno muttered. "This is now."

Dade Costello, in his long brown velvet mantle and Frisbee-shaped hat, passed in back of the sofa behind Bruno. "I told you so," he said, and moved on.

Bruno groaned some more. A cell phone rang from somewhere. Bruno automatically reached for his, but no one was on the other end. His expression was bleak as Ellie pulled out her own cell to take the call.

"Yes," she said. "I know." Her sweet face turned sour. "But . . . isn't it possible that . . . Yes, I suppose you're right. Still . . ." She listened, then sighed. "Okay . . . If you say so. Sure, you know I always do. Bye." She rang off, shot Bruno a blistering look, and walked off toward the bar, where another newcomer, attired in a pioneer woman's gingham dress and floppy bonnet, was accepting a drink from Cathy Rankers.

Angela La Belle came over to the sofa. Judith drew back, assuming the actress wanted to speak with Bruno. But Angela ignored the producer and spoke to Judith instead.

"I see the truffles finally turned up. At least one good thing happened tonight." With a swish of Scarlett's skirts, she turned away.

"You see?" Bruno whispered hoarsely. "You see how they turn on me? That's the way the business works. A hundred successes and one failure — that's all it takes to bring you down, to make you a nobody."

Judith glanced around the big living room. Still wearing their masks, Ben Carmody and Dirk Farrar were talking by the piano. Judith recognized them by their costumes. Dirk cut a dashing figure in his satin-slashed doublet and hose; Ben looked more like his sinister screen self in the nineteenth-century frock coat and top hat. Judging from their body language, neither seemed happy.

"Surely," Judith said, her naturally kind heart filling with sympathy for Bruno, "you don't really believe that you're . . . um . . . washed up in Hollywood?"

Bruno's eyes darted under the hood of his burnoose. "See? They're staying as far away as possible, like I'm poison, contagious. Do you watch pro football?" He saw Judith give a faint nod. "Then you know how the other players usually avoid a fallen teammate. They're superstitious, too; they think that if they touch the downed man, they'll be the next to get hurt. That's the way it is in the picture business. An injury, or a failure — or even a rumor of failure — can be career-ending."

Judith saw Chips Madigan as the computer geek, speaking with Angela by the buffet bar. Ellie was alone, studying the various pieces of china that sat along the plate rail. Dade was also by himself, at his favorite place by the French doors, staring out into the stormy October night. Dirk and Ben remained together, speaking and nodding in turn. Winifred apparently had gone into the front parlor with Morris the matador and Eugenia in her Carmen costume. The pioneer woman stood at the buffet, sampling food from the chafing dishes. It didn't seem like much of a party to Judith, but she reminded herself it wasn't her fault.

The doorbell distracted her. She waited a moment, thinking one of the company might be expecting more hangers-on. But the bell rang a second time, and Judith hurried to the front door.

"Trick-or-treat!" chimed two youthful voices.

Judith frowned at the spaceman and the alligator. "Aren't you out late?" she inquired, reaching for the silver bowl on the entry-hall table.

The spaceman, who had what looked like a fish bowl on his head, grinned through the filmy glass. "We're not little kids," he responded. "I'm getting my driver's license next week."

Considering that the spaceman was almost as tall as Judith — at least in the silver platform boots — she shrugged, then dumped four small chocolate bars into each of the pillowcases the youngsters held in front of them. "Okay, but doesn't that make you a bit old for trick-or-treating?"

The alligator shook its scaly green head. "We had to take our little brothers and sisters out first. Most of the people ignored us, so now it's our turn."

"I see," Judith said. "But it's still very late. You two should head home now."

The spaceman laughed and the alligator wagged his tail as they headed down the porch steps. As Judith was closing the door, they tossed a couple of thank-yous over their shoulders.

In the living room, nothing much had changed. The cloud of gloom still hung over the guests, so palpable that Judith felt as if she were looking through the blurred lens of a movie camera.

Bill and Joe entered at that moment, each carrying more platters of food. Spotting Bruno sitting in his favorite place on the sofa, Bill began to quack in an angry tone.

"Quack, quack-quack-quack!" He pointed to the melancholy producer. "Quack!"

Joe put a hand on Bill's arm feathers.

"Quack off. That guy looks pretty grim. Let him be."

Bill was slow to respond. "Qu-a-ck," he finally said in a reluctant voice.

Joe gave Bill a pat, observed the rest of the morose gathering, and spoke up: "Anybody care to dance? I'll put on some music."

Ellie laughed with a hint of hysteria and wandered out into the entry hall just as Winifred appeared with her Spanish-costumed duo. She glanced at Bruno, winced, and requested a stiff bourbon from Cathy. No one else responded to Joe's invitation.

Bill turned around, calling to an unseen Renie. "Daisy!" he shouted in his normal, if muffled, voice. "It's after midnight. Can we go home?"

Renie stumbled out of the entry hall. She seemed to be having trouble with her webbed feet. "I'll ask Judith," she said.

Judith excused herself and got up from the sofa. "I don't see why you shouldn't go," she said in a low voice. "This is one dead party. Arlene and Carl can help clean up." She glanced back at the buffet and sighed. "All that expensive food gone to waste."

"I put some pots and pans to soak in the sink," Renie said. "They should be scrubbed before you put them in the dishwasher."

"Okay," Judith said. "Thanks for everything. As it turned out, I didn't need so much help after all."

Renie nodded, her yellow bill bobbing up and down. "A real bomb, I guess."

"Right." Judith hugged Bill and Renie. Joe, who kept tripping over the hem of his choirboy's cassock, showed them out the back way.

When Judith returned to the living room, Winifred offered to introduce her to Morris and Eugenia.

"Morris Mayne is Bruno's studio publicist," Winifred said, a bit stiffly. "Eugenia Fleming is Bruno and Dirk's agent."

Judith allowed her hand to be shaken by the pair. Morris's grip was feeble; Eugenia practically pulled Judith's arm out of the socket.

"We so wanted to stay here at your charming B&B," Eugenia boomed in a deep voice. She seemed more than big; she towered over Judith's five-foot-nine and possessed a bust that could have triumphed in a head-on collision with an armored car.

"There wasn't room, I guess," Morris said, then cleared his throat. "Especially since my wife unexpectedly joined me on this trip."

Judith assumed that his wife was the pioneer in the sunbonnet and gingham dress.

"I'm sure you're enjoying the Cascadia," she said. "It's the most luxurious hotel in the city."

"It's fine," Morris said offhandedly. "The truth is, my wife's a real homebody. I was surprised that she wanted to come along."

Eugenia's dark eyes were flashing around the room. "Excuse me," she said, "I must speak with Dirk. I hardly recognized him in that doublet and the hat with those swooping feathers." With a click of the castanets she held in one hand, the agent stalked across the room to reach her prey.

Judith was left with Morris, who kept darting glances at Bruno, sitting alone and forlorn on the sofa. Sweetums, who must have come in when the Joneses went out, had planted his orange-and-white body at the producer's feet. To Judith's surprise, Bruno patted his lap. To her amazement, the cat leaped up and allowed himself to be petted. Maybe even Sweetums wanted to get into the movies.

"I should speak to Bruno," Morris murmured, removing his matador's cap. He was short, spare, and balding. "I simply don't know what to say to him. Perhaps I'll get a drink first."

Judith watched Morris accept a hefty martini from Cathy. The publicist then

143

stood off to one side by the door to the front parlor and gulped down his drink. Cathy removed her panda head, slipped out from behind the bar, and approached Judith.

"I'm dying of heat prostration in this stupid suit," she declared, and in fact, her face was dripping with perspiration. "I knew I should never have let my mother order my costume. I intended to come as Pandora, not a panda."

Judith couldn't help but smile. "That would have been more fetching in order to attract Ben Carmody."

Cathy shook out her long, damp blond locks. "Another idea of Mom's! I'm not even a Ben Carmody fan. He always plays meanies."

"Go home," Judith urged. "Joe and I can take care of the bar. I don't think this party is going to last much longer. In fact, your parents might as well leave, too. I'll go out to the kitchen and thank them."

Arlene, however, refused to leave Judith with such a mess. "Cathy can go, Carl can go," she asserted, "but I'm staying until the bitter end."

"I think we're already there," Judith said over the hum of the dishwasher.

"I'll stay, too," Carl volunteered.

"Really," Judith protested, "there's no

need. Joe and I can clean up by ourselves. It's late. Please, we'll be fine."

"Not entirely," Carl said, pointing to the sink. "You've got a backed-up drain."

Judith grimaced. "Renie! She never uses sink strainers. She says they don't work for her."

"What's to work?" Joe asked, gazing into the eight-inch basin of dirty water. "You put them in, turn the button on top, and there you go."

Judith shook her head. "Not for Renie. She says it's too complicated. I gave her a pair of brand new strainers for Christmas last year and she stuck them on her ears and said that's as close as they'd ever get to her double sinks."

Carl was still peering at the water. "Maybe if I used a plunger . . ."

"No, you don't," Joe said, taking Carl by the shoulder. "Go home, Hansel. Your gingerbread house awaits you."

Carl shot Joe a dark look. "With Gretel or the witch?"

"Gretel, of course," Judith said, patting Arlene's arm. "Go on, please. Poor Cathy has to get out of that panda suit."

With reluctance, the Rankerses exited with their daughter. Joe went into the living room to tend bar, and Judith scanned what was left of the crowd. On the window seat, Dirk and Angela were speaking with Eugenia in a serious manner. Chips Madigan was standing by the piano, framing imaginary camera angles with his hands. Dade, Ellie, and Ben were nowhere in sight. Winifred stood behind the sofa, where Bruno sat with Morris Mayne at his side. Sweetums remained tucked in the folds of Bruno's robes.

As innkeeper and hostess, Judith couldn't help but take Bruno's gloom personally. She knew it wasn't her fault, but it upset her to see a guest in distress.

As if sensing Judith's consternation, Eugenia slipped off the window seat and moved quickly across the room.

"I'm wondering if Bruno shouldn't leave for L.A. tonight," she murmured. "Of course it's none of my business, really. I'd mention it to Winifred, but she and I don't speak."

"Oh." Judith glanced from Eugenia to Winifred. "I see." She didn't really, but couldn't think of anything else to say. She hesitated, feeling Eugenia's hard-eyed stare. Judith cleared her throat. "Is there something I can do?"

"Why, yes," Eugenia replied. "You could ask what Winifred thinks of my suggestion. Only don't mention that it came from me."

"I don't think there's another flight to

L.A. tonight," Judith said. "The red-eye leaves shortly after midnight."

Eugenia waved a hand that was encased in fingerless black lace gloves. "Bruno doesn't fly commercial. He has his own jet."

"Oh." Judith started toward the sofa, aware that Winifred was also giving her a steely-eyed stare. Taking a deep breath, she decided to approach Bruno directly.

His eyes were dull as he gazed up at her from under the hood of his burnoose. "Yes?"

"Mr. Zepf," Judith began. She shivered slightly. The fire had burned out on the hearth, and the wind created a draft. Roman fashion wasn't intended for a chilly autumn evening in the Pacific Northwest. "Mr. Zepf," Judith repeated, "I want to say how sorry I am that your movie wasn't well received. Someone suggested that perhaps you'd like to fly back to Los Angeles tonight. What do you think?"

Bruno looked blank. "I don't think. I can't think. I mustn't think. Could you get me another Scotch?" He pointed to his empty glass on the coffee table between the matching sofas.

"Of course," Judith responded, and went over to Joe at the bar just as Dirk and Angela headed upstairs.

"Zepf needs zapping," Judith said in a low

voice. "I feel sorry for him. Do you suppose it's as bad as he makes out?"

"Judging from the funereal pall around here," Joe said, opening Bruno's favorite brand, "I'd say yes. I don't know much about the movie business, but a flop can ruin a career. And I don't mean just Bruno's."

"I never thought of it that way," Judith said softly, then gazed around the living room. Of the original guest list, Chips Madigan and Winifred Best remained. And Bruno, of course. Judith realized that even she was beginning to consider him an afterthought. In a fit of uncatlike compassion, Sweetums was still curled up on Bruno's lap.

Joe pointed to the elaborate buffet. "I'll wrap up some of the food and put it in the freezer. There's no sense in letting it go to waste."

Judith nodded. "They're not the type to take doggie bags with them. I'll start putting away some of the things from the bar in the washstand cabinet."

As she took the first half-dozen unopened bottles that belonged to the B&B into the dining room, Morris Mayne was at her heels.

"I must be on my way," he said. "There's not much more I can do for poor Bruno. Besides, as strange as it sounds for people in the picture business, my wife and I keep regular hours. Thank you for your hospitality." He ducked his head and scurried off toward the front door.

Judith was putting dirty dishes on a tray when a subdued Winifred Best came up to her. "I think Bruno wants to sit for a while with his thoughts," she said. "I'm going to retire for the night." Slipping her hands up the sleeves of her nun's habit, she seemed to strain for the next words: "Thank you for all you've done. I'm sorry this couldn't have been a happier event. Perhaps next time — if there is a next time — Bruno will want to stay in a hotel."

Judith watched Winifred leave the room, then noted that only Bruno and Eugenia Fleming remained. The agent was nibbling on truffles and standing at the piano, her free hand playing the fate motif from Carmen. Notes composed by the devil himself, Renie had once told Judith. An exaggeration, perhaps, but the minor chords certainly sounded like doom and gloom.

Out in the kitchen, Joe had just come up from the basement. "We've run out of room in the freezer," he announced. "How much of that stuff in there is worth keeping? You've got dates on some of those packages from six, eight years ago."

"Really?" Judith looked sheepish. "Then we'd better toss anything that old. Come on, I'll get some garbage bags and go down with you."

Joe looked up at the schoolhouse clock. "It's going on one in the morning. Can't it wait until tomorrow?"

Judith shook her head and put a sweater on over her Roman costume. "I want as much of this done tonight as possible. Otherwise I'll have a big mess in the kitchen come morning. That makes getting breakfast awkward. It won't take that long. Let's go."

But like so many household tasks, it took longer than Judith had predicted. Almost half an hour later the Flynns trudged back upstairs. Joe headed directly for the garbage cans outside while Judith returned to the kitchen.

Or almost. She rounded the corner into the hall and saw Bruno bending over the sink. Her initial reaction was that he was throwing up. Not that she blamed him. A sudden gust of wind roared over the house. She heard a garbage-can lid rattle, roll, and clank outside. She knew that Joe must be swearing a blue streak.

"Mr. Zepf," she called softly, moving down the hallway. "Can I help you?"

150

Bruno didn't move. His robes sagged around him and the headpiece was askew. Judith moved closer. She couldn't see his face above the sink.

Then, as she reached the kitchen table, she realized that Bruno's face was in the standing water from the plugged-up drain.

"Mr. Zepf!" she cried, fear seizing her like an iron clamp. She lurched at him, shaking his arm. "Mr. Zepf!" she cried again.

Bruno Zepf slumped farther into the sink, his burly upper body carrying him forward. With trembling fingers, Judith searched for a pulse. There was none. She felt faint, but kept shaking Bruno's arm. Then she noticed that the broken cupboard door was wide open.

And above the sink, suspended from the single light fixture, was a big black spider.

Chapter Seven

Judith didn't hear Joe come running down the hallway. She was aware of his presence only when he grabbed her by the shoulders and gently but firmly pushed her out of the way.

"Call 911," he ordered in a calm but emphatic voice. "I'll try to resuscitate him."

A flicker of hope sparked in Judith's breast. "He's alive?"

Joe didn't reply. He hauled Bruno onto the floor and started CPR. Judith couldn't remember where she'd put the phone. She finally buzzed the receiver from its base and heard it beep from the opposite kitchen counter.

How could she explain that a man might have drowned in the kitchen? Not a swimming pool, not a bathtub, not a hot tub, but a kitchen sink. Fumbling with the buttons on the phone, Judith felt giddy. She wouldn't give the details. She was afraid to, for fear of becoming hysterical. Or worse yet, disbelieved.

Finally she got a grip on her composure and informed the operator that there was a man near death. Or already there, Judith thought dismally. Help was required immediately. The operator told her to stand by, someone should arrive at Hillside Manor in just a few minutes.

"But," Judith said in amazement, "I haven't given you the address."

"Our system showed it on the screen," the female voice replied. "Besides, you've called here before, haven't you?"

"Yes," Judith said weakly. "So I have."

"The patrol car is close by," the operator assured her, "and the medics and firefighters have been alerted. You're not calling for your mother, are you?"

"No," Judith whispered, fixated on Joe, whose efforts appeared to be futile. "No."

"How's she doing?" the operator inquired. "I hear she's quite a character."

"Fine. Good. I . . . must . . . hang . . . up . . . now." Judith clicked off and, with a limp wrist, placed the phone on the kitchen table.

Panting, Joe looked up from Bruno's prone form. "It's no good. He's dead."

Judith crossed herself while Joe hung his head. "Damn," he breathed, "how did this happen? Was it an accident?" His eyes traveled to the light fixture. "Oh, hell! What's that thing?" He picked up a long cooking fork and poked at the spider. "It's fake."

"I need a drink," Judith said, her voice hoarse. She noticed that the balky cupboard door had swung open again and closed it with a shaky hand. "I can't believe this. Yes, I *can* believe this. But why me? Why us?"

"Hey," Joe said, reaching into the Flynns' private liquor stash, "it isn't personal. When I was on the job, I investigated at least a half-dozen homicides involving families that had already suffered through at least a couple of other murders."

"They were probably all crooks," Judith pointed out, wincing as she looked at Bruno, whose face was an unnatural color. She was about to turn away when she saw something round and white on the floor next to his body. Moving carefully so as not to touch the dead man, Judith fingered the object. "Aspirin," she said, holding it between her thumb and index finger. Not seeing the bottle she kept on the windowsill, she placed the pill on the counter. "Then you don't think it's all my fault?"

"No." Joe handed Judith her drink, then

stared at Bruno. "I wish I could figure out what happened. Does the spider suggest a setup?"

Judith gaped at him. "You mean . . . to scare Bruno to death?"

"Maybe just to rattle him," Joe replied, wearing his deadpan policeman's face.

As Judith gazed with compassion at Bruno's lifeless form, the familiar sound of sirens could be heard in the distance. "The neighbors." She sighed. "What will they think now?" She paused, a hand clutching at the deep neckline of her Roman gown. "The guests! What shall I do?"

"Nothing," Joe replied as the first of the sirens stopped nearby. "Yet. I'll get the door. You stay with the stiff."

Judith flinched. It was bad enough that she and Joe were drinking Scotch and standing over a corpse. But now her husband had reverted to his professional self, hard-boiled, keeping his distance, just-part-of-the-job. She, on the other hand, apparently had slipped into the role of Joe's longtime partner, Woody Price. Despite her not infrequent confrontations with corpses, Judith wasn't indifferent to the body on the kitchen floor. Surely Bruno had family who must be notified. Winifred would know.

Joe returned with two familiar figures in

tow. Darnell Hicks and Mercedes Berger had been summoned to Hillside Manor before, when a mobster had been gunned down outside of Gertrude's toolshed. Over two years later they still looked young, but not nearly so naive.

"What a shame," Darnell said, gazing down at Bruno. "How'd he get so soggy?"

Mercedes glanced at the sink. "What'd he do, stick his head in there and couldn't get out?"

Before Judith or Joe could respond, the medics and the firefighters arrived. "Come on," Joe said with a hand on Judith's elbow, "let's retreat into the dining room and give the folks some space."

"To do what?" Judith asked, moving through the swinging doors. "Oh, Joe, I can't stand it! It's got to be an accident, right?"

Joe didn't answer directly. "We'll find out more after the ME gets done. It may be tomorrow afternoon before we hear anything. Saturday nights can be pretty busy, especially on a holiday weekend."

Darnell Hicks gave a tentative rap on the swinging doors. "May I?"

"Sure," Joe said, going back into the kitchen. "What's up?"

"We're going to take the body to the

morgue." Darnell's brown eyes seemed intrigued by the Flynns' costumes. "Do you or Mrs. Flynn have any idea what happened to the guy? Was this a Halloween party?"

As Joe started to explain, Winifred appeared in the dining room. "What's going on?" she demanded of Judith. "Why are the police here?"

Judith put a hand out to the other woman. "Oh, Ms. Best, I don't know how to say this — except that Mr. Zepf is dead."

Winifred clutched at the front of her deep blue bathrobe. "Dead? As in . . . actually *dead?*"

Judith supposed that to someone in the movie business, *dead* didn't always mean losing one's life. "Yes, as in expired. We don't know what happened." She glanced over the top of the swinging doors into the kitchen. "They're taking him to the morgue. We'll know more later."

"Oh, my God!" Winifred swayed, then caught herself on the big breakfront. "His heart! Maybe he had a heart attack! He was complaining of a terrible headache earlier." She pulled out one of the dining-room chairs and collapsed onto it, her slim body convulsing.

Judith glanced at Joe, who was answering routine questions in the kitchen. She heard

157

a squeal from Mercedes Berger as Joe mentioned Dirk Farrar's name.

"Ms. Best," Judith began, "do you want to have the medics check you out?"

Winifred shook her head. "I must see Bruno," she finally said, but couldn't get to her feet. Winifred fell back into the chair as a knock at the front door made Judith jump. She hurried into the entry hall and peered outside. Under the porch light she could see Dade Costello, still in his costume and dripping wet.

"Mr. Costello!" she exclaimed, opening the door. "What are you doing out in this rain?"

Dade made an angry gesture toward the cul-de-sac. "What are *they* doing out here?"

Closing the door behind the screenwriter, Judith glimpsed the emergency vehicles, their lights still flashing. "I'm afraid I have bad news —"

"I don't need any more bad news tonight," Dade broke in. Without another word, he stomped upstairs.

"Oh, no," Judith groaned. Glancing at Winifred, who had her head down on the dining-room table, she hurried into the kitchen but had to step aside as the medics began to remove Bruno's body.

"Move, Jude-girl," Joe said, taking Judith

by the arm. "They're going out the back way, they need room for the gurney. I gave them as much information as I could."

Mercedes's blue eyes were huge. "Is it true?" she asked Judith. "Is Dirk Farrar really under this very roof?"

"Yes," Judith answered. "As far as I know." Nothing seemed certain on this wretched night. For all she knew, Dirk could have climbed out a window and been blown away by the gusting winds.

"What a hunk!" Mercedes was visibly palpitating.

Darnell's dark skin seemed to glow. "Movie people. Wow. You know, I hate to bring this up just now, but I've been working on a script, and I wonder if I could —"

"Patrolman Hicks," Joe interrupted in a solemn voice, "you're on duty. Let's get on with the job. Maybe I can mention your name to . . ." He paused, apparently wondering which guest would be interested in a script. "Chips Madigan, the director. Okay?"

"Really?" Darnell looked elated. "Golly. That would be terrific. Believe me, my script isn't just another piece of junk. I've got serious themes." He turned to his partner. "Come on, Merce, let's hit it."

The kitchen was clearing out. Judith put

both hands to her head and gave Joe a frantic look.

"What do we do now?"

"We wait," Joe said, sitting down at the kitchen table. "It may look like some kind of freak accident, but in fact they're going to have to send the homicide 'tecs in."

Judith was aghast. "Tonight?"

"Of course. You know the drill." He shot her a wry glance.

"But it's two in the morning, and we've got all these people upstairs, and —" She stopped, looked out over the swinging doors, then lowered her voice. "Winifred's still at the dining-room table. She either passed out or she's asleep."

But Winifred Best was wide-awake. Her head jerked up, then she slowly rose to her feet. "Where's Morris?" she demanded.

"Morris?" Judith echoed in a dull voice. "Morris . . . Mayne?"

Winifred thrust open the sliding doors and entered the kitchen. "Of course I mean Morris Mayne. The publicist. He must be at the hotel." She pulled her cell phone out of her bathrobe pocket and began to dial in a staccato manner.

Judith felt not only exhausted but helpless. "I'll make coffee," she said, and started for the sink.

"Hold it," Joe said. "You can't use the sink, remember?"

"Yes, I can," Judith shot back. "We'll plunge it. I can't imagine that it's seriously plugged up. Anyway, we've got a snake. If the plunger doesn't work, the snake should clear the line."

"You're missing the point," Joe said, his patience sounding thin. "The sink may be a crime scene."

"Oh." Judith stared into the murky water. "Oh, damn. You're right, I should have realized that." For the first time she saw something bobbing listlessly around in the sink. Judith reached out to touch it, then quickly withdrew her hand. "Evidence," she murmured. "It looks like my aspirin bottle. I found a pill on the floor."

"When I talked to Bruno the last time," Winifred said, clicking off the cell phone, "and he complained of a headache, I told him I'd seen some aspirin in the kitchen." For a brief moment she looked as if she were going to cry, then rallied. "Morris will be issuing a statement. He'll hold a press conference later for the early newscasts." She looked up at the schoolhouse clock. "That will be four A.M. our time for the seven o'clock news on the East Coast. Perhaps I should join him at the Cascadia. I doubt I can do anything here. Those cretins upstairs don't need to be consoled." With a swish of her bathrobe, Winifred started to leave the kitchen, but stopped abruptly. "Where is he?" she asked in a hollow voice.

Judith was puzzled. "You mean . . . Morris? I thought you just —"

"No!" Winifred exploded, waving a frantic hand. "Bruno! Where did you put him?"

In the dishwasher? Judith almost said as the giddiness she'd felt earlier tried to reclaim her emotions.

But Joe intervened. "His body was removed just minutes ago."

"Oh." Winifred's shoulders slumped. "Of course." Without another word, she left the kitchen.

The doorbell sounded. Joe got up to answer it while Judith gazed at the mess that still hadn't been — couldn't be — cleaned up. She, too, felt like crying.

But there was no time for tears. Joe, whose face had become so red that he looked as if he might explode, came storming back into the kitchen.

"It's Stone Cold Sam," he said under his breath, and then swore such a rapid blue streak that Judith — mercifully — could hardly understand him.

"Who," she finally dared to inquire, "is Stone Cold Sam?"

Joe stared at her. "You don't remember? Stone Cold Sam Cairo, my nemesis in the department? The world's biggest pain in the butt?"

"Oh!" Judith did remember. There had been several occasions when Joe had come home from work fuming because Stone Cold Sam had interfered with an investigation, offered unwanted criticism, and generally tried to make Joe's life miserable.

The stocky man with the goatee and mustache swaggered into the kitchen. Following him was a small young woman with short blond hair sticking up in peaks and an intimidated expression on her pretty face.

"You know, Flynn," the man said in a rough, deep voice, "it looks like you've got everything here, including the kitchen sink. Har, har."

Joe cradled his drink and leaned against the refrigerator. The gold flecks glinted in his green eyes, but with malice rather than mischief. "We don't know if we have a homicide or not," he said without inflection.

Stone Cold Sam Cairo chuckled, an unpleasant, grating sound. "Yeah, I guess it always took you a while to figure out the facts."

Judith didn't know whether to introduce

herself or not. Not, she decided. Any gesture of hospitality would annoy Joe.

Cairo, however, took matters into his own hairy hands. "Meet my new partner," he said, dragging the small blonde forward by the hand. "Dilys Oaks. Dilys, this is Joe Flynn, a former colleague, now retired. Don't be misled by the choirboy outfit. Joe can't sing a lick." Cairo glanced at Judith. "Let me guess. You're either a Roman empress, Joe's wife, or Joe's slave. Maybe the last two combined. Har, har."

"I'm Judith Flynn," Judith said, as noncommittal as Joe.

Cairo gave a faint nod. "Okay by me." He looked at the sink, and noted the phony spider, which swayed grotesquely from the overhead light. "Halloween stuff, huh? Nice touch. What was this movie guy doing, bobbing for apples?"

Joe didn't respond, which forced Judith to speak. "I think he was taking some aspirin. He had a headache."

"Hunh." Cairo steered Dilys to the sink. "What does this tell you?"

Dilys's smoky-gray eyes widened. "That the drain is plugged?"

Cairo put an avuncular arm around Dilys's narrow shoulders. "Think a little harder. Take in the whole picture. Remember, you're a rookie. This isn't like your first two cases with the drunks popping each other and the spousal murder-suicide."

"But," Dilys protested in her little-girl voice, "is it a homicide?"

Cairo removed his arm and wagged a finger at his partner. "There you go, young lady. Is it? How can we tell?"

"We don't have the body," Dilys noted. "Shouldn't they have waited until we got here before they removed it?"

Cairo nodded approval. "That's right. Haste makes waste," he added with a disapproving glance at Joe, who remained expressionless.

"I guess," Dilys said slowly, "you should have told them we were on our way. Now we'll have to wait for the autopsy."

Cairo shot Dilys a sharp, wary glance. "They should have known we were coming. But you're right, only the ME can tell us for sure how this guy died." He gave Joe an even darker look. "You know better, Flynn — why didn't you tell them to hold their horses?"

Joe stared up at the ceiling, looking innocent in his choirboy costume. "I'm retired, I'm old, I forgot."

Cairo grunted. "If you say so."

Joe said nothing.

But his former colleague wasn't giving up.

"Hey," Cairo urged with an expansive gesture. "Share your thoughts with us, for old times' sake. Reach out. We're listening."

"I never speculate," Joe said quietly.

"No kidding?" Cairo gazed at Joe with feigned shock, then swore as the faulty cupboard door swung open and rested gently against his right ear. "What's with this thing?" the detective demanded. "Ghosts?"

Judith shook her head. "The spring is sprung. Or something. It does that often."

Cairo glared at Joe. "Can't you or your slave here fix the damned thing?" He gave the door a vicious slam, rattling china and glassware in the cupboards. Judith gritted her teeth.

But Cairo's gaze was now on the spider above the sink. He turned to Judith. "What about you, Mrs. Flynn? Is that scary tarantula wannabe one of your Halloween decorations?"

"No."

"Oh?" Cairo grew curious. "Then who put it there?"

"I've no idea," Judith replied. "I didn't see it when I was in the kitchen before . . . before Mr. Zepf died."

Cairo nudged Dilys. "You hear that, young lady? Mrs. Flynn doesn't know how that nasty old bug got there. What's your idea?"

Warily, Dilys looked up at the spider. "Are you sure it's not real?"

Cairo reached up and gave the spider a spin. "Definitely fake."

Dilys gave a nod. "So maybe . . ." Her small voice trailed off.

"Yes?" Cairo urged. "Maybe what?"

"Maybe" — Dilys swallowed hard — "someone put the spider up there to frighten the deceased. You know, like a practical joke."

Cairo frowned at her. "Come now, isn't that pretty far-fetched?"

Dilys was blushing furiously. "Ah . . . maybe, but —"

"She could be right," Judith put in, unable to watch the young woman suffer further. "The deceased — Mr. Zepf — was superstitious about spiders. They terrified him. Someone had already tried to scare him by placing one of these phony tarantulas in his bed."

"No kidding." Cairo moved his frown to Judith. "You sure about that, Mrs. Flynn?"

"Absolutely," Judith replied. "There were several witnesses. Not to mention that Mr. Zepf became frightened by a very small but very real spider out on the back porch. I saw that with my own eyes." To Judith's satisfaction, Dilys had slipped behind Cairo and was making bunny ears above his head.

Maybe, she thought, the young detective wasn't quite as cowed as she pretended.

At that moment Angela La Belle and Ben Carmody appeared in the hallway that led from the back stairs.

"What's going on?" Ben asked, looking sleepy.

Joe turned to the pair. "Didn't Ms. Best tell you?"

Ms. Best hadn't. "What's to tell?" Angela inquired. "Bruno's dead." She was wearing a paper-thin wrapper over a sheer, short nightgown. "Are there any truffles left?"

Cairo's dark eyes were bugging out from underneath the black brows that grew together. "Now who's this, I might ask?" He leered at Joe. "Another one of your slaves?"

"This is Angela La Belle," Joe said woodenly, "and Ben Carmody. They're part of the movie company that came here with Bruno Zepf. You do have a list of possible witnesses, don't you?"

"Ah!" The question was ignored as Cairo beamed and put out a pawlike hand. "Celebrities! I'm thrilled." Despite the grin, it was obvious that Cairo would have preferred meeting a pair of real tarantulas.

Dilys, however, was goggle-eyed as she stared at Angela La Belle. "Ohmigod! I saw you in your first big movie, that musical —

168

Enjoy Your Pants! You have such a beautiful voice!"

Angela was scanning the kitchen counters, apparently for truffles. "Thanks. It was a small part. My voice was dubbed."

"But the dancing!" Dilys enthused. "Looking down from way up high on you with all the spinning and leaping and twirling and —"

"That was a double," Angela said, opening a couple of plastic containers. "I've got two left feet." She looked at Judith. "So they ate all the truffles?"

"I guess so," Judith replied. "Eugenia Fleming seemed especially fond of them."

"Bummer." Angela took in the official yellow tape that Stone Cold Sam Cairo was putting up between the kitchen and the dining room. "Oh," she said with mild interest, "is this a crime scene or what?"

"Bruno couldn't have drowned," Ben Carmody remarked. "Win must be wrong. He probably had a heart attack. Not that I blame him after what happened tonight."

Cairo whirled around with surprising agility for such a thickset man. "And what was that, young fellow?"

Ben gazed incredulously at the detective. "The premiere. What else? Bruno bombed. Big time."

"Ah, yes." Cairo rummaged in the pocket of his navy-blue raincoat. "What's it called?" He peered at a small notepad. "*The Gasbag*?"

"It might as well be," Ben said with a heavy sigh. "It's *The Gasman*," he added, emphasizing the final syllable.

"So," Cairo said, stuffing the notepad back inside his raincoat, "the deceased had suffered a big disappointment, had he? Did he have a history of heart trouble?"

Angela and Ben looked at each other.

"Ulcers, maybe," Angela said.

"High blood pressure?" Ben suggested.

"Ask Win." Angela pulled the folds of her wrapper more tightly around her body. "Win knows everything," she added with a sniff.

Cairo nodded sagely. "Let's have a word with this Win. That would be Winifred Best, correct?"

"Right," Ben said. "Come on, Angela, let's go back upstairs."

"But no further," Cairo called after them. "We don't want any of you fancy birds to fly the nest. Har, har."

Angela, who had started down the hallway, turned around and glared at the detective. "What do you mean? Are we stuck in this place for some weird reason?"

"That's right," Cairo said with a sharp shake of his head. "You're stuck until I unstick you. Surely you're enjoying the company of Mr. and Mrs. Flynn here."

Angela managed an ineffectual smile. "They're nice, but . . ."

"We've got meetings to take, lunches to do, people to . . ." Ben began in a not unreasonable voice.

"In due time, my lad, in due time." Cairo waved the pair off with a faintly sinister smile.

They had just disappeared up the stairs when someone knocked at the back door. Judith and Joe stared at each other. The rear entrance was reserved for family, friends, and neighbors.

"Mother?" Judith mouthed and started for the door.

Cairo put a hand to stop her. "Dilys will get that," he said. "It might be a reporter. Shoo him — or her — off, will you, my girl?"

The young woman cautiously opened the door to reveal a startling figure. A tall platinum blonde of more than a certain age stood on the threshold in an emerald-green satin lounging robe slit to the hip. She was carrying a paisley umbrella in one hand and a glass in the other.

Judith's jaw dropped. It was a neighbor, all right, it was sort of family, but it wasn't necessarily a friend.

Vivian Flynn, also known as Herself, was Joe's first wife and Judith's nemesis. Their visitor dropped the umbrella and swayed into the kitchen with a big crimson-lipped smile on her face.

"Stone Cold Sam!" she cried, setting the glass down by Judith's computer. She reached out her arms, embraced the detective, and kissed him three times. "It's been too long!"

Cairo, his chin on Vivian's shoulder, gave Joe a wink and a smile. A nasty smile, Judith noted, and thought the night would never end.

Chapter Eight

"Let's get out of here," Joe whispered to Judith. "We'll go into the front parlor."

Unobtrusively, Judith tried to edge toward the door. The crime-scene tape barred her way. Joe glanced at Cairo, saw that he was still in Vivian's embrace, pulled the tape aside, and with an arm around Judith, slipped out through the dining room. Dilys, though evincing curiosity about her partner and Joe's ex-wife, raised an eyebrow at the Flynns' departure but made no comment.

"Good Lord." Judith sighed, collapsing into one of the two matching armchairs in front of the stone fireplace. "I'm exhausted! And what's Vivian doing here?"

Joe's grin was off center. "You know Vivian, you've watched her for six years since she moved into the cul-de-sac. She keeps late hours. No doubt the emergency vehicles caught her attention."

Meanly, Judith figured it was more likely they'd roused her from an alcohol-induced stupor. Herself, as Judith preferred to call Vivian, had brought a glass with her. Maybe she'd come to borrow a refill. Despite Joe's efforts to get his ex to join AA, she continued to drink. Vivian Flynn wouldn't admit that she had a problem.

"Vivian obviously knows Stone Cold Sam," Judith remarked as Joe stirred the embers in the small fireplace.

"Oh, yes," Joe replied, adding some paper and a couple of small pieces of wood. "They go way back."

"They must." Judith stared into the fire, which was now sparking into orange-and-yellow life. It rankled her that Joe and Vivian had such a long — if rocky — past. The marriage had been a mistake from the start, a catastrophe set in motion by Joe's first encounter with a fatal teenage overdose. The cop bar he'd gone to afterward had offered strong drink and a stronger come-on by the woman perched atop the red piano. In fighting off the shadows of wasted fifteen-year-old lives, Joe lost his grasp on reality. When he awoke the next morning, he was in a Las Vegas bed with a new bride, the already twice-wed Vivian.

There was no going back, though Joe had tried. He'd called Judith from the hotel casino to try to explain, to beg forgiveness. But Gertrude had told him that her daughter never wanted to see him again. The irony was that Judith never knew about Joe's call, or his subsequent attempts to reach her. Brokenhearted and abandoned, she had married Dan McMonigle on the rebound. That union was also doomed from the beginning. When Judith learned years later what had happened to Joe, she realized that both of them had married alcoholics and were paying the price for their folly. Joe's folly more than her own, she had often thought, but no one had compelled her to marry Dan. It was only retaliation — and the unborn child she was carrying — that had sent her so recklessly to the altar. Eventually, she had begun to understand Joe's ties to Vivian. In addition to having been married twice before, she had a son by each ex-husband and was down on her luck. Joe was a sucker for the underdog. Having taken the vows, he felt obligated to live them, for better or for worse. And like Judith, Joe had endured more worse and no better.

Those long, mean years had tempered

both of them. It hadn't been just the chance meeting twenty years later that caused him to file for divorce. The marriage to Vivian had been a shambles for more than a decade; the only good thing that had come of it was a daughter, Caitlin. Perhaps it was proof of the dismal state of matrimony in the first Flynn household that had kept Caitlin, now forty, from seeking a husband.

The thoughts flickered through Judith's brain like the flames dancing in the grate. She could picture Joe and Vivian hosting a departmental party, with Stone Cold Sam Cairo running his hand up the welcoming slit in Herself's dress. She could see Joe chatting with his longtime partner, Woody Price, on the deck — if the Flynns had had a deck — and being introduced to a young woman named Sondra, who would later become Mrs. Price. Joe would tend the barbecue, rustling up steaks and burgers for many of the cops whom Judith met later in life, and for some she'd never known at all. Despite a decade with Joe, Judith still resented the wasted years during which Vivian had held him hostage.

". . . too long now," Joe was saying.

Judith realized she hadn't been listening. So caught up in her thoughts, so weary was her body, so enwrapped in what had been and what might have been, she hadn't heard her husband.

"I'm sorry," she apologized, "I faded out there for a minute. What were you saying?"

Joe gave her a sardonic look. "That they can't do much tonight. They need the ME's report to proceed if, in fact, foul play is suspected."

"Oh. Good," Judith said. "You mean they'll have to go away?"

"Right." Joe, who had sat down in the other armchair, turned as Stone Cold Sam Cairo entered the parlor.

"So you've got two wives in the same cul-de-sac," he said with another one of his leers. "Two wives, two slaves, and some sexy movie actresses upstairs. I guess you've got it made, eh, Flynn? Maybe I should retire right now. Then you could tell me your secret for the good life. Har, har."

"Don't count on it, Sam," Joe responded with a sour expression. "What's up?"

"Do you really want to know? Har, har." Cairo laughed again, then sobered. "I just heard from downtown. They won't know anything until midmorning. Bruno Zepf may be a big shot in Hollywood, but he's just another stiff on a busy Halloween weekend."

"His companions won't like that," Joe said.

"They're used to first-class treatment."

"So what are they doing here?" Cairo slapped his thigh and laughed even louder than usual.

"It's a fluke," Judith said, and wished she'd kept her mouth shut.

"A fluke?" Cairo looked mildly interested.

"A superstition," Judith replied as Herself and Dilys entered the parlor. "Bruno Zepf considered B&Bs lucky for his movies."

Cairo scowled. "Not this time."

"Goodness!" Vivian exclaimed, cradling her chimney glass, which was now almost full of what looked like bourbon. "To think that all these Hollywood people were here and I never noticed! That's what I get for being such a night owl! I miss the comings and goings during the day."

Judith felt obliged to offer Joe's ex a thin smile.

Cairo was moving restlessly around the room, his gaze darting between Herself's glass and Herself's décolletage. "I'd better chat up these folks, just to remind them they shouldn't wander off." His hooded eyes turned to Joe. "You want to tell 'em to rise and shine?"

"No," Joe responded. "I don't think that's necessary."

"Hey!" Cairo raised his voice and scowled

at Joe. "Who's in charge here?"

"You are," Joe retorted. "You tell them to rise and shine."

Cairo started to speak, stopped, and turned his scowl on Dilys. "You're it."

Dilys's gray eyes widened. "Me?" She hesitated, as if waiting for verification. "Okay." Obediently, she trotted out of the parlor.

"Now," Vivian said, slithering onto the window seat, "tell me about all these gorgeous hunks who are sleeping just over my head."

When Joe didn't answer, Judith stepped in. "There are only two actors, Dirk Farrar and Ben Carmody. The actresses are Angela La Belle and Ellie Linn."

In a dismissive gesture, Herself waved the hand that wasn't holding her drink. "Actresses! They're all made-up hussies. Surely there must be more . . . men."

Judith glanced at Joe, whose expression was blank. He and his ex remained on friendly terms, and not only because they had a daughter. It seemed to Judith that Herself was some kind of source of amusement to Joe. Or maybe she was a reminder, the living reinforcement of Joe and Judith's good luck in finally finding each other. Judith hoped it was the latter that made him so indulgent of — or was it indifferent to? —

Vivian's not-so-subtle charms.

In response to the question, Judith nodded. "There are other men, but they're not actors. They're directors and writers and —"

Herself waved again. "Aren't those types homely?"

Before Judith could try to reply, Cairo intervened. "Let's cut out the chitchat, ladies. I want to hear some specifics about this so-called accident. Tell me," he said, standing in front of the fireplace with his hands folded behind his back, "who discovered Zepf's body?"

"I did," Judith admitted, sounding miserable.

"You did, eh?" Cairo glanced at Joe. "Not the great detective over here?"

Judith didn't comment.

"All right," Cairo went on, "when did you find the stiff?"

Judith glanced at Joe. "Around one-fifteen, maybe later?"

Joe gave a faint nod.

"When and where," Cairo queried, "did you last see this Zepf character alive?"

Judith tried to focus on the question, though her brain was fogging over. "He was on one of the living-room sofas by the fireplace. That must have been about a quarter to one, when Joe and I began to clean up everything and take some of the perishable items down to the freezer in the basement."

Cairo flung out his hands. "So where's the basement?"

Joe sneered. "Under the house."

Herself burst out laughing; her bust almost burst the seams of her emerald-green robe. "Oh, Joe-Joe! You're such a scream!"

Stone Cold Sam Cairo did not look amused. "You know what I mean," he snarled. "How do you get to the damned basement?"

Judith spoke before Joe could further enrage Cairo. "Through the kitchen, the hallway, and down the stairs on the left."

Cairo looked thoughtful. "So it's quite a distance from where Zepf was in the living room. Who was with him?"

The fog enclosed Judith's brain. "I don't remember." She glanced at Joe for assistance, but none was forthcoming. "He may have been alone." She paused, straining in an effort to concentrate. "The cat — I think Sweetums was sitting on Mr. Zepf's lap."

Cairo scowled, but Herself laughed again, though this time the sound was soft and purring. "That lovely cat! Oh, Sam, you've never seen such a beautiful pussy. Not lately, anyway."

Cairo ignored Herself. His attitude seemed

to indicate that perhaps he was getting tired, too. Maybe frustrated as well, Judith thought in her exhausted haze. Before the detective could pose another question, Dilys returned to the parlor.

"They won't come down," she announced. "They won't even open their doors. The woman in Room One says we have no probable cause or any evidence of a crime having been committed." Dilys didn't bother to stifle a wide yawn.

"Not cooperating?" Cairo slammed his fist against the fireplace, hurt himself, and swore under his breath.

"Poor baby," Vivian murmured. "Let Mommy kiss your boo-boo." She advanced on the detective, allowing a great deal of bare leg to become exposed.

"Not now," Cairo growled. "I'll take a rain check," he added.

Joe looked at Judith. "Who's in Room One?"

"Winifred Best," Judith said, surprised that she could remember where Room One was located, let alone who occupied it.

"Ms. Best is right," Joe said to Cairo. "Why don't you go away?"

Rubbing his sore knuckles, Cairo bristled. "I want to hear the details about how this Zepf guy died."

"You *have* heard them," Joe asserted. "He came into the kitchen, maybe to get some aspirin, probably had a heart attack, and fell face first into the sink. Look, the guy had just had the biggest comedown of his career. His future was on the line. You never knew of someone to suffer a coronary after a life-altering shock?"

His face darkening, Cairo continued rubbing his knuckles, but made no comment.

"I'm curious about that cupboard door," Dilys put in. "How often does it open by itself?"

"Occasionally," Judith admitted.

"Interesting," Dilys remarked, then turned to Cairo. "Mr. Flynn has a point. We can't do much until we get the ME's verdict."

"Awwr . . ." Cairo grimaced, but nodded abruptly. "Okay, we'll hang it up for now." He loomed over Judith. "I gotta trust you, Flynn. We're shorthanded tonight because of the holiday weekend. You see to it that nobody goes near that kitchen, especially the sink. You got that?"

Joe nodded solemnly; Judith blanched. "But I have to serve breakfast for —" she began.

Cairo made a slashing gesture with his sore hand. "Forget about it. Your fancy guests can go out to eat. So can you."

"But Mother can't —" Judith began before Joe broke in.

"Sam's right. The kitchen is a potential crime scene. We'll manage." He offered Cairo a dubious smile.

"Trying to get rid of me, eh, Flynn?" There was nothing playful about the look in Cairo's chilly eyes.

The equivocal smile remained on Joe's lips. But he said nothing.

Cairo gave Dilys a nudge and took Vivian by the hand. "I'll see one of your wives home," he said. "You'll see me again tomorrow. Stay put." Cairo, Dilys, and Vivian left the house.

"Oh, Joe," Judith murmured, "I'm so tired! But what will we do about breakfast tomorrow?"

"We'll work it out," Joe said grimly. "You go to bed. I'll check things around here before I come up."

Judith started to protest but lacked the energy for argument. She did, however, have one last question.

"So you really think Bruno's death was an accident?"

Again, Joe said nothing.

Indeed, Judith was too tired to care.

To her great surprise and relief, a smiling Chips Madigan met her as she came down from the third floor just before nine o'clock the next morning.

"That's great!" he exclaimed, framing her with the ever-present viewfinder. " 'Early A.M., overcoming tragedy, ready to face the world.' My mother would be proud of you, Mrs. Flynn. She's had a couple of B&B guests die on her, too."

"Really?" Judith quietly closed the door to the third-floor staircase. "What happened?"

Chips made a face. "I'm not sure. I mean, it was so long ago that I don't quite recall. One was maybe a stroke. Maybe they both were."

Strokes, heart attacks, even aneurysms sounded comforting to Judith. Anything was better than murder. She smiled apologetically. "I'm afraid I can't make breakfast this morning. No one is allowed in the kitchen until the cause of Mr. Zepf's death becomes official."

Chips nodded. "That's what Win and Dade told us. Dade got his start writing for a TV cop show a few years back. He's our police expert. And Win — well, Win knows everything. Or so it seems."

"How is she?" Judith inquired. "I thought she was terribly upset last night."

"She was," Chips agreed. "She still is. She and Bruno were like that." The boyish-looking director entwined his first and second fingers. "But she's a survivor. She's had to be," he added on a grim note.

"I guess everybody in Hollywood has to be a survivor," Judith remarked, slowly heading for the front stairs.

"True." Chips's voice held no expression. "We're going out to forage. At least Win and Ellie and Ben and I are. Dade already left."

"He's a lone wolf, isn't he?" Judith remarked as she reached the top of the stairs.

Chips nodded. "A lot of writers are like that. They work alone, they prefer their made-up characters to real people."

"I can understand that," Judith said, though she really couldn't. People were the center of her world, her reason for being. Family, friends, and strangers — Judith held out welcoming arms to them all. She would never have been able to run a B&B if she hadn't loved people.

Judith risked a touchy question. "I got the impression that directors and screenwriters don't always agree on how a movie is made."

Chips flushed, his freckles blending in with the rest of his face. "You mean that little dustup with Dade the other night?" He didn't wait for Judith to respond, but shrugged in an exaggerated manner. "Typical. We call it artistic differences. It doesn't mean a thing."

"Yes," Judith said, "I see how that can happen. But you and Bruno Zepf must have agreed on how *The Gasman* was made, right?"

Chips cocked his head to one side, looking even more boyish than usual. "Directors and producers have their own differences. It wouldn't be normal if they didn't. We're all creative types, we all have our own ideas about how a picture should be made."

"Do you think Bruno had the wrong idea? I mean," Judith added hastily, "that he did something wrong to get such a strong negative reaction to his movie?"

"Yes," Chips said sadly. "Making the picture was wrong. A passion for filmmaking is one thing — Bruno had plenty of passion. But personal missions seldom make for good box office. The project was doomed from the start. Maybe," he continued on a mournful note, "Bruno was, too." With a shake of his head, he turned back into Room Five.

Judith headed downstairs. Joe had already gone to early Mass and was bringing back pastries and hot coffee in big thermoses. But Judith's priority was Gertrude. The old lady would be fussing, since her daughter usually showed up at least an hour earlier than this with breakfast.

Indeed, when Judith entered the toolshed Gertrude wouldn't speak to her. She was sitting in her usual place behind the card table, sulking.

"One of our guests passed away last night," Judith began.

Gertrude turned her head and stared at the wall.

"He may have had a heart attack. That's why I haven't been able to make breakfast. I can't go into the kitchen."

Gertrude uttered a snort of derision.

"It's possible that someone —" Judith stopped and bit her lip. There was no point in alarming her mother. "We have to get an official verdict from the coroner before I can use the kitchen."

Gertrude picked up a deck of cards and shoved them into the automatic shuffler. *Click-clackety-click-clack.* She removed the cards and began to lay out a game of solitaire.

"In about fifteen minutes, Joe will come back with pastries and hot coffee," Judith said, then added with a touch of irony, "I hope the trouble last night didn't bother you, Mother."

Gertrude, who was about to put a red six on a black seven, turned her small, beady eyes on her daughter. "I didn't hear a thing.

At least your latest corpse was quiet about sailing off through the Pearly Gates."

"Thoughtful of him," Judith murmured, so low that her allegedly deaf mother couldn't hear her.

"What kind of pastries?" Gertrude demanded, playing up an ace. "They'd better have that custard filling I like. Or apples, with that gooey syrup. The last time, Lunkhead brought something with apricots. I don't like apricots, at least not in my pastries."

"He'll do his best," Judith avowed.

"No blueberries!" Gertrude exclaimed. "They turn my dentures purple. I'd look like one of those trick-or-treaters who came by last night."

Judith frowned. "You had kids come to the toolshed?"

"Kids, my hind end! They were as tall as I am. I didn't give 'em anything. Nobody eats my candy except me." Gertrude slapped a deuce on the ace.

"What were they dressed as?" Judith asked, recalling the late arrival of the spaceman and the alligator.

"A cowboy with fancy snakeskin boots and a scarecrow that looked like he came out of *The Wizard of Oz*," Gertrude replied, putting up another ace. "I could hardly hear a word they said. That's when I told them to beat it. They did. They knew better than to mess with this old lady." With a savage gesture, she reeled off a black nine, a red eight, and a black seven.

"What time was that?" Judith asked.

"Time?" Gertrude wrinkled her nose. "What's time to an old lady on her last legs? There's not much of it left. If you were me, you wouldn't keep track of time, either."

Judith eyed her mother shrewdly. "You seem to keep track of mealtimes pretty well."

Gertrude played up several more cards. "What does it mean?" she said in a musing voice. "Think about it. Why do they say that?"

"What? You mean about time?"

"No," Gertrude replied with a scornful glance at her daughter. "*Last legs*. You don't talk about somebody's first legs, or their second or their third. If you got more legs as you went along, then they wouldn't give out on you. Your last legs should be your best legs, because they're newer." She paused, scanning the cards in her hand. "Now where's that ace of clubs? I saw it someplace."

Judith surrendered. She'd been curious about the trick-or-treaters because she wondered why they'd gone to the toolshed instead of to the house. But maybe they had. Renie or Arlene would have taken care of them. There'd be more tonight, she realized, since it was officially Halloween. At least the wind had died down and the rain had dwindled to a mere mist.

Joe had returned when Judith went back into the house. He was putting a variety of pastries and doughnuts onto the buffet, along with crackers and various cheeses. There was also a plate of cookies in the shapes of jack-o'-lanterns, bats, and witches.

"Cute," Judith remarked, kissing him on the cheek.

"Me or the cookies?" he responded, plugging in the coffee urn.

"Both," said Judith. "When should we hear from the ME?"

"Elevenish," Joe replied. "Then we'll know if the guests can leave."

Judith began to pace the living-room floor. "I'd hate to have to go through Ingrid at the B&B association to put up the guests who are coming in later today. We've got five reservations, you know."

Dirk Farrar entered the room, looking belligerent. "What's going on? Nobody's telling us a damned thing. We can't stick around forever."

"We were just talking about that," Judith

said. "We're still waiting to hear from the police."

"Screw 'em," Dirk said fiercely. "That SOB Bruno had a heart attack. It served him right. My price just went down at least five mil and next time — if there is a next time — I'll be lucky to get any points at all."

"But you're a huge star," Judith protested. "You've been in several big hits, including with Mr. Zepf. Or so I've heard," she added humbly.

The handsome, craggy features that had made females hyperventilate on five continents, and possibly Pluto, twisted with anger. "You don't get it. None of you people who aren't in the business get it. Last night's flop could be the end of Dirk Farrar!"

Joe may have been three inches shorter and twenty-five years older, but he stepped smoothly between the actor and Judith. "That could come sooner if you don't stop yelling at my wife. Back off, big fella, or I'll have to do a little cosmetic surgery on that famous face of yours."

"Why, you —" Dirk began, but suddenly stopped and threw up his hands. "Screw it. I don't need to make the papers for mixing it up with some old fart. That's why I usually have a couple of bodyguards around." He stepped back, then started to stomp off —

but not before he scooped three sugar doughnuts from the buffet.

" 'Some old fart?' " Joe echoed. "I don't like that *old* part much."

"You're not old," Judith insisted, patting her husband's cheek. "You're middle-aged. When Dirk Farrar hits sixty, all that cragginess will turn into bagginess. You have such a wonderful round face, you hardly have any wrinkles at —"

The phone rang. Judith let Joe pick up the receiver on the cherrywood table by the bookcases. When he turned his back on her, she was certain that he was speaking with Stone Cold Sam Cairo.

"Right . . . Yes . . . No . . . So be it." Joe hung up.

"Well?" Judith asked anxiously. "Is it . . . ?" She couldn't say the word *murder.*

Joe looked rueful. "A blow to the head apparently knocked him unconscious and he fell in the sink and drowned."

Judith was mystified. "You mean someone hit him?"

"Not necessarily," Joe replied. "It could have been that cupboard door swinging out. He may have bent over for some reason, reared up, and conked himself."

Judith remembered the aspirin she'd picked up from the floor. Perhaps Bruno had dropped it, ducked down to retrieve it, and then — unaware that the door had swung open — hit his head with such force that he blacked out.

"It's possible," she allowed, though with reluctance.

"You don't hear it coming," Joe said ruefully, then walked over to Judith and lowered his head. "Feel the bump about two inches above my hairline."

Judith touched the spot. There was a slight swelling. "The door? When did that happen? You never mentioned it."

"Friday," Joe said, avoiding her gaze. "You were gone. I didn't want to admit that I'd banged my head on the door, because I was supposed to fix it. I actually saw stars at the time."

Hands on hips, Judith stared at her husband. "You mean this is all our fault?"

"Yes," Joe said in a weak voice. "We may have killed Bruno Zepf."

Chapter Nine

"That's ridiculous," Judith declared. "How is it our fault that Bruno bumped his head on an open cupboard door? Maybe he opened it himself."

Joe gave Judith a bleak look. "The door was broken. That's negligence. That's our fault."

"My God," Judith moaned, "we could be ruined! If they find out about that door, they'll sue, they'll take every cent we have!"

Joe's expression turned grim. "What's the insurance for guests?"

"Substantial," Judith said, agitated. "I mean, adequate under normal circumstances. But not for something like this, if we're shown as being negligent and a big Hollywood celebrity gets . . . Think of the publicity! It's one thing to have a guest murdered by someone else, that can't be helped," Judith went on, her usual sound logic working in strange ways, "but an accident caused by the owners' carelessness?" She put her hands over her face. "Oh, Joe, I can't bear it! I feel sick!"

"Well, you can't throw up in the kitchen sink," Joe remarked, a touch of his characteristic humor surfacing.

Judith took a deep breath. "I'm in shock. And that poor man — if it's our fault that he's dead . . ." Her nausea remained though she pressed her hands against her face as if trying to subdue the sensation.

"Hang on." Joe put an arm around his wife. "We're not licked yet."

Judith peered between her fingers. "What do you mean?"

"I mean," he said quietly, "that we don't know for sure how Bruno ended up unconscious in the first place."

"You mean . . . Someone may have hit him with a different object?"

"No, there were slivers of wood and maybe varnish in what was left of Bruno's hair," Joe said. "Cairo was so busy giving me a bad time that the facts were a little hard to piece together."

Judith was still puzzled. "But what's the official verdict?"

"Death by misadventure. That means,"

Joe explained, pouring himself a cup of coffee, "that there's no evidence of foul play, but an investigation will continue."

"What about the guests?" she asked. "Are they free to go?"

"I suppose so," he said as the front doorbell rang. "I'll get it."

When Joe reappeared moments later, a tall, balding olive-skinned man wearing wraparound sunglasses and what looked like a very expensive Italian suit was right behind him.

"This is Vito Patricelli," Joe announced. "He's a lawyer, representing Paradox Studios. He just flew in from L.A."

The last person Judith wanted to meet was a lawyer. She reached out with an unsteady hand and tried to smile. "Hi, Mr. . . ." The name eluded her anguished brain.

"Patricelli," the attorney said smoothly, holding out a manicured hand. "I believe my clients are staying at your B&B."

"Clients?" Judith's brain was still numb. "Which ones?"

Vito Patricelli offered her a look that might have passed for compassion. "*The Gasman*'s cast and crew. I represent the studio, ergo, I represent Misses Best, La Belle, and Linn as well as Messieurs Farrar, Carmody, Madigan, and Costello. And, of course, the late Mr. Zepf."

"I see," said Judith, who almost did. "Excuse me, I have to sit down." She flopped onto the sofa and rubbed at her temples.

Joe took over. "I assume you want to meet with your clients. That door on the other side of the buffet leads to the parlor. There's also a door off the entry hall. Shall I get them?"

The attorney nodded. "I'd appreciate that. In fact, may I come with you?"

"Sure." Joe led the way out of the living room.

Judith put her head back on the sofa's soft cushions and closed her eyes. She saw strange visions, of her mother dressed as Cleopatra playing solitaire with chocolate cards, of Joe and Woody and Stone Cold Sam Cairo chasing each other in Keystone Kops costumes, of Skjoval Tolvang fending off Angela La Belle's advances with a crowbar.

The gentle squeeze on her shoulders brought her back to reality. Startled, she looked up at Joe. "I must have fallen asleep," she said in a sheepish voice.

"I wouldn't doubt it," Joe said, then gestured toward the parlor. "They're all in there. Every so often you hear somebody yell. It's usually Dirk or Angela."

"How long have they been meeting with Patricelli?" Judith inquired, moving around to remove the kinks she'd acquired in her neck and back.

"Not that long," Joe said. "Ten minutes at most." He stiffened as Vito Patricelli emerged from the parlor door that led into the living room.

"The meeting's concluded," Vito said in his unruffled manner. "I've made it clear to my clients where their responsibilities lie and what they must do to carry them out on behalf of Paradox Studios."

Joe was equally unflappable. "Which is?"

A faintly sinister smile played at Vito's thin lips. "That they are not to leave the vicinity until the studio knows exactly what happened to Bruno Zepf."

Judith didn't know whether to laugh or cry. She did neither, remaining on the sofa until the sullen guests exited the parlor.

Vito sat down opposite her, carefully arranging his trousers to make sure the crease stayed in the proper position. "I have some questions for you both," he said in that same, smooth voice.

Joe joined Judith on the sofa. "Fire away," he said.

Vito removed his sunglasses, revealing

wide-set dark eyes that seemed to have a fire lit behind them. "What time did Mr. Zepf die?"

"Around one A.M.," Joe answered.

"Are you absolutely certain?" Vito asked.

"We can't be precise," Joe said reasonably. "My wife and I weren't with Bruno when it happened. The time is an estimate, which is also what the ME gave us."

Only an almost imperceptible flicker of Vito's eyelids indicated any emotion. "But," he said, "you're positive that Bruno died after midnight?"

"Definitely," Joe replied. "Why is the time so important?"

The lawyer took a deep breath, then gave Joe what was probably meant to be a confidential smile, but looked a trifle piranhalike to Judith. "Let me explain two things. First, Paradox Studios insures all members of a shooting company when a picture is made. This is standard procedure, to make sure there's due compensation for anyone involved in the production suffering a disabling injury or" — he paused to clear his throat — "dying. The policy the studio took out on *The Gasman* expired October thirty-first, which is today. The problem is, did it expire last night at midnight or is it still valid until tomorrow, November first?"

Joe frowned. "Aren't such policies specific?"

"Not in this case," Vito replied. "There was also a rider concerning postproduction. Bruno had stated — verbally — that once *The Gasman* premiered, he wouldn't tinker with it. But last night he told Winifred Best and Chips Madigan that it was clear there would have to be some editing. He intended to pull the picture from release and postpone its general opening for a month."

Judith finally found her voice. "What does all this have to do with the guests not being able to leave?"

Vito tried to look apologetic, but failed. "I'm afraid I can't discuss that with you at present. But I'm sure you realize that the studio wants to conduct its own investigation into the cause of Bruno's death. You must be aware that the medical examiner's report is inconclusive."

"We're aware," Joe said with a dour expression.

"Good." Vito stood up, ever mindful of the crease in his trousers. "I hope this doesn't sound crass, but I believe you have a vacant room?"

"Ah . . ." Judith's jaw dropped. "You mean Bruno's? Yes, but —"

"If you don't mind, I'll spend the night

there," Vito interposed. "Right now I have to head back downtown to talk with the rest of the company at the Cascadia Hotel. Don't bother to show me out. I know the way." He slipped his sunglasses back on and gave both Flynns the slightly sinister smile. "I'm a quick study."

Despite the lawyer's assertion, Judith and Joe followed him as far as the entry hall. When the door had closed behind Vito, Joe put an arm around his wife.

"Let's go into the parlor in case the guests decide to come downstairs and commandeer the living room."

In the gray autumn light with the dead ashes in the grate and the single tall window streaked with rain, the room had lost its usual cheerfulness. The parlor seemed bleak, matching Judith's mood.

"Whatever are we going to do?" she groaned, slipping into one of the two matching side chairs. "Will the studio's investigation make us the culprits?"

"I've no idea," Joe admitted, "but one thing's for sure — Stone Cold Sam Cairo isn't going to rush around on our account. He's laughing up his sleeve over our dilemma because he hates me. Resents me, too, which is maybe why he hates me. I always had a better ratio of cases solved than he did. It was a competition to Sam, one-on-one. The bottom line is we can't rely on him."

Judith felt too dazed to respond.

"So we'll do our own investigating. I've got the experience, and you've got . . . a way with people." Joe lowered his gaze. It was difficult for him to admit that his wife's amateur tactics could ferret out murderers. "Between us, we may be able to get ourselves out of this jam."

"You mean," Judith croaked, "we informally interrogate them?"

"You do," Joe said, patting her hand. "I'll take a more professional stand. After all, I'm not only a retired cop, but a private detective." He offered her his most engaging grin. "Want to hire me?"

Judith grinned back, though she was still upset. "Of course. I'd better make arrangements with Ingrid for tonight's other guests."

Joe patted her, then started for the door. "I'm on the case."

"Oh!" Judith called after him. "One thing."

"What's that?"

She swallowed hard. "Do you honestly believe that Bruno may have been murdered?"

Joe regarded his wife with grim compassion. "I can't rule it out."

Judith's heart sank. "You sound like a cop."

He shrugged.

Judith tried to regain her composure. "One more thing."

"What?"

"Can I use the kitchen?"

When Judith drained the sink, she felt as if she were releasing the floodgates of evil. Joe had already removed the rubber spider and fingerprinted the entire area, including the wayward door, the window and windowsill, and the faucets. He'd ask Woody Price to run the evidence through the lab.

Judith called Ingrid at the state B&B association's office, but was informed that Ms. Heffelman had the weekend off. In her place was a soft-spoken woman named Zillah Young. Apparently Zillah was new to the hostelry business and didn't know of Judith's reputation for murder and mayhem. Without giving the details, Judith meekly asked her to assign the five Sunday-night reservations to other B&Bs in the area.

Finally, Judith had a chance to call Renie and let her know about the tragedy. It was shortly after eleven o'clock, and the Joneses should be back from Mass at Our Lady, Star of the Sea. Judith would either have to miss Mass or go in the evening. There was no way she could leave Hillside Manor at present.

The only guests that Joe had found upstairs were Dirk Farrar and Angela La Belle. Joe reported that both were furious. He also noted that they seemed to be sharing Room Three, which had belonged to Bruno.

"I told them to get out of there," Joe said. "I want to search that room thoroughly before Vito settles in."

"Will they go?" Judith asked, her fingers poised to call Renie.

"They stomped out of the house five minutes ago."

Judith sighed. "So there's nobody here for me to chat up. Heaven only knows where Dade Costello went. He seems to wander the neighborhood, thinking great thoughts."

"Or homicidal ones," Joe put in.

"Are you going to search Bruno's room now?" Judith asked.

"Yes. You want to come along?"

"No," Judith replied. "I have to call Renie, and then, if none of the guests are back, I'll go down to St. Fabiola's at the bottom of the hill for noon Mass. Oh, by the way, there's a book in Bruno's room called *The Gasman*. I heard he based the movie on it. It's old and looks as if it's been cherished. Chips Madigan said something this morning about Bruno being on a mission. I know it sounds silly, but I'm curious. Why don't you bring it down and I'll call one of my library mavens to see if they know anything about it."

"You never came across it when you worked as a librarian?" Joe inquired, referring to the weary years of Judith's first marriage when she worked days at the public library and tended bar at the Meat & Mingle in the evenings.

Judith shook her head. "I've never heard of it."

Joe left the kitchen while Judith dialed Renie's number. There was no answer except for Anne's voice on the machine.

"Anne Jones here. If you want to reach me immediately, call my cell phone or my pager. The numbers are . . ." After reeling off the digits, she added, "If you must speak to anybody else, leave your —" The message cut off abruptly, as if Anne didn't give a damn whether the rest of the Joneses ever got a phone call. Which, Renie asserted, Anne didn't.

Judith took a plateful of pastries out to the toolshed, where Gertrude picked over them with a persnickety air. Finally she selected two custard sweet rolls and three sugar doughnuts.

"Some breakfast," the old lady sniffed. "Isn't it time for lunch?"

Judith told her mother that lunch would be a little late. Gertrude sniffed some more.

By five to twelve, none of the guests had returned. Their absence made Judith nervous, but accepting it as a sign from heaven, she headed off to St. Fabiola's. The church was near the civic center, and was a half century newer than Our Lady, Star of the Sea. The amber brick edifice was only a few minutes' drive from Hillside Manor. At the bottom of Heraldsgate Hill on a quiet Sunday morning, traffic was light. Most of the businesses were closed, and the few that were open had just unlocked their doors to customers.

Judith arrived just after Mass had started, so she sat in a pew near the back. The lector was reading the first epistle when there was a commotion behind her.

Discreetly, she turned to look. At the side entrance, an elderly usher was struggling to keep a disheveled bundle of unsteadiness upright. It was a woman, Judith thought, and wondered if she was drunk or ill. At last the man steadied the unfortunate soul, propping her up against a confessional door.

". . . word of the Lord," intoned the lector from the pulpit.

"Oh, my Lord!" Judith gasped from the pew.

The disheveled woman was Renie. She was panting and limping, her clothes in disarray and her hair going every which way, including over her eyes. Judith hurried into the aisle and approached her cousin.

"What's wrong?" she whispered in a frantic voice. "Are you sick?"

Renie shook her head, brushing unruly chestnut strands of hair out of her eyes.

"Have you been attacked?" Judith asked.

Renie shook her head again. "Not exactly."

Judith gestured toward the pew where she'd been sitting. "Can you sit down?"

Renie nodded. The usher, whose wrinkled face was etched with concern, made a move to help both women.

"It's okay," Judith said softly. "She's not heavy, she's my cousin."

Chapter Ten

Renie all but fell into the pew. By now, several of the nearby worshipers were staring. But as she regained her breath and straightened her clothes, the curious returned their attention to the altar. Judith, however, still stared at her cousin with anxious eyes.

"Later," Renie mouthed.

It seemed like the longest Mass that Judith had ever attended. She had great difficulty concentrating on the liturgy, though she found no problem in praying for Renie and for herself. It seemed that they both were in a great deal of trouble. At last the priest gave the final blessing. Judith offered to help Renie out of the pew, but was shaken off.

"I'm okay now," she declared. "I won."

"You won what?" Judith asked as they started down the aisle.

"The fight," Renie said as they reached

the vestibule. "I got into a fight at the XYZ Market up the street."

"Oh, good grief!" Judith exclaimed, drawing more stares from the exiting churchgoers. "How did that happen?"

"Some middle-aged Amazon thought she was Wonder Woman and tried to edge me out at the checkout counter," Renie explained as they headed down the stairs to the door that led to the parking lot. "I'd already stood in line for ten minutes and I was afraid I'd be late for Mass. Bill had gone to ten o'clock at Our Lady, Star of the Sea. I was so pooped from everything that happened yesterday that I slept in. Anyway, this brazen broad ran her cart over my foot and said something like, 'Move it, shorty.' So I rammed her with my cart. Then we got into it, and the next thing I knew we were slugging it out over the counter and finally I put a plastic produce bag over her head. She surrendered." Renie wore a grim expression of victory. "So what's new with you this morning?"

Judith started to speak, and discovered that she had no voice. "I . . ." The single word was a squawk. "Joe . . ." Her husband's name was a guttural sound, as if she were gagging.

Renie looked alarmed. "What's wrong,

coz? Is something caught in your throat?"

Judith shook her head. The other church-goers were now swarming the parking lot, revving engines, and readying for departure. The cousins were blocking traffic. With a desperate effort, Judith mouthed the words, "Buster's Café."

"Buster's?" Renie looked bewildered.

Judith made chewing motions. Renie got it.

"You want me to meet you at Buster's? Okay, see you in a couple of minutes."

Buster's Café was old, a lower Heraldsgate Hill landmark. Buster himself still ran the place after inheriting it from his parents forty years earlier. Nothing much had changed in that time, or even before, but the food was decent and the rubber-soled waitresses could have won a restaurant Olympics for speed and efficiency.

It took each of the cousins less than three minutes to drive to the café, but almost ten to find parking spaces, even on a Sunday morning. Judith was out of breath when she arrived; Renie seemed to have regained her usual bounce.

"I can't have more than coffee," Judith said, "because I have to get home. If you think you've had a bad weekend, listen to this . . ."

Renie did, her brown eyes growing wider and wider. When Judith had finished about the same time that Renie's coffee had gone cold, an incredulous expression remained on her cousin's face.

"You can't lose the B&B!" Renie cried. "It'd be like removing your liver!"

"I know." Judith sighed. "It's not just a job or making money, it's who I am. The horrible part is that we may be at fault. We were negligent in not getting that cupboard door fixed. Why, you almost slammed into it the other day."

"True," Renie allowed, her expression full of concern. "But you don't really know what happened to Bruno."

"Also true," Judith agreed.

A brief silence fell between the cousins. "I'm not going to say it," Renie said at last.

"Whatever it is, I don't want to hear it," Judith responded, finally taking a sip from her water glass. "No matter what, I've already said it about twenty times since last night."

Renie said it anyway. "It can't be another homicide. That'd be three at Hillside Manor. On the other hand, if it is, you wouldn't be at fault." She paused after stirring extra sugar into her coffee. "When is a murder not a murder? How on earth do you and Joe expect to find out?"

"I'm not sure," Judith replied, looking worried. "I talk, I listen, while Joe sleuths in a professional way."

"Can Bill and I help?" Renie offered, her deep sense of family loyalty leaping to the surface.

While not nearly as compassionate, Renie ran a decent second to her cousin when it came to striking up a revealing conversation. As for Bill, whatever he disliked about idle socializing was more than made up for by his extraordinary perceptiveness. Being a trained psychologist didn't hurt any, either.

"Why not?" Judith said, brightening a bit.

"Well . . ." Renie grimaced. "We were planning on inviting our future in-laws over so we could make sure who was marrying whom, but the kids aren't positive that will work with their various and elaborate schedules. They insist we've met them already. I'll find out what Bill thinks. If he gives me a green light, we'll be over as soon as we can."

Driving to Hillside Manor, Judith breathed a little easier. To her relief, the cul-de-sac was empty, except for the patrol car that had crept close to the curb. She couldn't see who was inside, but assumed it was someone from the day shift. Darnell Hicks and Mercedes Berger would have gone home hours ago.

As she often did, Judith left her Subaru in

the driveway. She usually entered the house from the rear, but on this anxious Sunday she retraced her route to the front. Pausing on the walk, she drank in the entirety of Hillside Manor, acknowledging its age, soaking up its memories. The house was almost a hundred years old, built in the Edwardian era. The dark green paint and the off-white trim on the Prairie-style Craftsman had just begun to chip and fade. Next summer, Judith would have to hire a painter. If there was a next summer at Hillside Manor.

So many memories, she thought, ignoring the slight drizzle. Her Grover grandparents had bought the house in the twenties. Her father and Renie's father had grown up there along with four siblings. Gertrude and Donald Grover had raised Judith within its sheltering walls. After Dan died, Judith and Mike had returned, converting the house into a bed-and-breakfast. To Judith, it wasn't just a building, it was a sanctuary. She couldn't possibly give it up. Not ever.

With a dragging step, Judith entered through the front door, where her melancholia was swept away by angry voices coming from the living room. One voice soared above the rest.

"You don't live in our world, Mr. Flynn," proclaimed Angela La Belle. "You can't possibly understand what it's like to be in the picture business. If we aren't free to talk to people, to make contacts, to keep up on every nuance of the business, our careers are in jeopardy. Indeed, after last night's fiasco, all" — she paused, and Judith thought she glanced at Ellie Linn — "or *almost* all of us are already in deep doodoo."

It seemed to Judith the reference was not to Bruno's death, but to *The Gasman*'s flop. She couldn't help but flinch at the lack of humanity.

Joe remained unruffled. "Don't blame us. Talk to your studio suits. You all have cell phones, don't you?" He cupped one ear with his hand. "I could swear they've been ringing like a satellite symphony."

"It's not the same," Ben Carmody argued. "I planned to take a dinner meeting tonight with the number two producer in Hollywood. Number one now, with Bruno out of the picture. So to speak." The actor looked faintly sheepish, but continued, "After last night, there may not be any producers who want to talk to me."

"You're not kidding," Angela chimed in. "Now when my name comes up, they'll say, 'La Belle? She was in that disaster, *The Gasman*. I wouldn't touch her with a ten-foot pole.' It'll be like I have a contagious disease. There's no rationality in this business. Only success and its afterglow count."

The others enumerated their complaints, all of which swelled into a dirge of doom. Judith studied the gathering. Winifred was seated on one of the sofas by the fireplace with Chips Madigan at her side. Opposite them were Angela and Dirk. Ben Carmody leaned against the mantelpiece and, while not wearing his usual sinister screen expression, definitely looked morose. Dade Costello retained his lone-wolf status in his favorite place by the French doors. Ellie Linn also stood outside the circle, perched on the bay window seat with her feet tucked under her. It seemed to Judith that the young actress hadn't been nearly as vocal about the unfortunate movie premiere as her colleagues.

It was time, Judith believed, to cut someone from the herd. She singled out Winifred Best.

"Excuse me," she said in a deferential voice, "but could I speak with you privately, Ms. Best?"

Briefly, Winifred looked hostile. Or maybe just wary. But her response was sufficiently courteous. "Yes, if you like."

Judith led her guest into the front parlor. "It's really none of my business, but since

I'll have to fill out some forms, I should know what the plans are for Mr. Zepf's body."

"Oh." Winifred's face fell. "I've contacted his children — they're both in the L.A. area — and they're making the arrangements. My understanding is that the body will be shipped from here tomorrow. Under the circumstances, I should think any kind of service will be private. Very private." She uttered the last words through taut lips.

Judith wondered if the very private services were because the family was very private or because the deceased had suffered a huge professional catastrophe and the survivors were afraid that nobody would attend.

"Are his children grown?" Judith inquired.

Winifred nodded. "Practically. That is, they're both in college. Greta's at Pepperdine and Greg just started USC."

"Um . . ." Judith cleared her throat. "Is their mother also in L.A.?"

Winifred arched her thin eyebrows. "Their mother is in Dubai. She divorced Bruno several years ago and married an emir. She was an actress named Taryn McGuire. I wouldn't be surprised if you'd never heard of her. She did mostly TV and only appeared briefly in two or three feature films."

The name meant nothing to Judith. "I

suppose being married to Bruno wasn't easy," she said in a sympathetic tone. "That is, he really was considered a movie genius, wasn't he?"

"Brilliant." Winifred's eyes lit up and her voice became almost caressing. "He always had his dreams. Bruno attended every Saturday matinee, his attention fixated on the screen, his imagination catching fire. Early on, he understood what made a successful picture. It was born in him."

Judith felt as if Winifred were reading from a press release. Maybe she was; maybe she'd written it.

"It was only in the last six or seven years that he began to receive the kind of acclaim he'd always sought," Winifred went on. "Two years ago he made the short list."

"Which is?" Judith asked, puzzled.

Winifred offered Judith a pitying smile. "It refers to those few at the very top of their professions in the film industry. Like Spielberg or Cameron. And Bruno." Quickly, she turned away. "Excuse me. It's so hard to think of Bruno going out . . . with a failure."

"You seem genuinely fond of him," Judith said, surprised at herself for being so bold, even more surprised that she was using the word *genuine* with a Hollywood person.

Winifred drew back sharply. "Why

wouldn't I be? He gave me an excellent job."

Maybe it was as simple as that. Maybe gratitude was possible in the movie business. Maybe something other than ice water ran in the veins of Winifred Best.

"You'd been with Mr. Zepf a long time?" Judith said, keeping her voice low and casual.

"Yes," Winifred replied, still wary.

"You must have had excellent credentials to get the job as Mr. Zepf's assistant," Judith remarked, hearing a car pull up outside.

"Good enough," Winifred said, her expression shutting down. "Is that Morris who just arrived?"

"Morris?" Judith echoed, puzzled.

"Morris Mayne, the studio publicist," Winifred said, joining Judith at the parlor's tall window.

"No," Judith said, recognizing Woody Price's car. "It's a friend."

Winifred stiffened. "Not Vito?"

"No . . ."

"Who, then?" Winifred rasped out the question.

"Ah . . . An old friend of my husband's, actually." Judith didn't want to identify Woody as a cop. He had probably come to collect the physical evidence Joe had gathered. As much as she wanted to see Woody, she thought it best to stay out of sight. Joe could handle his ex-partner's arrival with a minimum of fuss.

But Winifred persisted. "Why is he here? He's not media, is he?"

"Heavens, no!" Judith's laughter was false. "He won't stay. I think he wants to borrow something from my husband."

Winifred looked relieved. "Morris has done an outstanding job of misleading the media about Bruno's death. So far, they have no idea where or how it happened."

Judith could hear Joe greeting Woody in the entry hall. To divert the other guests, she led Winifred through the parlor door that opened directly into the living room.

"Excuse me," Judith said loudly. "Since I can use the kitchen, I'll take dinner orders now. Does anyone have some particular craving?"

Only Ellie Linn seemed excited by the announcement. "Can I get some of my dad's famous hot dogs? I've really missed them the past few days, you know."

Judith nodded. "There's a Wienie Wizard just across the ship canal. Anyone else want something special?"

"Not wieners," Angela said with a sneer. "I'd rather eat rubber."

"Steak," Dirk said, giving Angela's shoulders a quick squeeze. "New York cut, an inch thick, rare."

"You know what sounds good to me?" Chips Madigan said in his ingenuous manner. "An old-fashioned chicken pot pie, like my mother makes."

Ben Carmody gazed at the ceiling. "Pasta. Any kind, with prawns and a really good baguette."

"If Vito is here," Winifred put in, "he prefers sushi, particularly the spider rolls."

Judith's innkeeper's smile began to droop. She hadn't planned on serving a smorgasbord.

"Wine," Ellie added. "You know — some really fine wines. I like a Merlot with my Wienie Wizards." She shot Angela an insolent look.

"Dade?" Judith called across the long room. "What about you?"

The writer, who had, as usual, been staring out through the French doors, slowly turned around. "What about what?" he inquired in his soft Southern voice.

"What you'd like to eat," Judith said, hearing the front door close.

"Chitlins," Dade said, and turned his back again.

"Winifred?" Judith said as Joe ambled back into the living room.

Winifred shook her head. "I'm not hungry." She paused, tapping her sharp chin. "A small salad, perhaps. Mostly field greens."

"I'll call a caterer. They'll be able to stop by the Wienie Wizard on their way here." Still trying to keep her hospitable smile in place, Judith hurried off to use the phone in the kitchen.

"Woody's heading for the crime lab," Joe whispered as Judith went past him. "He's doing some background checks, too."

It took ten minutes to place the order with the caterer, with Judith filling in various other items to tide her guests over until the next morning. She had just hung up when the phone rang in her hand.

"Now what?" demanded an angry Ingrid Heffelman. "Zillah Young just called me from the state B&B — on my day off — to say you'd requested changes for tonight. What's going on, Judith?"

"Hey," Judith retorted, "this Hollywood booking was your idea. I didn't ask to change the Kidds and the Izards. You forced my hand."

"That's beside the point," Ingrid replied, simmering down just a bit. "The Kidds were considering staying over for a day or two and moving to your B&B. They felt they'd missed out. I wouldn't be surprised if the Izards would still like to spend a night there for future reference."

"The Izards already checked out the place," Judith said, still vexed. "Anyway, there's nothing I can do. It's out of my hands."

"How come?" Ingrid was heating up again.

"I can't tell you exactly," Judith replied, trying to sound reasonable. "It has to do with an incident involving one of the guests."

"An incident?" Ingrid sounded suspicious.

"What would you expect?" Judith said, no longer reasonable but downright cross. "From the beginning, I figured this crew would be nothing but trouble. I was right."

"What kind of trouble?" Ingrid asked, then uttered a high-pitched squawk. "Not . . . ? Oh, Judith, not again!"

"I can't say. Really," Judith added in a frustrated voice, "I'm not allowed to tell anyone just yet."

"You don't have to," Ingrid said sharply. "I can read the newspaper. It's that Bruno person, isn't it? He died last night. I didn't put two and two together this morning because the story was so small and I was barely awake. Being *my day off and all.*"

"I'm sorry, really I am." Judith was about to say it wasn't her fault. But this time she couldn't. Maybe she was to blame. "Please, Ingrid, don't tell anyone. We're under siege from the studio, which is why the Hollywood guests can't leave."

"Oh, God." Ingrid expelled a huge sigh. "All right, I'll be discreet, if only for the state association's sake. You're right — it's my fault for putting them up at Hillside Manor. Given your track record, I should have known better." With an apathetic good-bye, she hung up.

Judith was still muttering to herself when Renie and Bill arrived at the back door.

"You told us we could come through the kitchen," Renie said, breezing through the narrow hallway.

"Where are the nuts I'm supposed to observe?" Bill asked in his rich, carrying voice.

Judith winced. "In the living room. We're expecting at least one more, I understand. Remember Morris Mayne from last night?"

"The publicist?" Renie said, hanging her jacket on the antique coatrack.

"The very same," Judith replied. "And Vito Patricelli, the studio lawyer."

"What happened to the agent, Eugenia Whatever-her-name-is?" Renie asked.

Judith sighed. "I forgot about her. Who knows? Maybe the entire crew from the Cascadia will show up eventually."

"Let's watch TV," Bill said upon entering the living room. "There's a pretty good NFL game on." As the guests stared at him, he marched over to the entertainment center next to the bay window, opened the oak doors, and switched on the big-screen television set. "Who's a Packer fan?" he asked, being a Wisconsin native.

"I am," Chips Madigan declared.

"I hate the Packers," Dirk Farrar asserted.

Dade actually expressed some interest. "Who are they playing? The Falcons, by any chance?"

Angela rose from the sofa. "I hate football. I'm not watching." She sailed past Judith and Renie, heading for the bathroom off the entry hall.

"Me neither," Ellie said, slipping off the window seat. "I've never understood how all those great big men like grabbing each other. It's not natural, you know." She wandered off into the dining room.

"The observation period?" Judith murmured to Renie.

"That's right," Renie said. "Bill insists you can tell quite a bit about people by the way they watch — or don't watch — sports. Have you chatted up Ellie or Angela yet?"

Judith shook her head. "Only Winifred. Dade's the one I'd really like to talk to.

Maybe if Green Bay isn't playing Atlanta, he'll get bored."

"I'll tackle Ellie," Renie said, making motions like a football player. "You can grab Angela when she comes out of the can."

While her cousin went into the dining room, Judith slowly paced the entry-hall floor. A couple of minutes passed. Angela didn't reappear. Judith fiddled with the guest registry and the visitor brochures she kept on the first landing. Still, Angela didn't come out of the bathroom. Judith began to wonder if the actress might be ill.

After another three minutes had passed, she rapped softly on the varnished walnut door. "Ms. La Belle?" she called, also softly.

There was no response. Judith pressed her ear against the old wood, but heard nothing. She rapped again, this time louder.

Still nothing.

Alarmed, Judith tried the knob. The door was locked from the inside.

"Ms. La Belle!" she called. "Angela! Are you all right?"

Renie and Ellie Linn appeared from around the corner.

"What's going on?" Renie asked with a frown.

Quickly, Judith explained. "I'm afraid Angela may be sick."

Renie's frown deepened. "The lock's one of those old-fashioned bolt things, isn't it?"

"Right," Judith said, "but it means damaging the door, which Skjoval Tolvang just rehung."

"Then leave Angela in there," Ellie said with a shrug, and walked away.

"We can't," Judith declared, scowling at Ellie's departing figure. "I'll get Joe."

Everyone in the living room seemed to be caught up in a third-and-three situation for the Packers except Joe, who was watching Bill watch the guests. Urgently, Judith grabbed her husband by the arm.

"Come with me," she commanded, keeping her voice down. "We have a lock problem."

"What lock?" he said, turning to Judith. "I thought you knew how to pick them."

"Not this one," Judith said, pointing to the bathroom door. "It's a bolt, remember? Angela La Belle is in there and won't answer."

Joe looked skeptical, but saw that his wife was upset and threw up his hands. "Okay, but if there's nothing wrong and she just wants to . . . well, sit around, then I'm going to be even less popular around here than I am already."

"Please, Joe," Judith begged. "Do it."

First, however, Joe knocked. Then he called Angela's name. There was still no response. Grasping the doorknob, he counted to three, then gave a mighty tug. The old wood shuddered, but stayed in place. He tried a second time. The bolt gave, but not enough to come free.

"Get Bill," Joe said to Renie. He was panting and beginning to perspire.

Renie hurried out into the living room, returning almost immediately with her husband. "Commercial break," she murmured to Judith. "Lucky us."

Joe held on to the knob and Bill held on to Joe. With a mighty effort, they pulled the bolt lock out of the door, which swung outward.

Angela La Belle was facedown in the bathroom sink.

Chapter Eleven

Having been privy to two, possibly three, murders at her B&B, and encountering corpses at various other sites, Judith couldn't believe that history was repeating itself in less than twenty-four hours.

In some tiny hidden corner of her mind, she honestly thought that nothing could sever her hold on reality. She'd seen everything, overcome so many obstacles, endured unaccountable hardships. Surely this was a dream, inspired by the discovery of Bruno Zepf's body the previous night. Flashing stars and crazy comets sailed before her eyes as Judith swayed backward. She would have fallen if Bill hadn't caught her.

Dazedly, she heard Bill shout at Renie to get a chair out of the dining room. More dimly, she caught snatches of Joe speaking — or was he shouting? — he sounded so far away — to summon 911.

"Call . . . Medics . . . CPR?"

Judith thought she heard Joe mention CPR. Maybe Angela wasn't dead in the bathroom sink. Or maybe Joe wanted CPR for Judith. As a former cop, he knew CPR. Maybe everybody needed CPR. . . .

Someone — Bill, she guessed, catching her blurred reflection off his glasses — was easing her into Grandpa Grover's chair at the head of the dining-room table. A moment later a slender hand held out a balloon glass with what looked like brandy in it.

"Take a sip," Renie urged. "I got this out of the washstand bar."

Judith didn't care if Renie had held up the state liquor store at the bottom of Heraldsgate Hill. Gratefully, she accepted the glass and inhaled deeply before taking a small sip. The darkness with its streaks of spinning lights began to recede; the dining room was coming into focus. Judith fixated on the middle of the table, where a Chinese bowl of gold and amber chrysanthemums sat in autumnal splendor.

But reality returned along with her vision. "Angela!" she gasped. "Is she . . . ?"

Renie gave a sharp shake of her head. "I'm not sure. I think Joe was asking if anyone knew CPR. I suspect he didn't want to do it himself in case something else —" She caught herself. "In case Angela doesn't make it. Dade Costello volunteered. Don't move, I'll take a peek into the entry hall."

Judith took another sip of brandy. Bill stepped behind the chair and began rubbing her shoulders.

"Dirk Farrar is passive-aggressive," he said quietly. "Winifred Best has low self-esteem. Chips Madigan has an unresolved Oedipal complex. His father may have abused him."

Bill's analyses, along with the brandy and the massage, brought Judith into complete focus. "You figured out all that in five minutes of watching the guests watch TV?"

"It was longer than that," Bill replied. "The Packers got stalled on the Bears' thirty-eight-yard line, punted, and the Bears made two nice pass plays before they kicked a field goal."

"Oh." Judith smiled faintly. "I'm still amazed at how quickly you pinpointed their personalities."

"I'm guessing," Bill said, finishing the massage. "Ordinarily, it'd take several sessions to peel the layers off a patient. But you're under pressure to figure these people out."

"Yes," Judith agreed as Renie returned to the dining room.

"Angela's alive," she announced, "but still unconscious. Fortunately, there was no water in the sink."

"And no cupboard door to hit her in the head," Judith murmured. "So what happened?"

Renie shook her head. "Nobody knows. Maybe she fainted."

"She wouldn't still be out cold," Judith noted, getting to her feet with Bill's help. "She's either sick or . . ."

"Or what?" Renie put in as her cousin's voice trailed off.

"I'm not sure." Judith's expression was grim as she moved unsteadily into the entry hall, where Dirk Farrar was kneeling over Angela's motionless figure. Dade Costello, apparently weary from his CPR ministrations, leaned against the balustrade and used a blue-and-white bandanna to wipe sweat from his forehead.

Dirk looked up. "She's alive. Her breathing's better. Where the hell are the medics?"

Judith's ears picked up the sound of the medics' siren. "They're outside," she said, and staggered to the front door.

Chips Madigan was already on the alert. "In through here," he told the emergency team, pointing to the entry-hall bathroom. As the trio made their way to Angela, Chips got down on one knee and framed an imaginary shot with his fingers. "Whoa! This is good! Medium shot, backs of uniforms looking great, equipment visible, love the red steel cases." The director stood up. "Two men and a woman. That's good, too. But the height differentials could be better. The woman's too tall."

Dirk Farrar had stepped aside as the medics began their task. The woman — who was indeed over six feet — waved the other onlookers away. "Clear the area," she commanded. "We need some room here."

Judith, Joe, Renie, and Bill returned to the dining room. The women sat down at the dining-room table; the men remained standing, Bill by the window, Joe next to the big breakfront that held three generations of the Grover family's favorite china.

"What could have happened to Angela?" Judith mused in a fretful voice. "Stress?"

"In a way," Joe said, rocking slightly on his heels. "That is, if you figure that stress can lead to drug addiction."

"Drugs!" Judith exclaimed. "You think Angela overdosed?"

Joe nodded. "I'm certain that the white powder you found in the downstairs bath-

room was cocaine. I'm having Woody ana-
lyze the residue to make sure. I found traces
of it upstairs in the bathroom that Dirk and
Angela shared when they usurped Bruno's
room."

"Not surprising," Bill remarked. "How
many show-business people have a drug
habit?"

"How many ordinary people do, too?"
Renie said with a touch of anger. "It's everywhere."

"Bruno!" Judith breathed. "What if he
overdosed, too?"

Joe, however, shook his head. "No traces
of drugs were found by the ME."

Slipping out of her chair, Judith tiptoed to
the door that led to the entry hall and
peeked around the corner. An oxygen mask
had been placed over Angela's face and an
IV had been inserted into her arm. The two
male medics were preparing to remove her
on a gurney. The woman was speaking in
low tones to Dirk Farrar. Judith couldn't
hear a word they said.

She barely had time to duck out of sight
before Dirk Farrar came into the dining
room. Without his usual bravado, he addressed Joe.

"I assume it wouldn't break any rules if I
went with Angela to the hospital?" he said.

"Go ahead," Joe responded. "What's her condition?"

Dirk frowned. "Not so good. But they think she'll be okay." He hurried out of the room.

"Halftime," Bill murmured. "Let's see how the other guests are taking all this." He, too, left the dining room.

Judith and Joe trailed behind him. Bill was correct: The Packers and the Bears had retired to their respective dressing rooms to regroup for the second half. Ben Carmody was on his cell phone; Chips Madigan was leafing through a coffee-table book on Pacific Northwest photography; a disconsolate Winifred Best was sitting in what had once been Grandpa Grover's favorite armchair; Dade Costello had gone out through the French doors and was standing on the back porch.

Winifred's head snapped up as Bill, Judith, and Joe entered the living room. "What's going on? What happened to Angela? Is she dead?"

Joe explained the situation, somehow managing to leave out the part about a cocaine overdose.

"Was it a cocaine overdose?" Winifred demanded, looking as if she were about to collapse.

Joe didn't flinch. "That's possible."

Winifred wrung her thin hands. "I knew it. I knew it. She can't get off the damnable stuff. How many times have they —" She stopped abruptly. "Where's Dirk?"

"He rode to the hospital with Angela," Joe replied. "I believe they're taking her to Norway General."

The siren sounded as the medic van pulled away. Judith went back into the entry hall and looked outside. A second van, apparently a backup, was also turning out of the cul-de-sac. The neighbors, who were accustomed to the occasional burst of mayhem at Hillside Manor, were well represented by the Porters, the Steins, and the Ericsons, who stood on the sidewalk with Arlene Rankers. Across the street on the corner, the elderly widow Miko Swanson sat at her usual post by her front window. However, there was no sign of Vivian Flynn, whose bungalow next door to Mrs. Swanson's typically had its drapes closed during the daylight hours. Feeling obligated to keep her fellow homeowners informed, Judith started onto the porch just as a black limousine pulled into the cul-de-sac.

Vito Patricelli emerged with Morris Mayne and Eugenia Fleming. With a weak wave in the neighbors' direction, Judith ducked back inside, where she collided with Winifred, who was hovering right behind her.

"Sorry," Judith murmured.

Winifred ignored the remark as she hastened to greet the newcomers, who barely acknowledged Judith's presence as they entered the house.

"Dirk called me on his cell," Vito said, his mouth set in a grim line and his sunglasses hiding the expression in his eyes. "We have to take a meeting. Now." He marched straight for the living room. "Ben, shut off that damned TV. Where's Dade? Where's Ellie?"

"Dade's out back," Chips replied, his tone indifferent. "I think."

Vito's head turned in every direction. "What about Ellie?"

"She went upstairs," Winifred said in an unusually meek voice. "I think."

"I'll get her," Judith volunteered.

Vito gave a curt nod. "You do that. And clear the room of any outsiders." He particularly glared at Bill, who maintained his stoic expression.

Joe had clicked off the television set. "Let's give these people some space," he said amiably.

Hands in his pants pockets, Bill meandered out of the living room. Renie, however, balked.

"Why don't you hold this session in a regular meeting room at the Cascadia Hotel?" she demanded. "There's the Regency Room, the Rhododendron Room, the —"

Bill turned around, grabbed his wife by the scruff of her neck, and hauled her away, muttering, "Don't make trouble."

"Hey," Renie protested, "they're such big shots, I just thought they'd rather . . ."

Halfway up the stairs, Judith didn't hear the rest of her cousin's contrary reasoning. Going all the way down to the end of the hall, she rapped on the door to Room Six. When there was no response, Judith's heart skipped a beat. Originally, Angela and Ellie had shared quarters. Then Angela had moved into Bruno's room with Dirk. Could Angela and Ellie also have shared a habit, one that would overcome their apparent dislike for one another?

Judith knocked again, much louder. When there was still no answer, she turned the knob and held her breath.

Ellie was lying on the double bed, wearing headphones and tapping out the beat of a song only she could hear. The young actress looked up in surprise as Judith moved into the room.

"What's up?" she asked, removing the headphones. "Are the Wienie Wizards here?"

"No," Judith replied in relief. "But Mr. Patricelli, Mr. Mayne, and Ms. Fleming are. Mr. Patricelli has called a meeting in the living room."

"Oh, drat!" Ellie switched off the CD player and slid off the bed. "What a busybody! When are the wienies coming?"

"Not until after five," Judith said.

"But it's only three o'clock," Ellie responded. "How am I going to sit through a stupid meeting without my wienies?"

"I'm sorry," Judith said, then frowned. "Don't you want to know what happened to Angela?"

"Not really," Ellie said, slipping into a pair of white mules decorated with multicolored beads. "Angela's on a collision course, if you ask me." She paused to glance in the big oval mirror attached to the dressing table. "Is she dead?" The question was asked without much interest.

"No," Judith said. "But I gather it was a close call."

"I don't doubt it," Ellie responded, yanking at shafts of her long jet-black hair. "Look at this — why can't I do what my stylist does to make this cut look right? Oh, I'll be so stoked to get back to Cosmo in

L.A. They should have let me bring him with me." She gave her hair a final tug. "Next time, I bet they will." Her small, perfect lips curved into a smug little smile.

"Next time?" Judith echoed.

"I mean," Ellie said, turning away from the mirror, "next time I have to make a special appearance. You know — like this premiere." Suddenly her usual perky expression disappeared. "Except I don't know if *All the Way to Utah* will get made. At least not soon. You know — with Bruno dead."

The title struck a familiar chord with Judith. "I've heard of that," she said. "What's it about?"

"Pioneers," Ellie replied, picking up a pink cashmere cardigan that matched her pink cashmere short-sleeved sweater and tossing it over her slim shoulders. "The Old West. You know — action, adventure, sex, big rocks, bonnets, seagulls, Mormons."

"Fascinating," Judith commented, though it sounded like a bit of a mishmash. "Do you have a big part?"

"Very," Ellie said, joining Judith at the door. "I not only play the female lead, but my name should go above the title."

"Really?" Judith knew that was good.

"Really," Ellie said over her shoulder. "Got to scoot. Vito can be an awful pest. Besides, I really need to talk to him."

Judith took the back stairs. Renie was in the kitchen, studying the contents of the refrigerator.

"What'd you do with all those leftovers?" she asked.

"We put most of them in the freezer," Judith replied. "There are still some cheeses and slices of Italian ham."

"Good," Renie said, checking the crisper drawers. "I'm starved. I didn't eat a serious lunch." With a gesture of triumph, she held up some smoked Gouda and a package of prosciutto. "Pass the crackers, coz."

Judith fetched a box of table wafers from the cupboard. "Where are the husbands?" she asked.

"Eavesdropping in the front parlor," Renie answered, putting two round slices of Gouda on top of the ham.

"Ah," Judith remarked. "That's good."

"Bill's taking notes," Renie said, making a sandwich out of the crackers.

"Did you get anything interesting from Ellie Linn?" Judith inquired, sitting down at the kitchen table.

Renie opened a can of Pepsi and sat down across from her. "You mean besides how much she hates Angela La Belle and Dirk Farrar?"

"And why is that?" Judith asked.

"Professional jealousy of Angela," said Renie, after swallowing a big bite of her concoction. "Maybe genuine dislike. Conflict of personalities. It can happen in any business."

"What about Ellie's feelings for Dirk?"

Renie shrugged. "Couldn't say." She ate another mouthful.

Judith took a pumpkin-shaped cookie from the jar on the table. "Did Ellie mention a film called *All the Way to Utah*?"

"Yeph," Renie replied, still chewing. "Geb wha? Ewwie's muvver wode the scwip."

"Her mother wrote that script?" Judith, who had learned long ago to decipher her cousin's words when she spoke with a mouthful of food, was surprised at the information. "I actually saw that script someplace. I think it was in the room that Dirk and Ben shared."

"Her mother," Renie began, having swallowed, "is a writer. Her name is Amy Lee Wong, wife of the Wienie Wizard. She's Chinese by birth, from Hong Kong. I gather she's written a few romance novels under the pen name of Lotus MacDermott."

"Interesting," Judith commented, looking thoughtful. "So Mrs. Wienie sold the script to — whom? Bruno?"

"Could be." Renie polished off the crackers, cheese, and ham, then took a long drink of Pepsi. "Ellie is supposed to star as the seventh wife of a Mormon bishop back in the 1850s. The narrative involves the Utah War, which occurred when there was a public outcry about the Mormon practice of polygamy. According to the script, one of the reasons that the persecution or whatever you'd call it ended was because the Mormon bishop took a Chinese wife. If I recall my Western history, it had more to do with the Mormons pledging allegiance to the Union when the Civil War broke out. Ben Carmody is supposed to play the bishop."

"My." Judith got up and took a can of diet 7UP from the fridge. "It sounds a bit implausible. I mean, the Mormons weren't famous in those days for being tolerant of other races."

Renie grinned at her cousin. "That's why it's a movie."

"I suppose," Judith said. "Except for the distortion, the film might have possibilities. Maybe that's what Ben and Ellie were discussing when we saw them at T.S. McSnort's."

"That's very likely," Renie said. "Since Ellie looked as if she had the upper hand, I wonder if she was talking Ben into it. Therefore, I wonder if Dirk Farrar wasn't her first choice."

"So where does Ellie get so much clout?" Judith remarked, sitting down again. "She hasn't made very many movies."

"Ah!" Renie grinned at her cousin. "Don't you remember who bankrolled Bruno for *The Gasman*?"

"Mr. MacDermott, the Wienie Wizard," Judith responded.

"Right," said Renie. "So naturally he would put money into the Utah film. If he has any left after the debacle with *The Gasman*."

"Hmm." Judith drummed her nails on the table and grimaced. "If Bruno was murdered, then we can eliminate Ellie and probably Ben Carmody as suspects."

Renie shook her head. "Not necessarily. The fact that the movie flopped at the premiere might make Bruno dispensable."

"What do you mean?" Judith queried.

"I can't explain it," Renie said. "Ask Bill. It may have something to do with the studio's insurance. Or Bruno having a flop, which would have made raising money for his next picture much harder. It was complicated. I got sort of mixed up."

Judith was about to speculate further

when the phone rang. She picked it up from the counter behind her and heard a vaguely familiar female voice.

"We're sure glad we didn't stay at your place," the woman declared. "And don't think we ever will!"

"Mrs. Izard?" Judith ventured.

"You're darned tootin' it's Mrs. Izard. And I'm speaking for Mr. Izard, too. Walt here says you must run a pretty half-baked bed-and-breakfast to let your guests get murdered in their beds."

"No one," Judith said firmly as she cursed Ingrid for breaking her word, "got murdered in their beds. In fact, no one got murdered that we know of, period."

Meg Izard chortled gleefully. "Whatever happened wasn't good. And doesn't that just go to show you? No matter how big a wheel, the Grim Reaper can still bust up your spokes when you least expect it."

The phone slammed down in Judith's ear. "Damn that Ingrid — she promised to be discreet about our . . . misfortune. And she usually is. I've always trusted her, even if we've had our differences. And," Judith went on, growing more annoyed by the second, "talk about a poor sport. Since Meg Izard and her husband didn't get to stay at Hillside Manor, the old bat wants to lord it over us because we're in a pickle."

Renie was trying not to smile. "Yes, it's a pickle, coz. At least the other displaced couple hasn't bugged you about what's happened."

"The Kidds?" Judith said, going to the refrigerator and taking out a package of bologna. "No. They were very nice about it. In the Izards and the Kidds, you see the two ends of the spectrum when it comes to guests. Some — most, really — are wonderful, and then others can be a huge pain." She deftly buttered two slices of bread. "I'm going to take Mother a snack. She's been shortchanged today."

Upon entering the toolshed, Judith expected a testy greeting. Instead, Gertrude was writing on a ruled tablet as fast as her arthritic fingers would permit. She barely looked up when her daughter arrived.

"I have a bologna sandwich with apple slices and some hot chocolate," Judith said as the old lady scribbled away.

Gertrude still didn't look up from the tablet. "Put 'em there," she said, nodding at the cluttered card table.

Judith moved a bag of Tootsie Rolls and a copy of *TV Guide* to make room for the small plastic tray. "What are you doing? Writing a letter?"

"Nope," Gertrude replied. She added a few more words to the tablet, then finished with an awkward flourish and finally looked up. "I'm writing my life story. For the moving pictures."

"You're . . . what?" Judith gasped.

"You heard me," Gertrude snapped. "That writer fella, Wade or Dade or Cade, told me that everybody's life is a story. So I told him some things that had happened to me over the years and he said I should write it all down. So I am." She gave Judith a smug look.

Judith was puzzled. Her mother had led a seemingly ordinary life. "What exactly are you writing?"

Gertrude shrugged her hunched shoulders. "My life. Fleeing Germany in my youth. Starting a revolution in primary school. Drinking bathtub gin and dancing the black bottom. Eloping with your father."

"You were a baby when you came to this country," Judith pointed out. "I don't recall you ever mentioned fleeing much of anything."

"We fled," Gertrude insisted. "We were fleeing Grossmutter Hoffman. Your great-granny on that side of the family was a real terror. She drove your grandfather crazy, and how she treated your grandmother — her daughter-in-law — is hardly fit to print."

Vaguely, Judith remembered scattered anecdotes about the autocratic old girl and her savage tongue. "Well . . . okay. But I never heard the part about the primary-school revolution."

"I've been ashamed," Gertrude admitted. "But this Wade or Dade or whoever told me to let it all come out. I was in third grade, and those girls at St. Walburga's grade school never flushed the toilets. It disgusted me. So I told my friends — Agnes and Rosemarie and Maria Regina — to stop using the bathroom and piddle on the playground. Protesting, you know, just like all those goofy people in the sixties and seventies who didn't know half the time what they were protesting against. Or for. Silly, if you ask me, burning brassieres and smoking funny stuff. What kind of a revolution was that?"

As she often did, Gertrude seemed to be getting derailed. "What about the bathroom protest?"

The old lady looked blank. "What bathroom? What protest?"

"At St. Walburga's," Judith said patiently.

"Oh." Gertrude gave a nod. "Well, we all got into trouble, and the principal, Sister Ursula, sent for our parents. We were suspended for two days, but by the time we got back, those toilets were flushed, believe me. In fact, the school's water bill went up so much they had to raise tuition three dollars a month."

"You were ashamed to talk about this?" Judith asked.

"That's right," Gertrude said. "Nice little girls didn't piddle in public. In those days, nice little girls didn't even admit they piddled at all. But I feel good about it now. We won a victory for hygiene."

"You did indeed," Judith declared, patting her mother's arm. "That was very brave."

"I hope that writer fella will like it," Gertrude said, preening a bit. "He told me he could use a good script about now. I guess he's in some kind of a pickle."

"Like what?" Judith asked.

Gertrude frowned. "I don't rightly know, except it had something to do with an ax."

"An ax?" Judith looked puzzled. "Or . . . acts?"

Gertrude waved a hand. "No, it was an ax. A hatchet — that's what he said. Some kind of a job he was supposed to do with a hatchet. Maybe he's got a part-time job as a logger. What kind of money do scriptwriters get? I'd like to charge him at least fifty dollars for my story."

"At least," Judith said vaguely. "Did Dade say anything else about this hatchet job?"

Gertrude shook her head. "Not that I remember. He seemed kind of off his feed, though."

There was no point in pressing her mother for details. If Gertrude remembered something later, fine. Besides, Dade Costello's moodiness seemed to be an integral part of his personality.

Or so Judith was thinking when she smelled smoke.

"Mother," she said, sniffing the air, "did you put something on your hot plate?"

"Like what?" Gertrude retorted. "You think I could roast a turkey on that thing? I can hardly boil an egg on it."

Nor did Gertrude ever try, preferring to have her daughter wait on her. Still, Judith went out to the tiny kitchen, with its sink, small fridge, microwave oven, and hot plate. Nothing looked amiss, nor could Judith smell anything burning. She went back into the living room.

"It must be coming from outside," she remarked, and headed for the door.

Gertrude didn't respond or look up. She was writing again, her white head bent over the card table.

The smell got stronger as Judith stepped

outside and closed the toolshed door behind her. The rain had stopped, but fog was settling in over the rooftops. She could barely make out either of Hillside Manor's chimneys. Perhaps Joe had started a fire to ward off the increasingly gloomy October afternoon.

Then she noticed the barbecue. It sat as it had all summer on the small patio by the statue of St. Francis and the birds. Like the kitchen cupboard door, the barbecue had been another source of Judith's prodding. Joe should have taken it into the garage at least two weeks earlier when the weather had made a definite transition into autumn.

Instead, it remained, and smoke was coming out from under the lid. Judith went to the patio and opened the barbecue. A sudden burst of smoke and flame made her step back and cough.

Reaching out with a long wood-and-steel meat fork that was lying nearby, she stirred whatever was burning. Peering with smoke-stung eyes, she saw that it was mostly paper. Quite a bit of paper, and attached to a plastic binding, most of which had melted.

Judith was no expert, but she thought that what was left might be a movie script.

Chapter Twelve

Joe hadn't yet detached the garden hoses or covered the faucets for the winter. Judith turned on the hose by the back porch and gently aimed it at the barbecue. The stack of paper hissed and sizzled, but didn't go out. When she increased the pressure, the smoke finally died down and the heat faded away. Standing over the barbecue, Judith stirred the ashes with a meat fork.

"I don't think I'll ask what you're doing," Renie called from the back porch, "but I thought you'd ordered food from a caterer."

Startled, Judith turned toward her cousin. "Somebody burned something in here. I'm trying to figure out what it was."

"Wienie Wizards?" Renie inquired, coming down the walk to the patio.

"Nothing so edible," Judith said. "It looks like a script."

"It does for a fact," Renie agreed, picking up a pair of steel tongs. "It's pretty well fried." She flipped through the ashes until she got to the last few pages, which were only charred. "If I touch them, they may burst into flame again, but it looks like a script all right. See — it's mostly dialogue on this top page with some directions in between."

"Can you see what any of it says?" Judith asked, shivering slightly as the fog began to drift among the trees and shrubs.

"Not really," Renie admitted, after putting on her much marred and thoroughly smudged reading glasses. Judith could never figure out how her cousin could see anything through the abused lenses. "Wait — here are a couple of lines I can make out: *Benjamin: You have never had cause to be . . .* I think the last word is *afraid*. The next line is dialogue by someone named Tz'u-hsi, who replies, *It is not strange to be a concubine, though I am called wife. Yet I am more than a stranger, I am a . . .* The rest of the page is too burned to read."

"A Chinese name," Judith murmured. "Ellie's role in the script written by her mother, *All the Way to Utah*?"

"Maybe," Renie allowed. "So who'd burn the script? And why?"

Judith started to stir the ashes again, thought better of it, and replaced the lid to the barbecue. Heading back into the house, she paused with her hand on the doorknob. "It was in Dirk and Ben's room," she said. "Room Four. The script was all marked up. There were even some obscenities, as if whoever was reading it didn't like it much."

"But which of the two actors?" Renie asked. "Ben or Dirk?"

"Ben, of course," Judith said. "He's supposed to costar, remember? Besides," she added, "I read a clipping, also in Room Four, about how Dirk had lost the lead in another Zepf movie because he and Bruno got into a fistfight at Marina Del Rey in L.A. I assume Dirk was permanently scratched from Bruno's A-list."

"Very interesting," Renie remarked. "So Ben gets to be a leading man instead of a villain because Dirk played smash-mouth with Bruno."

"I suppose so," Judith responded as the cousins went inside. "I guess nice guys do finish first."

"That's not the saying," Renie corrected. "It's the other way around."

"You're right," Judith said. "With everything that's happened in the last couple of days, my mind's a muddle."

The cousins had barely reached the kitchen when an insistent tap sounded at the back door. It was Arlene Rankers, looking desperate.

"What's wrong?" Judith asked, hastening to meet her friend and neighbor.

"What's wrong?" Arlene threw up her hands. "That's what I came to find out. Who got hauled off by the medics?"

Judith realized that the Rankerses wouldn't know of the events that had occurred at Hillside Manor since they left for home the previous night. "Have a seat," she said, pulling out a chair at the kitchen table. "I'll fill you in."

Which Judith did, though she was careful to omit specific details. Her good-hearted neighbor was famous for spreading the news over what was called Arlene's Broadcasting System, or merely ABS. Judith felt there was no need to make the situation any worse than it already was.

"Goodness!" Arlene gasped when Judith had finally finished. "You certainly get more trouble than you deserve. What can Carl and I do to help?"

Judith was about to reply that she was beyond help, but changed her mind. "Keep an eye on who comes and goes around here." That was easy; the Rankerses' kitchen windows overlooked Hillside Manor and the cul-de-sac. At the sink and the dinette table, Arlene had long ago established her personal observation deck.

"Fine," Arlene responded, "but can't you do that yourself?"

"Not really," Judith said. "There's too much going on. This is a big house. I can't keep track of everybody's movements."

"Not to mention that it's Halloween," Renie put in.

Arlene was uncharacteristically silent. She was staring at the table, arms slack at her sides, forehead creased in concentration. When she finally spoke, it was as if she were in a trance.

"Seven-fifty A.M., Joe leaves through the back door in his red MG. Eight-fourteen, the writer goes out the French doors and disappears around the west side of the house. Nine-oh-six, the red-headed youngish man leans out the second-story window by the stairs and looks every which way through something like a small camera. Nine-twenty-two, Joe returns with two white bakery bags, two pink boxes, and a Moonbeam's bag, probably filled with hot coffee. Nine-thirty-one, writer comes back and sits in lawn swing on front porch. Nine-forty, black Lincoln Town Car pulls into cul-de-sac. Writer jumps over porch rail and runs down driveway toward garage. Nine-forty-one, well-dressed man wearing sunglasses goes to front door and is let in." Arlene, wearing a bright smile, looked up. "How am I doing?"

"Wow!" Judith gasped in admiration. "So that's how you do it?"

Arlene looked blank. "Do what?"

"You know . . ." Judith faltered, never one to accuse Arlene of snooping. "Keep track of things. Help Carl run the Neighborhood Watch. Stay on top of events on the block. You must file everything like a computer."

"No," Arlene asserted. "Not at all. Now that I've said it out loud, I can barely remember anything."

Judith didn't quite believe her, but wouldn't argue. Any dispute with her neighbor brought grief in the form of Arlene's reversals and self-contradictions. "That's very helpful," she said. "After Vito — the man with the sunglasses — arrived, what happened next?"

Arlene's smile faded. "There is no next. Carl and I left for ten o'clock Mass at SOTS, went to coffee and doughnuts in the school hall, and stopped at Falstaff's on the way back. We didn't get home until almost one. I didn't notice anything or anybody until you showed up shortly before one-thirty."

"What about," Renie inquired, "since Judith got back?"

But Arlene shook her head in a regretful manner. "I got caught up in dinner preparations. Most of our darling children are coming over tonight. Except for seeing you and Bill arrive, I didn't notice anyone else until the medics arrived."

"Nothing in the backyard?" Judith asked.

Arlene's eyes narrowed. "The backyard?" She automatically swerved around to look in that direction, though she couldn't see anything from her position at the table. "No. What on earth did I miss?" She seemed genuinely aggrieved.

"It may have happened while you were on the sidewalk with the other neighbors," Judith said in a comforting voice. Quickly, she explained about finding the burned script in the barbecue. She had just finished when Joe came into the kitchen.

"They're adjourning to the living room," he announced. "I gather they may all be going out to dinner in a private room at Capri's."

Capri's, on the very edge of Heraldsgate Hill, was one of the city's oldest and most distinguished eateries. "I didn't think they were open on Sundays," Judith said.

"Apparently they are for this bunch," Joe

responded with a wave for Arlene, who was heading to the back door.

"But what about all the food I ordered?" Judith wailed. "It'll go to waste and I'll get stuck paying for it."

Arlene went into reverse in more ways than one. "Send it over to our house. I can use it to feed those wretched kids of ours. They eat like cannibals."

"Cannibals?" Renie echoed.

"You know what I mean," Arlene said peevishly. "They eat like your children."

"Oh." Renie nodded. "Now I get it."

Arlene hurried out of the house.

Judith was on her feet, gripping Joe's shoulders. "Well? What did they say in this latest meeting?"

"Spin-doctor stuff, mostly," Joe replied. "Morris Mayne has the burden of trying to make everything sound as if Bruno died for Art."

"Hunh?" Judith dropped her hands.

Joe shrugged, then opened the fridge and took out a beer. "You know — that Bruno was so disturbed over the possibility of failure that it broke his heart. He'd striven to be the best in his chosen profession, and anything less than a total triumph was too terrible to face. Blah-blah."

"So they think it was an accident?" Judith

asked as she heard footsteps climbing the main staircase.

"They want it to be more than an accident," Joe said as Bill also came into the kitchen, carrying a small notepad. "They want it to be a Greek tragedy. It plays better that way, as Dade Costello pointed out during the powwow. Morris Mayne was all for it."

"What's the official news release?" Renie inquired.

"Go scavenge for it after they've cleared the area," Joe suggested. "Bill and I could hear the ripping and tearing of many sheets of paper. Maybe you'll find what's close to a finished product."

Bill was now at the fridge, perusing its contents. "They issued an earlier statement, but it sounded very terse." He paused, scowling at the shelves. "Don't you have any weird pop?"

Judith knew that Bill preferred oddly flavored sodas that came in strangely decorated bottles. "Not really," she said.

"Oh." Bill firmly closed the refrigerator door. "Maybe I'll just have a glass of water."

He was turning on the faucet when Eugenia Fleming barged into the kitchen.

"Do you people know how to keep your mouths shut?" she demanded.

"No," Renie shot back.

"Yes," Judith said, giving Renie a dirty look. "I assume you're referring to the media?"

"Of course," Eugenia replied with a scornful glance at Renie. "Morris is very concerned that we can't keep the lid on this location much longer."

Joe stepped forward to face Eugenia, who met him at eye level. "Are you saying," he inquired, "that there's been no leak as to where the non–Cascadia Hotel guests are staying or where Bruno died?"

"That's so," interjected Morris Mayne, who had come up behind Eugenia like a small caboose following a large locomotive. "But eventually they'll put two and two together. I'm sure they've checked out most of the hotels by now. Eventually, they'll get to the bed-and-breakfasts. Once they tie in the emergency calls that have been made from here, they're bound to show up en masse."

Joe tipped his head to one side. "So?"

"So," Eugenia said, rising up on her tiptoes to look down at Joe, "we must insist on the utmost discretion — indeed, total silence — from all of you."

"Fine," Joe said.

Morris peeked out from behind Eugenia. "Really?"

Joe was nonchalant. "Sure."

Bill moved closer to Joe. "I have a question."

Both Eugenia and Morris looked surprised. "What is that?" Eugenia asked.

"Why should we keep quiet? It hardly matters to my wife and me what the media might learn from us." Bill's voice was, as ever, very deliberate. "Mrs. Jones and I could sell information about all these Hollywood shenanigans for quite a big sum."

Renie's eyes practically bugged out. "We could?"

"Of course," Bill replied. "Especially to the tabloids."

Judith and Joe exchanged uneasy glances. Morris seemed stunned. Eugenia was growing red in the face.

"You wouldn't dare!" she exclaimed. "Aren't these people your friends?" She waved a big arm in the Flynns' direction. "Do you know what legal straits they might be in?"

Bill looked unfazed. "They're not friends, they're my wife's relatives." He paused to pour himself more water. "What about a compromise? Why don't you let us in on what you know about anyone who might have had a motive to kill Bruno? Why not be up-front about Angela's drug habit? Why not" — the next word seemed to gag Bill, who despised buzz-words — "share?"

Eugenia whirled on Bill, who didn't budge. "That's blackmail! What right do you have to ask such a thing? Can you imagine the legal steps we could take to silence you?"

"My brother, Bub, is a lawyer," Bill said quietly. "Or maybe that wasn't a threat?"

Joe, who along with Judith was looking relieved now that Bill had tipped his hand, was nodding sagely. "I think this is a good idea." He gestured expansively. "Take a seat. We'll talk."

"No, we won't," Eugenia retorted. "At least not until we've consulted our legal counsel. Who, I might add, is waiting for us in the limousine. We're going back to the hotel." She turned abruptly, almost knocking Morris over.

"Have your suit call our suit," Bill said as the pair departed. "Bub's number is —"

"That's great, Bill." Renie could barely contain herself. She was leaning against the fridge, holding her sides. "You've got them worried."

"They should be," Bill said in a mild tone. "But I'd have preferred that they give us some information on the spot."

Judith heard the door slam. "Tell us what you overheard from the parlor," she urged.

Joe sat down at the kitchen table. Bill got out his notepad.

"As we mentioned," Joe began, "it was mostly spin-doctor stuff. They talked more about how to make it seem as if Bruno was such a dedicated artist that he couldn't survive failure. Eugenia — being Bruno's agent — was for that, but there was some disagreement, especially when they discussed whether or not *The Gasman* should be salvaged."

"Could it be?" Renie asked.

"Maybe," Bill put in. "They'd have to cut the running time by almost half. As it is, the film's not only a flop, but it's a distribution nightmare. At four hours, that means only one showing a night per house. That's economically unfeasible."

"So they wouldn't make a profit?" queried Judith.

"Not in domestic theaters," Bill responded, also sitting down. "But these days there are all the ancillary rights. There are so many other markets — offshore, cable TV, syndication, merchandising tie-ins. A movie can lose money in this country and still turn a profit. Not to mention that the studio could cut back on its advertising and promotion. I suspect they intended to spend huge sums before the general release."

Joe sipped his beer before he spoke. "You sure know a hell of a lot about Hollywood for a psychologist."

Bill shrugged. "Cinema is both a reflection of and an influence on contemporary life. Besides, I just like movies."

Judith, however, was looking for a more personal angle. "What about reactions? Did you catch any remarks or attitudes that might indicate animosity toward Bruno?"

"Plenty," Joe replied, "but nothing I'd call suspicious. Dade complained about what Bruno had done to the script. He also griped that Chips Madigan hadn't directed the movie the way the script indicated. Chips accused Dade of screwing up the original work." Joe glanced at Judith. "That must have been the book you saw upstairs, *The Gasman* novel."

"Did you find it?" Judith asked, having forgotten that she'd told Joe to look for it in Room Three.

"Yes," Joe answered. "I put it in a drawer by your computer. Anyway," he continued, "Dade reminded Chips that a movie is not a book. They started to get into it, but Vito cut them off."

"That," Bill put in, "was when Ben Carmody declared that the whole thing was a mistake from the start. He insisted that the movie would never have been made if Bruno hadn't been able to con a huge investment out of Heathcliffe MacDermott in order to boost his daughter Ellie's career."

"I'm sorry," Judith broke in, "but I don't understand how the financing works. If Bruno is an independent producer, how does the studio get involved?"

As was his fashion, Bill waited to organize his thoughts. Renie, who was long accustomed to her husband's methodical and precise mental processes, climbed up on the kitchen counter, popped the top on another Pepsi, and settled in for the long haul.

"Usually," Bill finally said, "it works this way: A producer like Bruno never invests his own money. Let's say he's already nailed down at least one big bankable star. Dirk Farrar, in this case. Maybe the estimated budget is seventy million dollars. He — Bruno — then goes to Paradox Studios and says he's got a project and he's got a star. Dirk's name is worth, say, twenty million at the box office. Paradox says okay, we'll get our investors to come up with another thirty million, then you — Bruno — raise the rest of it. Bruno goes to private investors, in this case because of the connection with Ellie Linn, he asks Heathcliffe MacDermott for ten million. The other ten million he gets from other sources — German business-men, Japanese investors, Italian bankers. I mention those three countries because they're big moviegoers. The studio then says they want him to use one of their direc-tors — maybe Chips Madigan — and one of their stars — Ben Carmody, perhaps — plus a cinematographer, a writer, an editor, some other actors already under contract to the studio. They'll share the profits with Bruno and they'll handle distribution. Thus, they're ready to roll."

"*The Gasman* had a hundred-million-dollar budget," Joe remarked. "Isn't that kind of high? And didn't Chips Madigan mention going over budget?"

"Did he?" Bill frowned. "Yes, you're right. I think I read something about that while the picture was being made. Did Chips give a reason?"

Joe scratched his head. "I didn't catch all of what Chips said. He was toward the other end of the room, by the bookcases. Dade, who always assumes his stance by the French doors, was even harder to hear. But I think — in essence — Chips put the blame on Bruno for shooting some of the scenes over again."

"That's possible," Bill allowed. "If that's the case, Bruno would have had to scrounge up more money to make the revised budget. The next thing I have in my notes is that Winifred broke in saying that Bruno had so much clout in the industry that he would have been green-lighted for any project. A number of people would back him because of his track record. Naturally, Eugenia Fleming agreed."

"How did Ellie react to all this?" Judith queried.

"She kept her mouth shut," Joe said. "In fact, she sort of simpered."

Judith gave her husband a skeptical look. "You could hear simpering through the parlor door?"

"It was open a crack," Joe replied. "Besides, she was standing next to it, fiddling with the CDs by the stereo."

Judith sighed. "This isn't very helpful."

"We did our best," Joe said with a touch of sarcasm.

Renie also seemed disappointed. "That's it?"

Bill carefully went through his notes. "There were undertones, of course."

Joe gave a little shake of his head. "Maybe so. That's your department, Bill. We cops tend to stick to the facts. But since it's you, go ahead. At least it'll please my wife."

Judith shot her husband a dirty look.

"You've certainly never been one to credit my intuition."

"Intuition doesn't hold up in court," Joe pointed out.

Judith sniffed, then turned to Bill. "I'll take all the undertones I can get."

"Let me see." He studied the notepad pages for some time. "What's missing is interaction between the absentees — Dirk and Angela — and the others. Ellie made a couple of cracks about both of them. Only Chips was inclined to defend them, though he wasn't very enthusiastic."

"Are Dirk and Angela lovers?" Renie asked.

"Probably," Bill replied, "though what that means in Hollywood these days, I couldn't say. They may have been sleeping together just for the fun of it while they were here. You have to allow for a certain amount of old-fashioned promiscuity."

"What about the cocaine?" Judith inquired. "Was that mentioned?"

"Only in passing," Bill responded, "though there was a cryptic remark made by Morris. When someone . . ." He addressed his notes. "It was Ben Carmody who said maybe Angela had learned her lesson. Morris agreed, observing that as they all knew, three times could be a charm."

"Curious," Judith murmured.

"Come on, Bill," Renie urged, "you know darned well you've got some other information tucked away."

"I'm sifting it," Bill said, putting the notepad back in his pocket.

"As usual," Renie remarked, accustomed to her husband's cautious but thorough approach to the deductive process.

Judith started for the kitchen's swinging doors. "I'm going to look for the news-release drafts before the guests come down to leave for dinner." She glanced back at the old school clock. "It's almost four. They should be a while."

Renie followed her cousin out to the living room, which was uncharacteristically untidy. As Joe had reported, there had been much tearing of legal pads, accompanied, no doubt, by a certain amount of tearing of hair. There were also empty springwater bottles and a few glasses, the latter apparently used for beverages foraged from the liquor supply in the washstand. The buffet had been raided, too, with the last of Joe's bakery goods reduced to crumbs. Someone had removed several paperback books and left them scattered around the window seat. Magazines from the coffee table had been dumped on the carpet, and a stack of tapes and CDs were lying by the stereo.

"Spoiled brats," Judith muttered, picking up some of the litter before perusing the discarded sheets of yellow paper.

"I'll help," Renie offered, already gathering up the books by the bay window.

"These people must never wait on themselves," Judith groused. "Frankly, I think it'd be awful to live like that. No wonder they get bored and take drugs. They'd be better off using a dust mop."

Renie had replaced the books and was now collecting the tapes and CDs. "Gosh, coz, some of these recordings are kind of old. Since when do you listen to heavy metal?"

"I don't," Judith responded, brushing crumbs from the matching sofas. "Half of those tapes and CDs are Mike's. He says he's outgrown most of them, but when I asked why he doesn't throw them out or give them away, he says someday he might want to hear them again. Of course he doesn't have room to store them up at the cabin." She sounded put-upon.

"He might be able to sell them," Renie said, glancing at some of the labels. "A few of them are real classics." She held up a tape. "Remember the Demures? They had one huge hit, 'Come Play with Me' — it's on this — and then the group fell out of sight."

"I vaguely remember it," Judith replied. "Didn't the lead singer have an unusual name?"

Renie peered at the tape. "Ramona Pomona. I hope it wasn't her real name. The two backup singers were . . . Hunh." Her eyes widened.

"What?" Judith inquired, pausing on her way to the kitchen with an armful of glasses and water bottles.

Renie gave Judith a curious look. "The backups are Jolene DuBois and Winnie Lou Best. What do you make of that, coz?"

"I'm not sure," Judith said slowly. "It may be a coincidence. Is there a picture of the group?"

"Yes," Renie replied, "but it's small and not very good. The girls all have their mouths open — presumably singing — and are waving their arms."

Judith moved next to Renie and looked over her cousin's shoulder. "You're right. Three dark-skinned girls with bouffant black hair. Let's see the liner notes."

"If you can believe them," Renie cautioned.

But the information was brief and not very enlightening. "It says," Judith read after taking the small folder from Renie, "that Ramona, Jolene, and Winnie Lou grew up together in Compton, California, and started singing in their high-school glee club before forming their own group. They got their first big break when they were discovered at a high-school dance in Glendale. *The trio,* and I'm quoting now, *toured for two years as the opening act for several of the biggest names in the business before becoming headliners in 1978. This is their debut album, featuring the red-hot single . . .* et cetera." Judith examined the notes closely. "This is copyright 1979. Mike would have been twelve. How old do you figure Winifred is now?"

Renie screwed up her face. "It's hard to tell. Fortyish? She would have been in her late teens back then. But maybe it's not her."

"And if it is," Judith noted as she slipped the liner notes back inside the plastic tape container, "so what?"

"So how do you go from being Ramona Pomona's backup with one hit single to Bruno Zepf's assistant?" Renie mused.

"Over twenty years," Judith said. "A lot of things can happen in that time, especially in a place like Hollywood."

"There's one way to find out," Renie said.

"How?"

"We could ask Winifred."

"Oh." Judith felt almost disappointed. "We could at that. I'll do it now, before they leave for dinner."

After depositing the dirty glasses and garbage in the kitchen, she headed up the main staircase for the second floor. Winifred was in Room One just off the landing.

A double rap on the door brought an immediate response. Judith was relieved; it seemed as if every time she knocked on a door, an anxiety attack ensued.

"What is it?" Winifred asked in an irritable tone.

"I wanted to show you something," Judith said, clasping the tape in her hand. "It'll take just a moment."

Warily, Winifred opened the door a scant four inches. She was wearing her dark blue bathrobe and her face was covered with cream. "What is it?" she repeated.

Judith wore her most ingratiating expression. "I think my son may be a fan of yours. Or at least he was several years ago." She opened her hand to reveal the tape. "Is this you?"

Winifred recoiled. "Oh, my God! Where did you get that?"

"It was in our collection," Judith replied equably. "Mike — my son — left some of his belongings here with us."

"You're lying." The astonishment on Winifred's face had been superseded by a steely-eyed look. "Where did you really get that?"

"I told you," Judith persisted, "in with our other recordings in the living room."

"That's impossible. This tape's a demo. It was never released." Without opening the door further, Winifred's slim arm reached out to grab the tape.

But Judith pulled her hand back. "I'm sorry. I don't understand. Is this you on the tape? Is that why you're upset?"

But Winifred's lips clamped shut as she slammed the door in Judith's face.

Chapter Thirteen

Judith stood rooted to the spot, staring at the tape in her hand. She jumped when Chips Madigan came into the hall, apparently heading for the bathroom between Rooms Three and Four.

"Whoa!" he called, a bath towel slung over the terrycloth robe that reached to his knees. "Sorry. Did I scare you?"

"Startled is more like it," Judith said with a weak smile. "I was lost in thought."

Ever the director looking for the perfect shot, Chips half knelt to frame Judith's stance by Winifred's room. " 'Shaken innkeeper, anxious about guest, medium shot.' " He stood up and moved nearer. " 'Close-up of innkeeper, looking weary and somewhat distraught.' How am I doing?"

"Better than I am," Judith answered, keeping her voice down. "How much do you know about Winifred's background?"

Chips fingered the towel. "Not much. I mean, she's been with Bruno a long time. As far as I know, she started working for him nine, ten years ago, after he made his first hit, *No Prunes for Prudence*. That was the small-budget independent picture that won a film-festival prize at PAW in Iowa City."

Judith was puzzled. "PAW?"

Chips nodded. "It's called THAW nowadays. I'm not sure what it stands for."

Judith hesitated before posing another question. Judging from his youthful appearance, she assumed he was in the same thirty- to thirty-five-age group as Mike. "Do you remember the Demures?" she asked, holding out the tape.

Chips looked bemused. "Yes . . . yes, I do. They had a big hit . . . What was it called?"

" 'Come Play with Me,' " Judith responded. "It's on this tape."

"Right." The director beamed at Judith. "It was a single, really popular the year I graduated from high school. We wanted to play it at our senior prom, but the principal wouldn't let us. It was kind of raunchy for those days. I grew up in a typical Midwestern town, sort of straitlaced. You know what they say — change starts on the coasts, and it takes a long time to get to the middle."

Judith smiled back. "One of the singers was named Winnie Lou Best. Do you think that's a coincidence?"

"Winnie Lou . . ." Chips repeated, then slapped a hand to his head. "You mean as in Winifred Best?"

Judith nodded. "I showed her this tape and she pitched a small fit. Why would she do that?"

"Golly," Chips said, "I've no idea. Maybe she's embarrassed."

The explanation was so simple that it made sense. "That's possible," Judith allowed, though a snippet of doubt remained. Before Chips could resume his walk to the bathroom, she held up a hand. "Quick question. Why is there so much controversy over the way *The Gasman* was filmed?"

"You mean the picture's length?" Chips responded.

"No, not exactly," Judith said. "I understand there were differing opinions about the story itself." Maybe that was more to the point. "That the result wasn't true to the original book."

Chips laughed. "You'd better ask Dade about that. Of course, he'll tell you I didn't direct the picture right. The fact is, I directed it the way Bruno wanted. Of course I wouldn't admit that publicly, but you're not in the business."

"In other words," Judith said, "Bruno dictated how you should direct?"

Chips shrugged. "It was his picture."

"You felt he knew what he was doing?"

A flush crept over Chips's freckled face as he began inching his way toward the bathroom. "I admit, I hadn't worked with him before, but until I signed on for *The Gasman*, he hadn't missed a beat. Of course, he directed his first six films himself. It was only for the last two — including *The Gasman* — that he'd hired another director. I had reason to trust him. All his films had been successful."

Through the window over the landing, Judith could see the fog swirling around the house. It was going to be a gloomy, damp night for the trick-or-treaters.

"What went wrong with this movie?" she asked, aware that Chips was trying to escape.

"Well . . ." He looked pained. He also looked around the hallway. In the process, he noticed the fog through the window. "Wow," he said softly. "Real fog. We didn't have that in the Midwest, where I was raised. In L.A., we have only smog, which doesn't create this kind of atmosphere.

Would you mind moving to your left about six inches?"

"What? Oh, sure." Judith sidestepped a half foot.

" 'Troubled innkeeper,' " Chips murmured, framing yet another shot with his fingers. "Fog in background symbolizes her ambiguous thoughts, as well as impending danger. I like this very much."

"About what went wrong," Judith said as Chips scooted around in a crouching position, seeking different angles. "Have you any idea what happened?"

"The length, for one thing," he replied, one eye closed as he peered through his imaginary lens. "Ah! That's perfect!" He stood up. "The ambitiousness of the project. The concept itself. The original material. The budget overrun."

"In other words," Judith put in, "everything?"

Chips gulped. "Sort of."

"I see," she said. "But you couldn't tell that from the start?"

"You wouldn't believe how Bruno could talk up an idea." Chips grimaced. "That's a talent in itself. After five minutes with him, you'd think he was going to make the next *Gone With the Wind*." He bobbed his head as a door shut somewhere on the second floor.

"Excuse me, I've got to take a quick shower before we go to dinner."

Dade Costello shambled down the narrow corridor that separated Room One from Rooms Two and Three. When he saw Judith, he merely nodded and kept going. He was halfway down the stairs before she called to him.

"Mr. Costello," she said, hurrying down the top flight and realizing that her hips were aching from all her recent exertions, "may I ask you a question about my mother?"

Dade turned to look over his shoulder. "Your mother? Oh, Mrs. Grover. Sure." He continued on down the stairs. "I was just going out for some fresh air before we took off to dinner."

"It's pretty foggy out there," Judith said when she reached the main floor. She pointed to Dade's leather vest, which he wore over a plaid shirt. "You should wear a heavier jacket."

"Think so?" He sounded dubious. "I'm not used to all this damp. Now what's this about your mother?"

"Are you really encouraging her to write her life story?"

"Sure," Dade replied, leaning one arm on the balustrade and propping a booted foot up on the umbrella stand. "Why not? She seemed to like the idea."

"She would," Judith murmured. "You aren't seriously thinking of buying it from her, are you?"

"I'm a writer," Dade said. "I don't buy scripts, I sell them."

"I don't get it," said Judith.

Dade shrugged his wide shoulders. "I'm interested in ideas. Your mother sounds as if she's had a colorful life." His casual demeanor evaporated, replaced by weariness. "Besides, I could use some good ideas about now. I feel tapped out."

Judith was mystified. "You mean — you'd buy ideas from her?"

"Not exactly," he replied, eyeing the door as if he were anxious to make his getaway. "It gets real complicated."

Judith let the matter drop. She was more interested in *The Gasman* script than in her mother's life story. "Was it so complicated with the book that *The Gasman* was based on? I mean, that was a very old book, wasn't it? Copyright may have expired."

"It had," Dade said without much interest. "I think. Anyway, whoever wrote it had been dead for years."

"How did Bruno come by the book? That is," she went on, not wanting to admit she'd been snooping in the guest rooms, "I used to be a librarian, and I've never heard of it. I'm assuming it was fairly obscure."

"It was at that," Dade drawled with a gleam in his eye. "I heard that one of Bruno's ancestors had written it. In a nut-shell, sophomoric and dull. Carp was the author's name, as I recollect."

"C. Douglas Carp," Judith said as the name on the title page sprang into her mind's eye. "Was it his grandfather or an uncle?"

Dade shrugged again. "I don't really know. There was a family tie, though. It was more textbook than novel, almost impossible to use as the basis for a script. Too much fact and not enough fiction. And too damned much territory to cover. I struggled for almost a year to get just the outline done."

"I gather you had your differences with Chips Madigan over the script," Judith said, trying to sound matter-of-fact.

"Chips!" Dade growled, making a slashing motion with one hand. "That punk. He and Bruno screwed up my script every which way. They — Bruno speaking for both of them — insisted I hadn't kept to the spirit of the book. Bull. There was no spirit. It was just a bunch of events strung together by a weak narrative. For all I know, old Carp may have paid to get it published. It was garbage, all nine hundred pages of it." He paused to pull out a pocket watch from inside his vest. "Hey, it's after five. I'd better get going. I think the limo's coming a little after six." He ambled to the front door.

"Psst!" It was Renie, lurking behind the archway that divided the entry hall and the living room. "Where've you been? I pieced the statement together."

"You did?" Judith hurried to join her cousin. "How is it?"

"Stilted," Renie said, flapping a half-dozen sheets of yellow paper at Judith. "It's the kind of corporate copy that makes me want to shoot all writers and fill up space with graphic designs instead."

Judith held out her hand. "Let me see."

"No," Renie retorted, "don't read this hodgepodge. I've written it out in what's probably close to the final draft." She held up the last sheet and began to read what she'd patched together: "*In the wake of producer Bruno Zepf's tragic passing last night, Paradox Studios launched an investigation to determine the cause of death. It is generally felt by studio executives and Zepf's close associates that* The Gasman *premiere's apparent inadequacies* — some choice of words," she inter-

284

posed before continuing, "*may have caused the producer to die of a broken heart. According to Zepf's agent, Eugenia Fleming, 'Bruno set the bar extremely high, not only for himself, but for others in the industry.* The Gasman *was a project he had nurtured for years, with roots going back to his youth. Having the picture receive such harsh criticism at its premiere may have been too much for him. He wasn't used to negative reactions, and he had worked himself into exhaustion. During the making of the film, he had to be hospitalized for a lengthy period. Obviously, his health was seriously affected. Bruno couldn't tolerate a lack of excellence, especially in himself.'* End of quote," said Renie.

"That's it?" Judith inquired, sitting on the arm of the sofa.

"No," Renie responded. "That's the end of what Eugenia said. There's more, but not much. In fact, there were about three concluding statements they might have used. The gist was that Bruno should be remembered for his many successes, rather than for *The Gasman*'s flop."

Judith didn't respond immediately. When she did, her words didn't pertain to failure or success. "Do you suppose Bruno really had health problems?"

Renie hesitated before answering. She

flipped through the discarded pages, then tapped her finger on several fragments of writing. "There are some notes about that, but they're cryptic. Here." She handed the page to Judith.

B's health, came first, written in an elegant if not very legible hand, presumably by Vito. "How do you read penmanship like this?"

Renie shrugged. "It's all those years I've spent reading CEOs' scribbles. Of course most of those people never got past the block-printing stage. They thought cursive meant cussing."

"*HBP,*" Judith read aloud. "High blood pressure?"

Renie nodded. "Probably."

"*Ulcer . . . ulcer . . . ulcer.* That's clear enough. So's *colitis.* What's this? *C?* It's under-lined twice. Then it says *treatment.* Cancer?"

"I couldn't tell," Renie said. "Maybe the C is for colitis."

"Do you remember a drug called thalido-mide?"

"Sure," Renie replied. "Years ago, it was prescribed as a sleeping pill for pregnant women in Europe. Unfortunately, it caused horrendous birth defects."

"True," Judith agreed, "but when we were in Good Cheer Hospital, I overheard a doctor and a nurse talking about thalidomide. It sounded as if it was being used for cancer patients."

Renie looked blank. "I don't remember that. Maybe you heard it after I'd been released from the hospital. You had to stay a few days longer."

"How could I forget?" Judith said with a grimace, then grew silent again. "High blood pressure could have killed Bruno. But wouldn't the ME be able to tell?"

"You'd think so."

Setting the sheet of paper down on the coffee table, Judith heaved a big sigh. "If only we could be sure that Bruno was murdered."

Renie looked askance. "Aren't you being kind of bloodthirsty, coz?"

"No, I'm being realistic," Judith retorted. "I can't bear to think that Joe and I may be at fault for Bruno's death. It's not just the possibility of a lawsuit, it's the moral implications. If we're to blame, I'll feel the most awful guilt for the rest of my life."

Renie's face hardened. "What about that stupid spider over the sink? Who put it there? Why? Was it just a prank to scare Bruno? Did it scare him into passing out in the sink?"

Judith stared at Renie. "How odd — I never thought about that. I mean, first there

287

was the real spider on the back porch, then the spider in his bed — he didn't pass out, by the way — and the one over the sink. Why would that one have more of an effect on Bruno than the others?"

"Maybe," Renie reasoned, "because Bruno was already distraught. Wasn't a spider a sign of bad luck for him? And hadn't he just had the worst luck of his career?"

"True," Judith allowed in a thoughtful voice. "Who put those spiders in the bed and in the kitchen? What," she went on, her voice rising as she stood up from her perch on the sofa, "if there are more spiders somewhere?"

"Good point," Renie remarked. "Have you looked?"

"No," Judith said, "but Joe searched the guest rooms. Still, it's odd that there weren't more than two. If you wanted to scare somebody with a fake bug over the course of a weekend, wouldn't you bring along, say, a half dozen?"

"I would," Renie said. "Better safe than sorry." She turned as Joe and Bill entered the living room.

"Bill made a chart," Joe said. "It shows all the relationships between the guests and their possible motives."

Sure enough, Bill held up a sheet of butcher's paper. He had used different colored pens, made a legend in one corner, and set down at least a dozen footnotes in the other. It was so elaborate that it resembled a diagram of the solar system. Or Einstein's theory of relativity. As far as Judith could see, it was equally hard to decipher.

"Goodness," she said for lack of anything more positive. "Does it . . . make sense?"

"It does to Bill," Joe replied.

"Of course," Renie murmured.

Bill revealed a long bamboo skewer to use as a pointer. "Bruno is here in the middle," he said, indicating the largest of the circles.

"Like the sun," Judith said softly.

Apparently, Bill didn't hear her. "This smaller circle closest to Bruno is Winifred Best. Note the lines coming from her. Can you read my handwriting?"

"Can I ever?" Renie remarked. "By the way," she said in an aside to Judith and Joe, "he can't spell."

Bill ignored his wife. "One line is for loyalty, another is for dependence, a third is for —"

"What's that thing that looks like a bug?" Renie interrupted.

"It's a bug," Bill responded, smacking the creature with his hand. He paused to use a handkerchief, wiping the victim off his palm.

"Not a spider," Judith noted.

"The spider's over here." Bill pointed to what looked like an asterisk. "Source unknown. To get back to Winifred —"

The phone rang. Judith went to the small cherrywood table and picked up the receiver. "It's for you," she said to Joe.

The others remained silent while Joe took the call. His expression changed from mild interest to surprise. "No kidding? That's . . . a shame. Sure, let me know." He hung up.

"Who was that?" Judith inquired.

"Dilys," Joe replied, looking preoccupied. "Stone Cold Sam Cairo is in Norway General Hospital with a heart attack."

"Oh, no!" Judith exclaimed. "How serious is it?"

"Serious enough, I guess," Joe said, trying to look sympathetic but not succeeding very well. "Dilys is waiting to hear who'll take over the case with her until he recovers."

"I was wondering why we haven't heard from downtown," Judith said. "I thought that Cairo and Dilys had taken the day off. At least the police haven't given up. I mean, they must still believe that Bruno could have been murdered."

"It's high profile," Joe said. "They have to stay on it, or they could get sued, too."

"Don't mention it." Judith nodded at Bill. "Go ahead, what else have you attached to Winifred's circle?"

"The possibility of a love affair," Bill replied, "or her wish to have one with Bruno. Men and women who work so closely together — especially in the Hollywood atmosphere where sex is so prevalent in every phase of life. Often, it doesn't mean anything. It's just casual sex. But sometimes it can be more, at least for one of the parties involved."

"Say," Judith put in, "what's Bruno's marital track record? Was he married to anyone besides the starlet who's now an emir's wife in Dubai?"

The others looked blank. Finally, Renie spoke. "Didn't Winifred say Bruno's kids were of college age? He must have married — what was her name?"

Judith thought hard. "Tamara . . . no, Taryn. Taryn McGuire."

Renie gave a brief nod. "Bruno must have married Taryn at least twenty years ago. It's hard to imagine that he never married anyone else. I saw on one of those discarded statements that he turned fifty-three this year. Surely he couldn't be the only man in Hollywood who had just one wife."

"True," Judith remarked. "But Winifred

didn't mention any other family except the two children. Let's face it, we don't know much about his background. Except," she continued with a wag of her finger, "he was related to the C. Douglas Carp who wrote *The Gasman* novel."

"Ah." Bill glanced at Renie. "I need an orange pen."

Dutifully, Renie reached into the box of markers on the coffee table and handed her husband the object of his desire.

Bill drew a rectangle on the chart. It could have been a book — or a box of cereal. "That's interesting," he noted. "Despite the fact that the novel wasn't very good, Bruno was deeply attached to it. Which suggests he was deeply attached to the author, maybe more so than to the book."

Joe gave Bill an approving nod. "You may be onto something, Mr. Jones."

Judith was peering at what looked like a stick figure wearing a big hat. Or maybe it was a halo. "What's that?" she asked.

Bill examined the clumsy sketch. "That's the alien suspect. See, it's from outer space."

"So's Bill," Renie murmured. "He can't draw, either."

"I don't understand," Judith admitted.

Bill tapped the figure twice. "We can't exclude an outsider. If you and Joe were in the basement when Bruno died, he could have let someone in, someone you never saw and don't even know exists. Thus, the alien suspect."

"That's not a bad theory," Joe remarked. "I tell you, Billy Boy, you may be going somewhere with this chart."

"Speaking of going," Renie said with a bored expression, "could we go on to something else?"

"No," Judith responded. "I think Bill has a very important point." She ignored her cousin, who was using her hands to make a conical steeple over Bill's head. "Why don't I call one of my buddies with the library system and ask about *The Gasman*?"

"Why?" Joe countered. "You said yourself you didn't remember anything about it."

"But I'm not eighty-five years old," Judith said, seeing Sweetums wander into the living room. "Delia Cosgrove is. She might recall something. Delia's been retired for years, but she's still very sharp. I ran into her last spring at the annual library tea."

"Forget Delia," Renie said with a curious expression. "Call my mother."

Bill looked askance. "Your mother?"

"Yes," Renie replied with a touch of defiance. "My father read all sorts of books, including some oddities nobody else probably ever heard of. Mom might remember."

Bill sucked in his breath. "I've gone to a lot of work here."

Judith started to speak, but Renie interrupted. "I'm going to call my mother right now." She picked up the phone and dialed as Sweetums sashayed over to Bill and sniffed the corner of his chart.

"Why don't we watch the end of the football game?" Bill muttered. "We might as well. This is going to take a long time."

"The game's over," Joe said as the doorbell rang. "I'll get it."

Without any sense of optimism, Judith stood next to Renie as Aunt Deb picked up the phone on the first ring.

"Hi, Mom," Renie began. "I've got a question for you . . . Well, yes, of course I want to know how you are, but I talked to you this morning for at least twenty minutes and . . . No kidding? How did get your big toe stuck in the drain? . . . Thank goodness for Mrs. Parker stopping by . . . I didn't realize Auntie Vance and Uncle Vince were coming down from the island . . . No, I won't tell Aunt Gertrude . . . Yes, I know how she and Auntie Vance like to argue . . . No, I realize you aren't one to quarrel . . . Yes, Aunt Gertrude can be a trial sometimes. You're very patient with her . . . I'm aware that she thinks she's the one who's being patient with you . . . Certainly Auntie Vance can have a rough tongue . . . She told you to put your big toe where? . . . Well, that is kind of coarse, but you know what Auntie Vance is like . . ."

Judith was distracted by the return of Joe with three deliverymen carrying several cartons and portable heating units. "Oh, dear," she sighed. "I forgot about the caterers."

"I'll handle it," Joe said grimly.

As the deliverymen began to unload the order onto the buffet, Renie eyed the food with longing. "I know it's foggy," she said into the phone. "Yes, I'll cover all my orifices when I go outside so that the damp won't harm me . . . Of course I'm wearing sturdy shoes." She glanced down at her flimsy brown flats. "No, this pair doesn't lace up to my ankles. I haven't worn those oxfords since I was twelve . . ."

Judith's attention drifted to the buffet, where Joe was ripping open boxes and dumping out heated bags. The deliverymen had already skittered out of the house after presenting an embarrassingly large bill.

Joe emptied a box of Wienie Wizards, dropping almost all of them on the floor. They bounced, but not very high.

"Wait!" Judith cried. "Let me do that.

You're angry, and you're making a mess."

Joe's jaw jutted. "Do you know what all this crap cost?"

"No, and I don't want to know," Judith shot back. "Not now. Let me call Arlene on my cell phone and see if she wants any of this food before you destroy it."

She started to get her purse from the kitchen when she heard the sound of hurrying feet on the stairs. "I smell Wienie Wizards!" cried Ellie Linn. "Yum, yum!"

In a flurry, Judith scooped the hot dogs off the floor and dumped them into a crystal bowl. "They're nice and warm. Be our guest."

"I already am." Ellie giggled, her dark eyes shining with delight. "Mmm . . . my faves!" She immediately pitched in, grabbing four wieners and four buns at once.

Finally reaching the kitchen, Judith dialed Arlene's number.

"What food?" Arlene asked in a puzzled voice.

Judith reminded her neighbor about the large order from the caterer. "I thought you wanted some of it for your family dinner tonight."

"What family?" Arlene asked. "They canceled. They all decided to stay home because of Halloween."

"Rats!" Judith muttered. "Okay, sorry to bother you."

"Why don't you freeze it?" Arlene suggested.

"Frankly," Judith said, "we're running out of room in the freezer. But you're right, I'll try to squeeze in some of the items that won't keep."

By the time she returned to the living room, Renie was finally hanging up the phone. Ellie Linn had disappeared, apparently going upstairs to savor her Wienie Wizards.

"Guess what?" Renie said, looking dazed.

Bill and Joe barely looked up from their places on the matching sofas. The TV screen showed Nazi planes swooping over England. Bill had one eye on the set and the other on his chart, which was spread out over the coffee table. Sweetums was weaving in and out between his ankles, the cat's great plume of a tail swishing back and forth.

"Go away," Bill snarled under his breath, "or I'll turn you into cat chowder."

"What is it?" Judith asked of Renie.

Bill spoke up before his wife could answer. "Get this damned cat out of here. And I could use a purple pen."

Renie swooped down, grabbed Sweetums,

297

and made a face at Bill. "The marker pens are under your chart, Galileo." She moved away, unceremoniously dumping Sweetums near the entry hall.

"My mother actually read *The Gasman*," Renie declared. "So, of course, did my father. He made her read it because he insisted it was a quick way to learn the history of the world."

"You're kidding!" Judith cried.

Joe hit the mute button on the TV's remote control; Bill didn't take his eyes off the screen.

"Does Aunt Deb remember anything about the book?" Judith asked, aware that her aunt's memory was much keener than her mother's.

"Well . . ." Renie made a face. "She admits she skimmed it. My dad enjoyed it because there were some obscure facts he learned and some misconceptions he had that the book cleared up. I gather C. Douglas Carp meticulously researched his material. Anyway, that sort of thing appealed to Dad. Mom didn't give a hoot, and thought the story itself was silly, and she didn't like all the wars." Her gaze shot to the TV, where London was being bombed into what looked like charcoal clumps.

"Oh." Judith was disappointed. "At least

we know that somebody besides Bruno read the book."

"There was one other thing," Renie said. "You know my mother — she's like you, coz. Her main interest in life is people."

Judith smiled faintly. It was a great irony that in many ways, Judith's personality was more like Aunt Deb's. Conversely, Renie had some of the same traits as Gertrude. Reacting to Renie's comment, Bill groaned, but Joe gave a thumbs-up signal. Both men felt they had a cross to bear when it came to their mothers-in-law.

"So?" Judith prodded.

"So," Renie began, "Mom had an old friend, Hattie McDonough, who married a man named Carp. In fact, I guess she married him back in the late twenties, about the time that my folks read *The Gasman*. Naturally, since Carp isn't a common name, Mom wanted to know if Hattie's husband and C. Douglas were related. Hattie — who, by the way, died a few years ago — said they were cousins. Bernie Carp — the one Hattie married — was from the Midwest. Iowa or Nebraska, Mom thought. Alas, Mr. Bernie Carp turned out to be a drinker, and Hattie divorced him before World War Two, *a war we all know who won by now*." Renie raked the TV screen with a scathing look.

Judith clapped her hands together. "Damn! Why didn't I think of this before? I'm going on-line to find out about Bruno's background. If," she added on a note of doubt, "I can figure out how to do it."

"I'll do it," Renie volunteered. "I'm semi-good at finding stuff like that. But only after I eat most of this food. Then you can start putting it away while I surf. Meanwhile," she added, pointing to Joe and Bill, "we'll leave General Eisenhower and General Patton in here to beat the stuffing out of the Führer all over again."

Five minutes later Renie was at the computer in the kitchen while Judith staggered past, carrying a load for the freezer. Directly behind Renie's chair, two of the boxes fell over and hit Renie on the back.

"Yikes!" she cried. "Watch the shoulder! I've had surgery, remember?"

"How can I forget?" Judith muttered. Favoring her artificial hip, she bent over to retrieve the boxes and dropped two more.

Renie jumped out of the chair. "Let me help. You can't carry all that at once."

"I guess not," Judith admitted. "How are you doing on the Internet?"

"I just got into one of the main sites," Renie said as she scooped up the fallen boxes. "I had to eat a little something first. Like the steaks."

"Those I could have frozen," Judith said, leading the way down the basement steps.

"I didn't really eat them," Renie admitted. "I had some of that field-green salad, a few tempura prawns, a piece of fried chicken, and some excellent lox on an outstanding bagel."

Arriving at the freezer, Judith shook her head. "All that in five minutes. How could you?" She always marveled at how much — and how fast — Renie could eat. She also wondered why she couldn't have inherited Renie's metabolism instead of Aunt Deb's compassion.

"You're right," Renie said as Judith opened the freezer. "You don't have much room. Maybe we should take this stuff out of the boxes and put it in freezer wrap."

"There's some right up here," Judith said, reaching for a roll on the shelf above the freezer. "So did you learn anything about Bruno's background yet?"

"No, I just got started," Renie replied, removing four prime New York steaks from one of the boxes. "I only learned his age, which indeed is fifty-three as of March ninth. The next thing I knew, I was being crushed by your cartons."

"Here," Judith said, moving some of the items in the freezer, "I've made some room.

We can put those steaks in this corner by the
—" She stopped and sucked in her breath.

Renie looked at her cousin with some
alarm. "What's wrong? Did you cut yourself
on something?"

"No," Judith said slowly as she brought
her hand out of the freezer. "But I did find
these."

She opened her palm to reveal four black
rubber spiders, stiff as boards and covered
with frost.

Chapter Fourteen

"Give me a clean piece of freezer wrap," Judith said to Renie. "I'll put the spiders in it just in case there might be fingerprints or fibers or something on them."

After securing the evidence, the cousins worked quickly to store the rest of the food. It was almost six by the time they returned upstairs to find the guests in the entry hall, awaiting their limousine.

On a whim, Judith approached them. "Hey, anybody lose some fake spiders?" She held them out in their shroud of plastic wrap.

Ellie, Winifred, and Dade all gave a start. The others looked mildly curious. Judith's eyes darted around the gathering, trying to assess the individual reactions.

"Where'd those spiders come from?" Ben Carmody asked. "They look like the ones in Bruno's bed and over the sink."

"I'm glad they're fake," Ellie said. "Those things creep me out even if they are phony."

"They devastated Bruno," Winifred noted. "Why do they look like they've been frozen?"

"Because they were," Judith responded. "Nobody wants to claim them, I see."

"Gosh, no," Chips said. "Why don't you put them around the door for the kids who come trick-or-treating?"

"I don't think so," Judith said, trying not to show disappointment at the lack of a revealing reaction.

"We shouldn't be late," Winifred said as a knock sounded at the front door. "By the way," she informed Judith, "we heard from the hospital. Angela is going to pull through, but it was a near thing. Dirk will be joining us at Capri's for dinner." Along with the others, she moved toward the door, where their chauffeur awaited them.

Joe ambled over to the entry hall after the guests had left. "What was that all about?"

"This," Judith said, showing him the frozen spiders. "You should have Woody check them out."

"Hidden in the freezer?" Joe cocked his head to one side. "Not a bad place, I suppose. Nobody twigged when you showed them off?"

"No," Judith admitted. "Oh, Ellie and Winnie and Dade gave a start, but that doesn't prove anything. I was hoping that either all of them except one, or none of them except one, would react. Or not."

"I think I understand you," Joe said, taking the spiders from Judith. "Dilys can handle this. She saw the spider over the sink."

Judith went back into the living room. Bill, with the sound on again, was now watching the Allies get revenge for London by blasting the bejeesus out of Berlin.

"You two sofa soldiers can graze at the buffet," she announced. "I'm not making a formal dinner."

In the kitchen, Renie was staring at the computer screen. "Interesting," she remarked. "Bruno was born in Iowa of an army mother and a German war groom. They moved to California when Bruno was very young. His dad got a job in Hollywood as a translator for German films. Young Bruno grew up obsessed by the movies. Hence his destiny, but only after two years of extensive travels in search of his roots. He was married briefly at the age of twenty, divorced before he was twenty-one, then took Taryn McGuire as his second wife when he was twenty-seven, divorced six years later, married a third time to a film cutter for five years, again divorced. The two children by Taryn are listed, ages eighteen and twenty."

"Does it give his mother's maiden name?" Judith asked.

"Yes," Renie replied, scrolling up the screen. "Father, Josef Zepf; mother, Helena Walls. No Carp. Sorry."

"What about wives number one and number three? Any names?"

Renie shook her head. "The first marriage was so brief they don't mention her. And the film cutter's name isn't listed, either. Since this is an official site, they may have been omitted because they weren't names in the industry. There are other sites, I'm sure."

"Check those," Judith urged. "There's got to be a Carp somewhere."

"I'll try," Renie said, "but sometimes it's tricky to get into the unofficial sites. At least it is for me. Meanwhile, I'll print out the stuff we've already seen. There's quite a bit of information about Bruno's films, of course."

In the living room, World War II had ended in Europe. The program had moved on to the Pacific, where General Douglas MacArthur was wearing his game face. Bill was adding another section to his chart.

"Joe," Judith said with a sigh, "I thought you were detecting."

"I am," Joe replied. "I'm like Hercule

Poirot, letting my little gray cells cogitate."

Bill gave Judith an accusing look. "You didn't let me finish explaining my chart."

"You're right," Judith said, sitting down on the sofa arm. "Really, I *am* interested. Show me."

While Bill wrestled with his unwieldy chart, Joe reluctantly turned off the TV as a mushroom cloud exploded over Hiroshima. Bill picked up his bamboo skewer just as Renie burst into the living room.

"Hey!" she cried. "I found something. There's a whole Web site devoted to *The Gasman* and its origins."

Judith turned to look at her cousin. "What does it say?"

"I don't know," Renie replied. "It's kind of long, so I'm printing it out." She saw her husband with his chart and pointer. "Oops. Sorry, Bill. Am I interrupting?"

"You usually are," Bill said with a long-suffering air.

"Go ahead," Joe urged, nodding at Bill. "I'd like to hear this, too. It might help me . . . cogitate."

"What's that new section?" Judith asked, noting that two more circles had been added.

"Morris Mayne and Eugenia Fleming," Bill replied with a tap for each of the turquoise circles.

"You're right," Judith said. "We can't ignore them. They were here last night, too. What else can you tell us?"

"I've been thinking about this," Bill began, tapping the corner of the chart. "We're talking about Hollywood, and we should keep a few things in mind. One is power. Who has it here? Bruno, of course. He was one of the most powerful men in the movie industry. That's a very exclusive club. Who else, then?"

Judith felt she was in the classroom with Bill, and automatically raised her hand. "Winifred? She was so close to Bruno."

Bill nodded solemnly. "That's right. If nothing else, Winifred would have had the power to say yes to a proposal or a script. Anyone in Hollywood can say no. But saying yes is a risk. Winifred was probably able to do that because of her close association with Bruno."

"Then Eugenia would have power, too," Judith conjectured, "because she's Bruno's agent?"

"Only to the extent of allowing access to the people in her stable," Bill replied. "Eugenia also represents Dirk, doesn't she? The amount of her power depends more on her clients' clout."

"What about Morris?" Joe asked.

"Morris Mayne is a studio flack," Bill said, tapping the smaller of the circles in his addendum. "Morris can be replaced on a whim. The only way publicists have any power is if they're keeping a secret. Let's say, covering up for Angela's overdose today."

"Blackmail," Joe said. "Morris is more likely a victim than a perp because he knows too much. Blackmailers are always vulnerable."

The room went silent for a few moments as the foursome reflected. Finally, Renie spoke. "Angela and Dirk are bankable. Doesn't that give them some power?"

"Dirk, yes," Bill said. "But not Angela. She's a big star, though I doubt that a producer or a studio could get a large investment on her name alone. Bruno could and did with Dirk."

"What about Chips Madigan?" Joe asked. "He's a successful director."

Bill shook his head. "Chips is under contract to Paradox. His power is limited. In fact," he continued, tapping at several of the smaller circles, "no one here really has power except Bruno, Winifred, and Dirk. Writers in particular are way down on the food chain."

"Ellie had power," Judith pointed out. "She was the reason Bruno got a big chunk of money for *The Gasman*."

Again, Bill shook his head. "That was a fluke. Ellie had connections, which isn't the same. Until now, her father wasn't a player."

"But," Renie said, "do people murder for power in Hollywood? I don't think I've ever heard of such a thing."

Bill pointed the pointer at Renie. "That's right," he said approvingly. "They don't. If Bruno was murdered, I doubt that power was a motive."

"You really think he was murdered?" Judith said eagerly.

Bill shrugged. "How do I know? But you and Joe seem to be operating on that premise. Judging from the studio's involvement, they are, too."

"So," Renie inquired, "what's the other factor besides power?"

"Factors, really," Bill responded, then studied his chart for a moment. "Image, for one. I realize it's not like it used to be in Hollywood, where studios manufactured images and personalities. Stars were shielded from bad publicity; they had to live up to certain standards. Of course they misbehaved, but either they were protected from the press or the reporters themselves turned a blind eye. Nowadays actors don't have that kind of buffer. And journalism is different — no turn goes unstoned, as they say. The tabloids not only exploit the stars' misdeeds, but they invent some of them." Bill took a deep breath. "All that being said, it's only human nature for actors to want to keep certain unsavory things from the public. Such as Angela's apparent cocaine habit."

"Dirk, too?" Judith offered. "If he and Angela were romantically involved, isn't it possible that he also had a coke addiction?"

"We don't know about Dirk," Bill replied. "Do we have proof?"

On the sofa, Joe stretched out his legs. "Only the coke dust my bride discovered in the downstairs powder room and traces I noticed in the bathroom Angela and Dirk used after they commandeered Bruno's room last night."

"But that could have been only Angela," Bill pointed out.

"What about the bathroom Angela and Ellie shared the first night?" Judith inquired of Joe. "Did you notice anything in there?"

Joe shook his head. "It could have been cleaned up, of course."

Judith persisted. "The night that Dirk roomed with Ben, they had access to Bruno's bathroom, because it's the largest and it's shared by Rooms Three and Four."

"Nothing there, either," Joe responded. "Angela may not have wanted to haul out her stash while she was sharing a room with Ellie. They don't like each other much. Ellie might have lorded it over Angela somehow. Haven't we figured that Angela used the bathroom on this floor to do coke?"

"That's right," Judith allowed.

"What else?" Bill asked, impatient with the latest digression. "We're talking image and reputation here, remember."

"Ellie's too young to have much of a past," Judith noted.

"Chips," Renie declared, "is too good to be true."

"Do writers care what people think of them?" Joe remarked. "Dade, at least, gives off I-don't-give-a-damn signals."

"All writers are weird," Renie said. "That's why they're so difficult to deal with."

Judith was staring at Renie. "Why do you think Chips is too good to be true?"

Renie shrugged. "Isn't he always telling you those endearing stories about his wholesome youth in the Midwest? Mother and apple pie — literally."

"It was chicken pot pie," Judith said, but Renie's comment caused her to wonder. "Could we check him out on the Internet?"

"Probably," Renie replied.

He pointed to the circle that represented Dirk Farrar. "The worst thing about Dirk —

from an image standpoint — would be to find out he was gay. He's Mr. Macho on the screen."

"Can't we rule that out?" Joe inquired. "He was banging Angela."

"He could be a switch-hitter," Bill responded.

"What about Ben Carmody?" Judith asked.

"Ben's a different case," Bill said. "He usually plays villains. Isn't the role in the Utah picture his first leading-man opportunity?"

"I guess," Judith said, "though I don't think all the different parts he played in *The Gasman* were bad guys."

"That's not the same," Bill pointed out. "Ben Carmody has built his reputation as an actor, not as a star. You see the difference?" Like any good professor, he waited for the others to nod their understanding. "As for Ellie, you may be right, Judith. She's not only young, but grew up in a prominent family. I suspect that her past is relatively blameless."

But Renie didn't agree. "She may have run over a cripple. She could have done drugs. She might have gone off on a lark with some friends and held up a convenience store at gunpoint."

Bill gave his wife a withering look. "She

may have been the homecoming queen and won a scholarship to Yale. Let's assume she's in the clear. You're just being contrary."

"True," Renie admitted, not looking the least contrite. "Still, I think there must be something unsavory about Chips. And where did he get a name like that anyway? It's got to be a nickname."

"You may be right," Bill said. "Midwesterners are very good at hiding things they don't want others to see, especially their dark side."

Bill ought to know, Judith thought, since he was a Wisconsin native. "Who've we left out?" she asked. "Winifred?"

"Yes." Bill tapped the circle nearest to Bruno's. "What do we know about her background?"

"I think she was a Demure," Judith said, walking over to the stereo, where she had slipped the tape behind a rack of CDs. She related Renie's discovery along with Winifred's reaction. "I'm sure it's her," Judith concluded, "but she doesn't want it known."

"Ah," said Bill.

"I remember them," Joe put in. "They were a one-hit wonder. Vivian used to sing their song when she did her piano-bar stints. 'Come Play with Me,' wasn't it?"

Judith gave her husband a censorious look. "I'm sure she did."

Joe waved a hand. "It was her job. At least I had a spouse who worked. Sometimes."

"She only worked because she got free drinks," Judith asserted.

"Truce!" Renie shouted, holding up both arms like a football official signaling a touchdown. "No fighting, no biting. Let's go back to Winifred."

Joe calmed down first. "So Winifred's ashamed of being a Demure? Why?"

"Because," Judith suggested, still bristling a bit, "they only had one big hit?"

"Another person deeply affected by failure," Bill murmured. He used the purple pen to make some marks by Winifred's circle. "Yet," he continued, making a squiggle with the orange pen, "she rebounded to become Bruno's assistant, a position of great power. So why," he concluded, adding a chartreuse slash, "wouldn't Winifred be able to laugh off her early experience in the music world?"

"Bill," Renie inquired, "have you any idea what all those marks mean?"

"Of course." With an expectant expression, he gazed at the others as if waiting for the brightest student to give the correct answer. "Well?"

"Because," Judith said slowly, "there was something shameful about that experience."

Bill nodded approval. "There has to be. What could it have been?"

"Guesswork," Joe said in a disgusted voice. "That's all we can do is guess. That's not a professional approach in law enforcement."

"We don't have anything else," Renie pointed out.

With a hopeful expression, Judith turned to Renie. "You couldn't find it on the Internet?"

"I doubt it, coz," Renie said.

"Then there has to be another way," Judith declared, getting up from the sofa and heading out of the room.

"Hey," Renie called after her cousin, "what are you going to do?"

Judith turned just before she reached the entry hall. "I'm about to crash the dinner party. Anybody care to join me?"

"Hey," Bill said sharply, "I'm not finished yet."

"Later," Judith shot back. "I feel useless. I'm frustrated. I'm getting out of here."

"Don't act like a moron, Jude-girl," Joe said with a scowl. "You can't go barging in on those people like that."

"Look," Judith said, almost stamping her foot but afraid to, lest she jar her artificial hip, "we're running out of time. The guests may be gone by tomorrow. You're not the one who worked your tail off to build this B&B. Do — or don't do — what you want, but I'm not sitting around waiting for a bunch of L.A. lawyers to fleece us." She turned on her heel and headed for the back hallway to get her jacket.

"Wait for me!" Renie cried, hurrying after Judith. "Our car's blocking the driveway. I'm coming with you."

Judith waited, though it took only seconds until her cousin was in the Joneses' Toyota Camry. A moment later Renie was reversing out into the foggy cul-de-sac.

"It's just as well to take your car," Judith said, fastening her seat belt. "It's newer than my Subaru. Maybe the parking attendants at Capri's won't act so snooty."

"They aren't as snooty as they used to be," Renie replied, heading onto Heralds-gate Avenue. The fog had settled in over the hill, making it difficult to see more than twenty feet ahead. Though Renie had a rep-utation — which she claimed was unearned — for driving too fast and erratically, she crept along the thoroughfare. "With all the new money in this town," she said, "especially among the younger set, it's hard to tell a millionaire from a millworker."

Capri's was located on the east side of the hill, closer to Renie's house than to the B&B. The cousins climbed Heraldsgate Avenue to the commercial district on the flat, then kept going north into a sloping residential neighborhood. They turned right in the direction of the restaurant, but within four blocks, Renie took a left.

"Hey!" Judith cried. "What are we doing?"

"You do nothing," Renie said. "I change clothes. I can't go into Capri's wearing this Loyola University sweatshirt and these black pants. They have a hole in them, in case you haven't noticed, which maybe you haven't because I'm wearing black underwear."

"Good grief." Judith held her head. "Okay, but don't take long."

Sitting in the car, she studied her own attire. The green wool slacks matched the green cable-knit turtleneck. Her shoes were fairly new, having been purchased at Nordquist's annual women's sale. She supposed she could pass at Capri's for a real customer.

As she continued to wait, Judith's mind wandered back to Bill's chart. Someone was missing. Who, besides the Alien Suspect? The answer came to mind almost immediately. Vito Patricelli wasn't represented among Bruno's satellites. But it appeared that he hadn't arrived in the city until this morning. Was that true? Judith used her cell phone to dial one of the airlines that served passengers from L.A.

"We have no one named Patricelli on our manifests in the last three days," the pert voice said.

Judith tried the other connecting carriers and got the same negative result. Maybe Vito had flown north by private plane.

She was about to call Boring Field, where many of the smaller aircraft landed, when Renie reappeared wearing a great deal of brown suede, including her pants, jacket, ankle boots, and handbag. She also wore a brown cashmere sweater.

"How many animals had to die to clothe you in that outfit?" Judith inquired as Renie slid into the driver's seat.

"A lot of cows with really rotten dispositions," Renie replied, starting the car. "None of the children were home. They must have gone a-wooing."

"Very likely," Judith agreed as they headed back up the hill to the turnoff for Capri's. "Really, I'm anxious to meet the future in-laws."

"So am I," Renie said darkly, "even

319

though I allegedly have already done so."

"Say," Judith said, "did you get a chance to look at the material you got off the Internet about *The Gasman* and its origins?"

"Not yet," Renie replied, slowing at a six-way stop and peering into the fog to see if there were any vehicles coming from the other directions. "It looks as if it came out to at least twenty pages. That includes art-work, of course."

"Who puts those sites together?"

"This one may have been done by the studio," Renie said, curving around in front of the restaurant and pulling into the drive-way. "Some of the sites are created by fans."

A blemish-free teenager with corn-tassel-colored hair and a big smile greeted the cousins.

"Which private party will you be joining?" he asked as Renie stepped out of the Camry. "That is," he added with an ingenuous ex-pression, "on Sundays we're not open to regular customers."

"How many parties are there?" Renie in-quired as Judith joined her under the porte cochere.

"Two," the youth replied with a discreet wink. "The Smith and the Jones parties."

Renie darted a glance at Judith. "I'm Mrs. Jones," Renie said, winking back.

"Ah." The young man made a flourish that was almost a bow. "This way, please. Derek will take care of your car." He nodded at a second fresh-faced adolescent who had been standing by the door.

"So which is which?" Judith murmured as they passed across the flagstone flooring, where they were met by a maître d' so handsome that he could have given Dirk Farrar a run for his money.

"We've got a fifty-fifty chance of getting the right party," Renie said out of the side of her mouth. "Serena Jones here," she informed the maître d' in her normal voice.

"I'm Charles," the maître d' informed the cousins. His smile seemed to assure them that he was their new best friend. Charles led the way up a winding black iron staircase, then turned right to face a paneled mahogany door. With a dazzling smile and a flourish that was indeed a bow, he opened the door.

"Your party, Mrs. Jones," he said.

Renie rocked on the heels of her brown suede boots. This was definitely the Jones party. All three of Renie and Bill's offspring sat at a table for at least a dozen other people, some of whom looked vaguely familiar.

"Hi, Mom," Tom said in greeting. "We thought you'd never get here. Where's Pop?"

Chapter Fifteen

"What is this?" Renie demanded when the maître d' had left and she regained her equilibrium. "What do you mean, 'Where's Pop'?"

"Didn't you get our note?" Anne said with an innocent look on her pretty face.

"What note?" Renie all but shouted. Then, realizing that she must be in the presence of her future in-laws, she tried to smile. "No. Where was it?"

Anne turned to Tony, who was seated four places down the table. "Where did you put the note, Big T?"

Tony's chiseled features were vague. "I thought Tom put it up by the hall closet."

"Not me," Tom said with a shake of his curly dark head. "You wrote it, Annie-Bannany. What'd you do with it?"

"I didn't write it," Anne retorted. "I thought —"

"Hold it!" Renie cried, this time unable to keep her voice down. But she managed a smile for her bewildered audience. "Your father and I never saw a note. We haven't been home since early this afternoon. How about introducing your poor old mother and your just-as-poor-and-almost-as-old aunt to these other folks?"

Anne and Tony both gazed at Tom as they always did when they expected the eldest of their lot to take responsibility. The others included a fair-haired young man who was growing something fuzzy that looked like it might become a goatee, a raven-haired young woman who looked as if she could be Native American, a red-headed girl who looked faintly ethereal, and a half-dozen middle-aged adults who looked as if they wished they were somewhere else. The whole group stared at Renie.

"We told you and Pop about the dinner tonight," Tom said, looking wounded. "Remember, it was Friday, and you mentioned having everybody over at our house. But we said we thought it'd be better to go out. You and Pop didn't say anything, so we assumed it was all set."

"Probably," Renie muttered to Judith, "they were all talking at once — and so loud — that we couldn't hear them."

"What's that, Mom?" Tony inquired.

"I said I guess we goofed." Renie looked unusually subdued. "I'll call Pop and get him over here."

"He won't answer the phone," Anne warned.

"He's not home," Renie said, delving into her brown suede purse for her cell phone.

Judith whispered into Renie's ear. "I'm out of here."

"Coz!" Renie cried as she hit the wrong button, causing the phone to emit a sharp squawk.

"Sorry," Judith apologized. "I have a job to do."

She scooted out of the room.

The only similar door was on her left. The other doors along the corridor were for rest rooms, storage, and other restaurant facilities. Grasping the mahogany door's brass lever, Judith took a deep breath. Now that her prey were at hand, she didn't know what to do. Barging in, as Joe had cautioned, wasn't a good idea. The door was too thick to allow her to overhear what was going on in the private dining room. Worse yet, the servers were all young men wearing tuxedos. A wild idea involving the impersonation of a waitress had struck her earlier. Not only was it far-fetched, it was impossible.

At that moment, one of the waiters appeared at the top of the stairs carrying a jeroboam of champagne. Swiftly, Judith fished into her purse, searching for a piece of paper.

"Young man," she said, blocking the door, "could you deliver a message to the Smith party? I'm with the Joneses, in the other private dining room."

The waiter, who was young, Asian, and very good-looking, was too well trained to show surprise.

"To whom shall I give the message?" he asked.

Having found a small notebook, Judith scribbled out a half-dozen words. "Morris Mayne," she said. "Tell him it's urgent. Thank you."

The waiter disappeared inside. Judith wondered if she should have slipped him five dollars. Or ten. Or twenty-five, considering that she was at Capri's.

Moments later Morris Mayne dashed out into the hall. "What is it? What's happened at the studio?" Not nearly as tall as Judith, he peered up at her through rimless spectacles. "Wait! You're the bed-and-breakfast lady, aren't you?"

"That's right," Judith said, hoping to look appropriately solemn. "I think we'd best go downstairs to the bar. Perhaps they'll serve us a drink."

"A drink?" Morris's sparse tufts of hair stood out on his round head. "Yes, I could use a drink. Though of course I've already had . . . Never mind, let's talk." He hurried down the winding staircase.

Charles the maître d' expressed great pleasure at serving the duo. Judith ordered Scotch rocks; Morris requested a Bottle Rocket. Judith had never heard of it, but it appeared to consist of several alcoholic beverages and a slice of kiwi.

"Tell me, please," Morris begged after Charles handed him his drink. "Why am I being recalled?"

"Recalled?" Judith's dark eyes widened. "Is that what I wrote? Oh, dear. My handwriting is so bad. I meant you'd been called by the studio to . . . well, I didn't quite catch the rest of it, so I thought I'd better come in person to make sure you got the message."

Morris slumped in relief. "Oh! Thank God! I thought I'd been fired!"

"Why would you think such a thing?" Judith asked, still wide-eyed.

Morris gulped down some of his Bottle Rocket. "Because of this *Gasman* mess. I mean," he amended quickly, "it's not exactly a mess, but it does present some problems. With Bruno dying and all, you see."

"Yes, that complicates matters," Judith said in a sympathetic tone. "What do you think will happen to the movie now?"

"Who knows?" Morris spread his arms, knocking over a candle on the bar. "Oops! Sorry, Charles." The gracious maître d' picked up the candle and turned discreetly away.

"Hasn't the studio given some instructions?" Judith asked, taking a small sip of Scotch. It was excellent Scotch, maybe Glenlivet. She sipped again.

"Paradox is waiting to find out what happened to Bruno," Morris replied.

"What do the studio executives think happened?" Judith asked.

Morris drank more Bottle Rocket. "Whew!" he exclaimed, passing a hand over his high forehead. "That's strong!" He leaned closer to Judith. "What did you say?"

She repeated the question. Morris reflected, though his eyes weren't quite in focus.

"Paradox is sure Bruno had a tart ahack. I mean" — he corrected himself — "*a heart attack*. He's had problems, you shee. *See.*" The publicist hiccuped once.

"You mean he'd had a history of heart trouble?"

Morris grimaced. "Not exactly." He hiccuped again and drew himself up on the bar stool, which luckily had a large padded back. "Strain. That's what Bruno had. He worked under a lot of strain. That's why he —" He stopped abruptly. "I shouldn't tell tales out of school, should I?"

"You're not," Judith assured him. "I'm not in the business. I don't count. I'm nobody."

"Thash shtrue," Morris agreed. "You're not." He took another gulp from his glass. "Anyway, Bruno worked too hard. That caushes strain."

"Yes," Judith said amiably. "And strain can lead to many things. To help him cope, of course."

"Cope!" Morris's arm shot out, striking a calla lily in a tall black vase. "Oops!" He giggled and put a hand over his mouth. "Mushn't drink this too fast. Had a lot of champagne upstairs." He jabbed at the ceiling with a pudgy finger.

"Yes, to cope," Judith said patiently. "People cope in many ways. Sometimes those ways aren't healthy."

Sadly, Morris shook his head. "True, too true. Like Bruno. Not healthy. Don't blame him. Too much presshure. Not all his fault. Blame Big Daddy Dumas."

Judith was taken aback. "Big Daddy Dumas? Who's that?"

Morris giggled some more and shook a finger at Judith. "Wouldn't you like to know?"

"Yes," Judith said seriously, "I would."

At the desk by the bar, the phone rang. Charles picked it up. He appeared to be taking a reservation.

"Phone," Morris said. "Musht phone the studio." He patted himself down, apparently searching for his cell. "Hunh. Musht have left it upstairs. Here I go." He picked up what remained of his Bottle Rocket and staggered off to the iron staircase.

Judith was on his heels. "But, Morris," she said urgently, "you can tell me about Big Daddy Dumas. I'm nobody, remember?"

On the second step, Morris turned around. "Doeshn't matter. Big Daddy's dead. Ta-ta." Clinging to the iron rail, he wobbled up the stairs.

Judith returned to the bar, took another sip of fine Scotch, and considered her next move. She was still in a quandary when Bill came through the main entrance.

"Hi, Bill," she said, waving from the bar stool. "You aren't really Big Daddy Dumas by any chance, are you?"

Bill stared at Judith. "Why do you ask?"

Judith stared back at him. "Do you know who I'm talking about?"

"Of course," he replied. "Dumas is a famous psychological case study from about twenty years ago. Where did you hear the name?"

Quickly, Judith explained. "So what do you know about this Dumas?"

Bill looked pained. "Dumas was a black gang lord in L.A. He was involved in drugs and prostitution. He was atypical because he didn't allow his hookers to take drugs, though he used them to sell the stuff. He was interesting from a psychological standpoint because the control he exerted over his girls was paternal, rather than intimidating or enabling. He was creating a familial bond between himself and the prostitutes. Almost all of them had had no father figure in their lives, or if they did, he was abusive. Big Daddy never had intercourse with the girls. He protected them and made sure they were checked out for disease. He acted like a real father, which was all the more intriguing because he was only in his twenties and had a large brood of children of his own. This was one of the first case studies that showed how young people got caught up in gangs and prostitution rings. It emphasized how the gang provides a surrogate family and a sense of belonging."

"What happened to Dumas?" Judith asked. "Morris Mayne told me he was dead."

Bill nodded. "I suppose Morris knows the story, being based in L.A. Dumas was quite a legend there for almost ten years. One of his girls killed him. He was also involved in the local music scene, though whether with promoting talent or just peddling drugs and sex, I can't recall. This particular girl, who was from Mexico, felt Dumas could help her get started as a singer for the Hispanic audience. He couldn't or wouldn't, so she stabbed him in a fit of rage, claiming he'd betrayed their family bond."

"A father–daughter quarrel," Judith remarked.

"Speaking of children," Bill said, starting up the steps, "I'd better join mine before Renie and our kids eat all the food."

Judith watched Bill disappear at the top of the staircase, then resumed her place at the bar. The glimmer of an idea was forming at the back of her brain.

Charles cleared his throat. "Will you be rejoining your party upstairs?"

"Ah . . ." Judith paused to take a quick sip from her glass. "Yes, in a few minutes. I had to get away."

"Oh?" Charles tried to hide his puzzlement.

"I mean, I know I just got here," Judith explained, "but those people can be very . . . difficult."

"The Joneses?" Charles inquired politely.

"Yes, the Joneses." Judith smiled confidentially. "They're relatives, you see."

"Yes," Charles agreed tactfully. "Sometimes family members can be taxing."

"If you don't mind, I'll finish my drink down here," Judith said, wondering if she should call a taxi and go home. Renie and Bill would be stuck with the future in-laws for at least an hour or two.

"Of course," Charles responded.

Before Judith could say anything else, a pair of hefty legs and sensible black pumps came down the stairway.

"There you are," Eugenia Fleming said in an accusing tone. "What's this about the studio calling Morris? And how did you get him so drunk?"

"He got himself drunk," Judith declared. "I've never seen anybody drink a Bottle Rocket before. It's a wonder he didn't launch himself across the lake."

Eugenia turned her head in every direction. "What lake?"

Judith gestured at the slanting windows that faced the length of the restaurant. "There's a lake out there. Two lakes, in fact.

And mountains. You can't see them because of the fog."

"Miserable weather," Eugenia muttered, planting one black pump on the single step up to the bar. "Now tell me what's going on with Morris and the phone call."

Judith feigned innocence. "I'm only the messenger."

"Morris was too drunk to call Paradox," Eugenia huffed, her majestic bust heaving. "I wouldn't let him, so I called for him. No one there knew anything about trying to contact him. Vito is very annoyed."

"That's a shame," Judith said placidly, then took another drink of Scotch. "Morris isn't in trouble, is he?"

"Of course he is!" Eugenia shot back. "We're all in trouble!" Abruptly, she put a hand to her large crimson lips. "That is," she said in a much softer tone, "this Bruno incident presents several challenges to all of us who are involved."

"I would imagine," Judith said, sounding sympathetic. "You've lost a very important client."

"Yes," Eugenia said, then turned to Charles. "Give me a shot of Tanqueray, straight up."

Charles complied. Eugenia downed the gin in one gulp. "Producers like Bruno don't come around every day," she grumbled. "In fact, I was with him from the beginning, right after he won that film-festival prize. You might say he owed a lot of his success to me." She gave Charles a curt nod. "I'll have another, please."

"Really?" Judith remarked. "How does that work?"

Eugenia scowled at Judith. "How does it work? I do the work, that's how. I start a buzz, build an image, play publicist as well as agent. It wasn't easy with Bruno," she said, downing the second gin. "He had hang-ups, phobias, problems. But I connected him to the right people. Nobody gives agents credit for the grunt work involved in building a reputation."

Judith inadvertently neglected the agent's efforts as she zeroed in on a word that had captured her attention. "You mentioned hang-ups?" Again, she wore her air of innocence.

"Family background," Eugenia said, snapping her fingers at Charles for another hit. "His parents may have moved to California, where Mr. Zepf worked in the business, but they were very strict. What would you expect with a German father and a Midwestern mother? It's a wonder Bruno's creativity wasn't stifled before he could leave home."

"I understand he went in search of his roots," Judith said, trying not to stare as Eugenia knocked back a third gin.

"He did," Eugenia replied. "He went to Germany to discover his father's past. Josef Zepf had come from Wiesbaden, the son of a shoemaker. Bruno loved Germany, especially the music and the literature. No doubt Wagner influenced him, which may be why his pictures always ran a bit long."

"As long as *The Gasman*?" Judith asked as Eugenia signaled for yet another drink.

"Not that long," Eugenia said. "But even the picture that won the film-festival prize — *No Prunes for Prudence* — was over two and a half hours."

"That's a lot of prunes," Judith murmured.

The agent, however, was in full spate, and apparently didn't hear the remark. "He visited England as well, since his mother, Helena, had been stationed there before being sent to Germany," Eugenia continued. Her voice had taken on a lilting quality, as if she were narrating a documentary on Bruno's life. Or quoting from an A&E *Biography*. Judith was reminded of Winifred's dissertation on Bruno. Maybe all his associates had been forced to memorize the producer's life story.

"After more than a year," Eugenia went

on, "he returned to the States. The farm in Iowa where his mother had been raised was gone, the fields plowed under for a development, but the house was still there. Grandfather Walls had died, but Bruno's grandmother still lived in the old house with its rickety steps and shutters which hung by a single hinge and clattered in the wind. Grandmother Walls was very old and ill. Bruno stayed with her until the end came, almost a year later."

"That's admirable," Judith said, thinking there should be a violin accompaniment to Eugenia's recital. "Bruno sounds very compassionate."

"Oh, he is. He *was*," Eugenia corrected herself with a start. "My God, I can't believe he's gone!" She requested a fifth drink. "To Bruno," she said, holding up her glass.

"To Bruno," Judith echoed, finishing her Scotch. She tried not to stare at the other woman, who seemed completely sober. Maybe her size accounted for her ability to drink like a fish. Bracing herself, Judith posed a question: "Who was C. Douglas Carp?"

Eugenia didn't bat an eye. "You mean the man who wrote *The Gasman* novel? Some relative, I believe. I never read novels, unless the book is adapted for a picture, and even

then I skim. Books are inevitably dull."
With surprising agility for her size and the
amount of gin she'd consumed, she slid off
the bar stool, planting her sensible shoes
firmly on the floor. "I must go upstairs. I do
wish you hadn't disturbed Morris with that
silly message. He's very drunk. Tsk, tsk."

Charles smiled at Judith. "Would you care
for another?" he asked, pointing to her empty
glass.

Judith shook her head. "I should go, I suppose."

"But I thought you were with the Joneses."
Charles looked a trifle tense. "Or am I mistaken? You also seem to know the people attending the Smith dinner."

Judith wondered if the maître d' suspected
she might be a groupie or a party crasher.
"Charles" — she sighed — "it's a long story.
Some members of the Smith group
are . . . ah . . . staying at my house." She refrained from mentioning that her house was
a B&B. "Mrs. Jones is my cousin. It's a coincidence that both parties are here at once."

"Ah." The maître d' offered her a conspiratorial smile and seemed to relax. "Then you
know these Smiths are movie people. I recognized Dirk Farrar right away. He came late,
though." The last sentence almost sounded
like a question.

"He came from someplace else," Judith said, "though he's staying with us. How did he seem?"

Charles looked around to make sure no one could overhear. But the lower part of the restaurant was still vacant. Even the waiters seemed to have gone to ground.

"I thought he looked kind of grim," Charles said, keeping his voice down. "Is that because of the producer who passed away last night?"

"That's part of it," Judith said, then curbed her tongue. She mustn't gossip about Angela La Belle. "I'm sure the poor reception *The Gasman* got at the premiere upset Dirk, too."

"I never read movie reviews," Charles said, then turned as the valet with the corn-colored hair came into the restaurant, looking worried. "What is it, Josh?" the maître d' inquired.

"There's a couple out in the parking lot who insist they want to eat here," Josh said. "They won't take no for an answer. I think you'd better talk to them."

"Excuse me," Charles said to Judith. "This happens almost every Sunday when we're closed to regular diners. In fact, this is the second time an insistent couple has shown up this evening. I won't be long."

Judith got up and strolled over to the big

windows. It was dark and the fog was thick. She couldn't see any lights, not even directly below the restaurant, which was located about halfway up Heraldsgate Hill. When she turned around again, she saw Charles leading a middle-aged couple inside and up the winding staircase. The man was big, bald, and bearlike; the woman was small, dark, and of Asian descent. Apparently, they had an entrée to one of the private parties upstairs, and Judith didn't think they were keeping up with the Joneses.

She could almost smell the aroma of Wienie Wizards wafting behind the couple as they disappeared onto the second floor.

Chapter Sixteen

Judith wanted very much to see Heathcliffe and Amy Lee MacDermott up close. She wasn't sure why, but it seemed important to talk to them. Unfortunately, she couldn't think of an excuse to get past the Smith party's mahogany door.

For several moments Judith stared down at the smooth black marble bar, where she could see her reflection. It was distorted by the slight grain, making her look old, tired, and ugly. A crone, she thought, and was disheartened.

What was she doing at Capri's, seeking clues to a murder that might not be a murder? Was she bloodthirsty, as Renie had remarked? Surely possession of material goods wasn't so important that it made her wish that one person had killed another. No, that wasn't the real reason she preferred murder over more mundane deaths. So why was she beating herself up so badly? Slowly, she turned to the windows again. There was nothing to see. The night was as dark and blank as her brain.

Yet Judith knew that if the fog suddenly lifted, the city's lights would glitter like stars on a clear winter's eve. The lakes and the mountains were there, if only she could see them. So were the answers to the riddle that was Bruno's death. Judith always had to know. If only the fog would lift from her brain, she could find the truth.

Charles hadn't come down from the second floor. There was still no sign of the waiters. Judith was curious. The guests must be getting served. How was the food coming from the kitchen, if not via the iron staircase?

Hurriedly, she crossed the restaurant to the far side, where she saw a plain brown door. Turning the knob, she discovered a narrow hallway on her left that presumably led to the kitchen. On her right was a staircase. Judith ascended to another plain door and opened it. She came out into another narrow hall, where she saw two identical doors.

The first one led into the main corridor, but judging from her position in the restaurant, the second door had to go into the Smith party's private dining room. In the shadows just beyond the door was a busing area. On tiptoes, she approached the second door and cautiously opened it just a crack.

". . . lose my investment" were the first words she managed to hear, and they were spoken by a nasal male voice she didn't recognize. Heathcliffe MacDermott, alias the Wienie Wizard? Judith peered through the sliver of open doorway. All she could see was Morris Mayne with his head down on the table and Dade Costello's blunt profile.

"Not necessarily," said a smooth voice that Judith identified as belonging to Vito Patricelli. "Paradox may not shelve the picture. They have an investment, too, even larger than yours, Mr. MacDermott."

"Idiots," snapped a waspish female voice that didn't sound like Winifred, Ellie, or Eugenia. "Idiots," the woman repeated. Judith figured the speaker had to be Mrs. MacDermott.

"I don't get it," declared Heathcliffe MacDermott. "The movie's a dud. If I made wienies like Zepf made movies, I'd be wearing a paper hat and peddling hot dogs at minor league baseball games instead of running a billion-dollar empire."

"The studio can make changes," Vito

said, his voice unperturbed. "They'll have free rein — under the circumstances."

"You beast," murmured Winifred. "How can you say such things when Bruno has been dead less than twenty-four hours?" Though Judith couldn't see her, it sounded as if Winifred was close to the service door.

"What kind of changes?" Ellie asked, not quite as pert as usual.

"Cutting, for one thing," Vito replied. "No one can argue that the picture should be shortened by at least an hour."

"Are you saying," Heathcliffe asked in a slightly confused voice, "that Paradox can do whatever it wants now that Bruno Zepf is dead?"

"Exactly," Vito responded. "The studio has the major chunk of money invested in the picture. They can do as they please."

Except for the creak of chairs and shuffling of limbs, a silence fell over the room. Judith glanced at the door to the stairs to make sure the coast was clear. As far as she could tell, no one seemed to be eating. Perhaps the group had finished its most recent course.

"What about *Utah*?" the unfamiliar female voice demanded. "What about my script?"

Judith heard Dade Costello snort.

Vito waited a moment to reply. "Your script?"

"*All the Way to Utah*," Amy Lee MacDermott retorted with anger. "Bruno bought it, and it's supposed to star darling Ellie."

"I can't answer that right now," Vito said, smooth as ever. "There hasn't been time for anyone to make that decision."

"Who makes it?" Amy Lee's voice had grown strident.

"Bruno's production company," Vito replied.

"Isn't that a weird setup?" Ben Carmody put in. The actor sounded uncharacteristically harsh. "Bruno had no second in command. He thought he was immortal."

"That's not true," Winifred said in a strong, stiff voice. "If anything happened to Bruno, I was to take over. I already had, when he was in . . . the hospital."

"Oh, that's right." Ben's voice brightened. "Then I guess any big decisions would be up to you, Win."

"Not necessarily," Vito interjected. "I suspect that Winifred's powers are limited to such situations as Bruno being temporarily out of the picture. So to speak." No one laughed except Dirk Farrar, and the sound wasn't pleasant. "There are two other factors involved, one of which is the studio's agreement to put money into *All the Way to*

Utah. But now that Bruno is dead — let's not mince words — Paradox would be free to pull out."

"They wouldn't dare!" Amy Lee cried. "They made a commitment!"

"It's not legally binding when the producer dies," Vito asserted. "But the other factor involves the heirs to Bruno's estate. Winifred, do you know if he made a will?"

"Why . . ." Winifred's voice sounded faint. "No," she went on slowly, "I don't believe he did."

"It figures," Dirk snarled. "From A to Zepf. Bruno thought he was the Alpha and the Omega, with no end in sight."

"Stop that!" Winifred shouted. "You're angry because you and Bruno got into a big fight and Ben ended up with the leading role in the *Utah* picture."

"Let's stop wrangling and back up here," Heathcliffe broke in, his voice sounding like that of a man obviously used to exercising authority. "What's this other factor, Mr. L.A. Lawyer?"

Vito cleared his throat. "That was what I was getting at when I inquired about a will. Since Bruno had no wife, his entire estate goes to his two children."

"His children?" Amy Lee and Ellie Linn shrieked in unison.

"That's ridiculous," the mother scoffed.

"That's stupid," the daughter declared. "Those kids aren't as old as I am!"

"How old?" Amy Lee demanded.

"Greta was twenty in June," Winifred said quietly. "Greg just turned eighteen a month ago."

"The son's name is Greg?" Ellie's voice had taken on a lighter note.

"Yes," Winifred replied. "After Gregory Peck. Greta was named for Garbo."

"Hmm." There was a faint simper from Ellie.

Judith saw Dirk Farrar's back at the door. She tensed, wondering if he might be about to leave the room.

"I don't give a rat's ass about that *Utah* crap," he said. "All I want to know is when the hell we can get out of this fog bank and go back to L.A."

"The matter should be resolved by tomorrow," Vito responded.

"It better be," Dirk shot back. "This place sucks scissors." His back moved away from the door. Apparently, he'd gotten up only to stretch his legs.

"Mr. Farquhar," Amy Lee said sternly, "don't speak so nastily of my *Utah* script. It's going to be a blockbuster. After all," she added with a sneer in her voice, "you were slated to star in it until you behaved so badly toward Mr. Zepf."

"The name's Farrar," Dirk shouted, "as you damned well know! And I'll tell you something else," he continued, not as loud, but just as intense, "I didn't really give a damn when Bruno canned me. I'd put up with enough crap from him with *The Gasman* and that lousy script he'd taken from Crappy Pappy Carp's book."

"Don't be so disrespectful!" Winifred exclaimed in dismay. "You're callous, Dirk. Everybody knows how self-centered you are, even more so than most actors. I suppose you intend to leave Angela lying in the hospital while you head back to Los Angeles."

"It's her own damned fault she's there in the first place," Dirk retorted. "I begged her to go into rehab. Besides, I'm not a doctor. What good can I do her hanging around the hospital?"

Judith was so caught up in the heated drama just a few inches away that she never heard the approaching footsteps. It was the tap on her shoulder that made her jump and let out a stifled cry.

I'm done for, she thought. *They'll throw me out in the street. They might arrest me. They might ban me from Capri's forever. They might put my picture up by the desk with a slash through it. "No Judith McMonigle Flynn."* With considerable trepidation, she turned around to confront the enemy.

"Learn anything?" whispered Renie.

"Coz!" A sudden silence had descended over the dining room. Judith was certain that the contentious crew had heard a suspicious noise. She gently shut the door. "What are you doing here?"

"Looking for the busing station," Renie replied, spying her goal behind Judith. "We need more napkins. You know how our kids eat. The tablecloth looks like an army field hospital."

"You're no slouch yourself," Judith retorted. "How's the dinner going?"

Renie made a doleful face. "Could these people be less fun? The parents are like mannequins. Thank God our kids have some animation. They're never afraid to speak out."

"Coz," Judith said, keeping an eye on the service door, "your family isn't merely outspoken, you're all very loud. Even Bill can bellow when aroused. The future in-laws are probably cowed."

Renie shot her a disdainful glance. "Okay, so we've got pep. But these people hardly eat a thing. The fiancé and fiancées are a little livelier. Heather is very smart — she's Tom's girl — and Cathleen — Tony's beloved — seems genuinely kind. As for Odo, he laughs at everything Bill says, which is good."

"Odo?" Judith responded. "His name is really Odo?"

"Yes," Renie replied, looking very serious. "You know the original Odo. Bishop Odo became pope just in time to launch the First Crusade."

Judith shook her head. "Funny, the kid didn't look militant. Or religious."

"He's not," Renie said. "At least as far as I can tell. I just wish the parents had more zip. They never flinched when our kids got into a shouting match. They didn't bat an eye when Tom threw one of Tony's socks in the consommé. And you know how Bill belches sometimes when he eats — well, the rest of them sat like statues when he practically blew up after taking a bite of jalapeño pepper by mistake." Renie shook herself. "I babble. What are you doing here? Or should I guess?" She nodded in the direction of the door behind Judith.

"It's been interesting," Judith said, edging around the corner to the hallway, "but I'm pushing my luck. I've been eavesdropping for over five minutes, and the waiters are bound to reappear."

"Care to join us?" Renie asked.

Judith grimaced. "I think I should go home. Mother must be famished. I'll call a cab."

"You don't have to," Renie said, piling linen napkins over her arm. "Bill drove your Subaru to Capri's. Just get the keys from the valet."

"Do I need the parking ticket?" Judith asked.

Renie shook her head as they approached the top of the winding staircase. "Tell them you're Mrs. Jones. And by the way," she said with a quizzical expression, "is there anything I should know about what you discovered while you were lurking outside that door?"

"Not now," Judith said, "but I've got quite a bit of information to sort out. Maybe I'll have made some sense of it by the time I talk to you later this evening."

"Sounds good," Renie said, heading for the private dining room. "Time to rejoin the stuffed animals."

Judith smiled at her cousin. But she was thinking less about the stuffed animals at the Joneses' table than about the wild ones at the Smiths'.

She got as far as a block away from Capri's when she had another, possibly impractical idea. Instead of going up Heraldsgate Hill, she took a left and swung back onto the main thoroughfare through the city. Just before reaching downtown, Judith took another left and pointed the Subaru toward the hospital district. In less than ten minutes, she was in the parking garage of Norway General.

Angela La Belle would no doubt be listed under an assumed name. Judith knew she'd have to think of a really good fib to tell the person behind the reception desk. Her role as Angela's innkeeper probably wouldn't cut any ice with the staff.

Inside the main doors, she checked the directory. Not ICU, Judith figured. Angela had been taken to the hospital several hours ago and was reportedly on the mend. She'd be in a private ward, of course. But under what medical heading? Not yet ready to show her hand, Judith approached the main desk and asked where emergency patients were taken after they were out of danger.

Specialty medicine sounded promising. Judith took an elevator to the seventh floor, then followed the arrows to the nurses' station in the middle of the corridor. A woman wearing a blue hospital smock over a print dress looked up from a patient chart. She wore half glasses on a silver chain and her white hair was in a severe pageboy that accented a hooked nose and prominent chin.

"May I help you?" she asked in a tone that indicated she'd rather stuff her visitor into the recycling bin that sat next to the desk.

Judith froze. The fib she'd been trying to conjure up still hadn't materialized. Briefly, she closed her eyes. Angela's pale face and tall, voluptuous figure floated before her. The well-defined features, the wide shoulders, the above-average height, the dark eyes, the blond hair that was undoubtedly colored by an expensive Beverly Hills stylist . . .

Inspiration struck. There was a physical resemblance as long as no one looked too closely. "I'm here to see my daughter." Judith leaned forward, striking a conspiratorial pose. "I don't know what name she's using, but to her adoring fans, she's . . . Dare I say it?"

"Say what?" the woman snapped.

Judith glanced at the name tag on the blue smock. "Perhaps you aren't aware of her real identity, Wanda. My daughter was brought in today with . . ." She feigned embarrassment. "A drug reaction."

Wanda's expression went from unpleasant to sour. "Oh, yes. One of those." She scowled at Judith, no doubt blaming her for the daughter's decadence. "May I see some ID?"

Momentarily flustered, Judith tried to

come up with another tall tale. "Her father and I," she began, fumbling for her wallet, "were only married for —"

The phone rang on the desk. Wanda held up a hand for Judith to be silent. After tersely answering some questions regarding the status of another patient, the aide hung up.

"Let's see that ID," she ordered. "I don't need your life story."

Judith handed over the wallet with her driver's license. Wanda gave it a piercing look, then nodded. "Miss Flynn is in Room 704, back down the hall and on your left."

With a gulp, Judith nodded and hurried off before Wanda noticed her astonishment at the coincidence.

The door to Room 704 was closed. Judith knocked in a tentative fashion, but when no one responded, she slowly opened the door. Except for the green and red lights on the various monitors, the room was dark.

Nearing the bed, Judith saw that Angela was on her side, turned away from the door. The IVs that trailed from her left hand looked all too familiar.

Judith thought she was asleep. But the actress must have heard someone approach. "What now?" she asked in a disgruntled, if subdued voice.

"It's Judith Flynn."

"Who?" Angela didn't bother to move.

"Judith Flynn, your innkeeper at the B&B. How are you?"

"Awful," Angela replied, still not moving. "What do you want?"

Judith sat down in the molded plastic visitor's chair. "You're my guest. Naturally I'm concerned."

"Bull," Angela muttered. "You're here to pry. Why should you be concerned? Are you afraid I'm going to peg out like Bruno did?"

"Of course not," Judith said a bit testily. "I'm genuinely concerned about your welfare. You gave us an awful scare today." She paused, waiting for a response. There was none, except for a restless flutter of the young woman's hands at the top of the bedsheet. "I also wanted to know," Judith continued, her voice a bit stern, "why you used my name when you checked into the hospital."

"I didn't use it," Angela said querulously. "Dirk checked me in. Or somebody. I was out of it."

"But why Flynn?" Judith persisted.

At last Angela turned to look at her visitor, though the movement made her wince. "Why? Because it's my name, dammit. You don't really think I was born Angela La Belle?"

"Ah . . ." Judith hadn't considered this possibility. "I see. I'm sorry I was impertinent. That is, I didn't mind you using my name, I just thought it was . . . odd."

"It's not odd," Angela insisted, her voice a trifle stronger. "I was born Portulaca Purslane Flynn. My mother was into plants and herbs. Even if I hadn't become an actress, I'd have dumped all three of those names just like my mother dumped me when I was two. Now how about getting out of here? My head hurts like hell."

"Shall I ring for the nurse to bring you more pain medication?" Judith offered.

"Are you kidding? These sadists are afraid I'll get addicted to aspirin."

"I'm sorry, really I am," Judith said. "I was in the hospital last January. I know how difficult the medical profession can be when it comes to administering painkillers."

"Don't be cute," Angela snapped. "You know damned well why they won't give me anything. I'm a coke hound. Now beat it, will you?"

"Of course," Judith said, standing up. "Really, I feel so sorry for you. Is it possible that you could kick the habit if you went into rehab?"

Angela scowled at Judith. "The goody-goody side of the Quick Fix, huh? Easier said than done, Mrs. Flynn." Suddenly her eyes widened. "Where are you from?"

Judith was taken aback. "You mean . . . where was I born?"

"Yes. Where? When?" The queries crackled like scattershot.

"I was born right here," Judith replied, "about two blocks away, in a hospital that's been turned into condos. Why do you ask?"

"Are you sure?"

"Certainly I'm sure," Judith answered, indignant. Then, seeing the disappointment on Angela's face, she understood the reason for the questions. "I'm sorry. I've only had one child, a boy. And I didn't become Mrs. Flynn until ten years ago."

Wearily, Angela turned away. "Never mind. I keep hoping someday I'll find my mother."

Even when she wasn't wanted, Judith was too softhearted to walk away. She remained standing, gazing down at Angela's blond hair and twitching hands.

"Do you want to meet your mother for revenge," Judith asked softly, "or for an explanation?"

Angela didn't respond immediately. Indeed, her whole body convulsed, then went slack. "I know why she gave me away," the actress finally replied, her voice muffled by the pillow. "She never really wanted me. My mother was a free spirit, a big-time flower child. I was just a burden in her personal revolution."

"Your mother sounds selfish and immature," Judith declared. "Who raised you?"

"An aunt in San Bernardino," Angela said. "She meant well, but she had four kids of her own. I was much younger than they were. I was always the outsider." Abruptly, she turned again to face Judith. "This is none of your business. Quit asking so damned many questions."

"I apologize," Judith said. "I can't help myself. I'm interested in people. I care about them."

"You're an oddity, then," Angela said. "Most people only care in terms of what they can get from you. The funny thing is, my mother didn't want anything from me. She didn't want me, period."

"She may be a villain," Judith said quietly, "but she's not the one who hooked you on drugs. Who did?"

Angela gaped at Judith. "What a rotten, snoopy question!"

"No, it isn't," Judith said reasonably. "Addicts have to start somewhere, and usually because someone coaxed or goaded them into it. You don't just walk into the supermarket and get cocaine on Aisle B."

"Why do you care?" Angela's voice was toneless. "It's abnormal."

"I guess," Judith said, "I'm one of those rare people who do care. I must be eccentric. Humor me."

Angela heaved a deep, shuddering sigh. "Why not? It doesn't matter now. It was good old Bruno."

Judith was surprised. "Bruno? Did he do drugs?"

"For years," Angela said, "right up until he overdosed midway through the making of *The Gasman*."

"Is that why he was hospitalized?" Judith asked, remembering Vito's medical notes including the letter C. For cocaine, apparently.

"That's right," Angela said with a bitter note. "It scared him, so he went into rehab. He's been clean ever since. Lucky him."

"Not so lucky since he's dead," Judith remarked. "You say he'd been an addict for years?"

"Yes." Angela looked bitter. "Some people can function forever on coke. Bruno thought so. I did, too. Maybe I still do. As Bruno told me, coke can enhance the creative process. He truly believed it did for him."

Maybe, Judith thought, that explained

The Gasman disaster. "It's more like Russian roulette," she asserted. "Eventually, you're going to reach the chamber that takes you out."

"Sure, sure. Easy for you to say." Angela made a face at her.

"So who got Bruno hooked?" Judith inquired.

Angela shook her head. "You're not going to get me to tell you about that."

"But Bruno's dead," Judith said as she heard the faint sound of the doorknob turning. A nurse no doubt, coming to take the endless vital signs. "What difference does it make?"

"Because the person who got him started is still alive," Angela said. "And if you ask me, very dangerous. You don't want to know."

But Judith did want to know. Despite the odds, even the risks, she had to know.

Yet she could get nothing more out of Angela. And to be fair, the young woman seemed not only agitated, but tired. Judith was heading out of the room when another click sounded at the door. She waited for the person in the corridor to come in.

But no one did, and when she turned the knob she discovered that the door was firmly shut.

Chapter Seventeen

Slowly, she opened the door and peered into the hallway. A pair of orderlies had their heads together by the elevators. Wanda was sitting at the reception desk. A doctor in scrubs was talking to a nurse at the far end of the corridor. None of them seemed interested in Room 704.

But someone was. As she'd turned the knob to open the door a few inches, she'd heard footsteps close by. Not the soft, almost noiseless tread of shoes worn by members of the medical profession, but high heels. *Tap-tap-tap.* They'd stopped abruptly just as Judith had looked into the corridor.

The door on the right of Angela's room was open. Moving as silently as possible, Judith looked inside. It was dark, but she could tell that the single bed was empty. On a whim, she opened the bathroom door and flicked on the light. Nothing. Leaving the light on and the bathroom door open, she went to the closet. Nothing there, either. But just as she was closing the closet door, she heard the *tap-tap-tapping* again. Quickly switching off the bathroom light, she hurried into the corridor. The tableau remained the same, except that the orderlies by the elevators had gone.

Judith walked softly to Room 702, on the other side of Angela's private room. There a light glowed above the bed, where an old man with paper-thin skin breathed with noisy effort. Judith gave up. She couldn't search every room. Besides, she reasoned, the high heels might have belonged to a visitor who had tried to get into the wrong room.

But she didn't quite believe it. Feeling defeated, she headed for the elevators. There was one good thing about her visit, though. As she exited on the main floor, Judith felt a sense of freedom at leaving the hospital under her own power. It hadn't been that way when she exited Good Cheer on a cold day in January. She'd been wheeled out to a cabulance and had spent the following week learning to walk again.

Fifteen minutes later she was back at Hillside Manor. Joe was sitting in the living room, studying Bill's chart.

"Where the hell have you been?" he demanded. "I was about to file a missing-persons report."

Judith explained everything except the hospital visit. She had a question of her own that wouldn't wait. "What about Mother? It's eight o'clock. She must be starving."

"Your mother is fine," Joe replied. "Arlene brought her dinner over a couple of hours ago. It seems that none of the Rankers clan showed up. Arlene was furious — right up until she insisted she hadn't wanted to see any of them in the first place."

"Dear Arlene." Judith sighed, collapsing next to Joe on the sofa. "A sea of contradictions. And a heart as big as Alaska."

"So what good did all your sleuthing at Capri's do for you?" Joe asked, putting Bill's chart aside.

"I'm not sure," Judith said, suddenly hearing her stomach growl. "Goodness, I haven't eaten in hours. What's left from the caterers?"

Joe peered at her. "You look beat. Let me fix you a drink and bring you something to eat. How about Winifred's field greens and Chips's chicken pot pie?"

"Sounds wonderful," Judith said, slipping

out of her shoes as Sweetums crept up to the sofa. "I should see Mother, but I'll wait until I get my second wind."

Joe had gone into the kitchen when the doorbell sounded a minute later. Wearily, Judith trudged to the front door. Eugenia Fleming and Morris Mayne stood on the front porch with three small trick-or-treaters. The youngsters, who had an adult waiting on the sidewalk, chorused their Halloween greeting. Eugenia practically trampled them as she entered the house.

"It's very damp out there," she complained. "Did Vito mention that he and I and Morris are staying in your vacant rooms tonight?"

"I'm . . . not . . . sure," Judith replied, scooping candy bars out of a cut-glass bowl in the entry hall. She stepped aside as Morris barged his way inside. Judith scowled at him, then addressed the children. "Two ghosts and a witch," she said, dropping two chocolate bars into each of the three pillowcases. "Very scary. Don't get a tummy ache."

The children said thank you with varying degrees of confidence, then turned around and ran off to join their adult companion. Judith managed to flag down Eugenia before she reached the second landing of the main staircase.

"Excuse me," Judith said, "but the rooms aren't made up yet. It's been a very busy day. Besides, there's only one vacant room. Bruno's," she added, lowering her voice. "We'll have to see if Ellie or Winifred or Chips or Dade will consent to share a room."

"Chips and Dade wouldn't share a bomb shelter if a nuclear device went off," Eugenia retorted. "You might have better luck with Win and Ellie. Just tell me which room is mine. I need to lie down. I'm quite fatigued."

Judith was forced into a quick decision. "Morris will stay in Room Three. You take Room Six, where Ellie's staying. I'll make it up as soon as I have something to eat."

Eugenia leaned over the banister, her bust looming like two large water balloons. "Now would be preferable."

Judith was about to snap back when Joe appeared in the entry hall bearing a tray with a Scotch rocks, a steaming chicken pot pie, a generous salad, and a hot roll.

"Take a seat, Jude-girl," he said as the doorbell rang again. "Dinner is served."

Judith shot Eugenia a frigid look and returned to the living room. Morris Mayne was reclining on the sofa, his shirt and tie loosened and his suit jacket covering the coffee table.

Joe stared down at the publicist. "Get the door, will you, Morris? And move that jacket. My wife's dinner is going there."

Morris looked affronted. "Pardon? I'm a guest, not a servant."

With a nimble move, Joe lifted one foot, caught the jacket on the toe of his shoe, and dumped it on the floor. "Maybe you didn't hear me. Get that door. If you want to lie down, use the stiff's room. It's behind Door Number Three. Move it. I'm not in one of my good moods."

Morris moved. He scrambled for his jacket, gave Joe a wary glance, and scooted out of the room. Sweetums, who had been napping by the sofa, woke up and chased Morris all the way up the stairs.

Judith beamed at her husband. "I always find it exciting when you play bad cop."

"Maybe we'll both have a chance to get excited when this crew of loonies gets the hell out of here," Joe grumbled. "Now sit and stay. And eat. I'll take care of the trick-or-treaters."

"How many have we had so far?" Judith asked.

"About thirty," Joe replied, heading to answer the doorbell on the second ring.

By the time her husband returned, she'd eaten half of the pot pie with its flaky crust and chunks of tender chicken. "Were they cute?" she asked.

"It was some of the Dooleys," Joe said, referring to their neighbors whose house was across the back fence by the Flynn garage. "I can never tell if it's their kids, grandkids, nieces, nephews, or just some strays they've picked up."

"Darn. I'd like to have seen them," Judith said, tackling the field-green salad.

"You wouldn't have wanted to see some of the bigger ones," Joe said. "About half an hour ago there was a scarecrow and a cowboy who were as tall as I am. I'd swear they were old enough to vote."

"Candy hogs," Judith said with a smile that quickly turned into a frown. "Did you say a scarecrow and a cowboy?"

"Right," Joe responded. "Why do you ask?"

"A *Wizard of Oz* scarecrow? Was the cowboy wearing snakeskin boots?"

"As a matter of fact he was," Joe said.

"They were here last night." Judith took her first sip of Scotch. "Doesn't that seem odd?"

Joe shrugged. "As you said, candy hogs. That's the problem with Halloween falling on a Sunday. It becomes a holiday weekend instead of just one night."

Judith didn't respond. But she was more than curious. She was alarmed.

★ ★ ★

Joe had offered to make up the rooms while Judith finished her meal and put her feet up. He'd just come downstairs when Dirk, Ellie, Chips, and Ben returned to Hillside Manor. With a few succinct words, he explained the new room assignments. Ellie didn't seem pleased.

"Win's such a fussbudget," she said with a scowl. "At least Angela didn't care if my clothes weren't hung perfectly in the closet."

Judith apologized for any inconvenience. "I had no idea that Mr. Patricelli, Mr. Mayne, and Ms. Fleming were all going to stay here tonight instead of at the hotel downtown."

"The Cascadia is in a pickle," Chips Madigan remarked. "We've got about fifty people there who can't leave town, and some tour group is coming in from Japan tonight. They're overbooked."

So, Judith thought, was she. There were other hotels, some high-class motels, and probably even a few B&Bs that were empty on a Sunday night. She had the feeling that it wasn't a lack of vacancies that had brought the trio to Hillside Manor, but Paradox Studios' desire to keep certain persons under Vito's eaglelike eye.

"Is it possible," she inquired, recalling

what she'd overheard the attorney say in the private dining room, "that you'll all be going back to L.A. tomorrow?"

"Maybe," Chips replied.

"Let's hope so," Ben Carmody put in.

"We'd damned well better be out of here by tomorrow," Dirk growled, then turned on his heel and stomped upstairs.

A smiling Ellie watched him disappear. "Goody. Now we can watch Ben's movie on TV." She turned to Judith. "It's okay, isn't it? Chips directed. You might want to see it, Mrs. Flynn. *The Virgin Vessel*. It comes on in five minutes, and it's really creepy. Perfect for Halloween."

Judith vacillated. "I'll watch the first part while I finish my dinner. But then I have some work to do."

Joe volunteered to turn on the set. Ellie assumed her usual perch on the window seat, even though it meant she had to lean a little to see the screen. Chips sprawled on the sofa across from Judith, and Ben settled into one of the big armchairs.

With the screen coming to life, Joe had just put down the remote when there was a knock at the back door. He went out through the French doors and appeared a few seconds later with Renie.

"I'm bored," Renie announced as the

movie's opening credits appeared on the screen. "Bill's exhausted from meeting the future in-laws, so he's going to bed even earlier than usual. I don't feel like reading, and there's nothing on TV," she continued, stopping in the middle of the room and blocking the screen. "Once the baseball season is over, there's not much I want to see on television."

"Keep it down," Ben called out.

"Did you pay for your seat?" Renie sneered.

"Get out of the way," Ellie demanded. "You're blocking the screen."

"Read a book," Renie shot back as she refused to budge. "Improve your mind."

"Coz?" Judith forced a tense smile. "Our guests are actually watching a movie. Or trying to. Would you mind sitting down?" She patted the empty sofa cushion next to her.

"They are?" Renie shrugged. "What movie? There are some of them that I actually like."

"*The Virgin Vessel*," Ellie said, no longer annoyed. "It's really, really scary. We should turn out all the lights."

"Atmosphere!" Chips exclaimed, jumping up and hurrying around the room to turn off the four lamps that were burning. "How's that? Fog outside, witches flying on broomsticks, the whole Halloween scene. Could it be more frightening?"

"I hate frightening movies," Renie declared. "They scare me."

"They're supposed to," Chips replied, resuming his place on the sofa. "It's more thrill than scare when the picture's directed properly."

Judith nudged Renie. "Chips directed this one," she whispered to her cousin.

"Jeez," Renie sighed. "I guess I'll shut up now."

Joe edged past Renie to collect Judith's tray. "There's a preseason NBA game on," he said quietly. "Care to join me upstairs?"

"If this thing gets too gruesome, I might do that," Renie responded.

The movie's opening shot followed a young woman in late-nineteenth-century dress down a dark, winding London street. She was obviously nervous, and stopped periodically to look over her shoulder. As she turned a corner, a light glowed from a narrow timber-fronted building. Expressing relief, she pulled the iron knocker on the door. To the accompaniment of creaking hinges and ominous music, the heavy door opened slowly. The young woman rushed inside. The door slammed shut behind her. Strong, hairy hands swung a big ax. She screamed in terror. The hands and the ax came down again and again as blood spurted, presumably from her unseen body.

"That's it," Renie said, getting up. "I'm going to check out the basketball game. If I wanted brutality, I'd watch hockey."

Judith didn't much blame her cousin but felt obligated to watch at least the first fifteen minutes of the movie. The scene changed to what appeared to be an interior of Scotland Yard. The policemen were discussing the crime spree that had been taking place in London's East End. They shook their heads a great deal and muttered "Baffling" several times.

"Wow!" Ellie enthused. "This is sooo good. Watch, Mrs. Flynn, Ben's coming up in the next scene."

Sure enough, Ben Carmody, dressed in the garb of a nineteenth-century gentleman, sauntered up the same street where the young woman had presumably been murdered. It was daylight, and Ben carried a cane. He stopped in front of the building where the ax-wielding maniac had done his dirty deed. Ben looked up to the second story. Then, as a stout woman carrying a wicker basket entered the street, he turned and disappeared around a corner. Judith suddenly realized she'd seen this before.

"Excuse me," she said, getting up. "It's after nine, and I'm going to take our jack-o'-lanterns in. The trick-or-treaters should all be home by now."

As far as Judith could determine, the fog-filled cul-de-sac was empty. Taking the trio of pumpkins inside, she found Renie in the kitchen.

"I thought you were going to watch the game with Joe," she said, placing the pumpkins on the counter.

"I'm stealing a Pepsi first," Renie said, opening the refrigerator. "Did you get scared, too?"

"Sort of," Judith admitted. "But I think I've seen that movie before, though I can't imagine why. Joe and I don't like horror films, either."

"Maybe you saw a preview," Renie suggested, opening a can of Pepsi.

"Maybe." Judith paced a bit. "That must be it. I certainly can't remember anything else about *The Virgin Vessel*. But the scene with Ben Carmody looked very familiar." She went to the sink and stared out the kitchen window. Suddenly something clicked in her brain. "Coz!" she cried, whirling around to face Renie. "Do you remember that man I saw a couple of months ago between our house and the Rankerses' hedge?"

"What man?" Renie looked blank. "I don't think you mentioned it to me."

"Maybe I didn't," Judith allowed. "It was after Labor Day, when Skjoval Tolvang was working on the house and the toolshed. Mr. Tolvang saw him first. He thought the man was a city inspector."

"Did you see this guy up close?" Renie asked.

"Fairly close," Judith replied, pacing a little faster. "He had a beard and glasses. He said he was looking for a Mr. . . . . I forget, it was an odd name. Anyway, he hurried off after that."

"Okay," Renie said. "And your point is . . . ?"

"My point," Judith said slowly, "is that the man I saw outside the house may have been Ben Carmody."

Renie thought Judith was imagining things, and said so. "Why on earth would you think that?"

"Because of his height and build," Judith said. "At the time he reminded me of someone. I've seen Ben in a couple of movies, and one of them was a costume picture from the same era as *The Virgin Vessel*."

"It's a stretch." Renie yawned. "Why would Ben Carmody be hanging around outside Hillside Manor in September?"

"That's what I'd like to know," Judith said, reverting to her old habit of chewing on a fingernail.

"Why indeed?" Renie said as they heard the front door open. "I doubt that Ben did any such thing."

Judith didn't respond, but went into the dining room to see who had arrived. It was Vito and Winifred. He seemed fresh and vigorous; she appeared weary and anxious. Judith informed Vito that he'd be staying in Room Three.

"Bruno's room," Vito said solemnly. "It's an honor."

"You may find Morris Mayne already there," Judith said. "Would you mind asking him to move to Room Five with Chips?"

The attorney informed Judith that he'd gladly pass on the request. "I appreciate getting the larger room," he said. "I have some work to do."

Winifred, however, wasn't pleased to hear that she would have to share her room with Ellie. "Why couldn't Ellie and Eugenia share Room Six?"

"Because," Judith said, clearing her throat, "you and Ellie are quite slim. Eugenia is not. Both your room and Room Six, where Ellie's been staying, have double beds."

Flattery didn't have any effect on Winifred, who remained glum but didn't argue further. Maybe, Judith thought, that was because Eugenia had admitted that she and Winifred weren't on good terms. Whatever the reason, Winifred immediately went upstairs while Vito peered into the darkened living room.

"What's going on?" Seeing the movie on TV, he didn't wait for an answer. "Ah — *The Virgin Vessel*. The role that made Ben famous. It was Chips's first attempt at directing. He was superb." Without waiting for a response from Judith, Vito slipped gracefully into the living room just as a willowy blonde met her fate at the hands of Mr. Ax.

Judith was still shuddering when she returned to the kitchen. "Let's go upstairs so we can talk privately," she said to Renie, who had fixed herself some cheese and crackers. "I can still hear the screams from the TV."

"You want to watch the NBA's preseason?" Renie inquired, getting up from the table with her snacks.

"Not really," Judith said. "We can go in Joe's office."

The cousins ascended the back stairs, then entered the door that led up to the family quarters. Judith sat down in Joe's swivel chair and placed her unfinished Scotch on the desk.

"Okay, so fill me in," Renie said, seating herself in the rocking chair that Joe used to relax his back.

Judith complied, and it took almost fifteen minutes. Renie made only the briefest of comments until her cousin had finished.

"You've got a lot of fragmentary information there," Renie pointed out. "Let's start with A for Angela. She's a coke addict who got started by Bruno. He went to rehab and it apparently worked. She's still hooked. Is that a motive for murder?"

"I doubt it," Judith said, hearing the wind pick up outside. "But her most recent movie with Bruno turned out to be a bomb, and Ellie was to have starred in the next one. That might be more of a motive than mere drug addiction."

"Revenge," Renie murmured. "What does Bill's chart say about that?"

Joe had fortuitously brought the chart up to the office before any of the guests could see it. "I don't think Bill got to revenge," Judith said, spreading the chart out on the desk. "Wait — he did. Bill and Joe must have worked on this while we were gone. Angela, Dirk, Ben, Dade, and Chips all have mauve marks, which stand for revenge."

"They're all associated with the Big Flop," Renie remarked. "But murder doesn't seem like the right way to rectify a career stumble. I can't imagine that any of those celebrities won't bounce back."

Judith studied the chart for several moments. "It's got to be something personal. It almost always is."

"You ought to know," Renie said with a grin. "I see Bill's keyed in jealousy, but he's marked it only for Angela and Ellie, with a slash for professional rivalry."

Judith shook her head. "Why would either of them kill Bruno?"

"Didn't you say you overheard something about Ellie's next movie not being made now that Bruno's dead?"

"That's my point," Judith replied. "Bruno was worth far more to Ellie alive than dead. Let's face it, the only person in the entourage who got violent with Bruno was Dirk Farrar. They had that big fight in Marina Del Rey. Which signifies to me that Dirk wouldn't hesitate to duke it out in a disagreement, but he's not the homicidal type. If he killed someone, it would be in a burst of temper with his bare hands."

"You're ruling out Dirk banging Bruno in the head with the cupboard door and shoving him in the sink?"

"There would have had to be an argument first," Judith asserted. "Dirk's very loud. Joe or I would have heard the two men quarreling, even from the basement."

Renie didn't say anything for a few moments. "You're convinced this wasn't an accident?"

Judith grimaced. "I'm not going down without a fight to prove otherwise."

"I don't blame you," Renie said. "The problem is, we don't seem to be getting anywhere. We don't even know who all the guests were last night."

Judith gave Renie a puzzled look. "Yes, we do. Except for Vito, the ones who came back here after the premiere are the same people who attended the midnight supper."

"So where's Mrs. Mayne?" Renie queried.

"The one dressed as a pioneer woman?" Judith shrugged. "I assume she's still at the Cascadia. Morris told me she wasn't much of a traveler. She probably didn't want to make another move."

"Let's find out." Renie reached across Judith to pick up the phone on Joe's desk. "If she'd dug in at the hotel, you'd think Morris would have stayed with her." A moment later she was asking for Mrs. Mayne. "That's Mrs. Morris Mayne," she said. "She and her husband checked in either Friday or Saturday."

378

There was a long silence from Renie. "Oh. Really? Well, thanks all the same." She replaced the phone and stared at Judith. "Mrs. Mayne checked out at noon."

Chapter Eighteen

"I don't get it," Judith said, stopping herself from gnawing on another nail. "Why would Mrs. Mayne be allowed to leave town when the rest of them weren't?"

"Maybe because she's not in the movie business," Renie suggested. "Maybe there was a family emergency in California."

Judith nodded absently. "Maybe she was never here."

Renie looked startled. "What?"

"I mean," Judith explained, "here in this house. We only assumed that the pioneer woman was Mrs. Mayne. Do you remember what she looked like?"

Renie hunched her shoulders. "No. She was wearing a big floppy bonnet. I don't think I ever saw her face."

Judith got up from the swivel chair. "Let's find out. We'll ask Winifred. She's still in

Room One, sharing it with Ellie."

But Winifred wasn't in Room One. As the cousins reached the second floor, they could hear her raised voice coming from Room Six. They could also hear Eugenia's bellow.

"Now what?" Renie said as they edged closer to the angry voices.

Signaling for Renie to be quiet, Judith pricked up her ears. The cousins stood at the door to Room Six like a pair of sentries.

". . . more harm than good," Eugenia shouted.

"That's not true!" Winifred rejoined. "It was Morris more than you!"

"Oh," Eugenia responded, her voice dropping a notch, "it was Bruno. It was always Bruno. But why was he killed?"

"Who says he was?" Winifred retorted. "I thought it was an accident."

"Nonsense," Eugenia snapped as Judith gave Renie a thumbs-up sign. "Think about it. How could anyone hit a cupboard door or get hit by it hard enough to knock themselves out? And even if they did, wouldn't falling in a sink filled with water snap them back into consciousness? Why do you think the studio has insisted we stay in this stupid town? Because they're doing their own investigating, that's why."

"I don't agree with you," Winifred huffed.

"If they're investigating, why haven't we seen any detectives around here?"

"We haven't been here all the time," Eugenia said in a reasonable voice, which still carried as if she were speaking into a bullhorn. "The investigators may be working with the local police. Or maybe they're arriving tomorrow."

"Vito said we could leave tomorrow," Winifred said, sounding sullen.

"Vito said maybe," Eugenia responded. "Let's stop wrangling. I'd like to retire for the night in peace."

"Until you got here," Winifred complained, "*I* could retire in peace. Now I have to share my room with that little twit Ellie."

"Ellie's simply immature. And spoiled, but she has talent," Eugenia pointed out. "She's limited, of course."

"You mean because of her race?" There was steel in Winifred's voice.

"No," Eugenia replied, "I'm referring to her acting range. And her looks, which have nothing to do with the fact that she's half Chinese."

"You meant race," Winifred accused. "It always comes down to race, doesn't it?"

"For you, apparently," Eugenia snapped. "I often find that different-colored skin is also very thin."

Judith and Renie exchanged pained expressions.

"That's not true!" Winifred cried. "But can you argue that Hollywood has always been fair to minorities?"

"Certainly not," Eugenia said in a self-righteous tone. "But look at you. You've managed to claw your way up to the top. Of course some would say you used more than your brains to get there. I wouldn't use *Winifred Best* and *ethics* in the same sentence."

"Ethics? What have ethics got to do with this business?" Winifred demanded.

"You know perfectly well what I mean," Eugenia asserted. "A certain lack of ethics is one thing, but criminal means are —"

"Ladies!" a masculine voice cut in. "Please! I can't stand any more of this quarreling. I'm trying to rest."

Renie mouthed "Morris?" at Judith, who nodded. "He's in Room Five," she whispered. "He's sharing with Chips. The bathroom connects between Five and Six, remember?"

"This whole situation is intolerable," Winifred declared. "Do you both realize that all three of us are out of a job?"

"No, we're not," Morris replied. "I work for the studio as well as for Bruno. Eugenia has other clients. As for you, Win, someone will have to stay at the helm of Bruno's production company at least for a while. Who knows? His children may want to keep the company going."

"No, they won't," Winifred asserted. "I know them. They're utterly irresponsible. They couldn't run a convenience store."

"Win's right," Eugenia conceded. "Besides, there's the problem of bailing out *The Gasman*. It may prove very complicated, not to mention the harm done to Bruno's reputation."

A door opened in the corridor. Judith and Renie both jumped as they turned around to see who had caught them eavesdropping.

It was Joe, coming from the family quarters. "Jeez," he said in a low but vexed voice, "could you be more obvious?"

Judith gave her husband a sheepish look. "Okay, we're done here anyway. But this is how we sleuth."

"Unprofessional," Joe murmured, heading for the back stairs. "I'm going to lock up for the night. It's ten o'clock straight up."

Judith glanced at her watch as the cousins followed Joe downstairs. "You're right. I suppose they're still watching the movie in the living room."

"I suppose," Joe said. "It was scheduled to run until eleven."

"I should go home," Renie declared as they reached the main floor.

"Don't," Judith urged as she saw the computer printouts on the kitchen counter. "We never had a chance to go over the material you found on *The Gasman* and its origins."

"Oh. Well . . . sure." Renie began sorting the pages as Joe headed for the front door to lock up.

A terrified scream erupted from that vicinity, causing Renie to drop several sheets on the floor. But the exclamation of "Wow!" followed by "Way cool, Ben!" from Ellie and a couple of masculine chuckles indicated that the scream had come from another hapless movie victim.

Judith heard Joe say something to the guests that she couldn't quite make out. A moment later he was back in the kitchen. "Everybody's here except Dade," he said. "He has a key, right?"

"He should," Judith said. "That's odd. Has he been back since they all left Capri's?"

"Chips said he hasn't," Joe replied, removing a can of beer from the fridge. "Dade arrived here with some of the others, but never came in the house."

"Typical," Judith remarked, "though why

he'd want to walk around on such a foggy, windy night is beyond me."

"The wind's blowing the fog away," Joe said, then yawned. "I'm going to watch *Sports Center* and head for bed. It's been a long day. In fact, it's been a long weekend." He kissed Judith, gave Renie a hug, and headed back upstairs.

"I'm organized," Renie announced. "I've skimmed some of this stuff, especially Bruno's filmmaker's approach to the narrative. Naturally, he sounds like a genius."

The cousins sat down at the kitchen table. More screams could be heard from the living room. "Wouldn't you think they must have killed off most of the cast by now?" Judith murmured.

"We wish," Renie remarked, underlining points of interest with a red pen. "Dade should be writing a movie about what happened after this crew arrived at the B&B. Who needs spooky London streets or the human race's time line?" She paused, shuffling some papers. "Okay, here's some information on C. Douglas Carp."

"Crappy Pappy Carp," Judith said suddenly. "That's what Dirk Farrar called him."

"You can call him Pappy, you can call him Crappy, you can even call him Sappy," Renie said, handing two pages of underlined information to Judith, "but don't call him Slaphappy. Carp was a diligent scholar of some repute. He wrote *The Gasman* when he was twenty-two."

"Goodness," Judith responded. "That's impressive."

"It may account for why my father read the damned thing," Renie noted. "Dad was probably swayed by Carp's credentials." She flipped through a few more pages. "This is what I found on Carp himself. I haven't read it yet. Shall I read to you?"

"You can also carry me up to bed and tuck me in." Judith sighed. "I'm not sure I can get up those two flights of stairs again."

Renie offered her cousin a sympathetic smile. "You should put an elevator in this place. And not for the guests." She cleared her throat and adjusted her much-abused glasses. *"Carson Douglas Carp was born in Cedar Falls, Iowa, in 1907, the son of Louis Franklin Carp and Annabelle Ernestine Carp (née Morgan). An outstanding student, Carp began his epic novel of civilization,* The Gasman, *while still attending Northern Iowa State Teachers College. While Carp's fictional style has been criticized by some as tedious, pedantic, and maladroit, his meticulous attention to historical detail and his accuracy have merited praise from others. Although the novel never sold well except to libraries, his next work, a nonfiction treatise on the Dahlak Archipelago, was eagerly awaited by scholars. Unfortunately, Carp suffered from severe alcoholism, and died at the age of thirty-eight, leaving the two-hundred-thousand-word tome unfinished. His son, William Euclid Carp, and his daughter, Marguerite Louisa Carp, attempted to find a publisher for the work in the mid-1960s, but without success.*"

"No kidding," Judith said. "Where's the Dahlak Archipelago?"

Renie shrugged. "Wherever it is, I doubt that it's a major book market."

"Pappy," Judith said thoughtfully. "Whose Pappy?"

"You mean in reference to the guests?"

"Yes. Nobody would call someone Pappy — especially a man who died quite young — unless he was their father or the father of someone they knew."

Renie rested her chin on her fist. "I'm not sure why it matters. Aren't you grasping at straws?"

"Of course I am," Judith said testily. "I'm desperate."

"Okay." Renie's tone was unusually agreeable. "Pappy Carp is dead. He died in 1945 or thereabouts, right? Which means that if any of these people are his offspring, it has to be someone over fifty. Bruno's out — his father was a German war groom. Dade, Chips, Ben, Dirk, and Angela are too young. Did you say Angela's real last name is Flynn?"

"I did. It is." Judith was still a bit testy.

"Rule Ellie out because her father is alive and hustling hot dogs," Renie said. "That leaves Eugenia, Morris, and . . . Vito?"

"Vito wasn't here for the postpremiere supper," Judith pointed out.

"Are you sure?"

Judith gave Renie a peculiar look. "What do you mean?"

"How do you know that someone didn't change costumes? Or that there weren't two Arabian sheikhs or a pair of matching Gutenbergs?" Renie demanded.

Judith considered the idea. "But never in the same room at the same time," she murmured. "It's a thought. There's another thing we might have overlooked — Chips is from the Midwest."

"Even if he appears younger than he really is," Renie noted, "he couldn't be over fifty."

"Grandson, maybe?" Judith suggested.

"Oh." Renie got up from the chair at the counter and went to the refrigerator to claim another Pepsi. "That could be. On the other hand, Chips often talks about his mother, but not his father. I wonder why?"

She paused, then shook her head. "It can't be Chips. What's the motive?"

Judith gave Renie a helpless look. "I've no idea. Unless the novel was written by Chips's father — big stretch, I know — or grandfather, and Bruno stole it. Remember, I told you that the book had keepsakes in it. Obviously, it had been treasured by someone for many years." She suddenly jumped up. "Keepsakes! What's wrong with me? Where did I put that book?" Frantically, she looked around the kitchen as the wind rattled the windows.

"Ah!" she exclaimed, snapping her fingers. "I didn't put it anywhere. Joe brought it down from Room Three." Cautiously bending down to favor her artificial hip, Judith opened the bottom cabinet drawer next to the wall. "Here it is. Let's see if we can learn anything from these keepsakes."

Renie wore a resigned expression but said nothing. The cousins had just sat down at the counter again when Sweetums sidled up to Judith. He had a partially eaten chicken breast in his mouth, which he began to wrestle around the kitchen floor.

Judith scowled at the cat. "Where did you get that? Here, let me have it."

Sweetums wasn't in the mood to oblige. He backed away, with the chicken still in his teeth. Judith chased him into the pantry, where he got under the lowest shelf, just out of reach. In recent months, Sweetums had figured out that his human was limited in her capacity for capturing him.

"Damn!" she cried as she heard the cat chewing lustily on the chicken. "He must have gotten that out of the garbage. I'd better make sure the can didn't blow over." Grabbing her jacket from its customary peg, she headed outside.

Driven by the wind, the fog swirled around the backyard like smoke from a beach fire. The light in the toolshed appeared and disappeared as if it were coming from a lighthouse. Gertrude kept late hours, requiring less sleep as she got older. Of course, Judith thought as she hurried to the garbage cans and recycling bins by the side of the house, her mother dozed off frequently during the day.

The big green bins were intact, but one of the garbage cans had blown over, spilling half its contents. From inside the house, she could hear more screams emanating from the TV. The terrified cries set her teeth on edge. She was beginning to wonder if the events of the past two days and her fears for the future were triggering an emotional collapse.

As Judith set the can upright, a loud

banging noise behind her made her jump. Peering through the eddies of mist, she saw nothing. Gingerly, she began putting the garbage back into the can.

She was about to replace the lid when something brushed against her leg. Judith let out a small squeal, then looked down to see Sweetums depositing bare chicken bones on her shoe.

"Nasty!" she exclaimed under her breath. "If my nerves weren't going to pieces, I'd pull your tail."

Sweetums responded with a growl, then trotted off down the driveway. Judith started back to the porch, but decided to make a quick visit to her mother. She felt guilty for hardly seeing Gertrude all day. As she headed down the walk to the toolshed, the wind rattled her nerves along with the Rankerses' wind chimes. The usual gentle tinkling sounded more like an out-of-tune brass band.

But the fog was definitely dissipating. She could see the toolshed clearly, though the lights had now gone out. Judith stopped, debating whether or not to bother her mother. She decided against it. Gertrude would only berate her for being neglectful. Judith didn't need any more problems on this particular All Hallows' Eve.

She'd started up the back-porch steps when she heard another clatter nearby. It sounded like another garbage-can lid. More annoyed than nervous, she trudged around to the side of the house.

Within a foot of the cans, Judith stopped dead in her tracks. There, down the driveway in a maelstrom of fog, an unearthly creature seemed to levitate before her eyes. She suppressed a scream as her legs wobbled and her eyes grew huge. The pointy hat, the stiff shaggy hair, the windblown garments, and the shoes with the turned-up toes almost convinced her that witches did indeed fly the skies on Halloween.

The image was enhanced when a cat with its fur standing on end suddenly appeared out of the mists. The animal hurtled straight for Judith. In fright, she flung herself against the wall of the house, and only recognized Sweetums when he hid himself between her feet.

"P-p-poor k-k-kitty," she stammered, glancing down at the cat. "P-p-poor m-m-me."

Then she looked up, and the eerie apparition was gone.

A frowning Renie was standing on the steps. "Where've you been? The back door blew shut, and I thought maybe you got locked out." Seeing Judith's pale face under the porch light, she gasped. "Hey, what's wrong? You look like you've seen a ghost!"

"A witch, actually," Judith said, clinging to the porch rail as Sweetums crept along beside her. She felt dizzy, her teeth were chattering, and her feet seemed glued to the steps. "I may be having a nervous break-down. I need a drink."

"I'll fix it," Renie volunteered, but first put a hand under Judith's elbow. "You are a mess. Easy does it." Carefully, she guided her cousin through the back door.

"How does Bill describe his patients who've gone mad?" Judith asked, slumping into the nearest kitchen chair.

"Clinically?" Renie responded, going to the cupboard where the liquor was kept.

With vacant eyes and mouth agape, Judith nodded.

"Crazy as a loon," Renie replied, pouring her cousin's drink. "Tell me about the witch."

It took Judith two big sips just to get started. She scowled at the glass before she spoke. "I'm not only insane, I'm turning into a drunk."

"Hardly," Renie said. "You've been through a lot the last few days."

"So I have." Judith sighed, beginning to pull herself together. "But I'm not seeing things. I don't think." She proceeded to tell Renie about the apparition in the driveway.

"A witch?" Renie said when Judith had finished the horror story. "Maybe it was. It's Halloween."

"At this hour?" Judith glanced up at the schoolhouse clock, which showed eleven on the dot. As if to underscore the time, applause and cheers could be heard coming from the living room. "Then why didn't whoever it was come to the door?" Judith asked, clutching her drink as if it were a talisman against evil.

"Maybe the witch went to the toolshed," Renie replied. "Your mother was probably still up, and with the TV on and the lights out in the front of the house, whoever it was may have thought everybody had gone to bed."

"That's possible," Judith allowed, then gave her cousin a piercing look. "You don't believe that. You're just trying to make me feel better."

Renie winced. "Well — I'd like to make you feel better. Frankly, you look like bird poop."

"Thanks. I feel like bird poop."

"I'd better go home," Renie said as the

movie watchers broke up and headed for bed. "Is there anything I can do before I leave?"

Judith slumped farther into the chair. "We still don't know who Crappy Pappy is."

"Does it matter?" Renie asked gently as she stood up.

"No." Judith's voice was lifeless. "Nothing does."

"Coz!" Renie gave Judith a sharp slap on the back, then let out a little yip. "I keep forgetting, I'm supposed to favor that arm and shoulder for a while longer."

Judith looked up. "Are you okay?"

Cringing a bit, Renie moved her right arm this way and that. "I think so." She sat down across from Judith. "Maybe I should wait a couple of minutes. I only started driving again in July. Even though the surgeon assured me I couldn't dislocate it again, I don't want to take a chance and wreck the car."

"Don't mention dislocating our body parts," Judith said, though there was evident relief in her voice. She hadn't wanted Renie to leave just yet. "I worry about my hip all the time. Unlike your shoulder, there are certain things I can't do because it'll dislocate. I suppose that's next — more major surgery."

"Oh, coz!" Renie shook her head. "Don't fuss so. You'll only —"

A banging at the front door startled both cousins. "The witch?" Judith gasped.

"Dubious. Stay here, I'll get it."

"No," Judith said, already on her feet. "Rest your shoulder."

With considerable trepidation, she went through the dining room and the entry hall. Except for the small Tiffany-style lamp on the table by the stairs, the rest of the house was dark.

"Who is it?" Judith called through the door.

"Me," came the voice on the other side. "Dade. Dade Costello."

"Oh!" Relieved, Judith hurriedly unlocked the door. "Come in. I thought you had your key."

"I did," Dade said, rubbing at the back of his head. "I guess I lost it."

"Oh, dear," Judith sighed. "Do you think it's in your room? When did you use it last?"

Dade shrugged. "I don't know that I've used it at all. Or did I?"

Judith couldn't remember, either. But she didn't want a key to Hillside Manor in the wrong hands. Disconcerted by the latest calamity, she said the first thing that came into her head: "Wasn't it kind of miserable for a walk this evening?"

"I didn't walk that much," Dade said in his soft Southern drawl as he started for the stairs.

The response further muddled Judith. "Wait," she called after the screenwriter. "Do you have your room key or was it with the one to the house?" Guests were always given the two keys on a simple ring with their room number taped on the room key.

"Let me see." Dade rummaged in the pockets of his cargo pants. "Here," he said, holding up a single key. "It says Room Two. That's me."

"Yes," Judith answered. "But you're sure you don't have the house key lying loose in your pockets?"

"I already checked." He shrugged again. "Sorry." Once more, Dade started up the stairs.

"One other thing," Judith said, standing by the banister. "Who was C. Douglas Carp related to?"

He paused, frowning. "Hunh. I think Carp was some relation of Bruno's."

"Are you sure?" she pressed.

"Well . . ." Dade looked up into the stairwell. "Carp was his father-in-law at one time. Yes." He nodded to himself. "Bruno was married to somebody whose maiden name was Carp. C. Douglas must have been her daddy.

Bruno always referred to him as Pappy."

"The father of which wife?" Judith hoped she didn't sound eager.

Again, Dade looked puzzled. "It wasn't the second wife," he said slowly. "I met her at the Cannes Film Festival a couple of years ago."

"That was the actress?" Judith prompted.

"Right. Taryn, Taryn McGuire. But she doesn't act anymore. She's married to an oil sheikh. They brought their yacht to Cannes to attend all the parties."

"What about the first and third wives?" Judith persisted. "Did you meet either of them? Wasn't the third wife in the movie business?"

"Right," Dade said. "She was a film editor or something. I never met her. I think her name was Mary Ellen."

"But you don't know if her maiden name was Carp?"

"I've no idea." Dade looked apologetic.

"I assume you never met wife number one," Judith said. "I understand that was a youthful marriage."

"Way before my time," Dade said, still leaning on the banister. "She was the one Bruno rarely talked about. When he did, he was critical. I'll say this for him — he never bad-mouthed the other two wives."

"Why was he so hard on the first one?"

Dade grimaced. "I guess she was kind of a terror. I recall Bruno saying he ran into her someplace where he least expected. He always called her Spider Woman."

Judith stared up at him. "Did that have something to do with his superstition about spiders?"

"I don't think so." Dade yawned. "Sorry, Ms. Flynn, I'm beat. I'm afraid I haven't been much help." Once more, he started up the stairs, but this time he was the one to stop his own momentum. "Why do you need to know about Bruno's wives?"

Judith offered him an uncertain smile. "I'm just curious. You know — when someone dies under your roof and all . . ." She let the sentence trail away.

"Oh. That makes sense. I guess." At last he continued on up the stairs and out of sight.

Wearily, Judith trudged back to the kitchen. Renie was wearing her suede jacket and holding her huge handbag.

"What was that all about?" she asked.

"Dade Costello. He lost his house key." Judith made a face. "But guess what? Bruno referred to his first wife as Spider Woman."

Renie looked surprised. "Really? Who was she?"

"Dade doesn't know," Judith said, espying *The Gasman* novel on the counter. "Did you find any of the keepsakes interesting?"

Renie started ticking off items on her fingers. "The usual pressed flowers and leaves, a faded red ribbon, a pair of ticket stubs from the 1968 World Series between St. Louis and Detroit, another pair of stubs from the 1975 Iowa State Fair, a lock of what looked like baby's hair, a young woman's photo, a newspaper clipping of C. Douglas Carp's obituary, and a recipe for prune pie."

Judith looked thoughtful. "Let's see the obit."

Renie flipped through the book, then handed her the yellowed clipping.

"Hmm," Judith said. "Nothing here that wasn't in the other account of his life and times. By the way, did you come across a picture of a young woman?"

Renie flipped through the pages. "Yes, here it is. Anybody we know?"

Judith studied the youthful face with the innocent expression. "I don't think so. And yet . . ." She held the photo out for Renie's perusal. "There is something familiar about her. Or maybe I'm imagining things. Do you recognize this face?"

But Renie didn't. "Why," she inquired in a wistful voice, "are you fixated on Mr. Carp?"

"Because," Judith replied in a peevish

tone, "I don't know where to go with this damned mess. I still think the motive for this crime — if it was a crime — is personal. I don't believe that anybody under this roof killed Bruno for professional reasons. Somebody has a secret that was worth committing murder for, or somebody just plain hated Bruno."

Renie set her handbag down on the floor and leaned against the counter. "As in hated him for personal reasons?"

Judith nodded. "Exactly."

"A woman scorned?" Renie suggested.

"Possibly."

"Which woman? Wives one through three, or someone who wanted to be number four?"

Judith sighed along with the wind, which was now a dull moan. "It's possible. We know nothing about the personal lives of Eugenia Fleming or Winifred Best."

"Eugenia?" Renie wrinkled her pug nose. "Hardly the type you'd expect a bigwig producer to marry."

"We might say Eugenia isn't the right type," Judith pointed out, "but that doesn't mean Eugenia would agree."

"Winifred?"

"She's been a wife, in a way," Judith said. "Women who work closely with men are like wives."

"True," Renie said. "I've seen it in the corporate world. The business partner, the executive secretary, the special assistant. It's not usually a sexual relationship, but sometimes it is. And of course one of the parties may suffer from unrequited love."

"I think we can scratch Ellie and Angela," Judith mused. "They owe their careers to him in some way — despite the Big Flop — but I can't picture either of them panting with desire for Bruno."

"Power's a great aphrodisiac, though," Renie noted. "Still . . ." She gave a shake of her head.

"We're on the wrong track there," Judith said. "We're back to professional motives. I wish we knew why Winifred is so reluctant to talk about her brief career as a singer."

"Because it was so brief?" Renie offered.

"I think it's more than that," Judith said. "I think that the brevity of her musical career could be a secret worth keeping."

Renie didn't bother to stifle a big yawn. "I've got to head home. The fog's just about gone and the wind's dying down. If I had to, I could drive with my feet."

"That might be an improvement," Judith murmured. "Sometimes you're not so hot at using your hands."

"Funny, coz," Renie said sarcastically.

"Talk to you in the morning."

As Renie left via the back door, Judith glanced at the schoolhouse clock. It was almost midnight, the witching hour on Halloween.

Maybe she wasn't losing her mind. Maybe she wasn't even losing her nerve.

But she still believed she could be losing Hillside Manor.

Chapter Nineteen

"The airport's still closed," Joe announced as he brought in the morning paper. "That's bad news."

"I didn't know it was closed," Judith responded with a frosty look.

"It's the fog," Joe said. "Haven't you noticed it settled in again during the night?"

"I haven't had time to notice anything," Judith retorted. "I've been too busy figuring out what to serve our unwanted guests for breakfast."

Joe rested his chin on her shoulder. "Need some help?"

Judith jerked away from her husband. "Help? Like what, plugging in the coffeemaker? I already did that."

"Hey!" Joe sounded offended. "What's wrong?"

She whirled on him. "What's wrong?

Are you kidding?"

Joe held up his hands in a defensive gesture. "Take it easy, Jude-girl. I know you're upset, but this morning I'm going to call Dilys at headquarters and find out what she's —"

"Dilys!" Judith exploded. "Where's she been since Saturday night? Sunbathing? And what have you been doing except studying Bill's stupid chart?"

"That chart's not a bad idea," Joe said, still relatively calm. "Woody and I used to put together something like —"

"Woody!" Judith cried in exasperation. "I thought he was helping you. Has he been kidnapped by Gypsies or did the floating bridge between here and the Eastside sink again?"

Joe threw up his hands. "Okay, okay! Don't knock Woody. He's been running background checks on these goofballs all weekend. I expect to hear from him soon."

"And he won't have one single thing that will help us," Judith declared, dumping two pounds of bacon into a skillet. "Toast." She bit off the word. "That's it, toast, bacon, and scrambled eggs. They can take their weird food cravings someplace else if they don't like it."

"Hey, has Woody ever failed when it

comes to being helpful?" Joe asked, getting two dozen eggs out of the fridge. Judith started to grab them from him, but he pulled the cartons out of her reach. "I'll fix these. I do a better job of it."

Judith refused to acknowledge that Joe definitely had a way with eggs. "I'm not criticizing Woody per se," she asserted. "I meant that any information he comes up with — and I'll bet there won't be much — isn't going to help us in this particular instance."

"You don't know that," Joe countered. "I don't see why you won't sit back and let the police and the studio's investigators figure out what happened. They're pros."

"You used to be a pro," Judith shot back. "I thought you still were with your private detective jobs. But you don't seem very involved in this whole, horrible situation."

"That's because I'm retired from the force," Joe said with obvious resentment. "I don't have the resources anymore. Once you've been a cop, you realize that most of the time law enforcement personnel know what they're doing."

Judith didn't respond, but gave him a skeptical look. Maybe he was right. Maybe he didn't have faith in his ability to work without the backup provided by a full-fledged police staff. Maybe, she thought with a pang, he didn't care about Hillside Manor as much as she did. It was even possible that in retirement, he disliked the constant parade of strangers going in and out of his home.

The phone rang as Joe was whisking eggs, green onions, and slivers of red pepper in a big blue bowl. Judith answered, and somewhat sheepishly wished Woody Price good morning. Without looking at Joe, she handed over the receiver.

"Good morning!" Eugenia Fleming's booming voice and majestic presence filled the kitchen.

Judith pointed to Joe, who had put one finger in his ear. He immediately began moving down the hall and out of hearing range.

"Sorry," the agent apologized, speaking with less volume. She was already dressed, wearing a tailored pants suit with a no-nonsense silk shirt.

"You're up early," Judith remarked, trying to be polite. "I usually don't serve breakfast until eight."

Eugenia checked her watch against the schoolhouse clock. "Seven-forty on the dot. I'm a morning person, which can be a disadvantage in Hollywood. Except for people who are actually involved in shooting a film, everyone else tends to work late into the night."

"The coffee's ready," Judith said. "Would you like a cup?"

"Certainly," Eugenia replied, surveying the kitchen with a critical eye. "Black, please."

Judith poured the coffee into a Moonbeam's mug and handed it to her guest. "I'm curious," she said in a casual tone. "Why was Morris Mayne's wife allowed to go back to L.A. when the rest of you weren't?"

Eugenia choked on her first swallow of coffee. "Well . . ." she began, gathering her aplomb, "that situation was different."

"Oh?"

"Yes." Eugenia cleared her throat. "Different." She winked.

Judith gave the other woman a quizzical look. "I don't understand."

"You don't need to." Eugenia winked again.

Enlightenment dawned. "You mean," Judith said, "Morris came here with someone who wasn't his wife?"

"Now," Eugenia said, wagging a finger, "don't be too hard on Morris. His wife is a genuine recluse. She hasn't left their house in fifteen years. You can hardly blame the man if he sometimes gets lonely when he travels. It's sad, really. I admire him for staying with her."

"Yes," Judith said slowly, "you have a point. So the woman who came here with him after the premiere was his . . . ah . . . companion?"

It was Eugenia's turn to look puzzled. "What woman?"

"The one dressed as a pioneer," Judith replied, turning the bacon in the cast-iron skillet.

Eugenia shrugged her broad shoulders. "I've no idea what you're talking about. Morris's . . . companion remained at the hotel."

Joe's conversation with Woody ended just as Eugenia took her coffee into the front parlor.

"Eat your words, Jude-girl," Joe said, wielding a whisk in a bowl of eggs. "Woody came up with some interesting stuff."

"Criminal stuff?" Judith asked in surprise.

"If it was, would you stop treating me like I had bubonic plague?"

So frazzled were Judith's nerves that she actually had to think twice before answering. "Yes, sure, go ahead." Her attempt to smile wasn't very successful.

Joe didn't respond until he'd put a quarter

pound of butter into a huge frying pan. "Nothing on Eugenia, Morris, or Chips," he said, keeping his voice down in case Eugenia was still in hearing range. "Ellie has a stack of speeding and parking tickets as high as the Hollywood Hills. Ben got busted a couple of times for possession."

"Of what?" Judith asked, getting plates out of the cupboard.

"Weed." He shrugged. "Dirk has been arrested four times for assault, but the charges were always dropped."

"Does that include the incident with Bruno at Marina Del Rey?" Judith asked.

Joe nodded. "It seems Mr. Farrar has to prove his macho image on both sides of the camera."

"Unsure of his manhood? Low self-esteem?" Judith murmured.

"Rotten disposition, no self-discipline." Almost forty years as a cop had caused Joe's patience with people's foibles to erode long ago.

Judith placed the silverware settings next to the plates on the counter. "What about the others?"

"I'm not finished with Dirk," Joe said, taking a break from his cook's duties to refill his coffee mug. "He was also involved in a messy paternity suit a year or two ago. He lost, and is paying for the kid's upbringing."

"Is Mom anyone we know?"

Joe shook his head. "Dirk was on location in Spain when he met Mom. She was an extra in a Basque uprising."

"No help there," Judith said.

"Only in terms of support payments." He offered more coffee to Judith. "Dade's had a couple of DWIs. He wiped out a Rolls-Royce on Sunset Boulevard and ran his Range Rover into a palm tree in Benedict Canyon. Not recently, though."

"He doesn't seem like much of a drinker," Judith remarked as she set out a dozen juice glasses.

"You never can tell," Joe said, reaching for a chafing dish high up in the cupboard. "Here's one you expected — Angela La Belle's been busted three times for coke possession. Bruno was arrested twice. On one occasion, they were together."

"That's not surprising," Judith said, "since Bruno supposedly got Angela hooked in the first place. Did they do time?"

"No," Joe replied, reaching for a second chafing dish. "Their clever lawyers — Vito, maybe? — got them off with fines, community service, and promises to go into rehab."

"Anything on Vito himself?"

"Nothing criminal," Joe replied, "though

412

I suspect that like any successful L.A. attorney, he may have a few slightly unethical tricks up his sleeve."

Judith narrowed her eyes at her husband. "You still look a bit scrofulous to me. Why am I supposed to heap you with praise and affection?"

Joe held up his index finger. "For one reason, and one reason only. Ahem." He paused so long for dramatic effect that Judith was poised to pounce on him. "In 1979, Winifred Lou Best was arrested twice, once for possession of cocaine and once for resisting arrest along with a man named Bartholomew Anthony Riggs, aka Big Daddy Dumas."

"Wow!" Judith's eyes sparkled as she threw her arms around his neck. "Now that is news!"

"What did I tell you?" He chuckled as she planted kisses all over his face. "I'm plague-free."

"More than you know," Judith said, finally releasing her husband. "Morris mentioned Big Daddy Dumas last night at Capri's. He was a pimp and a drug dealer. But Morris said Big Daddy was dead. He also said . . ." She frowned in recollection. "What was it? Oh! To blame Big Daddy for. . . . Damn, I forget."

"Sounds like Big Daddy was a bad daddy," Joe remarked.

"That's the odd thing," Judith said. "Bill had heard about him via a case study. According to Bill, Big Daddy wasn't all bad. He was good to his girls, he treated them like family. But that's not the point. Now we know why Winifred doesn't want to discuss her past. It's possible that Big Daddy helped the Demures get their start in the music business. Maybe the three singers were in his stable of hookers. That might explain why the group didn't have more than one hit. Their lives couldn't have been conducive to the discipline required by a serious music career. For all we know, the other two may have overdosed, gone to prison, or were murdered in a drug deal gone sour."

"Anything's possible," Joe allowed. "What happened to Big Daddy?"

"A dissatisfied hooker/would-be singer killed him," Judith replied. "Not one of the Demures, but a Latino girl."

"So maybe," Joe conjectured, "Big Daddy was the muscle who got Win and the other two started in the music business. When he got whacked, the Demures lost their leverage."

He picked up the plates and silverware

from the counter. "Here, let me set up the dining-room table."

"What?" Judith was lost in thought. "Oh, thanks. I'll cook Mother's breakfast now. I feel bad, I've hardly seen her lately."

"Don't worry," Joe called from the dining room. "She hasn't improved."

As Judith prepared Gertrude's meal and set it on a tray, the house seemed very quiet. Typical for early November, she thought, with the fog not only isolating but insulating Hillside Manor from the rest of the world. The calm, however, was not reassuring.

As usual Gertrude was up and dressed before eight o'clock, She sat behind the card table, not bothering to look up when her daughter arrived with breakfast. More surprisingly, the old lady was humming in an off-key manner.

"Hmm-dee-dee-hmm."

"Good morning," Judith said, forcing a bright smile. "You seem cheerful this morning."

"Hmm-mm-hmm-mm." Gertrude picked up her TV Guide and riffled through the pages. "Hmm-dee-dee-hm-hm."

Judith wasn't in the mood to play games with her mother. She placed the tray on the card table. Gertrude ignored it. "What is it?" Judith asked. "Aren't you hungry?"

"Dee-dee-mm-hmm."

"Mother!" Judith's patience fled. "Stop that humming! What's going on?"

Slyly, Gertrude looked up from the *TV Guide*. "Oh, it's you. I suppose you expect a tip now that I'm going to be rich. Forget it, I'm spending every dime on satin bloomers, lace hankies, and a walker with a motor on it."

Puzzled, Judith sat down on the arm of Gertrude's Davano. "What's going on? Did you win the lottery?"

"That's for suckers," Gertrude declared, even though she frequently conned Judith into buying lottery and scratch-card tickets for her. "You'll find out when the armored car pulls up with my loot."

Judith fought an urge to shake her mother until the old girl's dentures rattled. "What then?"

Gertrude shot her a contemptuous look. "How do you think, dummy? By selling my life story to the movies. That nice young Southun gentleman is writin' the script," she went on, her speech suddenly tinged with a drawl straight out of the cotton fields. "He's promised me a piece. Up front, too, but no points. Ah couldn't expect that for my first story, could Ah?"

Judith didn't know whether she was more

amazed by Dade's offer or her mother's use of movie jargon, which, judging from the drawl, was straight from the writer's mouth. "Are you sure he's not kidding you?"

"He's not the kind to spoof," Gertrude replied smugly, the drawl gone. "He's on the up-and-up. He says I'm great. In fact, I'm part of the Greatest Generation. I've lived through a bunch of wars, a big Depression, a whole slew of newfangled gadgets, going to the moon, riots, earthquakes, volcanoes, and bathtub gin. Not to mention your two lunkhead husbands and listening to Aunt Deb talk my ear off on the telephone."

It almost made sense. It was, in fact, not unlike the concept of the simple gasman viewing the history of the world. Judith was speechless.

"So what have you got to say for yourself now, Toots?" Gertrude demanded, finally picking up a fork and studying her meal.

"I think it's . . . terrific," Judith said at last. "If it all works out."

"That nice Southern boy says it will," Gertrude replied glibly. "What did he call it? 'An intimate portrait of the twentieth century.' See here?" She tapped a small piece of paper. "I wrote it down so I wouldn't forget."

Judith still had some reservations. "Have you signed a contract?"

417

"Nope," Gertrude said. "But some guy named Vito or Zito or Tito is writing it up. Still, I figure I'd better get an agent first. I can't read all that fine print. Literally."

Standing up, Judith reached out to hug her mother. "It sounds promising. I hope everything turns out the way you hope it will."

"It will," Gertrude said complacently. Then she frowned. "I just hope they hurry."

"You mean because the Hollywood people may be leaving soon?"

Gertrude shook her head. "No. Because I may be leaving soon. Even the Greatest Generation can't live forever."

By the time Judith got back to the house, she was surprised to see that several guests were sitting down to breakfast. In the kitchen, Joe was hustling eggs, bacon, and toast.

"The estimated time of departure is ten-thirty," he informed her in a low voice.

Judith gave her husband a startled look. "They're leaving? But the fog hasn't lifted."

"Vito says the studio has given them the go-ahead," Joe replied, placing toast in a rack. "The weather forecast predicts the fog will be gone by noon."

Judith stood rooted to the spot. "Should we be glad?"

"I don't know," Joe replied, heading to the dining room with the toast. "I couldn't get a feel one way or another from Vito."

When he returned moments later, Judith inquired after Angela. "Is she going, too?"

"No," said Joe, pouring more eggs into the pan. "They're sending her directly to rehab at the Ford Madox Ford Center on the Eastside. According to Vito, she'll be there at least a couple of months. Maybe this time the cure will take."

As Joe tended the stove, Judith peeked over the swinging doors that led into the dining room. The conversation seemed lighthearted. Maybe the movie people had put their differences aside now that they were leaving what they considered a fog-bound backwater. Everyone was there. Everyone except Winifred.

Winifred Best seemed to be the least likely of the guests to sleep in. A wave of apprehension came over Judith as she started for the back stairs.

The phone rang. Judith grabbed it from its cradle, hoping that Dilys Oaks was calling with good news for Joe. Instead, it was Phyliss Rackley, calling with bad news for Judith.

"I can't breathe," Phyliss announced in a voice that was anything but short of wind. "I

419

must have tuberculosis. Where's the nearest sanitorium?"

"They don't send people there for TB anymore, Phyliss," Judith asserted. "They can cure it with antibiotics. Call your doctor."

"I can't," Phyliss replied, then coughed with what sounded like feigned effort. "I'm fading fast. I need an iron lung."

"That's for polio," Judith said crossly. "Are you telling me you won't be here today?"

"How can I?" Phyliss asked, forlorn. "The Lord is coming for me. I saw Him this morning in my closet."

"Tell the Lord to come out of the closet and put you on the bus to Hillside Manor," Judith huffed. "I've got a big mess here today, and I'm worn out. Furthermore, it's All Saints' Day and I have to go to noon Mass."

"You and your Roman rituals," Phyliss complained. "What kind of sacrifice do you make this time? A gopher?"

Judith refused to waste time discussing the sacrifice of the Mass to Phyliss. She'd already explained it on at least a dozen occasions. "I really need you, Phyliss. Do you think you could make it by noon? The fog's supposed to lift by then."

"Well . . ." Phyliss seemed to consider the request. "I'll see. Maybe the Lord can work a miracle cure." She coughed some more for effect. "Kaff, kaff."

Hanging up, Judith continued on her way upstairs, then went the length of the hall to Room One, which Winifred had shared the previous night with Ellie Linn. Knocking gently at first, she got no response. She rapped harder. Still no reply. She was about to hammer on the door when she decided simply to open it.

The door was unlocked. A billow of smoke engulfed Judith. Flames licked at the bedclothes just as the fire alarm sounded and the sprinkler system went off.

Winifred lay awkwardly on the bed, her eyes closed, her mouth agape. Even as Judith screamed for help, she braved the smoke, fire, and drenching water to reach the motionless woman. Coughing, gritting her teeth, and ever aware that she could dislocate the artificial hip, she grabbed Winifred by the feet and attempted to tug her off the bed.

Despite Winifred's slimness, Judith could move her no more than a few inches. The water was pouring down, dousing the flames but turning the room into a nightmare of sizzling vapors. Judith gasped, coughed again, and yanked at a pillowcase to put over her mouth. She barely heard the pounding of feet on the stairs or Joe's shouts as he reached the second floor.

A moment later he was in the room, arms flailing, trying to push Judith out of the way. He missed. Judith, with the wet pillowcase protecting her nose and mouth, caught Winifred around the knees and, with a mighty wrench, moved her into a sitting position against the headboard.

At the same time she felt — and heard — an odd sound in her hip. She collapsed on the floor.

"Don't move!" Joe yelled as he picked up Winifred and carried her into the hall.

Dazed, Judith choked, coughed, and shivered in a huddled mass near the door. The fire, which had spread to the lace curtains on the other side of the room, was now sputtering out. Sirens could be heard in the distance. Someone must have called 911. Again.

"Winifred . . ." Judith murmured as Joe bent down to put his arms around her shoulders. "Is she . . . ?"

"Never mind Winifred," he said, his voice husky. "Can you stand?"

She wasn't sure. What was worse, she was afraid to try. To her surprise, Dirk Farrar entered the room. "I can lift her," he volunteered.

"We both can," Joe retorted.

They did, carefully moving her out of the room and placing her on the settee in the hall. Winifred was lying on the floor by the door to the bathroom between Rooms Three and Four. Dade was leaning over her, once again trying to revive a fallen comrade.

"She's alive," Eugenia announced.

Dade looked up. "She's coming 'round."

"Thank God," Judith gasped, then tried to sit up with Joe's help.

Vito Patricelli's customary calm was ruffled; he'd removed his sunglasses. "What happened? How did the fire start?"

He was ignored by both Flynns as the emergency crew charged up the stairs with Eugenia Fleming in their wake. Somewhat to her surprise, Judith didn't recognize any of the rescuers. Maybe, she thought a bit hazily, that was because it was a Monday. She couldn't recall anyone ever dying or almost dying at Hillside Manor on a Monday. This must be a different crew. Somewhat giddily, she wondered if eventually she'd know them all — police, firefighters, medics, maybe even a coroner or two.

"Clear the area!" one of the firefighters shouted.

From somewhere on the stairs, Judith could hear a vaguely familiar female voice giving orders for the rest of the guests to stay put. The girlish tones sounded more like Ellie than the buglelike Eugenia. But the voice belonged to a newcomer.

The medics had moved Winifred down the hall. "We'll work on her here," one of them announced with a slight Spanish accent. "Everybody else get lost."

Finally, Joe got Judith to her feet. "Can you walk?" he whispered.

She bit her lip, then wiped at her eyes, which were still smarting. "I'm not sure," she replied unsteadily. But one foot went in front of the other. There was none of the agonizing pain she'd suffered from previous dislocations. Perhaps the sensations trying to move Winifred had only been a warning.

The others had already trooped downstairs, except for Vito, who lingered in the hallway.

Eugenia was standing under the arch between the entry hall and the living room. Cautiously, Judith stepped over the tan fire hoses.

"Where is that woman?" Eugenia demanded, fists on hips. "It must be all her fault."

Judith stared. "What woman?"

"Your cleaning woman," Eugenia snapped.

"What kind of a person is she to cause such a mess?"

"My —" Judith stopped, allowing Joe to help her onto the sofa.

Eugenia followed, a bulldog running down a cat.

"I let her in while I was waiting for you to serve breakfast," Eugenia said, incensed. "How did I know she was a pyromaniac?"

Judith forced her brain to kick-start. "No. That couldn't have been my cleaning woman. I spoke to her on the phone just before I went upstairs looking for Winifred. She lives a good four miles from here."

"What did this person look like?" Joe asked, all business.

"Why . . ." Eugenia paused. "Like a cleaning woman. Which is who she said she was. Gray-haired, thin, homely."

Oddly enough, the description fit Phyliss Rackley. But that was impossible. Ignoring her hip, Judith jumped up. "Where is she now?"

"How do I know?" Eugenia shot back. "She went upstairs just before the others came down to breakfast."

"Christ!" Joe took off at a run, apparently heading for the back stairs. The sound of water thundered overhead. Through the big bay window, Judith could see two firefighters climbing up to the roof.

"Oh, no!" she wailed. "My poor B&B! It's ruined!"

It was only then that she realized the fire wasn't the only thing that had laid waste to Room One. So overcome with shock and fear had Judith been at the time, she had failed to take in the more minor damage.

Winifred's room had been ransacked.

Joe returned a few minutes later with Dilys Oaks. Judith realized that it was the young policewoman's voice she had recognized earlier.

"Nothing," Joe said, out of breath. "We couldn't find any trace of the so-called cleaning woman."

Judith turned to Eugenia, who had just finished a call on her cell phone. "Did you notice a car outside when you let this woman in?"

"A car?" Eugenia looked indignant. "How could I? It's too foggy to see past the front steps. I don't know when I've been in such a miserable place. Except Croatia, perhaps."

"Look here," Judith said, her temper flaring, "you were the one who admitted this woman. Why didn't you let me open the door?"

"You weren't here," Eugenia retorted.

"Neither was your husband. Besides, your cleaning woman had a key. Apparently, she was having trouble turning it."

Judith frowned. She must have been in the toolshed with her mother. Maybe Joe had gone to the bathroom. It wasn't really fair to blame Eugenia for the disaster. If, Judith suddenly thought, Eugenia was telling the truth. As for the key, perhaps the intruder was faking it. Or, it suddenly occurred to her, someone had found Dade's missing key. But who?

A firefighter, moving clumsily in his bulky safety suit, entered the living room. "We think everything's under control," he announced, then turned to Joe. "The fire itself was just about extinguished by the sprinkler system. But there's quite a bit of water damage. We'll stick around to check things out, but if there's danger to the wiring, you'd better think about staying somewhere else for a while. Also, it may take some time for the investigators to do their job and for the insurance adjusters to estimate the amount of damage."

"That's impossible!" Judith exclaimed. "This is a bed-and-breakfast establishment! We can't shut down. And we certainly aren't going to move out."

With regret, the firefighter shook his

head. "Sorry, ma'am. I'm afraid you'll have to do both. Safety first."

Before Judith could argue further, the medics appeared on the staircase with Winifred on a gurney with her eyes closed and an oxygen mask over her face. Vito was right behind them.

"They're taking her to the hospital to treat her for smoke inhalation," the lawyer announced from the entry hall, a frown on his usually imperturbable face.

"I don't get it," Judith put in, moving with care. "The fire had just started. There was plenty of smoke, but not enough to render Ms. Best unconscious. She wasn't asleep; she was in her bathrobe lying atop the bedcovers."

The medics didn't respond as they wheeled Winifred out of the house and disappeared.

Vito started to follow, but Eugenia waylaid him with a firm hand. "Mrs. Flynn's right. What's going on with Win?"

With a pained expression, Vito leaned down to whisper in Eugenia's ear. She gave a start, then scowled. "The medics told you that? I don't believe it!" she snapped, then turned on Judith as Vito exited the house. "Your cleaning woman knocked Winifred unconscious!"

"What?" Judith shrieked. *"That wasn't my cleaning woman!"*

Eugenia shrugged her broad shoulders. "As you say. Vito is accompanying Win to the hospital. I understand this wretched house has to be evacuated. Don't worry, we're all but on our way."

Returning to the living room, Judith began to pace the floor.

"Take it easy," Joe warned. "You're listing a bit to starboard."

"I'm fine," Judith snarled. "I didn't dislocate, I just . . . twinged." She stopped by the piano at the far end of the room. "I can't believe this. Even if we don't get sued, we're out of business for God knows how long!"

"Come on, Jude-girl," Joe urged, "try to relax a little. It's not like the place burned down." He looked at Dilys, who had her back turned to both Flynns and was on her cell phone. "An APB has gone out on the mysterious cleaning woman. If there was one," he added, lowering his voice.

Dilys clicked off to face Judith and Joe. "Unfortunately," she said, "the description isn't very helpful. Ms. Fleming thought the woman was wearing dark clothing. The rest of her appearance is quite ordinary. With all the new apartments and condos on this side of the hill, there must be a hundred women

429

like that within three square blocks of here."

Judith abruptly sat down on the piano bench. "No," she said slowly, "there's only one."

Chapter Twenty

There was no time for Judith to explain. The battalion chief came into the living room to consult with the Flynns. His main advice was to contact their insurance agent as soon as possible. Joe agreed, saying he'd drive up to the top of the hill as soon as the local office opened at ten.

"What about the damage?" Judith asked in a plaintive voice. "How bad is it?"

"We'll let you know as soon as we can," the chief said kindly. His name was Ramirez, and he spoke with a slight Spanish accent.

Judith winced. "You're sure we have to move out?"

Ramirez nodded. "It may not be for long. It's the water damage, mostly. That's often the case with a small fire. Only the bedcovers, curtains, and carpet were destroyed. The rest of the fire merely scorched the bed itself, the mattress, and one wall. By the way, who tossed the room?"

Joe and Dilys both stared at Judith. "Um . . ." She put her hands to her cheeks, which seemed to have suddenly grown quite warm. "I forgot to mention that. It must have been the intruder who knocked out Ms. Best."

Ramirez frowned. "So that's what I heard someone talking about. Where are the police?"

Dilys took a step forward. "I am the police," she declared. "My backup should be along shortly. The patrol cars are already on the lookout for the perp."

The battalion chief seemed disconcerted. "You mean . . . All these people in this house and no one . . ." He gave himself a good shake. "Excuse me. It's a big house. In fact, haven't you had a couple of other 911 calls in the past few days?"

To Judith's great relief, Dilys stepped in to spare the Flynns the burden of an explanation. "To begin with," she said, guiding Ramirez out of the living room, "this is a B&B. The current guests are somewhat unusual in that they . . ."

The pair disappeared into the front parlor. Judith glanced at the bay window. The ladder remained; water still poured down the side of the house. Judith couldn't have felt worse if she'd suffered a physical blow.

"What did you mean," Joe inquired, "when you said there was *only one woman?*"

"I'll tell you later." Judith noticed the guests leaving their breakfast table. "My," she said in sarcasm, "I'm glad we didn't spoil their appetites."

Joe gave her a quick hug. "Hang in there. It's going on ten. I'll head out now to see Fred Sheets at the insurance agency."

Judith said something that sounded like "Mrph."

A moment later Dilys stuck her head back into the living room. "I'm going to confer with my backup. They seem to have gotten lost." She winked. "At Moonbeam's."

"Great," Judith said through gritted teeth, then threw her hands up in the air. "Mother! I'd better tell her what happened. She must be frantic."

Gertrude, however, was in her usual place, leafing through a film directory. "Hi, Toots," she said, barely looking up. "Abbott or Costello or whatever his last name is brought this to me. It's got all the directors and actors and moving-picture people listed. It's too bad Joan Crawford's dead. People used to say she looked like me."

"Mother . . ." Judith began.

But Gertrude interrupted. "Anyways, Dade — yes, *Dade*, I remember his first name now — left me his card and one from some woman named Fleming. She's supposed to call me when she gets back to Los Angeles." The old lady pronounced it "Los Ang-elees." "Boy, there sure are a lot of names in this book." She tapped the cover. "I never heard of most of them." Finally, Gertrude looked at her daughter. "Where's lunch?"

"It's ten o'clock," Judith said, then pointed to the breakfast tray. "You didn't eat all your eggs."

"They have funny stuff in them," Gertrude said. "What did you do, mix the eggs with an old salad?"

Judith refrained from saying that Joe had made the eggs. She also refrained from telling her mother about the fire. As long as Gertrude's deafness had obscured the sirens, there was no point in upsetting the old girl. At least not yet. Judith had other things on her mind.

Back in the house, the guests were scurrying about, completing their packing, hauling their luggage downstairs. They seemed as eager to leave as Judith was to see them go.

"Incredible," Ben Carmody said to Judith

as he put on a black leather jacket. "How did Win set fire to her room?"

Looking guileless, Judith shrugged. "Who knows? Does she smoke?"

"Hell, no," Dirk declared. "She's no drinker, either, at least not at nine in the morning."

Judith kept mum.

"She'll be fine," Ellie said, hooking her arm through Ben's. "I'd like to work with her on *All the Way to Utah*."

"Win's spunky," Chips said. "Maybe she'll be able to leave for L.A. later today."

Again, Judith made no comment.

Vito slipped a white envelope into her hand. "The studio wants to compensate you for your trouble. This is a promissory note for five thousand dollars. As soon as everything is cleared up in L.A., you'll get your money."

Judith's smile was off center. "Why . . . that's generous. I think." For all she knew, the money would cover only the caterers. Of course it was better than a subpoena.

Dade was the last one out the door. He was halfway down the steps when he stopped and turned around. "Tell your momma I'll be in touch. I'm pretty excited about this project."

Judith still couldn't believe Dade was serious. "You are?"

"I sure am," he responded. "That little lady has some mighty swell tales to tell. I like her style." With a salute, Dade ambled along after the rest of the party.

The limos had barely pulled away when Judith heard a knock at the back door. Maybe it was Renie, though she rarely got up until ten o'clock, and even then, it took her another hour to become fully conscious.

It wasn't her cousin who'd come to call. It was an even more unlikely person to show up so early in the day.

"Goodness!" Vivian Flynn exclaimed. "You've had more excitement, I see. Those sirens woke me up. I only managed to get dressed about five minutes ago, and then I saw the limos in the cul-de-sac. What's going on now?"

"One of the guests had an accident," Judith replied, leading Herself into the kitchen. "A small fire upstairs. She'll be okay, I think. Would you care for coffee?" The offer came with a tug of reluctance.

Vivian, however, waved a hand. "No, but thanks anyway. As long as I'm dressed" — she ran a hand over her ensemble, which consisted of a black wool suit with slits in the skirt, a frilly white blouse, sling-back stiletto heels, and a perky black beret adorned with faux pearls — "I think I'll pop over to

Norway General to see Stone Cold Sam."

"I hear he's doing well," Judith said.

"He's doing wonderfully," Herself declared, then giggled behind her hand. "But I feel sooo guilty!"

"About what?"

Vivian giggled again, then made a face. "About the heart attack. I mean, it wasn't as if we were doing anything really outrageous."

Judith's mouth was agape. "You mean . . . ? Stone Cold Sam was . . . ah . . . with you when he had the heart attack?"

Vivian's false eyelashes fluttered. "With me. Yes."

"Oh." Judith gulped. "I see."

"You'd better not!" Herself said, wagging a finger. "Naughty of you to peek!" She giggled some more. "That's why I feel guilty. I went to see him last night, and I was so upset I ended up on the wrong floor. I almost panicked when the room I thought was his turned out to be empty. I was afraid he'd passed away. I practically ran all the way to the elevator. I thought he was in 706, but it was 906. Silly me."

An alarm bell went off in Judith's brain. She stared at Herself until the other woman stared back with a puzzled expression.

"What's wrong, Judith?" Vivian inquired. "You look like you don't feel well. I've noticed that you haven't really looked very good since your surgery. Did it age you terribly?"

Judith was accustomed to Herself's barbs, but on this occasion, they were the least of her worries. "No," she said tersely. "I'm just tired. It's been a difficult weekend."

"So it seems." Vivian reached into her cobra-skin handbag to retrieve a pair of black kid gloves. "I must be off. I'll give Sam your best. By the way, I hope that nothing was badly burned. Except for those handsome firefighters on the roof, everything looks fine from outside."

"It's not too bad," Judith said, hoping the statement might be true.

"Good," Herself responded. "Toodles." She departed through the front door on a wave of decadence and a whiff of Chanel No. 5.

For at least a full minute, Judith stood in the hallway, thinking hard. She had been certain that the person wearing high heels at Norway General was Winifred, coming to see Angela. She had ruled out Eugenia, who always wore sensible shoes, and Ellie, who preferred sandals and sneakers. The idea that Winifred had wanted to ensure Angela's silence concerning the source of Bruno's cocaine addiction was out the window.

She considered going upstairs to see what was happening on the guest floor. But she didn't really want to know. Besides, she was leery of overdoing it with her hip. The first order of business was almost as painful as the fire itself: She had to call Ingrid Heffelman to change the current set of reservations.

With a heavy sigh, Judith looked at the calendar on the wall above the computer. She hadn't flipped the page to November. Saying good-bye to *Sculptor's Studio*, she stared at the new painting. It was Grant Wood's *American Gothic. Born 1892 in Anamosa, Iowa,* the tag line read, *he taught in the Cedar Rapids public schools and later was an artist in residence at the University of Iowa. Wood was strongly influenced by German and Flemish painters of the . . .*

Judith's brain was going into overdrive, but was short-circuited by the voice of Battalion Chief Ramirez, who was calling from the entry hall.

"Everything's under control," he said, pulling off his heavy gloves. "We'll come by later today to check things out and see what help we can offer once your husband has finished talking to your insurance agent."

Judith thanked the firefighter, then waited on the porch until the hoses were rolled up and the fire truck drove away. A small white sedan was pulled up to the curb by the Rankerses' driveway. Something about the vehicle chafed at her memory, but she shrugged it away. Small white cars were as common as the autumn fog. *My brain's in a fog,* she thought. Rarely had she felt so low in her mind.

As the firefighters disappeared out of the cul-de-sac, Judith heard a sound just off the porch on the other side of the Weigela bush. Walking down the steps, she turned the corner and peered through the fog.

A gray-clad figure appeared like a wraith out of the mists. Judith stood very still, her heart in her mouth. Then, as the figure came closer, recognition dawned.

"Mrs. Izard!" Judith exclaimed. "What are you doing here?"

Meg Izard clutched at her imitation-leather purse with one hand and held the felt picture-frame hat in place with the other. "Just passing by on our way out of town," she said, her usually cold gaze showing a spark of life. "I didn't think anybody was home. Walt and I saw somebody leave the house. We thought it was you. What's going on with the firemen?"

"A small fire," Judith replied. "Guests are sometimes heedless."

"I'll bet," Meg said, looking away toward the Weigela.

Judith retreated to the bottom of the porch steps. "Despite the problems we had with your reservation, do you plan on staying at Hillside Manor when you visit again?"

"We'll see about that," Meg replied with a scowl. "The weather here's dismal."

"September is lovely," Judith said. "So is early October."

"September's no good," Meg said, adjusting the round felt hat before her hands tightened again on her purse. "We never miss the state fair." She started to move past Judith on the walk.

"Where's Mr. Izard?" Judith asked, a hand on Meg's arm.

"He's wandering around, having a smoke," Meg replied. "You can't smoke in these rental cars, you know."

"We permit smoking," Judith said. "Why don't you come in for a few minutes? The fog's supposed to lift soon. Then driving will be safer, especially in an unfamiliar city."

"Well . . ." Meg flexed her fingers on the black purse. "I'll come in for a bit. Never mind Walt. He's happy just moseying around outside."

Judith led the way into the house. "Have a

seat at the dining-room table," she offered.

But Meg went straight into the kitchen, where she fumbled with her purse.

"Would you prefer sitting in here?" Judith inquired.

"No. Just give me a minute to catch my breath." She stood by the sink, looking down. After almost a full minute, she turned and followed Judith into the dining room. Meg sat down with her purse in her lap and her shabby gray coat unbuttoned. "I take cream," she announced.

"Fine," Judith said, going back into the kitchen. She fixed Meg's coffee and poured a glass of orange juice for herself. "Are you headed for the airport?" she inquired when she was seated at the big oak table.

Meg nodded. "We got a flight out at two. If the fog lifts."

"It should," Judith said. "So you always attend the Iowa State Fair," she remarked in a casual tone.

"Haven't missed it since I was two," Meg answered with a hint of pride. "Best fair in the Midwest."

"Do you and Walt own a farm?" Judith asked.

"A small one, just outside Riceville." The corners of Meg's thin mouth turned down. "Walt's dad sold out to one of those combines years ago. They cheated Mr. Izard. Now we've only got some chickens, a couple of cows, and a cornfield. It's been a struggle, believe me."

"Farming certainly has changed," Judith remarked. "But you must do okay. I mean, you and Walt are able to take vacations like this one."

"First time since our honeymoon," Meg said, with her usual sour expression. "We wouldn't have done it now except it's our silver wedding anniversary. That, and with —" She stopped abruptly, her thin shoulders tensing under the worn wool coat.

Recalling Walt Izard's gaunt frame, Judith gently posed a question. "Is your husband ill?"

Meg scowled at Judith. "No. Why do you ask? It's none of your beeswax."

"That's true," Judith admitted. "I'm sorry. It's just that I'm interested in people. Sometimes it gets me into awkward situations."

Meg's face softened slightly. "Well . . . you can't do much about serious sickness. Trouble is, the doctors can't either. Folks like us can't afford big-city specialists like some."

"Maybe not," Judith responded, then paused before speaking again. "Shall I tell you a story?"

"A story?" Meg wrinkled her long nose. "Why do I want to hear a story?" But a flicker of interest kindled in her eyes.

"You'll want to hear this story," Judith said, placing her elbows on the table and leaning closer to her guest. "It's about a young girl from a small town in Iowa who fell in love with a romantic young man."

Meg tensed, her hands tightening on the purse in her lap. But she said nothing. In Judith's mind's eye, she tried to picture the thin, haggard woman across the table as a young girl — the girl in the photograph that lay between the pages of *The Gasman*.

"This young man had a vivid imagination," Judith continued, "and he wooed her with all the passion of his creative nature. Unfortunately, the girl got pregnant. Her family insisted on a wedding. Since the young man had roots in the area, he gave in, and they were married. His bride made the mistake of believing he'd keep his vows. She trusted him, even if she thought his ambitions were out of reach. She couldn't understand why farm life in Iowa didn't suit him. But he had bigger dreams, and moved on, leaving her behind." Judith paused, recalling the lock of hair. She looked Meg right in the eye. "What happened to that baby, Mrs. Izard?"

444

Meg sat stony-faced for a long moment. When she finally spoke, her lips scarcely moved. "He was stillborn. My so-called husband had already left me. I named the poor baby Douglas, after my father. We buried him next to Pa in the family plot."

"I'm sorry," Judith said softly. "Do you have other children?"

Meg shook her head. "I couldn't. Something went wrong at the time of the birth."

Now it was Judith's turn to be silent. The fog seemed to permeate the kitchen, like a sad, gray pall. "Your first husband took something else besides your happiness, didn't he?" she finally asked.

Meg sat up very straight. "You mean . . . the book?"

Judith nodded. "That's what you came for earlier this morning, isn't it? The book. Your copy of the book."

Meg's jaw dropped, but she recovered quickly. "That Best woman — she was the one who all but stole it from us."

"Not your personal copy, though," Judith put in. "Bruno took it with him when he left you, didn't he?"

"I could have killed him right then and there," Meg declared. "Pa's book was his monument. It was all that we had left of him, except for the manuscript he never finished. And no one would buy that one from us. Foolishly, we let the copyright on *The Gasman* run out in 1985. We thought, what's the use? There was never more than the one printing. Then Bruno . . ." She spat out his name as if it were tainted with gall. "Then he used the book to make this big, big movie. Winifred Best had gotten hold of the rights for him. Walt and I couldn't believe it when we saw it on a TV show about Hollywood. Millions of dollars. And we were practically on food stamps. After all those years — thirty-one, to be exact — that son of a bitch uses Pa's book to make himself even more rich and famous."

"You never forgave Bruno, did you?" Judith asked quietly.

Meg shook her head decisively. "Never. How could I? He ruined my life, he destroyed my future, *he stole Pa's book*. It ate at me, like a cancer."

"Cancer," Judith repeated. "You have cancer, don't you?"

Meg's body jerked in the chair. "How do you know?"

"I found a piece of label from a prescription bottle in Bruno's room the morning after he died," Judith said. "It was for thalidomide. If it wasn't for Bruno and it wasn't for Walt, then it had to be for you. I'd heard that the drug was being used again, this time for cancer patients. Thalidomide has proved effective in retarding end-stage cancers. I think that scrap of label was dropped when you were exploring the upstairs. You didn't notice because you were too busy destroying Angela's costume and putting the rubber spider in Bruno's bed."

Meg's gaze dropped along with her shoulders. "That medicine helps. But it doesn't cure. I've got blood cancer. Multiple myeloma, if you want to put a fancy name to it."

"I'm so sorry," Judith said, feeling as if she had to apologize for too many tragedies in Meg's life. "When you learned Bruno was premiering his movie here in town, it must have come as a shock to discover that he and his company were registered at the same B&B you'd chosen."

"Not really," Meg said on a weary sigh. "It figured. Our first trip in twenty-five years, and somehow Bruno managed to foul it up for us. I guess that was the last straw. It was right after that when I found out about the cancer."

The damp air seemed to seep into Judith's skin; she felt faintly chilled. The ticking of the schoolhouse clock sounded unnaturally loud in her ears. For all she knew, Meg had a gun in her purse. It seemed heavy, judging from the way Meg held it. Judith braced herself before asking the next question. "Did you intend to kill Bruno?"

Meg smirked before speaking. "Of course I did. I'd wished him dead every day of my life. But then I saw him again, after so many years." She looked away and bit her lip. "I had to talk to him, to tell him what a skunk he was, to make him *give me back my book.* And of course money from him would have been nice. I don't know how Walt will manage without me. He hasn't been the same since the farming went bad." She looked away, into the corner of the dining room, with its quaint washstand, porcelain ewer, and pitcher. Judith thought the sight must have reminded the other woman of home.

"Bruno was so snotty to me," Meg went on, "so mean, like he was after we were married. When I first began to show with the baby, he called me Spider Woman. He said that with the big belly and my scrawny long arms and legs, I reminded him of a spider."

"How cruel," Judith said with a shake of her head. "Bruno sounds as if he was held captive by his ego, even then."

"He was nice only in the beginning," Meg said, "when he was trying to seduce me. I was so green. I'd never met anyone like him."

Judith started to reach out to comfort Meg, but thought better of it. "Don't blame yourself," she said. "You were a farm girl from a small town. He was in search of his Iowa roots, and already had the aura of Southern California about him." She paused, knowing that Meg had a need to talk about the confrontation with Bruno. "Night before last must have been very hard when you finally faced him again."

"It was and it wasn't," Meg responded, her sharp features hardening even more. "I was glad that when I finally saw him, he was feeling miserable. How the mighty have fallen, I thought to myself. But then he got nasty. When Bruno went to take some pills he had in his hand, he opened the cupboard by the sink to fetch a glass. Then he dropped one of the pills. When he bent down to get it, he reared up so fast that he banged his head on the cupboard door and knocked himself silly. He fell right into the sink with all that water in it. For a second I thought I should haul him out." Her face twisted with bitterness. "Then I thought, to hell with him. He never cared about me, why should I care about him? So I held his head under the water until he stopped flailing around. Then

I put the spider over the sink and left." Meg's pallor had a strange glow. She'd won the final battle with Bruno.

For a long time neither woman spoke. Judith forced herself not to look in the direction of Meg's purse.

"Your brother, Will," Judith said at last, recalling the information on the Internet. "You mentioned at some point that he lives here. He's William Euclid Carp, isn't he?" Silently, she cursed herself. She'd never thought of looking up Carp in the phone book.

Meg nodded. "He moved out this way a couple of years ago. He couldn't stand trying to make a living selling farm equipment anymore. The market had fallen out of that, too. I figured that this trip would be my last chance to see him. Will was real pleased. But sad. I'd asked him to scout out this place so we could find it without running around all over a strange city. By then, we'd been displaced, and knew from you that Bruno was coming here for his big shindig."

"Ah!" Judith exclaimed softly. She couldn't believe she'd been such a dunce. The tall, old-fashioned figure she'd seen alongside the house wasn't Ben Carmody; it was William Euclid Carp. "But you were the pioneer woman at the party," she said. It was a statement, not a question. *American Gothic*, Judith had thought the first time she'd met the Izards. Gothic, as in grotesque. Out of the corner of her eye, she could see the calendar with the Grant Wood painting.

"What else could I be?" Meg replied. "That was Great-Grandma Carp's dress and bonnet I found a long time ago in the attic. I brought it with me. I couldn't afford a fancy-dress costume. I'd heard about the ball on TV, and I figured I'd confront Bruno afterward at your B&B."

"Did Walt dress up?" Judith inquired. "I don't recall seeing him at the party."

"He never came inside," Meg said. "He and Will put together some makeshift costumes. Walt was a scarecrow. Will was a cowboy. Those were easy to do, after all the scarecrows we've had on the farm. Will had herded cattle for many years. He still had his boots and his vest and his cowboy hat. They didn't blame me for what I'd done, but they fussed. They were afraid I'd be found out. Will was especially worried, so he and Walt tried to keep tabs on what was going on here after Bruno died."

So the witch wasn't a witch, but a scarecrow, thought Judith. Another mistake she'd made, though understandable. In the fog,

451

the pointed hat, the turned-up shoes, the ragged garments, the strawlike hair, and the fact that it was Halloween had made the illusion credible.

"Who found the missing key to Hillside Manor?" Judith asked.

"Walt." Meg smiled thinly. "It was in your driveway. He picked it up on a . . . whim, I guess. I tried to use it this morning, but before I could make it turn right, some fat old bag came to the door."

Judith had another query for Meg. "Why did you hit Winifred Best and start the fire?"

Meg's jaw jutted. "I thought she had my book. She said she didn't — Bruno had it. But that didn't make sense. Bruno was dead, so where did it go? She swore she didn't know. That's when I hit her. Then I went all through her room, but I couldn't find the book. I got mad." Her eyes grew cold as marble. "I struck a match and set fire to the bedclothes. That woman may not have had my book on her, but she's had Bruno all these years. *It wasn't fair.*"

Judith tried not to gape. Could Meg still love Bruno in spite of everything he'd done? Sometimes love and hate were so hard to distinguish. Maybe it was obsession. Yet Bruno Zepf had inspired love in several women, perhaps including Winifred Best.

"And there was this," Meg added, releasing the grip on her purse. She fumbled a bit before she held out a black rubber spider. "I came to leave this. Sort of a . . . what do you call it? A calling card, maybe."

"An epitaph," Judith murmured. "Why did you put the other spiders in our freezer?"

"Walt did that," Meg said, looking askance. "Don't ask why Walt does things. Sometimes I think he's a little tetched. Losing his pa's farm, you know."

Judith suddenly recalled another seemingly inexplicable incident. "And the truffles that were sent here?"

"Truffles?" Meg scowled. "I don't know what a truffle looks like."

"They're kind of . . . disgusting," Judith explained, "but they taste wonderful."

Meg continued scowling, then suddenly let out a sharp yip of laughter. "I sent Bruno a cowpie, straight off the farm."

"Oh!" Gertrude had been right to flush the parcel's contents down the toilet. "I see."

Meg toyed with the spider for a moment, then pushed it across the table to Judith. "Here, you keep it as a souvenir. What are you going to do now, call the cops?"

Judith gazed at the gray, gaunt face. Meg Izard was already condemned to death.

"I have to," she finally said.

Meg reached into her purse. "Okay," she said. "But not yet." In her hand was a .45 revolver. No doubt it had been used previously to shoo away unwelcome birds and even more unwelcome strangers on the Izard farm.

Judith tensed in her chair. Her feet were planted firmly on the floor, her fingers gripping the table's edge. "Why would you shoot me?" she asked in a voice that didn't sound like her own.

"I want my book," Meg said, now holding the gun with both hands. "Give me my book."

"Okay." Judith forced herself to move. "May I?"

"Yes." Meg stood up. "No tricks, just my book."

It had never been harder for Judith to walk, not even when she'd taken her first tenuous steps after hip surgery. Slowly, agonizingly, she made her way to the drawer by the computer. Keeping one hand in full sight, she reached down to get the book.

"Here," she said, still moving with difficulty. "Here's your book."

Meg removed her left hand from the gun and took the heavy volume from Judith. "Thank you," she said with great dignity.

She clasped *The Gasman* to her flat breast and slipped the gun back into her purse. "Good-bye."

Judith stared as Meg walked toward the entry hall. The other woman moved slowly now, almost decorously, to the front door. Trying to control a sudden spasm of trembling, Judith started to follow. But Meg had closed the door behind her before Judith could get beyond the dining room.

"My God!" Judith exclaimed under her breath, and leaned against the wall.

She took several breaths before she could go on. Finally, she reached the door just as the shot rang out. Judith had expected it. She didn't want to look outside, but she had to.

Meg Izard was lying facedown at the sidewalk's edge. Her copy of *The Gasman* had fallen in the gutter.

Judith inspected the items on the silver tray and decided to start breakfast with the fruit compote. "How's your omelette?" she asked of Joe, who was sitting in a plush armchair with his tray on his lap.

"Excellent," he replied. "I couldn't have made a better one myself. The Cascadia Hotel has one of the best chefs on the West Coast."

"I have to admit it," Judith said with a pleasurable little smile, "this is heaven."

"As long as we've been turned out of our house, we might as well make the most of it," Joe said, his green-eyed gaze taking in the extensive hotel suite with its lavish old-world appointments. "Especially since Paradox Studios is paying for it."

"I can't believe they ended up paying us," Judith remarked, admiring the thick slice of Virginia ham on the white Limoges plate. "Twenty-five thousand dollars, plus our expenses. And the insurance money for the fire — I'm wondering if we shouldn't keep the B&B closed for a while. Business gets increasingly slow this time of year. We could make some renovations I've been thinking about."

"You decide," Joe said.

"We might even enlarge the toolshed for Mother now that she's gotten used to being out of it for a few days while the major work is being done to the house."

"I still say all the noise of the construction wouldn't have bothered her," Joe asserted. "She's deaf, she's daffy."

"She's also selling her life story to the movies," Judith pointed out. "At least she hopes so."

Joe merely shook his head. He didn't notice that his wife was staring at him.

"I'm not so hungry anymore," Judith said softly. She put the tray aside. "At least not for breakfast."

"What?" Joe looked up from his marmalade-covered toast. He grinned. "Well, now. Maybe I'm not either. But do you really want to let things cool off?"

"That depends on what you're talking about," Judith replied.

Joe set his tray down on a French marquetry table and moved toward her. "You're right. Seize the moment." Instead, he climbed onto the king-size bed and seized his wife around the waist.

"Oh, Joe." Judith sighed, her lips against his cheek. "This is perfect!"

A knock sounded at the door.

"Damn!" Judith breathed. "Shall I get it?"

Joe buried his face in the bare curve of her shoulder. "No," he said, his voice muffled.

The knock sounded again, louder, more insistent.

"We'd better answer that," Judith said through clenched teeth. "Whoever it is will go away fast enough." Pulling her terrycloth robe closed, she slipped off the bed and went to the door.

Gertrude stood in the hallway. "Where's my breakfast?"

Judith gaped at her mother. "Didn't you order from room service?"

"Of course not," Gertrude shot back. "You know how I hate to use the phone." She and her walker clumped past Judith and into the room. "Lunkhead here can order for me. And what's this leaving a newspaper outside my door? I'm not paying for it. I get my news on TV. Why are people always giving me things to read that I don't want? Even that nice Dade Whoozits brought me some goofy script when he was here, all about the Mormons. Now why would I want to read such a thing? I'm not a Mormon. I'm a Catholic and a Democrat. I just put that script in the barbecue and set a match to it. I think I'll do the same thing with that newspaper. It's not even local." Gertrude ran out of breath, but not for long. She glared at Joe. *"Where's my breakfast?"*

Judith proffered her own tray. "Here. I've lost my appetite."

As Gertrude sat down in the armchair Joe had vacated, Judith cast a longing look at her husband. Joe simply shook his head.

"Hey," Gertrude cried, "where are my dentures?"

"In your mouth," Judith responded a bit testily.

"Oh." Gertrude began to eat. After swallowing a mouthful of omelette, she stared at her daughter. "Where's that danged cat?"

"In your room, remember?" Judith said.

"Maybe not," Joe put in. He gestured at Judith. "Let's go look for him."

Judith started to protest, caught the gleam in Joe's eyes, and agreed. They'd search for Sweetums.

"Take your time eating, Mother," Judith called over her shoulder as they headed for Gertrude's adjoining room.

Hand in hand, Judith and Joe hurried out of the suite.

If life wasn't perfect, this was the next best thing.

The employees of Thorndike Press hope you have enjoyed this Large Print book. All our Thorndike and Wheeler Large Print titles are designed for easy reading, and all our books are made to last. Other Thorndike Press Large Print books are available at your library, through selected bookstores, or directly from us.

For information about titles, please call:

(800) 223-1244

or visit our Web site at:

www.gale.com/thorndike
www.gale.com/wheeler

To share your comments, please write:

Publisher
Thorndike Press
295 Kennedy Memorial Drive
Waterville, ME 04901

X